Foreshadowed

By G.M. Persbacker

Greenhaven Projects, LLC
Greenhavenprojects.com

Acknowledgements

Where do I begin?

I suppose the beginning will have to do.

I think it all started sometime back in 2006 or 2007, right around the time that I joined the Flights of Fantasy women's book club. I decided to finally write down the story that had been taking shape in my mind over the course of several years, and upon hearing about my literary aspirations, those amazing women not only offered me encouragement, they agreed to read my work a chapter at a time as I completed it and give me feedback. Trust me when I say that this book would not exist without their persistent demands to know what came next! This one is for you, ladies.

I also want to give a big shout out to my amazing editor, Sarah, who saw what this book could be and gently pushed me to make the necessary changes, and to my cover artist, Devvan, whose enthusiasm kept me going when my own was beginning to dim.

And to my husband, Chris – for everything.

Author's Note

When building an entire world, there are a lot of details to keep track of that the reader doesn't necessarily have to know, but that are nonetheless essential to keeping the story consistent. And while most folks are happy to keep such minutia "behind the curtain", I am aware that some people enjoy the ability to look up an unfamiliar term or know how the author intended certain words to be pronounced. Therefore, I have included a few reference sections at the end of this book to satisfy this group of readers. Enjoy!

Powerful as the Sight is, it must be understood that not every prescient vision will be realized, and that nothing is certain until it is past. Even then, there is room for doubt, for history has been known to lie.

The seers who serve Fate are only mortal, and no mortal being may know the sum and total of the future. Those with the Sight merely catch glimpses of what may be. Some are promises, some are warnings, and some are a little of both.

We are not infallible. For this, we should be grateful.

-Excerpt from the *Primer on Prescience*

Prologue

1292 AHS (After Human Settlement on Kaestra)

Dawn was usually Danielle's favorite time of day. But not today.

She gazed down at the still body of a young woman, one of her fellow seers, who cradled a mirror of polished black stone in her lifeless hands.

They had arrived just before sunrise, wordlessly picking their way around the remnants of the stone arch that had once defined the entrance to the garden. It had been reduced to rubble, as had the other stone figures within the garden's tall hedges.

There were five of them present: the three senior oracles, the First Guardian, and a young priest serving in the outer court of the Order of Kae-Madri. Danielle understood why she and the other senior oracles were there, but she could only guess at why Surai and the priest had come. Those guesses left a bitter taste in her mouth.

The initial silence that had been a mark of respect in the near darkness felt oppressive now, and as the light grew stronger, so did Danielle's urge to act.

With effort, she tore her gaze from the dead girl. Second Oracle Peyton and Third Oracle Maeve were openly grieving, which was to be expected. They were not much older than the child they mourned. Neither was she. But among the seers they were seniors, the leaders of their order.

Then she considered Surai. The First Guardian was nearly seventy years old, more than twice Danielle's age. But she was a woman in her prime, who likely had more years ahead of her than behind. Normally, Danielle did not dwell on the greatly foreshortened life span that came with the Sight, but today was different.

At least Surai had the good grace to look contrite. It was only fitting considering that the goddess she served had murdered the young woman before them. Danielle was about to say something to break the silence, when a small sound from the priest drew her attention.

His tawny skin flushed with embarrassment as the others focused on him. He ducked his head, but not before she noticed his pained expression.

"You knew her." It was not a question, yet her tone of voice made it a command.

"I loved her," he said flatly.

Danielle sucked in a breath. "I'm sorry. We share your grief."

The priest shrugged and met her gaze. "We both knew I would outlive her."

"What is your name?"

"Lucas." He paused. "Valori told me that seers must become accustomed to loss. You die so young."

"This was no ordinary death, even for a seer."

The First Guardian looked at her sharply. "Careful," she said.

"Would you have me lie to him?" Danielle snapped.

"This isn't the time or the place."

"I disagree. What better place or time could there be than the scene of the crime?"

Surai was incredulous. "Is that all you see here?"

Danielle bent down and reverently took the mirror from Valori's grip. She held it high and said, "I see a dead seer and a record of a vision too powerful to be viewed. And even if you hadn't come, I would have sensed Kaestra's presence here. *She* did this. You can't deny that!"

Surai's face went blank, and Danielle felt a shiver of fear run down her spine. The older woman closed her eyes, and when she opened them again, it wasn't Surai who gazed out of them. The First Guardian's grey eyes seemed to glow, barely able to contain a soul that was vast and powerful and in no way human.

Kaestra was calm as she said, "I deny nothing."

Fear warred with anger, and anger won.

"Why?" Danielle demanded, giving her fury free rein. "Why take her life?"

"There was no other way." The goddess was implacable. "The vision needed to be shared."

"What vision could be worth more than Valori's life?"

"A vision of my death."

Horror leached all the fury from Danielle, and she shivered. "How?"

"I do not know. The vision is not something that can be expressed in words." The goddess glowered at Danielle. "If it were that simple, I would have spoken through one of my daughters, as I do now. It is not yet clear how this will happen, or why. But the warning needed to be shared."

"How can you not know?"

"No mortal being may know the sum and total of the future."

Those words, a direct quote from the *Primer on Prescience*, pierced Danielle at her core. She stammered. "But you—you—you are a—a goddess."

"Yet I am mortal," Kaestra replied. "I have a physical form, and I can die."

Danielle said nothing for a long moment, struggling to grasp that concept. "But if you die…"

"All that lives upon and within me dies as well," the goddess finished.

One life weighed against *all* life. Danielle closed her eyes against tears. When she opened them again, Surai was leaning against Lucas for balance, fully herself.

"Did you hear that?" Danielle asked.

Surai nodded.

Danielle looked down at the mirror. "The power behind this vision is too potent, too raw. None of us can view this safely. What good is a warning we can't read?"

Maeve sniffed and cleared her throat. "The power that inscribed the vision in the mirror will fade in time, but the message itself will remain. One day, it will be safe to look at what Valori gave her life to record."

While it was true that the residual energy used to imprint such recordings eventually dissipated, Danielle had never seen so much used. Kaestra had done more than impart the vision to Valori. She must have used the girl as a living conduit and recorded the vision with her own power.

"It will take years," Peyton added. "Maybe decades."

Danielle thought that estimate was optimistic, but before she could comment, Surai spoke softly.

"Even a century is no more than a moment to a planet. Kaestra imparted this warning *now* with full awareness of the time needed before it could be viewed. I am sure of it."

Danielle considered that, then inclined her head toward Valori. "There will be many questions about this."

Surai nodded. "How do you wish to answer them?"

"I have no wish to answer them at all."

"Then don't."

The abrupt response startled Danielle. "We have to say something."

Surai shrugged. "A seer died last night in the thrall of a vision that overwhelmed her. That is all you need to say. No one needs to know that Valori successfully recorded said vision."

"And what about this?" Danielle waved a hand to encompass the destruction around them.

"Blame me." Lucas said abruptly. "I'm a sorcerer. I'm in the Magicians Order in addition to serving in the outer court of the kae-madri. You can say that I lost control when I found her body."

Danielle blinked in surprise.

"It is a convenient explanation," Surai said.

"So be it, then." Danielle held up the black mirror. "The existence of this vision will be a secret among the senior oracles, to be passed down to our successors as required."

"And we will not speak of it again," Surai added, indicating herself and Lucas.

Danielle nodded. If Surai felt no need to share this with others among the kae-madri, that was her decision. She sighed with relief and renewed sorrow. "We will return to the seers' cloisters and send someone back with a litter."

Lucas stepped forward. "I can carry her."

"It's a long way to our chapel."

He was undeterred. "I'm stronger than I look."

"Very well, then. Maeve and Peyton will guide you. I will follow shortly.

Danielle watched the trio leave the garden with their burden. The cremation would need to be performed soon.

"Will her ashes be scattered in the seers' memorial field?" Surai asked, as if reading her thoughts.

Danielle considered the question and asked one of her own. "You have an alternative?"

With a graceful gesture, Surai indicated the garden in which they stood. "Perhaps this would be a more fitting resting place."

Valori had come here to record her vision. Danielle had no doubt that the girl knew she was going to die in the process, and *this* was the place she had chosen to spend her final moments.

"Agreed."

Surai placed a hand on her shoulder. "I *am* sorry for your loss, Danielle. This was a tragedy."

She looked the First Guardian in the eye. "It must be difficult being bound to a deity who can be so cruel."

Surai shrugged. "Kaestra is the world mother. She is both kind and cruel."

Danielle sighed. "She was not kind today."

"Is Fate any kinder, First Oracle?" Surai asked pointedly.

"I was born with the Sight, Surai. I had no choice."

As they left the garden together, Surai responded in a voice so low that Danielle could easily pretend she didn't hear her. "Neither did I."

Chapter 1

"We need to complete the firebreaks to the north!" A hoarse voice shouted to be heard above the throngs of residents who were being escorted out of buildings and herded southwards.

Another voice shouted back, "Crews are already on their way! We need to get these civilians evacuated to the other side of town."

Kimmo Samburu, governor of Tikal, gazed at the chaos in mute frustration. The northern sky was black with smoke, and the wind carried the smell of burned vegetation. Poma was not a large city, but it was densely populated, and the fire moving quickly along the valley was an imminent threat.

One of his guards suggested the fire might have been an attempt on his life, but Kimmo dismissed the idea. He might not be universally loved, but he couldn't imagine anyone would destroy an entire city just to get rid of him. Besides, a fire started on a relatively distant farmstead was hardly an effective assassination technique. No, he was certain that his presence in Poma was a mere coincidence. But that didn't mean that he could ignore the catastrophe that was unfolding right before his eyes.

His secretary, Kenta, hurried toward him with a grim expression on his face.

"Did the Mage Hall respond to my request?" Kimmo asked as soon as the young man was within earshot.

Kenta nodded. "They are sending two masters, but it will take some time. None of the master mages have been to Poma before, so they will need to teleport to the nearest city they are familiar with and then make jumps using line of sight to get here. Archmage Sarosha has also directed adepts from Zolin to journey here as fast as they are able."

Kimmo held his temper in check. In wasn't Kenta's fault that the news he brought wasn't what he wanted to hear. "Do they have estimates on time of arrival?"

11

Kenta's eyes dropped to the ground. "They expect the masters to be here within the hour, maybe sooner. The adepts are already on the train, which is scheduled to arrive in about forty minutes."

Kimmo grabbed the arm of the first official-looking person who passed nearby. "Are you in charge here?" he asked her brusquely.

"Obviously not." The woman dressed in the golden-brown uniform of a merlin snapped back, gesturing to the insignia at her breast pocket that marked her as merely a rank-and-file officer.

Kimmo bit back a curse. "Do you know who I am?"

She grimaced. "Governor Samburu. I apologize for not being awed, but right now, I have bigger concerns. Perhaps you didn't notice, but there's a fire racing toward this city." Then the merlin's demeanor softened a bit, and he could see how exhausted she was under the attitude.

"We're getting firebreaks in place; that should buy us some time. Are there any local mages here to help?" Kimmo asked.

"A few, and they're doing what they can, but the fire spread too far too fast. They just don't have the raw power to contain a blaze this size."

He closed his eyes and took a deep breath. "Can you point me in the direction of whoever is in charge?"

She directed him to a large building at the near end of the business district that was normally used for receptions and conferences.

"Thank you, Officer." Kimmo said more gently, "I intend to do everything I can to help."

When Kimmo and his small entourage entered the indicated building, they were immediately brought to one of the smaller conference rooms where a weathered looking woman with sharp features stood at the end of a long table, giving out orders and receiving reports with brisk efficiency.

When he introduced himself, she dismissed the others, seeming to know what he was after. When he asked if she knew what had set off the blaze, she kept her expression neutral, though her eyes looked cold.

12

"It started at the Baya farm."

"I know *where* it started. I asked if you knew *how* it started."

She stared at him for several seconds before responding. "The Baya family has had some bad luck the past few seasons and were tight on money. They needed a new hearthstone, and instead of buying one from the mages in town, they let the boy who usually recharges their magical devices try to configure one from a piece of raw magestone. The boy didn't have the skill or training to recognize that the stone was flawed. When he tried to set the spell, the stone exploded."

"Where is the boy now?"

"Dead. The blast killed him instantly. Judith Baya was in the house and if she hadn't been on the other side of a stone wall, she would be dead, too. The rest of the family were in the fields, and they evacuated as soon as they saw the fire."

"Who else knows?"

"No one yet. I took her statement myself, and I'm keeping it quiet for now. Is that all? We need to get this fire under control. Inquiries can wait until things have settled. I'm sure I don't have to tell you what's going to happen when the people find out that this was caused by a sorcerer lacking Mage Hall training."

He left shortly after that and took Kenta aside. "I need you to get me on the next train to New Avalon."

Kenta frowned. "It would be much faster to request that one of the masters teleports you there once they arrive."

Kimmo shook his head. He'd be traveling for the better part of two days, but he wasn't about to ask the Mage Hall for transportation. A minor inconvenience to him was no reason to distract them from what really mattered.

"Make arrangements for the train. And send a message to the Archdruid. I will need to speak with her as soon as I arrive."

*＊＊

Archdruid Celeste Amru didn't bother with formalities. As soon as she received word that Governor Samburu had arrived at the New Avalon station, she had a coach bring him directly to her residence. Her housekeeper escorted him to her office and left the two of them alone. By way of greeting, Celeste handed the man a glass of bourbon. He drained it in two swallows and held it back out to her, saying nothing.

She sighed and refilled the glass, pouring one for herself as well. When they both had drinks in hand, she asked, "Do you want to sit down?"

"I've been sitting for hours," he replied.

"Fine." She pointedly took a seat behind her large desk. "Stand if you want. Or pace."

"I assume you've heard about the fire in Poma."

She rolled her glass between her hands. She knew what he wanted, and she knew what her answer had to be. But she also sympathized with his situation, so she offered what she could. "I have already asked First Guardian Patricia to send guardians to Poma to see if they can help the land recover more quickly."

He glared at her. "I didn't come here to request aid from the Order of Kae-Madri."

"I realize that. But I wanted you to know that I've made arrangements anyway."

He drained his second drink almost as quickly as he had the first and then slammed the empty glass on her desk. "Damn it, Celeste! We need to do something. People could have died in that fire. We could have lost the entire town."

"What exactly do you want me to do, Kimmo?" she said flatly. There was no use in trying to soothe him until he had a chance to vent his temper.

"Talk to the other governors. Put forward a proposal to control all sorcerers who aren't formally trained."

She narrowed her eyes up at him. "No."

"This isn't about taking away people's rights—"

"Yes, it is," she said sharply before he could continue. "That is exactly what you are proposing."

"This is about keeping people safe," he growled back. "And not just ordinary people. This is about protecting untrained sorcerers from themselves as well. We did have one casualty at Poma: the young sorcerer who inadvertently started the fire."

Celeste sipped at the deep amber liquid in her glass, rolling it on her tongue before swallowing to give herself time to shape a reply. After a long moment, she said softly, "It's a dangerous road to start down, Kimmo. And that's why you want me to propose this rather than introducing the idea yourself."

He seemed to be calming down a bit, and after pacing back and forth a few times, he dropped into one of the chairs across from her. "I've only been in office two years, and I don't have any family with magical talent. Coming from me, this could be taken the wrong way. But you are well respected by the entire Council of Governors, and you're a sorcerer yourself. No one would question your intentions."

Celeste let out a brittle laugh and shook her head. "Maybe not, but there would be considerable speculation as to whether or not I've taken leave of my senses."

"Please, Celeste." His tone had changed from angry to pleading. "Something needs to be done. This isn't an isolated incident. There have been other accidents, maybe not as severe, but bad enough. And I've been getting a lot of letters from constituents who are worried that this is only the beginning. As more people develop magical talent, the risks increase."

"Have the writers of these letters identified themselves? Maybe they've requested a meeting to discuss their concerns?"

"This is a sensitive subject. No one wants to be known as stirring up trouble that could impact their neighbors."

At just over forty, Kimmo was still young, and as he himself had pointed out, he was very new to his position. But she hadn't thought of him as naïve before this. "I wouldn't put too much credence in complaints submitted by anonymous sources," she said. "For one thing, you have no way of knowing if these letters are really coming from your own people, or how many individuals are sending them. This could be nothing more than a tiresome effort by one or two malcontents with an axe to grind."

"I'm not the only governor receiving such letters. I bet you've gotten some yourself."

Celeste stood and came around the desk to lean against the corner closest to him. "I have." In fact, she had received far more than a few in the last year, but since the majority were from unidentified senders, she didn't trust the motives behind them. "But that doesn't mean that I am going to propose something to the Council that could result in sorcerers being stripped of their rights as citizens of Tarya. If you question why I am taking this stand, I suggest you brush up on your history, specifically the Isolation Years on old Earth. Do you want a repeat of those past atrocities?"

Kimmo gulped. "I'm not suggesting we do anything like that."

She laid a hand on his shoulder. "It's a slippery slope, my friend."

He closed his eyes tightly for a moment, and Celeste suspected that he was holding back frustrated tears. Softly, he said, "We need to do something."

Celeste spent the next half hour saying soothing things while Kimmo finished off two more glasses of bourbon. By the time he left, he was calm, though she suspected the alcohol was owed more credit for that than she was. He wasn't wrong about the problem, but she knew without a doubt that he was wrong about the solution. Still nursing her first drink, she sat down to write a letter to the Archmage to see if there might be another way to address the current difficulties.

Jaron Sarosha welcomed the Archdruid into his home with a low bow. As Archmage, his rank equaled hers, but he was somewhat new to his position and a bit awed by her. "You honor me with your visit, Lady Amru."

She looked amused. "It is you who honor me, Lord Sarosha. I was relieved that you were willing to entertain me on such short notice."

Lady Amru was tall for a woman, thin, though certainly not frail, and she carried herself with grace and dignity. Her earth-brown skin showed only the faintest lines of age, and her eyes were much like his own, a brown so dark as to appear black from a distance. Her face, handsome rather than pretty, was dominated by those eyes and framed by steel-gray hair plaited into dozens of intricate braids that cascaded down her back and over her shoulders.

He led her to the parlor and invited her to sit. "Can I offer you any refreshments?"

She shook her head. "Later, perhaps. I suspect that I will want a strong drink before the day is over." She tilted her head at him. "May I ask a favor?"

"Of course, Lady."

"Can we *please* dispense with the formalities? I would much prefer you to call me Celeste."

"Of course, Celeste," he said in a more relaxed tone. "And you should call me Jaron."

She smiled. "Thank you, Jaron. I wasn't just being polite, you know. I do appreciate you seeing me on such short notice."

"Your letter was rather vague," he prompted.

"There was just too much to put into a letter. You know about the fire in Poma?"

"Of course." He didn't bother to hide his frustration.

"Let me fill you in on some of the details you probably *don't* know about." She began to describe the current situation, which was interwoven with political intricacies that Jaron would have been happier remaining ignorant of. Though sadly, much of it he already knew—or had guessed.

"If I understand you," he said when she was finished, "at least some of the governors want to enact restrictions on sorcerers who lack formal training, but none of them want to be the ones to propose it."

"You've cut to the heart of it," Celeste said.

"And what does this have to do with me?" he asked. "I'm not on the Council. Even if I were, I would never propose such a thing. Not because of how it might reflect on me but because it's wrong. Pure and simple."

"Tell me, Jaron: do you think that the current system is working? Do you think that having untrained sorcerers using magic without safety measures in place is a good idea?"

There was no accusation in her tone, just open interest in his assessment of the situation. It was for that reason that he felt comfortable answering her.

"No. We're failing people. Every time there's an incident like the one in Poma, I have to deploy mages to deal with it as best they can, so I know better than anyone how bad things can get when someone overreaches. But it isn't as if there are rogue sorcerers around every corner deliberately wreaking havoc. Most of the time, it's someone with good intentions, little training, and poor judgment."

She nodded. "So. How do we make things better?"

Jaron looked at her incredulously. "You've got to be kidding. If it were that simple, something would have been done long before now."

"I was surprised when you were chosen to succeed Branek. You're quite young to be a master mage, much less leader of the Mage Hall."

Jaron was thrown off by the abrupt change of subject. "I know that I'm inexperienced, but—"

She cut him off with a gesture. "You don't need to justify yourself to me. The majority of mages voted for you. That's enough."

18

"Some say I was only nominated because the rest of the mages wanted the youngest person they could get after Lord Branek died in office."

"Others, because you are currently the most powerful mage alive."

Jaron felt his cheeks grow warm and dropped his gaze to the floor. "Which do you believe?"

"Both."

He jerked his head up to meet her eyes.

"You are young," she said pointedly. "You are powerful. And you are now the undisputed leader of the Mage Hall. Branek was old and set in his ways. He was never going to change the status quo because the status quo kept him comfortable. But you have every reason to embrace change, and you have the means to make it happen."

"It's a bit more complicated than that."

"Details," she replied dismissively. "I'm not asking you to solve this overnight. I am asking that you find a path forward and that you use the power that has been given to you to pave it. You don't face reelection. Unless a majority of the other mages declare you unfit, you will be Archmage until you choose to step down."

"Or until it kills me," he said. Then he groaned as he realized how tasteless that statement was, given Branek's recent death.

Celeste didn't seem to mind. "Hopefully not."

"And what will you and the other governors do while I am blazing this new trail?" he asked.

"Very little, I'm afraid. I am currently on my way to Maliae to meet with the council. If it goes as I expect, we'll spend a week debating and arguing and will accomplish nothing.

"As the Archdruid, you lead the Council of Governors. Can't you do anything?"

"I lead the Council to the extent that I formally conduct the meetings, nothing more. You do realize that the title of Archdruid is just what the governor of Avrin is called, right? It doesn't convey any special power."

"But Avrin is the capital of Tarya."

Celeste shrugged. "It's still only one province of nine. I'll admit that I have some influence over the other governors due to my experience, but not enough to make any real difference."

"Would it help if I offered to speak at the meeting?" He didn't really want to do that, but he understood the importance of cooperation in such matters.

"No." Celeste said firmly. "And I would prefer that you didn't share what I've told you with anyone you can't trust to remain discreet. If asked about my visit, you can say that I was taking the opportunity to offer you belated congratulations."

"Why? Are these matters really that secret?"

"Every governor on the Council has received letters in the past year demanding that something be done to control sorcerers. Some even suggest that binding the power of any sorcerer with minor talent at an early age would effectively solve the problem."

Jaron swallowed bile at the thought. "No," he said weakly. "There's no way an idea like that would gain any traction."

"It won't," she assured him. "At least not anytime soon. But the other governors are nervous about these demands, not to mention the increased frequency of magic-related accidents. When we last convened, we agreed to keep this matter within the Council. This information could only promote further unrest if widely known. The last thing we want is to give potential malcontents a public forum. The Council also decided that any investigation would need to be conducted independently of the Mage Hall."

Comprehension came quickly. "You think that a mage is behind this."

"The letters are well-written, demonstrate a deep understanding of how magic works, and present frighteningly compelling arguments. They point to someone educated and gifted in persuasion as well as magic."

"They suspect a master, don't they?"

"Frankly, a few of the other governors suspect that you're behind it."

"What?" he exclaimed.

She laughed without mirth. "Think about it. You are powerful, intelligent, and extremely young to have risen to such a high position. It makes a certain kind of sense."

"You don't—" he began, but she cut him off.

"Of course not. I don't even think that all the letters were written by the same individual, though I wouldn't be surprised if there is a single person directing this campaign."

"Wait a moment," he said with a frown. "Are we talking about a few dozen complaints against sorcerers, or a conspiracy?"

"That remains to be seen."

"Do you expect me to find out who is behind this push for regulation of sorcerers?"

"No," she replied gently. "I think that I've placed a large enough burden on you already. You have a new trail to blaze, remember?"

He remembered all too well.

"I hope your faith in me is not misplaced," he said.

"I'm a good judge of character, and I believe that you will do well. But I advise that you exercise caution when deciding who to confide in from this point on. You'll need allies, but you should choose them wisely."

Jaron swallowed hard. "Some of my own people may be involved in this push to control sorcerers with limited talent. If they are, they probably won't be inclined to cooperate with any alternative solutions."

She nodded and gracefully rose from her seat. "I hate to say this, but you need to watch your back."

He stood and held out his hand to her. "Thank you, Celeste. I may not like the news you've brought, and I'm not sure how I feel about the task you've set for me, but forewarned is forearmed, as they say."

She looked him in the eye as she grasped his offered hand and squeezed firmly. "For what it's worth, Jaron, I believe that you have what it takes to make a difference in all this mess. Trust your instincts, and you'll be fine."

***

The Hall of Mirrors was deserted when Perrin Kiaru passed through the long room before descending to the vault that lay beneath it. The First Oracle was unsurprised by the emptiness. Few people visited during the day, much less at the crack of dawn.

He'd asked the other senior oracles to meet him in one of the private viewing chambers this morning. He sensed them already waiting for him, so he hurried to retrieve the mirror from its resting place.

Second Oracle Chu-Lin Sadray and Third Oracle Reed Valancy stood within the simple circular chamber, their impatience palpable.

"We're here," Chu-Lin said sharply, her blue eyes dull with sleepiness.

"I know it's early. I wanted to be sure we wouldn't be disturbed."

"Don't mind Chu-Lin," Reed said gently. "She's not a morning person."

"The sun is barely up," Chu-Lin countered. "This scarcely qualifies as morning."

Perrin took a deep breath, hugging the mirror to his chest. "There is something I need to share with you."

Reed snapped to attention. "Which vision is that?"

"The first recorded vision of Seeress Valori Lunais."

"And the last," Reed added.

Chu-Lin paled. "Why have you brought *that* here?"

"I've been having a recurring dream for the last few months, and it led me to this vision."

Reed was incredulous. "A few months? Why didn't you mention this sooner?"

"I was hoping I would receive another message that would make more sense."

"Were the dreams that vague?" Chu-Lin asked.

"I dreamed about Valori's death, as if I were witnessing it firsthand."

"And that led you to her prophecy." Reed nodded. "Something has changed. We need to look at this again."

"Why?" Chu-Lin shuddered. "Every senior oracle for the last forty years has seen it. I remember it well enough."

"But something has changed," Reed repeated.

"Recorded messages *don't* change." Chu-Lin was adamant.

"But our responses to them *do*," Perrin said firmly.

Before Chu-Lin could stop him, Perrin placed the mirror in the stand at the center of the room and initiated the spell to activate the projection.

Barren, empty land surrounded them. Dead land. The scale of the devastation was more than the aftermath of war or natural disaster. Not a single sign of any kind of life remained.

When the ley lines came into view, the true nature of horror became clear. The kaema that flowed through the veins of Kaestra was...tainted. The very life blood of the planet had been turned to poison. Kaestra was dead, as was all the life she supported.

Chu-Lin closed her eyes, but Perrin knew it would do no good. The record was more than a visual imprint; it assaulted every sense. It felt cold enough to burn. The air smelled stale and left an acrid taste in the throat. And the absolute silence chilled the soul.

Perrin held his breath until the scene began to shift. Gradually, another set of images depicting a healthy and whole world overlaid upon the first. The double vision was both unsettling and reassuring.

A few moments later, three bright but indistinct glowing shapes coalesced out of the air and began to move toward one another. Perrin watched them draw together, feeling hope rise within him. Threads of light emerged between the shapes to form a triangle of power. The energy of that triangle felt clean and fierce and *alive!* At its center, a column of light erupted with great force, plunging down into the ground and up into the sky.

From that glowing pillar, bright energy raced along the ley lines, cleansing them of the poisonous taint and leaving nothing but pure, uncorrupted kaema in its wake. As the ley lines were cleansed and replenished, the image of the wasteland faded, leaving only the scenic beauty of their planet to surround them. Perrin quietly wiped tears from his eyes. He glanced at Chu-Lin, who was weeping without restraint, and then at Reed who looked—entranced.

The images around them blurred and faded. The last thing Perrin saw were the three glowing shapes disappearing as the vision ended.

"Has it begun?" Chu-Lin asked with a sob.

Before Perrin could reply, Reed spoke. "It has."

Perrin drew a sharp breath. The Third Oracle was in full trance, body rigid and eyes unfocused. Questions leaped into Perrin's mind, but before he could voice them, Reed spoke again. "The three are born. The threat approaches. Events are in motion."

"What must we do?" Perrin asked the power that flowed through Reed.

"Our secrets must be kept. The chosen are not ready and must be protected."

"How can we protect them? Who are they?"

"Silence will protect them. Only the daughters may know they are here. We must watch and wait."

Before he could ask anything else, Reed swayed on his feet. Perrin and Chu-Lin converged on him, catching him before he could fall.

"Do you remember what you said?" Chu-Lin asked.

Reed's expression was grim as he regained his balance. "It's started."

"The chosen are born," Chu-Lin whispered.

"I wonder if they are human or kaesana?" Perrin mused.

"They feel human to me," Reed replied.

Reed's response was unsurprising. The vision had come through a human vessel, and few of the prophecies he was familiar with involved the kaesana. And yet, he had a strange feeling that the dragons had a role to play in this, even though they had largely withdrawn from active stewardship of the planet. The source of that feeling remained elusive, however, so he chose to keep it to himself.

"And we can't tell anyone yet." Chu-Lin sounded desperate. "We still need to bear this burden alone."

"Not entirely alone," Perrin said. "Only the daughters may know they are here. That must refer to the Order of the Guardians. That's what kae-madri means: the daughters of Kaestra."

"Not yet," Reed said softly.

"Why?" Chu-Lin was clearly uncomfortable.

"We should wait until the kae-madri approach us. I think that they will know when the time is right."

"How will they know if we don't tell them?"

"They know Kaestra. They'll know when she is in need."

"But will the chosen ones be ready?"

After a weighty silence, Perrin said, "We wait for now. The three are *born*. I don't think that three children, much less infants, can counter a disaster. Let's give them time to grow up." Before Chu-Lin could argue, he added, "In the meantime, we stay watchful. If we see evidence of this threat, we will reach out to the First Guardian."

"So be it," Chu-Lin said softly. Reed merely nodded.

Perrin took the mirror from its stand and gestured for the others to precede him from the room. As they left, Chu-Lin turned and laid one hand gingerly on the mirror, her eyes closed.

"Are you all right?" he asked.

She shuddered and met his eyes. "Valori gave her life just to record this message. What will the three who are chosen to save the world have to give?"

**

"Lady Karimah is here to see you, Master Tarvis," Alicia announced with a bright smile.

"Her proper title is Adept," Tarvis corrected mildly.

His petite and pleasant housekeeper set her fists on her hips and glared at him. "As far as I'm concerned, she is a lady as well as an adept, and it's no disrespect to call her so." Before he could respond, she added, "I'll show *the lady* in and then fetch you some tea."

Tarvis was still shaking his head after her when Karimah entered the room. Her light brown skin was slightly flushed, and she brushed back several strands of long black hair that had escaped her braids. He rose from his chair and greeted her with genuine warmth. "You look a bit windblown, my dear."

She huffed. "There's a storm coming. I'm glad I made it here before it started raining."

While she settled on the couch, Alicia returned. Tarvis eyed the tray she held with some surprise. "Honey crisps?" he asked attempting to convey only mild interest.

The twinkle in Alicia's eyes told him that he'd failed to hide his eagerness. "Lady Karimah has always been fond of my honey crisps," she replied with a nod to his guest. "If you need anything else, just send for me."

With that, she left the room and closed the door behind her.

"*I'm* rather fond of your honey crisps," he said to the closed door. Then he turned to Karimah and added, "But I don't often see them at teatime."

"Maybe you should invite me here more often."

As they settled to enjoy their tea, he tried to keep the conversation light and pleasant for as long as possible. The small sitting room felt like an oasis of comfort on such a gray and blustery day, and he didn't want to disturb the peace with dark conversation. Sadly, Karimah was too shrewd to believe that this was strictly a social call.

"Let me guess," she said after about five minutes of small talk. "Lord Sarosha has sent another request for your assistance."

He nodded and sighed. "Yes, though only a request. The boy is still too damned polite to issue a proper order."

"Don't you think it's a good thing that he shows you some respect?"

"He shows respect, yes, but he won't listen, not when it comes to anything important."

"Has there been any news from the Council of Governors?"

"None. And at this point, I'm not sure that anything useful will come from that direction. And before you ask, the Senate has been silent as well. I think the High Court of Ovates has taken notice, but as long as Jaron continues to deal with the matters they send to him, I doubt that they will do much to make any meaningful reform."

Karimah remained silent for a long time, her expression distant. Finally, she spoke. "If we cannot rely on the government or the judiciary, perhaps we need to try a new tactic."

"Such as?"

"Talk to Jaron directly. Explain your concerns and share your ideas for correcting the situation."

"No!" The word erupted out of him before he could stop himself.

"Do you hate him so much?"

That surprised him. "I don't hate him at all."

Karimah looked at him speculatively and he turned away from her. He didn't hate Jaron, but he did hate what his leadership was doing to the Mage Hall. He was young and reckless and held little regard for tradition. His ideas were too progressive, and he refused to listen to the counsel of those with greater experience. He couldn't trust Jaron to do the right thing.

"From his point of view, I'm probably ancient." Tarvis muttered, prompting Karimah to laugh.

"Eighty-two is hardly ancient, even to a pup of thirty-five" she said with a soft smile. "But it's true that his perspective may be somewhat skewed by his youth, and I agree that something must be done. However, unless you have a plan to challenge his position, I don't think you have much choice but to work with him."

He shook his head in mute reply.

She sighed. "Look at the bright side. As the headmaster here, you can do as you please. Jaron granted you full autonomy."

He nodded, recalling how much that gesture had surprised him. He had to admit that Jaron had been a gracious winner. He had offered him his pick of positions within the Mage Hall, and when he'd requested the post of headmaster of the satellite Mage Hall in Athens, Jaron had agreed without hesitation. He had yet to implement all the changes he wanted to make, but there was no question that he was free to do so.

"You could use your position here to your advantage," Karimah continued before he could become completely lost in his own thoughts. "There may be no other masters here yet, but look at how many adepts agreed to join you. They didn't uproot themselves on a whim. They came because they prefer to work under your hand than Sarosha's. And more than a few of them are young, even younger than Jaron. There might even be future masters among them."

There was at least one that Tarvis knew of. "Maybe, but I'd need an overwhelming majority to depose Jaron. By the time I get it—if I get it—it could be too late."

"Too late for what?"

He stood and walked to the window, staring into the rain that was now coming down in a steady drizzle. "All this trouble with sorcery gone awry."

"You're really worried."

"Yes." He turned to face her. "There are simply too many sorcerers out there, most of whom will never have sufficient power to become mages. But limited as they are, they still draw on kaema, which is a finite resource, despite what most people choose to believe."

"Do you really believe such weak sorcerers pose a threat to the ley lines?"

"It's hard to be certain since sorcerers aren't required to register with any recognized authority, but my estimates suggest that as many as five percent of the population has some trace of magical ability, and the numbers keep growing with each generation."

"Is that really enough to cause problems?"

"We're talking about hundreds of thousands of people. That's more than enough to cause problems."

"The only way to fully control the use of magic is to control the people who have magical abilities. That means binding the power of any sorcerer who isn't fit. Even if you were Archmage, you couldn't do that, Tarvis. You'd need the backing of the Council of Governors and the Senate to even suggest that sort of measure."

"There may be another way." He needed to confide in someone, and she was the only one he knew he could trust with this, at least for now.

"What other way?"

"We don't need to bind the power of individual sorcerers if we can control the flow of kaema."

She shook her head. "That makes no sense. You can't control kaema. It's all around us. Not just concentrated in the ley lines, but in the soil, in the water, in the air. How can you control something that permeates everything?"

"I've been studying this. I've found references to a way to bind kaema into a form that can only be accessed with a key. I realize that capturing all kaema would be difficult, but we might be able to store the majority of it, similar to the way the ley lines do. With proper controls, that should be enough to ensure that kaema would always be available for mages to use, and it would prevent most of the abuses we've been seeing."

"I don't doubt your abilities, but what you are proposing sounds rather impossible."

At that, he pulled out a small piece of gray kaeverdine, the material commonly referred to as magestone, and handed it to her.

"What's this?" she asked, examining the stone carefully.

"If I'm right, it's a starting point."

Chapter 2

Aria hesitated before opening the door to her office, dreading yet another confrontation with her anguished son-in-law. Mariah's death was hitting everyone hard, especially Larin.

Mariah had been generous and kind, and her serene nature had made it a joy to be in her presence. It was little wonder that so many had loved her. She'd accepted everything that life had brought to her with grace—even her own death. Aria could still feel the tiny squeeze that Mariah had given her hand moments before she fell into the sleep from which she never woke. There had been reassurance and contentment in that small gesture, and Aria knew that her daughter's spirit was at peace.

When Aria finally entered the room, she was shocked to find her husband alone.

"You let him leave?" she accused. "In his condition?"

"Of course not." Micail gestured to the far end of the room where the young man was sprawled across the sofa. He appeared to be sleeping soundly, but Aria didn't like the way he lay there with his limbs at odd angles.

"He finally fell asleep?" She couldn't quite believe it. Larin hadn't eaten or truly slept in days.

"Not voluntarily." Micail tossed a small syringe onto the desk. "Don't worry about waking him. Sanell assured me that he'll be out for at least twelve hours." He snorted. "The stuff worked fast, too. I barely had enough time to get him to the couch, and slender as he is, he's no lightweight."

"We should have Sanell take a look at him," she commented as she straightened Larin's limbs and brushed his golden-brown hair back from his face.

"Already arranged. He'll send a couple of apprentices shortly to bring him down to the infirmary. At the very least, he'll probably need intravenous fluids."

"Should we summon a healer?"

"Sanell is a skilled physician. He can take care of him."

"Physically, yes. But the rest?"

"Magic won't help, Aria. No. I know what you're thinking, and trust me, no ethical healer would touch his mind to try to erase his pain. He needs to work through it and get past it. We all do."

"I wasn't suggesting anything so drastic." It hurt that he believed she would think of such a thing, but she also had to admit that her thoughts had begun to drift in that direction.

Micail took her into his arms. "Sweetheart, I know you want to help him, but we're doing everything we can."

Aria knew better than to argue with him. "Did he fight you?"

"He was exhausted and distracted. He never saw it coming."

"He'll be angry with you when he wakes up."

"I doubt it. There's no room in him for anger right now."

Micail was right. Larin was utterly consumed by grief. She and Micail had lost their only child, but as fierce as their anguish was, it was dwarfed by what Larin appeared to be feeling.

"Perhaps we should have told him," Aria said, wondering if it was the shock that gave Larin's pain such an edge. "We might have been able to prepare him for—"

"No." Micail cut her off. "He knew she was ill. She never hid that from him. Breaking her confidence would have changed nothing. We owe it to Mariah's memory to move on with our lives. Larin needs to understand that."

"I think he's trying to kill himself." Aria almost choked on the words. "Not consciously, perhaps, but if he keeps this up, he'll sicken and die as surely as she did."

"Unacceptable!" Micail said with more than a hint of temper. "He has his children to think of."

Aria's eyes filled with tears at mention of the children. She had only just come from Riahn's bedside where she'd held him while he cried himself to sleep. His sister was less than a year old, far too young to understand what had happened. Shae-Lydra had taken her away to canyi Shaendari the previous day at Aria's request.

Always perceptive, Micail asked, "Shae-Lydra is sure she'll have enough milk for Glasnae and Naeri? The baby's wet-nurse could have gone with her."

"Naeri's almost weaned. Lydra will have enough for both."

Micail sighed. "She's that old already?"

"She's eight, only a year younger than Riahn, remember?"

"They grow so fast." His eyes grew soft with memory. "She was such a little thing when she was born. It still amazes me that a newborn dragon isn't much bigger than a human infant."

"They have more time to grow," Aria pointed out.

"True enough." He took a deep breath. "Naeri will enjoy having Glasnae at the canyi, and the baby will be better off with the Shaendari for now. Too much grief here and no one with enough time to give the girl the attention she needs."

"I know. That's why I asked Shae-Lydra to take her."

Micail hugged her close. "You could go to Canyi Shaendari, too. Take Riahn and get away from here, at least for a few days."

"I'm the governor of Maliae. I can't just leave."

"Even governors are allowed time to grieve, love. And I can mind things in your absence. As it is, your stewards have already arranged everything to give you as much peace as possible."

Reluctantly, Aria shook her head against his shoulder. "I'm tempted, but I can't. Not yet. Glasnae is better off with the dragons right now, but Riahn should be here with his father, and I can't leave him, or Larin." She glanced at her unconscious son-in-law. "The boy is like a son to me."

"To me as well, but he's not a boy. He's a man, and sooner or later he needs to act like one. I've already done as Mariah requested and added Larin's name to the list of candidates."

Aria bit her lip. "Is there any way to postpone the election?"

"Not unless you've changed your mind about retiring in the next five years. Mariah was your elected heir. It takes time to properly train a successor."

Aria swallowed hard. "No, I've served long enough. I'm ready to step down, but you know as well as I do that there's a good chance that Larin will be elected. I'm not sure that he's ready to deal with that."

"Larin was already learning how to govern at Mariah's side. He always expected to help her, just as I've helped you over the years."

"That's not the same thing. Now the full burden will fall on him."

"Larin may not have expected this, but Mariah did. She knew she wouldn't live to be governor, but she bowed to the wishes of the people and fulfilled her obligation as best she could. She always believed that Larin would make a good governor, and I agree."

Aria nodded mutely. There were several other candidates, including those who had lost to Mariah when the initial election had been held ten years earlier, but she didn't think they stood much of a chance. The people of Maliae had always shown a preference for members of the reigning governor's household as successors.

Micail held her in silence for a long time, allowing her to draw strength and comfort from him. It was so tempting to take his suggestion and go to her dragon-kin, but she couldn't wallow in grief at the expense of those who needed her. She also recognized that Micail was right about Larin. He could not be allowed to continue this way. He had responsibilities as well. He needed to come to terms with Mariah's death and move on.

Aria pulled back a little, and Micail loosened his hold but didn't let go entirely. He looked into her eyes, and the love she saw there comforted her. "Mariah had a happy life."

"And she's left an enduring legacy. Those children of hers will do great things someday."

"We just need to get them over this hurdle first."

Micail grunted. "If we can get their father out of the pit he's fallen into, they'll be fine. But that will be no easy task."

Inspiration struck Aria. "While Sanell sees to Larin's body, I'll see what I can do about bolstering his spirit."

Micail's eyes narrowed slightly. "What do you have in mind, woman?"

"There are times when a man needs his mother," she answered simply. "I'll send word to Linia and ask if she can stay for a while after the memorial services."

"You two never got along very well." There was a hint of warning in his voice.

Aria flushed. "I know. But Larin is her son, and I think he'll listen to her. She can be tough and no-nonsense, but that might be just what he needs. I certainly haven't been able to get through to him."

"All right. But Glasnae stays with Shae-Lydra," Micail insisted. "Linia is a good woman at heart, but I don't think she has the right temperament to handle her granddaughter just now."

"Mariah named Shae-Lydra as maternal guardian to both children. Riahn's old enough that he should stay with his father, but Glasnae is still just a baby. No one could convince Lydra to give her up at this point. You should have seen the look in her eyes when I handed her over. Lydra already thinks of Glasnae as her own."

That seemed to satisfy him, and he released her after one last hug. "All right, then. Do what you think is best, sweetheart. But keep in mind that Linia has a way of taking over. I don't want you to suffer because she's here."

Aria stepped away from him and set her face in a stern mask. "I know my place. I have a province to govern and people to care for. Linia will have her hands full with Larin. She won't have time to meddle in my affairs, and I won't give her the opportunity."

She opened the door for Micail, a gentle dismissal, before he could reply. He turned on the threshold to face her, his expression quizzical. She forced a smile and asked him to make sure that Sanell's apprentices were on their way to fetch Larin. He nodded and left the room, and she closed the door behind him.

She sat at her desk to draft a message to Linia, careful to avoid looking at Larin. The sight of his face, marked by grief even in sleep, was more than she could bear. She'd managed to keep her own exhaustion and pain at bay, but it was only a matter of time before she succumbed. She was determined to fulfill her responsibilities as best she could, but once the memorial services were over and the election was done, she would go to her dragon-kin at Canyi Shaendari. There, she wouldn't be Governor Maylan, ruler of Maliae. There, she would just be Aria, a mother who had lost a child and needed to grieve.

***

An hour earlier, when the room had been filled with people, it had felt incredibly small. Now that only the four of them remained, it was cavernous. Larin slumped in his chair, wondering how he was going to do everything expected of him. He felt hollowed out and wanted nothing more than to retreat to the rooms he had shared with Mariah, crawl into bed, and cradle the pillow that still held her scent.

Aria caught his eye for a moment and then looked away. She had been withdrawn ever since his mother arrived four weeks ago. He knew they didn't get along well, but Aria seemed distant even when Linia wasn't in the same room. Then he reminded himself that she was grieving, too.

The conversation between Linia and Micail had been going on for the better part of an hour, ever since the other candidates and dignitaries had taken their leave. Larin had ceased to pay attention some time ago and was only waiting for a long enough pause to announce that he was going to bed. He couldn't muster enough energy to interrupt outright.

Micail's voice betrayed his rising impatience. "I don't know how many ways I can say this, Linia. The other candidates have privately conceded, but the results will not be official until all the votes are in, and that will likely take another week. There will be no formal announcements until then, but you certainly don't need to stay."

"I'm not about to let my son face this alone. He needs someone at his side, and you and Aria will have your hands full. This will be difficult enough for Larin without the added social pressures. I can protect him and deflect unwanted attention. He is still in mourning, after all."

"The whole province is in mourning!" Micail was truly angry now. "No one will be anything less than considerate of Larin, and the formalities will be low-key and brief. There won't be a string of parties."

"Please!" Aria's voice was stern. "Larin is sitting right here. Stop talking about him as if he weren't even in the room."

There was a sudden tense silence, just the opening Larin had been waiting for. "I'm going to bed," he said flatly, rising to stand on shaky legs. Linia stood and approached him but stopped short when he met her gaze. He had no idea what he looked like, but if it was enough to give his mother pause, he needed sleep more than he thought.

"We should have adjourned long ago," Aria said softly. "I'm sorry, Larin. It was thoughtless of us to keep you here when you're obviously tired. Everyone is too keyed up right now. We could all do with a good night's sleep."

Larin nodded appreciatively and walked to the door. His mother wished him a good night but said nothing else. He wasn't surprised. No doubt she was looking forward to the opportunity to continue the debate in his absence, but he doubted that Micail or Aria would oblige her, at least not for long.

When Larin closed the door behind him, he heard a few muffled sounds that indicated that someone was speaking again, but he paid no attention. He walked through the corridors without giving any heed to his surroundings, following the path to his rooms by rote.

Only when he was safely in his suite with the door closed and locked behind him did he allow the pent-up tears to fall. Memories of Mariah flooded his mind: The way her nose crinkled when she laughed at one of his stupid jokes. The feel of her fingers gripping his hair, pulling him toward her for a kiss. The two of them playing hide and seek with Riahn. The sound of her voice as she sang Glasnae to sleep.

A pang of guilt assaulted him at the thought of his children. He knew he'd neglected them since Mariah's death, but he didn't know what to do for them. Riahn was nine, old enough to understand and young enough to grieve without shame or restraint. He'd held his son and cried with him, but he could no more ease Riahn's pain than he could his own.

As for Glasnae, he hadn't even seen her since Shae-Lydra had taken her to Canyi Shaendari. At the time, he'd numbly agreed with Aria that it was for the best. Now, he was simply relieved that he had no immediate responsibilities where the baby was concerned. She was far too young to understand what had happened, though she no doubt missed her mother's presence. His throat tightened at the thought that she would probably have no memories of Mariah when she grew up.

He promised himself that he would do better. Once he learned to live with this gaping hole in his heart, in his life, he would be a better father to his children. He would reconnect with his son. He would bring Glasnae back home and give her the attention she deserved. He would do better. He just needed a little time.

He stripped out of his clothing, then rolled everything into a ball and tossed it in a corner. He crawled naked into bed, on Mariah's side. Snuggled into the space that had been hers, he found a small measure of peace. It was as if some part of her was still there, as if her love could still reach him. It was the only comfort he had.

Gradually, he drifted off to sleep. The image of a raven-haired beauty with deep blue eyes filled his mind, and he surrendered to the loving embrace that he could now only savor in his dreams.

Chapter 3

Jaron successfully fought the urge to teleport directly to Tamara's house. She'd told him the boy was suffering an episode of uncontrolled release of kaema—what they called a poltergeist—but that she had the situation under control, and he believed her. She was very experienced at helping young sorcerers learn how to tame their power, but Andris Odara was not just another budding sorcerer. Andris was special.

He still set a quick pace and arrived flushed and out of breath just in time to see the whirlwind that surrounded the boy slowly subside. Tamara tossed him a hard look before returning her attention to the child. "It's all right, Andy. It's over." She moved toward him very slowly, arms open in a welcoming gesture.

"I'm sorry." The boy sobbed and dropped to his knees.

"There's nothing to be sorry for," she said as she closed the distance between them, "You're still learning. We've talked about this. These things happen. It was very thoughtful and clever of you to come outside. You did well."

"I can't control it." The boy's voice sounded hoarse. "I didn't mean to get angry, but when they said that Gina couldn't play with me, I just…"

"I know." Tamara crouched down and gathered him into her arms. "I understand. I would have been angry, too. And you *can* play with Gina. Those boys had no right to say you can't."

"Really?" There was such sweet hope in that young voice.

"Really." Tamara snuggled him close, rocking back and forth. "I'll talk to her parents myself. I promise."

Jaron kept his distance while Tamara comforted Andris. The boy hadn't seen him, and he suspected that his presence would only cause more upset. That was probably why Tamara had asked him to take his time when she sent for him. It wasn't long before the boy's head fell against her shoulder. Still holding him close, she stood up and carried him toward the house.

Come in, she sent mind to mind, clearly not wanting to wake the child in her arms.

He followed her into the house and watched as she laid the little boy gently on the couch in the sitting room. She smoothed back the tangled golden curls from his face and kissed him lightly on the forehead before shooing Jaron out of the room and into the kitchen.

"Should we shield the room?" he whispered as he took a seat at the kitchen table.

"No" she replied in a soft, but normal tone of voice. "I used a sleeping spell, and he was already exhausted. He won't wake easily."

"How bad was the poltergeist?" he asked, avoiding the term "magical seizure" so often used by non-sorcerers that seemed to equate magical ability with illness.

She sat down opposite him and sighed. "Bad enough. He felt it coming and ran outside, so there's no physical damage done. I just wish I could get through to him that this is a natural part of being born with magical ability. He blames himself whenever something like this happens, but he's just too young to fully control his power. His parents have always been understanding, so I know that the guilt doesn't come from them."

"I hope I'm not putting too much pressure on him."

She looked at him for a long moment before responding. "No, we've been careful about his training, and I don't think that any of the adults he's exposed to have been anything but supportive."

"You can't say the same for the children." It wasn't a question.

"We want to believe that all children are innocent, open, and accepting, but we know better. Andris is a sweet, sensitive, and affectionate child. That makes him an easy target for bullies."

"Who?" he asked more sharply than he should have.

She shook her head. "No. It's not your place to get involved. Jonas and I are his foster parents. We'll deal with it."

He knew better than to argue with her, so he tried another tactic. "Who is Gina, and why did the boys tell him he couldn't play with her?"

Her expression said that she knew exactly what he was up to, but she replied anyway. "Gina is a girl that Andy goes to school with. For some reason, the boys like to tease her. Andy stood up for her, and they told Andris that boys can't play with girls. They said that Gina's parents would punish her if they found out that they were friends."

"Where are the other boys now?"

"When things turned bad here, I called Caleb. He ran over and took them out to the orchard. He'll keep them busy for another hour or so and then take them home."

"You could have asked me. Andris is my personal apprentice after all. I have a responsibility to handle this sort of thing."

Exasperation radiated from her in waves. "Really, Jaron? You think that a mage who teaches basic magic to youngsters is unqualified for the task? You think that I should have summoned the *Archmage* to deal with a handful of children who had just witnessed another child in the first throes of a poltergeist? I can't even begin to think how they would have interpreted *that*."

She had a point. "Fine. So, if I wasn't needed to control the situation or deal with the little monsters responsible, why exactly did you call me?"

"They're not monsters."

"I respectfully disagree. Now, why did you call me?" He tried to hold her gaze, but Tamara stared down at the table.

"He's so young to be so powerful," she said.

"We knew that when he first came here. Is it more than you can handle?"

She still wouldn't meet his eyes. "I'm strong enough to deal with the poltergeists, but I don't know if I can really help him."

"You're doing a wonderful job, Tam. He's only been here a few months and he's already exerting better control than when he arrived. That is as much due to your efforts as mine."

"That's not what I mean, Jaron." She squeezed her eyes shut as if holding back tears. "He's hurting. His misses his family, especially his sister. No matter how many times we tell him that coming here isn't a punishment, no matter how much love and affection Jonas and I shower on him, he still feels as if he's been exiled from his home. And let's face facts, that's exactly what has happened. His parents had no way of dealing with his power. It's a lucky thing that Hayden recognized the situation for what it was before someone got hurt."

"We can't send him home, Tam. He needs the support of people powerful enough to deal with situations like the one that just happened. He needs to be taught by a master. We're doing what's best for him."

"Are we?" Tamara asked in a small voice.

"What else would you suggest?"

"I love Andy as much as if he were my own, so please don't hate me for saying this." She took a deep breath. "You might want to consider binding his power."

Jaron stared at her in shock. Tamara was one of the last people he'd expect to say such a thing. She finally lifted her head to look at him. Her expression was tortured. There was no other word for it. He knew that as awful as it was for him to hear such a suggestion, it was even more painful for her to make it.

He reached out and took her hands in his own. "We have no way to just limit his power—we can only take it away entirely. Do you really think that would be in his best interest?"

"You're not the one holding him when he cries himself to sleep at night. He's alone, Jaron. Even here at the Mage Hall, he has no real peers. His power is already greater than the average fully trained mage, and he'll only get stronger as he grows up. It won't be long before I don't have the power to contain his poltergeists."

"By the time his power outstrips yours, he'll have the control he needs."

"Even assuming I believe that, it doesn't change the fact that he has no one to relate to. He will always be set apart. It isn't fair."

"I can't do it, Tam. Even if he asked me to, I wouldn't do it. No matter how difficult it is for him now, I have no doubt that he would regret losing his power. Magic is part of who he is. Taking that away from him, no matter how good the reason, would be wrong."

She nodded, and Jaron got the distinct impression that she was relieved. "There must be something we can do." She wiped the tears from her eyes.

"Maybe there is," Jaron began hesitantly, trying to decide if he should share an idea that he'd been toying with over the last few weeks.

Tamara seemed to recognize his reluctance, and prompted gently, "I'm open to suggestions."

He gave her hands a squeeze. "I do have an idea, but it will mean a lot more work on your part. I don't want you to feel cornered into accepting. You can say no. If you don't want to, I'll think of some—"

"Stop it, Jaron!" she exclaimed, pulling her hands away. "At least tell me what you have in mind before you try to talk me out of it."

"Would you be willing to take on another fosterling?"

"Another one?" she asked. "But Andy would stay with us, right?"

"Of course," he assured her. "You would end up with two children instead of one. I could scale back your course load to give you more time at home."

"Most of the children here are so much older than he is," she said slowly. But Jaron could see that she was already warming up to the idea.

"His sister is four years older than he is, and they get along quite well."

"Do you have anyone in mind?"

"No. I thought I'd take a look at the current applications. That would be better than trying to shift a child who has already bonded with a foster family. I would, of course, review any candidates with you first. And if it doesn't work out, we can find an alternate family for the second fosterling."

"That doesn't seem entirely fair to the other child."

"The goal is that every child at the Mage Hall receives the attention and support they need. Not all fosterlings land in the right home the first time around. This wouldn't be any different."

"Are you sure?"

The light in her eyes made him sure. "Yes. I'll take a look at the applicants and let you know in a few days if any seem like a good match."

***

Later that night, sitting in his office with a small stack of files, Jaron flipped open the folder on the top of the pile and looked at it again, wondering if he was only seeing what he wanted to see.

The application was for a boy a little less than a year older than Andris. The child was strong magically, but not so strong that he needed extra tutoring in control. In fact, he seemed to have mastered control, which was highly unusual given his age and level of power. There wasn't any pressing need for the boy to be admitted to the early program, but if his intellectual abilities were even close to what his teachers suggested, it would be worth bringing him into the Hall for special instruction.

The aptitude tests indicated a child advanced well beyond his years who was especially gifted in mathematics, pattern-recognition, and problem-solving. The letters of recommendation and notes from instructors added another layer of insight, describing a boy who was easily bored in standard classes and difficult to challenge. Reading between the lines, Jaron also got the impression that he was somewhat isolated from his peers and that he even had some difficulty relating to his own parents, neither of whom possessed any magical talent.

He closed the file and folded his arms across his chest. It was almost too perfect—as if fate had provided him with exactly what he was looking for before he had even known to look.

He shook his head and stood up to stretch. He was entitled to a little kindness from fate. After spending the last few years struggling to maneuver the Mage Hall through the minefields of political intrigues and internal grandstanding over the management of non-mage sorcerers, it was nice to see something good come of his efforts.

At least no one had faulted him for his expansion of the early admissions program for the very gifted. The other mages were all too happy to encourage those with great power. And if his policy to take on paying students of lesser ability was still a bone in the throats of some people, at least they had ceased to vocalize it at every opportunity.

He sat back down to prepare to draft a formal letter of acceptance to the parents of a young boy named Kylec Dracami.

***

The boy sat quietly in his chair, eyes downcast, hands folded in his lap, and legs swinging slowly back and forth. He had barely spoken a handful of words while his parents were present, and then only when asked a direct question. He was the very picture of a respectful, perhaps even shy, child. And Jaron wasn't buying it for a minute.

Taking a seat across from him, Jaron leaned forward and rested his arms on his knees to be closer to the child's eye level. Kylec was tall for his age, with light brown skin that he suspected would hide all but the deepest of blushes, dark brown hair shading toward auburn, and hazel eyes that were just a bit too knowing for a six-year-old.

"You can drop the act," Jaron said with a smile.

Kylec raised his head, his expression innocent and slightly confused. But there was a cunning in his eyes that he couldn't quite hide. "Sir?" he asked politely.

"You're not shy, and you're not intimidated by me in the least. Since I know that, there's no need for you to pretend."

Kylec's eyes narrowed, clearly assessing. "Are you reading my thoughts?"

Jaron shook his head. "I would never invade your privacy like that. Besides, given your level of awareness, I think you'd know if I tried."

This time, the surprise wasn't at all feigned. The boy tilted his head to one side and said carefully. "I want to study here. My mother said that I needed to be polite if I wanted to get in, so I'm being polite."

Jaron chuckled. "I take it that your parents believe that polite children are to be seen and not heard?"

"Not exactly," the boy began carefully. "They don't mind if I talk, as long as I act my age. I'm not very good at that, though."

That simple statement coupled with the letters of recommendation from Kylec's teachers provided Jaron with all the insight he needed. The child was perceptive and clever, and no doubt many of the adults in his life, including his parents, found him unnerving to be around.

"I'm not very good at acting my age either," Jaron said with a grin.

"But you're a grown up," Kylec responded.

Jaron winked at the boy. "Not everyone would agree with you about that."

Kylec leaned back and crossed his arms over his chest, staring at Jaron with a mix of hope and suspicion for several moments before nodding to himself. "You were smart when you were my age, weren't you?" the boy finally asked.

Jaron nodded. "I was. And I'm smart enough now to recognize potential when I see it."

Kylec's expression brightened. "You mean I can come to school here?"

"Yes."

"Promise?"

"Promise," Jaron affirmed, holding out his hand. "Shake on it?"

The boy took the offered hand and shook it firmly.

47

That small act of faith seemed to offer the boy all the reassurance he needed, and he soon turned talkative. What followed was a meandering conversation about his favorite subjects, his hobbies, and his opinions of the various teachers he'd had.

When the subject came around to friends, the boy became more subdued. "Most kids don't like me very much."

"Maybe they're jealous," Jaron suggested.

The boy snorted. "Most are just scared. Which is fine by me. I prefer to be alone than put up with bullies."

"Do you get bullied a lot?"

"I used to. But I'm fast, and I'm strong, and bullies are cowards deep down. Now they leave me alone."

Jaron frowned. "You use magic to fight back?"

He snorted again, grinning broadly. "Of course not. You don't need magic to handle bullies. Most of the time, you don't even need to fight if you think things through. I'm quick and smart. Tricking someone into falling into a compost bog is a lot better than getting in trouble for fighting. And a lot more fun."

Jaron grinned back, and at his prompting, Kylec filled in the details of that adventure. He was equally impressed by the boy's determination to stand up for himself and the forethought and restraint he exercised in the process. The more they talked, the more he liked this child and wanted to spend time with him.

After sharing a few carefully edited stories of his own somewhat adventurous youth, Jaron brought the conversation back to friends. "So, you don't currently have any close friends near your own age?"

"It's okay," the boy replied, almost dismissively. "Like I said, I don't mind being alone."

"I understand that. But what if there was someone you got along with? Someone who wouldn't be intimidated by your intelligence or power?"

Kylec's expression turned thoughtful. "I don't dislike other kids. And I don't pick fights. If you're worried that I won't get along in class, I promise it won't be a problem."

"I'm sure it won't be," Jaron said softly. "But I want to make sure you have the opportunity to meet others you might have more in common with."

The assessing look was back in Kylec's eyes. "Okay."

"Children your age aren't admitted to the dormitories, you know. You would need to be fostered with a family while you're here."

"I know."

"The family I have in mind currently has one other fosterling, a boy just a little bit younger than you."

Jaron knew he had piqued the boy's interest when Kylec sat up straighter and leaned forward ever so slightly. "What's his name?"

"Andris." Jaron replied smoothly.

"And he's here because he's smart, too?"

"I don't think he's quite as clever as you are, but yes, he is smart. Though he originally came here because his magic ability is very strong. Do you think that's a problem?"

"As long as he doesn't use his power to pick on other people, it's not a problem."

"Andris would never do that," Jaron said with conviction. "But he does lose control sometimes."

"You mean like a poltergeist?"

Jaron thought about that question for a moment. He was glad that Kylec used what he considered the proper term. It meant that at least some of the adults in his life had a positive view of magical talent and understood the challenges young sorcerers faced. But according to his records, Kylec had never experienced that kind of uncontrolled outburst of kaema. For a child with such significant magical talent, that represented a remarkable level of control, and he was curious to see what Kylec's opinion of the subject was.

"Exactly. Does that idea frighten you?"

Kylec shrugged. "No. I've seen it happen to a couple of other kids with talent. It's got to be scarier to feel than to watch. I'm glad I don't get those."

"You've never had one?" Jaron asked for confirmation.

"Nope," Kylec responded matter-of-factly. "My tutor, Jasper, said that I have really strong shields, so the magic doesn't just spill out. And I don't actively pull in kaema unless I have a really good reason."

The expression that accompanied that comment held such mischief that Jaron was torn between fascination and dread, and he decided to forge ahead before he got sidetracked any further. "Would you like to meet Andris?"

"Sure!" Kylec replied with enthusiasm, jumping up from his chair. "Right now?"

Jaron took the boy's hand to lead the way. "I can't think of a better time."

***

Camp Fraxin, the merlin training camp in Ashton, was directly adjacent to the Mage Hall and consisted of a few dozen stone and wood buildings, neatly arranged around a massive open green. The architecture was simple and sturdy, as befitted such an installation, but the craftsmanship of the construction was of the highest caliber, and there was a certain kind of beauty to the clean lines and logical arrangement of the structures.

The same pragmatic design could be seen in the central green space, which was divided into a large parade ground along with several smaller practice fields meant to accommodate the various exercises and forms of combat training.

Master Aidan Varano stood on the top of the low retaining wall that surrounded one such practice field, a square of approximately fifty feet on a side, sunken about three feet below the surrounding ground level. From his vantage point Aidan had an excellent view of the seven pairs of combatants who faced off, waiting for the signal to begin. Sergeant Randon Blake whistled sharply from his position beside him, and the air filled with the sounds of wooden swords clashing against each other. Jaron, paired with a merlin cadet less than half his age, was attacking and defending with what Aidan thought was a fair display of skill. The boy was a bundle of energy who bounced from one location to the next with remarkable agility, but his strikes looked half-hearted.

"Damn it, Ben. You'll never land a blow that way!" Randon called out. "You're too timid. Get in there and attack! With the way Jaron moves, you should have enough time to strike and retreat before he has a chance to react."

Aidan grimaced on his friend's behalf. Apparently, Jaron wasn't as skilled as he'd thought.

"And you, Jaron. You've got to be faster than *that*. You're practically moving in slow motion! Your blade should be in place to block his attack the moment he starts to move, not halfway through the thrust."

Ben began attacking with more determination, and Jaron struggled to keep up. They circled. Ben moved in with a thrust, and Jaron raised his blade just in time to deflect it. He took a step back and feinted to Ben's right, then turned to thrust toward the boy's left side. But Ben was too quick and spun out of the way, pivoting to catch Jaron under his left arm with the tip of his blade.

"Point!" Ben declared.

Jaron nodded to acknowledge the hit and moved back to the starting position. Before they could resume their bout, Randon whistled again, calling a halt to the training session.

"Fifteen-minute break!" he yelled. "And then be back here for drills."

There was a collective groan from the cadets as they returned their practice weapons to the rack. Jaron set his sword in its place and trotted over to them. Aidan grinned down at him. "Are you going to stay for drills?"

"Might do you some good," Randon commented sharply when Jaron just shook his head.

"I think I've had enough exercise for one afternoon," he replied. "Besides, I have other commitments today."

Randon snorted. "I'll grant you're in decent shape for a mage, but any one of my cadets could run circles around you."

Aidan laughed but quickly took a step back when the sergeant rounded on him. "Maybe you should join your friend here and take up a practice sword from time to time."

"I'd rather get my exercise in a less combative way."

"Fencing exercises mind and body. You might be surprised by how much both could improve."

"Aidan's mental agility is quite remarkable as it is," Jaron said in his defense.

"The offer stands." Randon growled and walked away toward the barracks.

Jaron waited until the sergeant was out of sight before he leaned against the wall. Aidan dropped down beside him. "You don't want him to see just how tired you are, do you?"

"Would you?"

Aidan considered for a moment and replied, "I guess not."

"Thanks for meeting me here. Michaela is on her way."

"I don't mind, but I would like to know why you asked us to meet you here rather than somewhere on campus."

"I have another meeting scheduled for this evening. I wanted to talk to you both beforehand, but I also wanted to get in some exercise. I figured we could talk on the way back to the Hall."

Aidan frowned. Something about the situation didn't feel quite right. "What's been eating at you lately?"

"What do you mean?"

"All this sparring is more than just exercise, Jaron. Something is bothering you."

"I've been fencing for years."

"Yes, once, maybe twice a week. You've been down here almost daily the past few weeks. So, what's bothering you?"

"Am I interrupting?" Michaela asked sweetly as she approached. "Or is this an open conversation?"

"Michaela!" Jaron greeted her with more enthusiasm than seemed warranted, and Aidan suspected he was only glad to have an excuse not to answer his question. "Let's walk back to the Hall. I'll explain on the way."

"Jaron!" She put her hands on her hips and huffed. "I just came from the Hall. Now you want to go back?"

"He's multitasking, Michaela," Aidan offered. "Our Archmage is so busy that the only way he can get enough exercise these days is to schedule walking meetings."

She glanced at the rack of sparring swords and then looked at Jaron. "Fine," she said with more than a hint of tartness. "But if you try to hit me with a stick, I'll smack you upside the head before you see it coming."

"Don't worry," Aidan replied with a smirk. "According to Sergeant Randon, Jaron is so slow that he'd never move quick enough to block you even if he *did* see it coming."

"Well, then. I guess I should have made an effort to get here sooner. It sounds like I missed quite a show."

They fell into step easily enough, and Aidan was reminded of their childhood years when Jaron would sneak off campus to practice with the merlins and he'd tag along. They walked in comfortable silence for several minutes, giving Jaron time to catch his breath and gather his thoughts. Aidan wasn't sure what was going on, but he was certain that it was something important.

Jaron broke the silence with a question that caught Aidan by surprise. "Do you think that I've done the right thing in taking Andris as my personal apprentice?"

Michaela answered before he could collect his thoughts. "I think that you've done very well by Andris. He's come a long way in a short time."

"I agree with Michaela," Aidan added. "Considering his age, and how powerful he is, his control is impressive. What's really worrying you, Jaron? You can't possibly think you're lacking as a teacher."

"A few weeks ago, Tamara confided in me that he's lonely and homesick. After discussing some of the difficulties he's been having, she agreed that it might help if she took in another fosterling. Give him a sibling of sorts here at the Hall."

Michaela smiled. "What a lovely idea, Jaron. Let me guess, that little darling, Meredith, right? Isn't she just about the same age as Andy's sister?"

Aidan didn't think that it was a good idea to try to recreate Andris's home life at the Hall, but before he could comment, Jaron replied, "No doubt she would have been Tamara's first choice, but I asked her to let me review the candidates first. In the end, she agreed with my recommendation."

When Jaron didn't continue, Aidan prompted, "And do you plan to share the name of the child you've convinced her to take in?"

"Yes, but first I have to ask you something else." He took a deep breath. "Do you think I inadvertently isolated Andy from his peers?"

While Aidan understood the concern, it was illogical. "Andris is exceptionally powerful. That's what sets him apart. Being your apprentice is a minor thing in comparison."

Michaela nodded her agreement with Aidan. "Few Archmages take on personal apprentices, but it isn't without precedent. Lord Branek had two in his younger years: Tarvis Neroon and Sandra Neems. The rest of the Hall held them to a higher standard perhaps, but I don't think either suffered because of it."

"Sandra is so vivacious that it would have taken more than special status to keep her from making friends. As for Tarvis...well, he is a bit of a loner."

Aidan shook his head. "Tarvis is a very private man, but I wouldn't call him a loner. Besides, I don't think his apprenticeship was the determining factor in that, do you, Michaela?"

She snorted. "Branek fed his ambitions and stroked his ego, but Tarvis always set himself above the rest of us."

"Do you think that's what I'm doing with Andy?" Jaron still sounded genuinely concerned.

"Of course not!" Michaela and Aidan replied nearly in unison.

Michaela continued. "You can't compare the two, Jaron. I've known Tarvis for decades, and I've spent a fair amount of time with our little Andy. Two people couldn't be more different. Andris doesn't believe that his power places him above everyone else. I think he sees his abilities as both a gift and a responsibility."

"And a burden?"

"To some extent, yes," Michaela admitted. "But under the circumstances, that is to be expected. As he develops more control and learns how to *use* his talents, the feeling should fade."

Aidan watched the tension slowly drain out of his friend and asked pointedly, "Why the sudden concern, Jaron?"

Jaron took a deep breath and said, "I'm thinking of taking on a second apprentice."

The pieces fell into place for Aidan, and he groaned. "Let me guess, the second fosterling you're placing with Tamara and Jonas, right?"

Michaela frowned. "Whatever for, Jaron? If you're worried about Andy being lonely, placing a second child with Tam makes a world of sense, but why burden yourself with another student? To make a point that Andris isn't the only one worthy of having the Archmage as a teacher?"

"Does it sound that ridiculous?"

"Not ridiculous, just unnecessary," Aidan replied.

"I wasn't planning on it originally," Jaron admitted, the corner of his mouth turning up in a slight smirk that was all too familiar to Aidan.

"No more stalling. Which child are we talking about?" Aidan asked, suspecting he knew the answer.

"Kylec Dracami," Jaron replied levelly.

"Did I meet him?" Michaela asked, frowning as if trying to place a face to the name.

"No, you didn't," Aidan supplied. "You would have remembered him if you had."

"He's that remarkable?" she asked.

"You could say that." Aidan gave Jaron a hard look. "He's not in the same league as Andy."

"No one is," Jaron countered. "Myself included. But then again, no one is exactly in Kylec's league, either. Well, you might come close."

"What does he mean, Aidan?"

"I conducted Kylec's initial power assessment and placement tests. Assuming he follows the usual developmental pattern, he'll be a powerful adept one day, *maybe* even a master. But what makes this boy special is his intellect. Put simply, he's a mathematical genius."

"Doesn't that make him better suited to be Aidan's apprentice than yours, Jaron?"

Jaron shrugged. "Eventually, I suspect that Aidan will take over his training, but I can stay ahead of him for a while. I may not have Aidan's skill, but I'm not exactly devoid of talent. And this way, I can keep my two one-of-a-kinds under my wing, and perhaps they can take some comfort in sharing the status of being apprenticed to the Archmage."

Michaela nodded. "There is a certain logic to it, and I can't see any harm in it for either child. Of course, if they don't get along, you could have a problem."

Jaron grinned. "Ah, we're already off to a positive start. I brought Kylec over to Tam's three days ago. When I spoke with her this morning, she told me that they are getting along remarkably well and that the little squabbles that have cropped up are the good-natured type to be expected between siblings, foster or otherwise. I realize that it's still early to be sure, but I am cautiously optimistic that they'll do well together.

"Kylec's parents are heading home tomorrow, and I'm meeting with them tonight to finalize the arrangements for the boy. Since you don't seem to have any objections, I'll inform them of my intention to take him on as my apprentice."

"It sounds like you have everything well in hand, Jaron," Michaela said with obvious approval.

Aidan scowled. "I won't argue with your plan or fight you over which of us would make a better mentor for Kylec. As you said, I'll likely be teaching him eventually. But I want you to admit to Michaela, and yourself, exactly why you felt the sudden urge to make this boy your protégé."

When Jaron didn't respond and Michaela flashed him a baffled look, Aidan explained that while he had been conducting the child's assessments, he'd been reminded of another precocious boy who had come to the Hall early.

"Yourself?" Michaela asked.

"No." Aidan pointed at Jaron. "Him. It's no wonder Jaron is looking forward to teaching Kylec. It will be like teaching a younger version of himself."

"Hmm," Michaela said thoughtfully. "If that includes his penchant for mischief, perhaps it's only fitting that he assumes this responsibility."

"Mischief?" Jaron scoffed. "The boy just has inventive ways of dealing with difficult situations."

She arched an eyebrow and glanced meaningfully at Aidan. "Inventive, you say? Such words were used to describe the two of you on more than one occasion. Just stay sharp, Jaron, if you want to keep a step ahead of your new apprentice."

If Michaela's warnings had dimmed his enthusiasm at all, Jaron didn't show it. They were back at campus before a truly appalling thought occurred to Aidan. "Did you even think to warn Tamara?"

"Warn her about what?" Jaron asked.

"You've just placed one child with a precocious ability for devising extremely complex spells with another child who has more than enough power to cast them."

When that thought fully sunk in, Jaron replied, "This could get complicated."

Michaela sighed. "No, it's quite simple. We just need to make sure that discipline is maintained, at least as much as possible." She patted his arm. "Go clean yourself up and give the boy's parents the good news. In the meantime, Aidan and I will talk to Tamara and Jonas and let them know that life is likely to be *interesting* for the next several years."

Jaron grinned and headed to his house. Michaela took Aidan's arm and started leading him toward Tamara's house near the edge of the campus. "I didn't volunteer for this," he grumbled.

"Nope," she agreed. "You were drafted."

"Why?"

She threw back her head and laughed. "Because you and Jaron will undoubtedly need to help Tamara with her charges from time to time, and at least one of you should tell her so in person."

"This wasn't my idea!" Aidan protested. "I shouldn't be dragged into it."

"Do you remember all the times I pulled you and Jaron out of one scrape or another when you were young?"

"Yes," he replied reluctantly.

"Do you remember arguing that it was all Jaron's idea, and you just went along with it?"

"Yes," he grumbled.

"And what was my answer back then?"

"I don't remember," he lied.

"I pointed out that *you* were supposed to be the clever one, and if Jaron outsmarted you, it was because you let him." She gave his arm a squeeze. "I saw the look on your face. You might be worried about what kind of trouble these children could get into, but you're also intrigued by the potential of such a friendship."

He didn't remember feeling that way, but now that she said it, he knew it was true. If the boys lived up to their promise and forged a bond strong enough to last into adulthood, they could accomplish great things together. It would be amazing to see, assuming the rest of them survived it.

"Okay, Michaela. I'll talk to Tamara, and I'll help out in any way I can."

"Oh, Aidan," she said with another laugh. "That is so sweet of you, as if you actually had a choice."

Aidan didn't respond to that. After all, he was supposed to be the clever one.

***

Among the nine provinces of Tarya, Maliae was unique. With the notable exception of Avrin, each of the other provinces derived its traditions from a different segment of the myriad of ancient cultures from old Earth. The people who had founded Maliae had taken a quite different approach: they had gone native.

Even the name Maliae came from the kaesana language rather than any human tongue and loosely translated to "joyous union." The name represented the bond that the humans shared with their kaesana neighbors. Maliae had the highest percentage of joined families of any province, as well as the highest concentration of kaesana clans living within its borders. It was also an exceedingly large and diverse province with a vast array of resources. The resulting culture that had developed was rich and vibrant, but the intermingling of human and kaesana customs bordered on the strange.

It was this strangeness that set Tarvis's nerves on edge as he observed the tavern from his secluded corner table. Rough-hewn stone was the dominant building material, and the walls undulated in a manner designed to simulate a natural cavern. Baskets overflowing with plant life were suspended from the ceiling amid the lightstones, giving the impression of sunlight shining through a forest canopy. Some people might have found the effect charming, but Tarvis did not.

He idly stirred the contents of the bowl in front of him. The kaesana influence was even apparent in the food. The night-hearth stew that the establishment provided to its late-night visitors was a thick concoction of cooked grains in addition to meat and vegetables and was seasoned with unfamiliar herbs. The taste was tolerable, but he had barely touched it. He couldn't quite reconcile the stew-like flavor with the porridge-like consistency. He lifted his mug and took a long drink. At least the ale was good.

Karimah returned from the ladies' room a few moments later, looking faintly wary. The glamour she was using was expertly crafted, but she seemed uncomfortable in her own skin. Her natural coloring was warm and dark: rich brown skin, golden brown eyes, and straight black hair. She had transformed herself into a pale, curly-haired blond with ice blue eyes. Even if she hadn't also altered her features, the change would have been startling.

When she sat back down beside him, he leaned over and whispered, "Perhaps you should try a more subtle disguise next time, my dear. I can only imagine how you reacted when you looked in the mirror."

She frowned at him, clearly unamused. "At least *I* still look my age."

He laughed. He *had* made himself look considerably younger. The persona he'd adopted for this foray was that of a merchant looking for new business opportunities. As a young man trying to work his way up through the company, he would be expected to be outgoing and enthusiastic in pursuing new contacts. Gossip was a time-honored tradition among traders, especially among those looking to make career-advancing connections, and Tarvis was planning to use that to his advantage.

Karimah's role would be that of senior manager. The people they met would show her deference and respect but would expect her to stay in the background while he did the grunt work of negotiating. They'd already met with representatives from two separate trade companies and had yet another meeting planned. In each instance, they were careful to collect contact information rather than provide any themselves. After all, the porcelain patterns contained within their carefully assembled portfolio were as fictitious as the faces they currently wore.

"You're enjoying this game of yours too much," Karimah accused.

He shook his head. "This isn't a game. This is a necessary step to achieving our goal."

"I still don't see why. If you're successful in containing and controlling the kaema in the ley lines, it won't matter what people think. You'll decide who has access to kaema and who doesn't."

"Of course, it matters. It will be a lot easier to maintain control if people support what we've done."

"I don't think you can expect support on this, no matter what rumors you spread."

"Not at first, perhaps. People rarely react well to sudden change. But in time, they'll come to realize that everyone is better off."

"As you pointed out, there are a lot of unaffiliated sorcerers out there. They aren't going to be happy about losing what power they have."

"Their numbers may be growing, but they are still a small percentage of the population. Once we've succeeded, I expect that those without magical ability will be relieved to know that only the most qualified individuals will have access to kaema."

"Maybe. But if that's the case, they won't really need convincing, will they?"

"I thought you approved of my plans?"

Karimah looked profoundly unhappy. "I approve of your plan to control magic and prevent its misuse. But your methods feel wrong, Tarvis. A lot of innocent people could get hurt."

He understood her concerns but was confident that he could prevent that from happening if he handled it carefully. "I have been stressing that the people are not to blame, that it's the overly free use of magic that is the problem. I'm being extremely cautious, and very subtle."

"You're invading people's thoughts. It's one thing to try to control the ley lines, but it's quite another to try to control other people's minds."

He was grateful for the interruption when he spotted their target: a burly redheaded man they had met briefly earlier in the day. Tarvis made eye contact with the man and nudged Karimah. "I believe that our next contact just arrived."

She followed his gaze and groaned.

He closed his eyes and sighed. "Please let this go."

"I'm sorry. I agreed to help, but it's difficult to watch. This isn't like you. You're not this ruthless."

So easy to let her believe that, but it wouldn't be right. "I *am* this ruthless when I have to be. That's why I can do the right thing when Jaron cannot. I am prepared to do whatever is necessary to protect our future. Jaron is an idealist, and he makes people feel safe even when they aren't."

Their contact reached the table and nodded to Tarvis and Karimah in turn, smiling broadly. "Terrence, Karin. Business is thirsty work, is it not?"

"Pull up a chair, Gavin," Tarvis did his best to adopt the same hearty mannerisms as the trader.

Gavin did so, and they launched into a discussion about the wares. As expected, Gavin suggested that hiring a mage to transport the goods might be a better option. "Not that I'm refusing, mind you, but breakables don't fare so well on long hauls. Your stuff looks awful fine, and we don't handle much that's delicate."

"Teleportation is expensive," Tarvis countered with a rehearsed frown. "Only adepts and masters can do it, and their fees are high. We would have to be very selective about which communities we sold in, and we were hoping to expand our market a bit more."

Gavin turned thoughtful. "There are ways of protecting more fragile items. Not as pricey as hiring an adept, but I'm afraid it will add somewhat to the cost of carriage."

"What did you have in mind?" Karimah asked on cue.

"Well, there are plenty of sorcerers about who can craft shields to protect breakables during a journey. They charge quite a bit less than Hall-trained mages since they don't pay tithes to the Hall, and a lot of them also have other skills that can be handy on a long trek. We haven't hired any on in several seasons, but I can put out feelers to work up some quotes for you."

Tarvis made a great show of looking nervously at Karimah before replying, "I'm not so sure we'd be comfortable with that."

"Why not?" The man looked perplexed. "You're not uncomfortable with magic, are you?"

"Not at all," Karimah said, "but we prefer to hire only fully-trained professionals, not amateurs."

"I wouldn't call them amateurs, Karin. I would never hire someone who wasn't competent."

Karimah glanced at Tarvis and then down at her watch, before replying, "I'm sure you wouldn't." Then she smiled and excused herself. "Terrence is well acquainted with our policies and can discuss this matter with you further. It's been a long day, and I'm quite tired. I hope you don't mind if I retire."

"Of course not." Gavin, looking faintly relieved, offered his arm to help her to her feet. Then he bowed deeply as she took her leave.

Mindful of the need to maintain the proper appearance, Tarvis sent her a silent message and she turned back to him briefly, her expression carefully stern. "Do not forget yourself, Terrence. While I have complete confidence in you, you are not authorized to finalize any contracts without my consent."

He replied in an appropriately meek tone of voice. "Of course. I will report to you regarding our progress first thing in the morning."

As soon as Karimah left the room, Gavin plopped back down in his chair and leaned toward Tarvis, his voice tinged with sympathy. "She keeps you on a short leash, eh?"

"She's very traditional. I won't say that I disagree with her, or with the company's policies, but it can be frustrating."

"Well, a bright young man like yourself should be moving up soon. Give it another couple of years, and you'll be the one in charge of the deals."

Tarvis smothered a self-satisfied smile. The man was playing right into his hands. "I hope so. In the meantime, I have to abide by the rules."

"Rules that won't allow you to work with sorcerers who aren't mages?"

"Our company's official policy limits our involvement with magic-users to fully trained mages, with the exception of magical healing, in which case we rely on the services of qualified healers."

"That must add a lot to your costs."

"I thought it odd myself at first, but a person who achieves the rank of mage or higher can be expected to have a certain level of skill and integrity. The Mage Hall sets high standards for its people and expects those standards to be maintained. Now, I'm not saying that most unaffiliated sorcerers aren't good people, but I'm not so sure that every person who *can* use magic *should* use magic."

Gavin looked confused. "Most people who can use magic aren't strong enough to be mages, but many of them are quite skilled."

"I don't doubt it," Tarvis said, forcing a glum expression, "but I've seen and heard of things that make me wonder if it would be better if such people kept their skills to themselves."

Gavin looked mildly irritated as he asked, "What sort of things?"

Tarvis hid his disappointment. He'd been hoping that all he'd need was the right choice of words to convince the man, but stronger measures were clearly called for. Fortunately, Gavin was not only completely devoid of magical talent, but his weak mental shields also indicated that his psychic abilities were minimal as well. It took remarkably little effort for Tarvis to slip beneath the man's defenses and craft a subtle compulsion spell.

Gavin's eyes went out of focus for a moment. When they cleared again, he leaned a little closer to Tarvis and said in a voice that was equal parts curiosity and nervousness, "What sort of things?"

Tarvis proceeded to recount a series of carefully prepared tales describing incompetent sorcerers and the disastrous outcomes of their mistakes. It wasn't hard. Considering the number of magical accidents he'd been called upon to clean up after over the years, he didn't lack for raw material.

His message was clear: when self-trained sorcerers offered their services in place of mages and healers, it often led to disastrous outcomes, regardless of the intent of the practitioner. He was careful to avoid any suggestion that the individuals were inherently corrupt or willingly did harm. Instead, he focused on the idea that they simply lacked the power and proper training to be effective, and that their ineffectiveness could have serious and unpleasant consequences.

The spell he wove around Gavin's mind ensured that the other man listened carefully, believed every word of the stories he heard, and would eagerly repeat them. It also wormed its way into his subconscious and established a deep sense of distrust of unregulated magic that would color his future experiences. By the time he and Gavin said their farewells and he made his way back to his rented room, Tarvis was confident that the seeds he had planted in Gavin's thoughts would take root and spread.

Chapter 4

1463 AHS

The tall cliffs that surrounded the crumbling city offered a breathtaking view as Shae-Lydra gazed down from her perch. The Ruins spread out below, filling the small valley. Kaesa Daerisa. Center of the World. The last and greatest of the kaesana cities, now often called "The Ruins" by humans and kaesana alike.

At one time, most kaesana lived in grand cities such as this one, and their civilization had rivaled any that the humans ever aspired to. But that was all long ago.

As a matriarch of her clan, Shae-Lydra knew the history better than most, and it made her sad. Not the loss of such greatness, but the cost of it. Her people lived more simply now, and she was glad. One only had to look at the stresses and struggles humans imposed upon themselves to see the value of living free of such burdens.

Still, the ruins of Kaesa Daerisa were beautiful, and she couldn't help but wish that she could have seen it in its full splendor. The other cities had been carefully dismantled in an attempt to restore the ecosystems of Kaesa Atera, the world humans had come to call Kaestra. The task had taken generations to complete. This last city was still a central part of kaesana life, though no one lived there anymore. The Ruins were now a place for the clans to gather to tell the old tales, exchange new ones, and perform certain sacred rites, such as The Dance.

While she took joy in the delight her youngest children expressed in seeing this marvel, there was also sorrow. Today marked her eldest child's passage to adulthood, which meant that he would soon be leaving his childhood home—and her—to join another clan.

"There's Vanek!" Naeri shouted and pointed to the distant figure of her older brother performing an elegant swoop. Naeri dutifully held her mother's hand while the wind lifted her wings, and she fought the temptation to join the dancers who flew below her. Mirsa clung fiercely to Lydra's leg, even as she craned her neck to look where Naeri was pointing. Mirsa was not kaesana but was every bit as much Lydra's child as Vanek and Naeri were. She was the daughter of her human sister-in-heart who had died five years earlier, and she considered Lydra her mother in every way that mattered.

Shae-Lydra leaned down to stroke the little girl's head and spoke reassuringly to her mind, *I will not let you fall, love.*

I know, Atar, the child answered in kind, *but the wind is very strong, and it's a long way down.*

Lydra suppressed a sigh. It both saddened and puzzled her that Mirsa was afraid of heights. The girl had been raised among the Shaendari Clan since she was less than a year old, and there had never been any mishaps or accidents that would give her cause to be fearful. But Lydra also admired Mirsa's bravery. She faced her fear, which was why she was able to stand here on the edge of the cliff.

Lydra returned her attention to The Dance and its backdrop.

The Dance was symbolic of the dance of life. Beautiful, intricate, and challenging, it was both a celebration and a rite of passage. With her younger children by her side, Lydra watched the young adults from all the scattered clans perform the complex flight through and around the old city. They circled the few ancient spires that still stood, rising into the sky. They swooped beneath the remaining arches, and the places where arches had once been. They wove and swirled past each other, sometimes coming precariously close to the edge of a structure or to one another. Some dove down sharply, only to rise just before hitting the ground. Others traced the path of the river that wound through the center of The Ruins, one hand or foot reaching down to sample the waters.

The Dance always stirred up deep feelings within her, but today's ceremony made her heart ache more than any other. After today, Vanek would leave her. He would, as all young males eventually did, move to another clan. She trusted that he would visit her often, but it wouldn't be the same. As if sensing her thoughts, Vanek flew close enough to the edge of the cliff to catch her eye and waved to her and his little sisters. Naeri sniffed and Mirsa turned away and pressed her face against Lydra's leg, hiding her tears. Both girls adored their older brother.

Reaching down once again to offer the human child another reassuring pat, Lydra fought back tears of her own. She suspected that it wasn't only Vanek that she would soon be parted from. Lydra had taken Mirsa knowing that she would eventually have to send her back to her father and the rest of her human family. The past few years had been precious, and she was grateful for them, but now that their time together was coming to an end, she wasn't ready to let go.

When the musicians sounded out the last triumphant notes that concluded the ritual performance, the dancers flew to the cliffs where their families waited. Lydra embraced her son warmly, eyes shining with pride and unshed tears. Vanek bent down and lifted Mirsa into his arms and then helped her clamber up to sit on his shoulders, her hands holding on tightly to the curved horns on his head.

"Careful, little sister," he warned. "You mustn't pull those off, you know."

Lydra smiled when Mirsa playfully replied, "If they're loose, maybe you should have a healer check them." It was a common exchange. Naeri laughed and flew up to perch similarly on her mother's shoulders, and they walked back to the place where their clan had made camp.

***

Later that night, when most of the clan was sleeping in great piles of limbs and wings around their campfire, Lydra went back to the cliff's edge where they had stood in the afternoon. The moonlight gave the ruins a strangely ethereal quality. It was almost like looking into another world. Lydra wondered for a moment if she had been granted her wish and was seeing the city as it was long ago. The buildings didn't look so decayed now. The forest growth that had intruded into the city looked tamer, almost planned. Unnerved, she shook her head to clear her vision.

She startled at the sound of someone approaching and spun around to see Pataerin standing a few paces away. He walked toward her and draped one outstretched wing over her shoulders, his arm encircling her waist. She leaned her head against him, taking the comfort he offered wordlessly. Pataerin was her lover and her friend, and so much more. With him, she could almost understand why some humans sought a lifelong partner.

"I missed you, love," he said softly after some time had passed. "You look beautiful in the moonlight, but wouldn't you prefer the warmth of the fire?"

"Your warmth is more than enough," she answered, still focused on the view.

"Things change, Lydra. That is what The Dance is all about. You know that."

"I don't want to lose my children."

"You won't," he assured her. "Vanek's chosen clan isn't that far away, and he will visit us often."

"And Mirsa?"

"She's not leaving anytime soon."

Lydra wished she could believe that, but her instincts said otherwise. "She's almost six years old. By human custom, she should have started school last year. And in just a little over two years she'll enter her service years. We can't keep her any longer than that."

"Foolish custom, using children for labor."

"That's not what the service years are about, and you know it. They teach the young discipline and self-reliance. It's not all that different from the chores we give our own children."

Pataerin grumbled. "If that's the case, she can do her service with us. She can gather plants in the forest with Naeri, and even though she's small, there's no reason she can't learn to hunt in a few years."

He made it sound so simple, but it wasn't. "We can't teach her everything she needs to know, Pataerin. She needs to learn about human ways and customs."

"We've taught her well enough, and it isn't as if she has no human company. With so many families joined to our clan, there's a steady stream of humans for her to spend time with. And Aria brought you those books so you could make sure she learned what she needs to keep up with her peers."

The more he tried to convince her that they could keep her, the more she realized that they couldn't. She looked sideways at him, taking note of the way he was watching her and realized that he'd been pushing her toward that conclusion all along.

"You know we can't keep her," she accused.

"And so do you," he replied smoothly. "I don't want to see her leave any more than you do, but we both know that she needs to be with her family."

"We are her family!" Shae-Lydra cried. "I am her atar, the only mother she has ever known. Vanek and Naeri are her siblings as surely as Riahn is. And you are her devya. She chose you, Pataerin. She chose you." Lydra choked on a sob.

"Yes," he said with quiet pride. "And I will forever be grateful for the honor she granted me. But she also has a father. He deserves the chance to be with her too."

"If Larin really wanted to be with her, he could have visited more often. Or asked us to bring her down to Maliae Keep."

"Larin is still bound by his grief, Lydra. He hasn't been whole since Mariah died."

Lydra recognized the truth of those words. She had nearly let herself be consumed the same way. Mariah had been a rare friend, someone who knew her as well as she knew herself. Losing her had torn a hole in Lydra's heart. Mirsa could not fill the empty place her mother left behind, but her presence had given Lydra a reason to heal. Now she wondered if taking the girl had denied Larin that.

Always attuned to her moods, Pataerin said softly, "You did what was right for Mirsa. Larin has been too wrapped up in his own pain to be a proper father to either of his children. Aria said as much. If Riahn had been any younger, she would have sent him to the canyi as well."

A new wave of guilt crashed over her at the thought of Riahn being neglected. Pataerin glared at her. "Larin may not have supported his son the way he should have, but Micail and Aria were there for him. And you've seen Riahn. Losing his mother was a tragedy, but the boy is doing fine."

"Must you always anticipate me?"

He pulled her closer and whispered in her ear. "I thought females appreciated male attention. Isn't predicting your responses just proof that I've been paying attention?"

She wanted to be annoyed with him, but it was difficult to do when he was nuzzling her neck.

"Now you're trying to distract me," she murmured.

"Is it working?"

"Yes." She sighed. "But distracted or not, I can't be entirely happy right now."

The nuzzling stopped and he hugged her tight. "I know that. But I can't allow you to be entirely sad, either. Today is supposed to be a happy day. A new generation of young kaesana have crossed into adulthood. Our race lives on. The Dance endures."

"And Mirsa?"

"Maliae Keep isn't far from home. We'll see her often, even after her father comes to fetch her."

"It won't be the same."

"No, it won't be," he agreed.

She swallowed hard and snuggled against him, accepting the comfort he offered.

"I should start calling her Glasnae, so she gets used to it," she said after a long pause.

"Probably," Pataerin agreed. "And I should do the same."

"You are her devya, after all."

Pataerin looked out over The Ruins, and said solemnly, "She was born without wings, but her spirit is like ours. She will never join The Dance, but she is a true child of Kaesa Atera. Whatever the future holds for her, wherever her life may take her, she's ours."

Lydra allowed him to lead her back to the campfire. Pataerin was right about Mirsa. She was a human child, and she needed to learn to live with her own kind. But she would always have a home among the kaesana, and she would always be Shaendari. That much would never change.

Chapter 5

Jaron whistled a tune, enjoying the late spring day as he walked toward Tamara's cottage. It was perfect weather for fishing, and since his boys had a few days off before they left for their respective homes, he'd decided to surprise them with a little excursion to the lake.

He was just rounding a bend in the road when raised voices stopped him in his tracks.

"Come on, freak, can't you fight back?"

"Just leave me alone," Andris replied with a hint of temper.

"Why? Can't the almighty Odara defend himself?"

Jaron created an invisibility field around himself and continued moving toward the cottage. He saw no need to announce his presence. He was close enough to step in if things got out of hand, and he was curious how his young apprentice would respond.

When the cottage and the cluster of boys in front of it came into view, his temper spiked. Not one boy taunted Andris but five, all of them at least a couple years older than him. He recognized them as mage apprentices but didn't know any of them well enough to recall their names. One was holding Andris's hands behind his back while the others laughed.

He was about to intervene when Kylec stepped out of the front door. "Sure, he can defend himself," Kylec said, sounding confident, even amused. "But why should he? Andy knows how much I enjoy dealing with bullies, so why should he waste the effort?"

"And here comes Dracami to the rescue," one of the other boys sneered. "Just walk away. We're not here for you today."

"Let him go."

"Why don't you make me?"

"If you insist."

Andris squirmed sharply just as Kylec grabbed the boy holding him, allowing him to pull away. It was obvious to Jaron that it had been a coordinated move, and it was equally obvious that this group of ruffians lacked the brains to see it.

Andris skipped out of reach and immediately shielded himself. No one would be able to touch him now, and after a moment of consideration, Jaron decided to stay out of sight and observe how things played out. Kylec released his hold on the other boy and stepped back. "Get out of here. You've got no business here."

"Why should we?" The one who'd been holding Andris spoke with the authority of a leader. It was clear that he expected the others to back him up without question.

"Because we don't want trouble. But if you insist, I'll give you more trouble than you can handle."

"I suppose that means you'll go tattling to Lord Jaron, just like the teacher's pet you are."

"I've never done that before, so why should I start now? I can fight my own battles just fine."

"Yeah, and you can fight Odara's too, huh?"

"Sure. Like I said, I think beating down bullies is fun, and this way Andy doesn't have to blow you to bits."

"Perfect little Andy wouldn't hurt a fly." The leader scoffed. "He knows the consequences of misusing his power. He'd let us beat him to a pulp before he'd lay a hand on us. He's too terrified that the masters will bind his power."

"Wow, you guys are really thick." Kylec shook his head. "Andy is the Archmage's personal apprentice. Do you really think that Lord Jaron would punish him like that just for defending himself?"

"Everyone knows the only reason Lord Jaron took him as an apprentice was to control him. After all, one of the Archmage's duties is to protect people from dangerous sorcerers. Oh sure, he's giving Odara a chance, but everyone knows he'll bind his power in the end."

Jaron rocked back on his heels, stunned. He knew that a certain amount of bullying went on in the Hall despite his efforts to stamp it out, and he knew that Andris had been a target in the past, but this level of cruelty was a shock.

Andris looked stricken, which fueled Kylec's temper. "You don't know how lucky you are that Andris is so forgiving. Unfortunately for you, I'm not nearly so nice."

"Let it go, Ky," Andris said. "They know they can't do anything to us."

"Shut up, freak."

"Andris isn't a freak." Kylec snarled out the words.

"Says the other freak."

"Leave. Now."

"Don't like the truth, do you? All those brains and you still haven't worked it out yet. No one wants you here, Dracami. We're all tired of your better-than-everyone-else attitude and showing the rest of us up every chance you get." The boy pointed to Andris. "And we don't need him around, making everyone walk on eggshells, treating him like he's made of glass because they're afraid of what will happen if he loses his temper. Why don't you take your own advice and leave? Why don't both of you just get out. We don't need a pair of freaks like you making life harder for the rest of us."

Kylec took a step toward the leader. "I'm not going anywhere, and neither is Andy. If you want a fight, I'll give you one. I'll even let you throw the first punch."

That was all the prompting the boy needed. He stepped forward and swung without another word. Kylec dodged the blow with ease and danced just out of reach. "Is that really the best you can do?"

"Kylec, just stop. Tamara will be home soon. Please, just let it go."

Jaron couldn't understand the concern in Andris's voice. Kylec's shielding abilities were more than adequate to protect him from a bunch of schoolyard bullies, even fellow apprentices. Then he took a good look and saw the reason for Andris's concern. Kylec hadn't bothered to shield at all.

The leader growled out a string of obscenities and attacked with a barrage of blows. Most missed, but a few grazed their target, which finally pushed Kylec into attacking back. The scuffle that ensued was energetic but not particularly damaging to either party.

Jaron didn't approve of fighting, but he'd had his own fair share of scrapes and knew that it was just another facet of childhood. That didn't mean that he was going to let this incident go without an appropriate response. He made careful note of each face so he could deal with them later while he waited for the combatants to tire themselves out.

Admiration for Kylec's fighting abilities began to overpower his initial reaction of disapproval. Until the other boys joined in.

It happened fast. One minute, it was just two boys slugging it out. The next minute, Kylec was on the ground with five assailants kicking and hitting. Shock held him immobile for just a few seconds, which was all the time it took for Andris to react.

It wasn't a poltergeist. Andris was holding it back…almost. There was no change discernible to non-magical senses, but Jaron felt raw, unformed kaema flowing out from Andris in a spiral. The power swirled around the boy before grounding itself. It didn't seem to be immediately dangerous, but Jaron could see that the effort to keep it under control was taking a terrible toll on the boy.

Andris didn't shout, but his voice seemed to reverberate through the air, and it certainly commanded attention. "Get off him. Now!"

The boys backed off almost immediately, turning to stare at Andris with abject fear. Kylec stood up. He looked beat up, but not beaten. His attention was focused on Andris, and he didn't even glance at his attackers when he spoke to them. "If you value your skins, I strongly suggest that you leave."

They turned tail and ran. Kylec swallowed hard, and Jaron sensed a very impressive shield forming around him as he approached Andris, whose expression was positively tortured.

"Are you okay?" Andris whispered.

"I'm fine, see?" Kylec said with a shadow of a grin. "Andy, I'm okay. You need to calm down and let it go."

"I know."

"Andy, just calm down."

"I'm trying."

Jaron dropped the spell that hid him from sight and stepped forward, but before he could intervene, Tamara raced toward them. She stopped a couple of paces away, locked eyes with Andris and spoke very calmly and deliberately. "Andris. Look at me and focus. Let it flow…smooth and slow now. Stop drawing it in. Just release what you're holding. Easy does it…smooth and slow…release it just a little at a time."

Jaron hesitated. No one paid him any attention, and even though Tamara looked concerned, she didn't seem afraid.

With the help of Tamara's quiet coaxing, Andris managed to stop drawing in kaema and ground the excess power he'd already raised. When it was done, his shoulders sagged, and his eyes looked sunken with fatigue. With the immediate danger gone, Tamara's face darkened with temper.

"What happened here?" she demanded.

Kylec sounded uncharacteristically sulky. "Arthur and his gang were giving Andy a hard time."

"And you thought that challenging them was better than letting me know there was trouble?"

Kylec turned defiant, which Jaron thought suited him better. "If we run to you every time someone tries to bully us, it will only make it worse. We need to prove that we can handle ourselves."

"We?" she asked with narrowed eyes. "So, you're speaking for Andy now?"

"Kylec defended me," Andris said in a small voice.

"And while he was defending you, you could have sent for me."

"I didn't think of it until it was too late."

Jaron decided the time had come for him to step up. "If I may interject, I arrived a few moments before you, and frankly it just looked like a harmless fight between two boys at first. I don't think Ky or Andy expected it to escalate the way it did."

"I appreciate your input, Lord Jaron, but I'd like to remind you that fighting is against the rules of the Mage Hall, as well as *my* rules. If Kylec and Andris had simply shielded and returned to the house, this incident would have ended before it began." She spoke with stiff formality, and then added silently, *I will deal with you later.*

Jaron tried not to wince and was almost relieved when she turned her attention back to the boys. "Jonas is working in the infirmary today. Kylec, I suggest you head over there and have him examine you. Right now, you're too full of adrenaline to feel just how badly you came out of this little fight of yours."

Kylec hesitated and she added, "Go."

He went.

Then she turned to Andris. "Drop the shield."

Jaron hadn't noticed that Andris's shield was still up, but he dropped it at Tamara's command. She laid one hand on his shoulder and closed her eyes for a moment. When she opened them again, she said, "You should go to the infirmary, too. If Healer Laramy isn't available, tell one of the other healers on duty that you strained yourself fighting back a poltergeist."

"That's not exactly what happened," Andris protested.

"It's close enough for them to give you some relief."

Andris walked off in the same direction Kylec had gone a few moments earlier. When he was out of sight, Tamara turned toward Jaron, and he wondered if he could hold back his questions long enough to take the edge off her temper. As he met her eyes, he hoped even harder that she didn't realize how long he'd been watching the fight.

"I'm sorry, Tam. I was about to break things up. I just didn't move quickly enough."

When she didn't say anything, he risked a question. "Is this how he's avoided any poltergeists over the past two years?"

The tears that sprang to her eyes were wholly unexpected, but he didn't let it worry him overly much. After all, given her condition, a certain amount of moodiness was understandable. She hugged herself as she replied, "When he gets upset, he still draws in too much kaema, but it doesn't explode out of him anymore. He can hold it back enough that it doesn't do much at all when it escapes. But grounding it takes a lot out of him. It puts a terrible strain on his nervous system."

"Why didn't you tell me about this?" Jaron asked quietly. He knew better than to be angry, but it hurt that no one had confided in him about this.

"Andy asked me not to," she replied just as quietly. "He's been so proud that he hasn't had a poltergeist in almost two years. He didn't want to disappoint you, and I think he wanted to prove that he could deal with this on his own."

"Tamara, you of all people must realize how dangerous this is to him. I'm shocked that you didn't come to me."

"It's not that simple, Jaron." She sighed deeply. "The first time it happened, I wasn't here. Andris trusted me enough to tell me only after I promised to keep it a secret."

"He grounded it on his own that time?"

"Kylec helped. I think he can do it alone, but it's easier for him if there's someone there to help keep him calm and focused. I just don't know if he'll be able to do so in a completely new environment."

"At the dormitories next term, you mean."

"Exactly."

"It's only a ten-minute walk from here to the junior dorm, Tam. They'll be able to find you whenever they need you." He smiled reassuringly. "And you'll be able to find them."

"Besides," he concluded, "You'll soon have your hands full with a child of your own."

Tamara unconsciously touched her abdomen. She was only a few months along, but Jaron could just make out the slight protrusion beneath her blouse. "I will always have time for Andris and Kylec, even after my daughter is born."

"I know that Tam." He smiled warmly at her. "I never meant to suggest otherwise, but they're growing up. They're ready for this."

"You'll have to warn the resident faculty members about Andris," she said with resignation.

"I don't want him to feel any more self-conscious than he already is, so let's not make a major issue out of this. It should be enough to inform the Master-in-Residence for the junior dorm."

She looked confused. "Who?"

He grinned. "Each dorm will have a master living there throughout the term to oversee the other faculty supervisors. It will improve relations between our senior teachers and the students."

"And it will give the children more incentive to behave."

"Really? I hadn't thought of that."

"So, who did you coerce into this?"

"Michaela volunteered for the junior dorm for the next year. No coercion required."

Tamara's expression slowly softened into a smile. "That will make it easier. Andy already trusts her."

"That settles the situation with Andy, but I'm also worried about Ky."

She smirked. "Yes, our dear Kylec. Well, I guess that the next time he convinces Andris to create a pond in their bedroom, Michaela will have the joy of dealing with it."

Jolted out of his train of thought, he replied sharply, "Honestly, Tamara. That was over a year ago. And it was nothing more than a harmless illusion."

She narrowed her eyes at him. "Harmless illusion? The water sloshed, the mud squelched, the frogs hopped, and the room smelled like a swamp!"

"It was a very good illusion," Jaron conceded.

"There was a pond in my house, Jaron. Illusion or not, no woman wants to open a door and discover a pond in her house."

"Point taken, Tam."

"All right then." She nodded with a hint of finality.

He was about to leave when he realized that she'd very nearly sidetracked him. He didn't think it was deliberate, but he couldn't be entirely sure.

"While I appreciate your concerns and will certainly take them into account, that isn't what worries me about Ky."

She looked at him thoughtfully for a long moment. "You're referring to his willingness to jump into a fight?"

"Not exactly. I'm wondering why he would jump into to fight without taking any precautions. He didn't bother raising any kind of shield until Andris started releasing kaema. He was up against five older students, and he didn't even try to protect himself."

Tamara replied with a mixture of suspicion and annoyance. "I won't ask just how long you were standing there. I expect that it will only make me angry again, and I'm really not in the mood."

He didn't bother to respond to that. Instead, he said, "It was reckless, Tam. I need to know if this was an isolated incident or if it's typical for him."

She shrugged. "It may not be quite as reckless as it seems. He uses magic to defend himself when necessary, but Kylec prefers a physical response when he's challenged like this. I used to think it was his way of playing fair, since none of the other children can match his magical skills, but I've come to realize it's more than that. He wants to prove he can take whatever they can dish out, and for the most part, he can. He's energetic and...competitive...and..." She trailed off for a moment. Then she glared at him and added sharply, "You should understand well enough. Just think back to when you were his age, and you can answer your own damn questions."

Jaron wouldn't admit it, but he knew she was right. And while it didn't make him particularly happy, it did somewhat alleviate his concerns. So, he set aside his own worries in favor of reassuring her.

"It's going to be fine, Tamara, I promise." He kissed her lightly on the cheek. "Let Michaela deal with boys when they're in the dorm, and you can deal with them when they're visiting you."

"You think they'll still make time to visit?"

"Of course, Tam. They love you." He grinned. "And your daughter is going to have two very devoted and adoring foster brothers, who will jump at the chance to teach her all their favorite tricks."

She glared at him. "Shoo. You've given me far too much to think about."

He bowed and left. She had given him plenty to think about as well.

***

"Governor Tierney!" Steward Samuel's voice was ragged. "We've got most of the animals under cover. Carl and Dana are rounding up the stragglers."

Larin looked up at the mass of black clouds swirling overhead and shivered. Only ten minutes ago, the sky had been clear and blue. "Five minutes—no more," he replied sharply, "Livestock can be replaced. People can't."

The man nodded and hurried to obey. Larin turned and went back into the Keep. *Please, gods, don't let it be her,* he prayed silently.

He found Mage Danai outside the family gathering room. The double doors were open, and he could hear a child sobbing, just out of sight. He met Danai's eyes, and her expression confirmed his worst fears. He gestured for her to follow him inside. He didn't know what frightened him more: the damage the storm could cause, or that it was the manifestation of a child's temper tantrum.

He found Glasnae curled up in a ball behind the couch at one end of the room. His mother stood nearby and admonished her granddaughter. "Stop this, child. You need to ground the power you've raised."

"I can't!" the little girl choked out between sobs.

"Yes, you can." The words might have been encouraging if they hadn't been delivered in such a frustrated tone.

Larin kept his own voice as calm as he could. "Stop it, Mother. You're not helping."

"She's out of control, Larin. Something needs to be done."

"Glasnae?" Danai knelt and spoke in a soothing tone, extending one hand toward the little girl. "Glasnae, take my hand. Just take my hand."

Larin watched his daughter reach out toward the mage hesitantly. Danai kept her expression calm and encouraging, waiting for Glasnae to come to her. Unfortunately, his mother wasn't so patient, and he could hear the undercurrent of fear in her voice as she said, "Just grab her and force her to ground it, Danai. We need to act before someone gets hurt."

Glasnae withdrew her hand as if slapped and inched further away, hugging herself tightly.

Larin hissed. "Mother, please let Mage Danai handle this."

His mother glared at him but remained silent as Larin gently took her arm and eased her away, giving Danai a clear path to approach Glasnae.

The mage crawled on her hands and knees until she was right next to the child. She carefully sat beside her without touching her and said softly, "It's not your fault, Glasnae." She shot a hard look at Linia, warning her to keep silent, and Larin reinforced the message by gripping his mother's arm a bit more tightly. The gesture earned him a sharp glance, but he didn't care. He had more important concerns than his mother's temper.

Danai continued to coax, and after a few more moments passed, Glasnae took the woman's hand. Larin looked out the window, but all he saw was the reflection of the room in the glass. It was too dark to see what was going on outside, though he could hear the distinct sound of hail pounding against the stone balcony above the roar of the wind. He held his breath, half his attention on the sounds of the storm, the other half on Danai's soft voice as she tried to calm his daughter.

Several minutes passed before the hail stopped, but it *did* stop. A few minutes later, the wind died down, and a few minutes after that the sky brightened enough for Larin to see the courtyard beyond the window.

He took a step toward the glass doors that led to the balcony and approached with caution, afraid of what he would see. Relief flooded through him when he realized that the damage was fairly minimal. The courtyard was a mess, to be sure. Windblown debris littered the space, and the hail was several inches deep in places. But the buildings were intact and mostly unscathed.

Samuel looked up from below and caught his eye. Larin opened the door and carefully stepped out onto the balcony. "Anyone hurt?" he called down to his steward.

The man shook his head. "A few bumps and bruises. Nothing serious. And the horses and other animals are okay, too. Most of the animals had more sense than their handlers and ran to shelter before the first obvious sign of trouble."

Larin smiled weakly. "I guess we should be grateful for that."

"Is it over?" Samuel asked.

The question jolted through Larin, suggesting that man knew the source of the storm. It was unsettling, but Samuel was waiting for an answer, so he replied, "Looks like it is. Please assess the damage and report back to me with a list of needed repairs."

"Yes sir!" the man called back, looking relieved.

Larin walked back into the room and closed the door behind him just in time to see the beginning of a fight between his mother and Danai.

Linia was practically screeching. "If you can't control her, we'll have to find someone who can."

"The child needs help. She's trying to control her power. Can't you see that?"

"She needs discipline."

Danai noticed his approach first and directed her next words to him. "Governor Tierney, your daughter's power is simply too great. She needs the kind of support and instruction that only a master mage can provide."

"Isn't there anything more you can do?" He didn't really want to have this conversation.

"I've done all I can. She's far more powerful than I am, Governor. All I can do is try to guide her, but it's obviously not enough. A master could take her through the process directly, step by step."

"Do you think that a master would be willing to come here?"

"It would be better if Glasnae went to the Mage Hall."

Larin shook his head. "She's too young."

"That's not true. Lord Jaron is accepting children with exceptional power well below the age of apprenticeship. He would welcome her."

"I don't know. Maybe—"

His mother cut him off before he could finish the thought. "You can't be serious." She looked at each of them in turn. "Just be honest, Danai. The child is a danger to everyone around her. I agree that she needs to be seen by a master, but only so that her power can be bound once and for all."

"Lord Jaron would never approve of binding a child's power."

"Why not?" Linia countered. "One of his duties is to protect Tarya from dangerous sorcerers. Glasnae is dangerous. You've already demonstrated that trying to train her is a complete waste of time."

"I told you that she needs to be taught by a master." Danai sounded outraged.

"Ladies!" Larin said sharply.

Both women turned to him. Danai looked contrite. Linia looked annoyed. He swallowed his own anger and said softly, "Danai, please send an inquiry to the Mage Hall to see if they can send someone to evaluate Glasnae. It isn't that I don't trust you, but I'd like a second opinion."

"I can do that," the mage said carefully, glancing at Linia. "There are some adepts who are specifically trained to evaluate potential students."

Larin nodded, and before his mother could comment he turned to her and said, "I intend to do whatever is best for Glasnae. It may be that binding her power is the right thing to do, but if there is any chance that she can be trained, she deserves that chance."

"A chance for what, Larin?" Linia's tone was more exasperated than angry now. "It isn't as if we're talking about maiming the child. Most people have no magical ability at all. It's hardly essential to living a normal, productive life. And in Glasnae's case, she stands a better chance at having a normal life if her power is bound now. In a year or so, she won't even miss it."

Larin didn't respond right away. His mother did have a point. Glasnae was struggling so much to control her power that she might well be better off without it.

Danai interrupted his train of thought. "Governor, that may be the easiest path to take, but that doesn't make it right. And considering that Glasnae was fostered with her dragon-kin, I believe that losing the ability to do magic would be a real loss to her."

"She spends too much time with those creatures as it is," Linia said. "She's human, not kaesana. Frankly, I think that the time she spends with them has made the situation worse."

"That's not true!" Danai protested. "The kaesana have been able to help her in ways I can't."

"There's no sense in arguing." Larin scrubbed his face with his hands, feeling weary to the bone. "Right now, we need to deal with immediate matters."

"We should get Glasnae to bed," the mage said. "She must be exhausted."

Larin realized that they had just spent the last several minutes arguing about Glasnae's future as if she wasn't even in the room. Swallowing hard, he walked over to where she had been hiding, hoping he could smooth things over. But when he looked behind the couch, she was gone.

"Did either of you see Glasnae leave?" he asked. When there was no response, he looked at Danai, an unspoken question hanging in the air between them. She shook her head, her expression distressed, almost fearful. Ignoring his mother completely, he spoke directly to the mage. "Let's organize a search."

***

Larin's voice was rough with emotion and fatigue. "You found her? She's safe?"

It had been nearly four days since Glasnae had gone missing. Search parties had been sent out in all directions, but his real hope for finding her had lain with his son.

Riahn nodded. "We need to talk."

"About what?" Linia asked sharply as she entered the room.

Riahn glared at her. "I want to talk to Father alone. As for where Glasnae is, she's safe. That's all you need to know."

"All I need to know!" Linia shrieked. "How dare you! I am your grandmother, and you will show me proper respect. You can start by telling us where your sister is hiding this instant. She's had us worried sick, running off like that."

"She only ran because she was terrified. I'll tell you where she is as soon as Father and I come to an understanding about her future. Now, please give us some privacy."

Larin stared at his son. His tone was polite, but the anger beneath it was unmistakable. Before his mother could respond and turn the conversation into a full-blown fight, he stepped in. "Mother, if you would please give us a moment alone, I'd appreciate it."

"There is nothing that either of you need to say that can't be said in my presence."

"I want a private word with my son," Larin said firmly. He could feel his mother's thoughts brush against his own, but he deliberately shut her out, refusing whatever silent message she wished to impart. Her eyes grew wide in surprise before her expression turned blank.

"Very well," she said stiffly, "but I hope you know what you're doing. Riahn is an adolescent, not an adult, and Glasnae is still a child. I suggest you keep that in mind before giving in to whatever demands the two of them have conspired to make."

She left, firmly closing the door behind her.

Larin turned his attention back to his son and noticed that Riahn's expression looked distant. Then he felt a subtle *something* and Riahn's eyes came back into focus.

"What did you just do?" he asked.

"I shielded the room." Riahn was unapologetic. "I don't want her eavesdropping."

Larin knew that his son had some limited magical talent, but this came as a surprise. "When did you learn how to do that?"

"There's an adept stationed at the training camp. He gives lessons in basic magical techniques to any cadets who have demonstrable ability."

"You're learning magecraft?"

Riahn shrugged. "Sort of. I'm not gifted enough to be a mage, and even if I had the power, I'm not sure I could handle the math. But I am learning a few simple spells suited to a warrior."

Larin just nodded, not trusting himself to comment. Ever since Riahn decided to join the merlins, he'd been struggling with the idea that his son wanted to be a warrior.

At eighteen, Riahn physically bore a strong resemblance to his mother. He had the same slender build, dark hair, fair skin and deep blue eyes. Because of that physical resemblance, Larin too often thought of Riahn as his mother's son, rather than a person in his own right. And Mariah had been a gentle soul who shied away from violence of all kinds. She had even avoided hunting with her kaesana kin.

But Riahn was not so gentle, despite his usually quiet demeanor. When Larin forced himself to look below the surface, he saw the young man as he really was: passionate, determined, even fierce. And very protective of his little sister. It was the latter that made him hold his tongue and wait for his son to speak first. He knew with terrible certainty that Riahn would protect Glasnae from any perceived threat, even if it came from their own family.

After a few moments, Riahn took a deep breath and said softly, "I found her and brought her back to the Keep. She's safe and sound."

Maliae Keep was the size of a small village. Telling him that she was at the Keep wasn't pinpointing her location. "Don't you trust me enough to tell me where she's hiding?"

"Will you let them bind her power?"

"I may not have a choice."

"Yes, you do. I know enough about the Mage Hall to know that they wouldn't bind her power unless you insisted."

"I wouldn't insist," Larin said with complete sincerity. "I never wanted that, Riahn. I was scared. We all were."

"Not as scared as Glasnae." Riahn was angry, but Larin didn't think that his anger was directed at him. "She tried to get back to Canyi Shaendari, but the clan had already left for The Ruins, so there was no one in range to hear her call. She's spent the past few days hiding in the forest below the cliffs. When I found her, she begged me not to let you send her to the Mage Hall. She's afraid they'll take away her magic and that she won't be able to go back to her real family."

The last statement cut deep. "We're her family, too."

Riahn's expression and voice softened. "She knows that, but she doesn't feel like she belongs here, and right now, she doesn't feel safe here. She doesn't trust Linia."

Larin wasn't surprised that Riahn didn't refer to Linia as his grandmother. There had never been an abundance of affection between them, and this latest incident likely killed any warmth he might have felt. He almost didn't ask the next question, but not knowing would have been a constant ache in his heart. "Does she trust *me*?"

Riahn didn't answer right away, and when he did, Larin suspected that he was blunting the truth. "Not completely. She doesn't think that you would deliberately hurt her, but she isn't sure that she can rely on you to protect her, either."

"I will protect her. Riahn, you have my word on it. I won't allow her power to be bound unless there is absolutely no other option. I'll fight for her. I promise."

He looked into his son's eyes and wondered when he had lost the innate trust that children are supposed to have in their parents. He realized that he'd likely lost it so long ago he might as well have never had it. After Mariah died, he hadn't been much of a father at all, so he had little claim to a father's privileges.

He was beginning to think he'd lost completely when Riahn finally said, "I believe you. But it may take some time to convince Glasnae."

"She needs help, Riahn," Larin said anxiously. "Whether she trusts me or not, I love her and want to keep her safe. And right now, her power is more than she can handle. She needs help."

"What kind of help?" Riahn sounded suspicious.

"Danai said that the masters at the Mage Hall can help her."

"You promised not to bind her power."

"They won't bind her power. They'll teach her how to control it. They'll show her how to use it safely."

Riahn shook his head. "If you send her to the Mage Hall, she'll panic. And she'll run."

"What other choice do we have?" Larin ran his fingers through his hair, pulling against his scalp to try to ease the pain in his head. "I might be able to find a master living nearby."

"I'm sorry, Father, but the damage is done. I don't think that Glasnae will trust any mage other than Danai right now, much less a master."

"I don't see what other options we have, unless you think she should move back to Canyi Shaendari. I understand that Shae-Lydra was working to help her control her power."

"That would be a good idea for the time being, but it isn't a reasonable long-term solution."

"Then what?"

"We could take her to New Avalon in Avrin."

When Larin didn't respond immediately, Riahn continued. "The druids don't teach the same kind of magic that the mages do, but they do teach the basics. And they also have highly skilled people at the Druidic College who should be able to help her."

Larin swallowed hard. Mariah had been a novice of one of the druidic orders once. She'd left New Avalon before taking the vows of a priestess and accepted the nomination to become governor of Maliae at the same time she'd agreed to his proposal of marriage.

He'd never fully understood why she'd left the order. There was no law prohibiting a priestess from marrying or serving as governor. But Mariah had turned firmly away from that path and put it behind her. To the best of his knowledge, she had severed all ties with the people she'd left behind in New Avalon, and though she usually shared everything with him, she'd resolutely refused to discuss the time she'd spent there.

Riahn must have read the direction of his thoughts in his expression. "This has nothing to do with Mother. I'm not suggesting that Glasnae enter the priesthood. Even if she did show such an inclination, she's far too young to be considered for a novitiate."

"The magicians are a druidic order, not a guild," Larin reminded his son.

Riahn nodded. "I know that. But Glasnae doesn't need to learn ritual magic or other advanced teachings. She needs to learn control

91

and basic magical skills. The Druidic College offers that kind of instruction openly."

"And if she wants to learn more?" Larin asked, still uneasy about the idea for no reason he could put into words.

Riahn smiled. "Once she learns how to control her power, she won't have any further reason to be fearful. At that point, she could leave Druidic College and go to the Mage Hall for training. She'll be able to choose for herself."

"You've given this a lot of thought."

"So has Glasnae. I knew that the only way I'd get her to come home would be to reassure her that she wouldn't be forced into something. Right now, she's afraid of the mages. What she really wants is to go back to Canyi Shaendari and stay there, but I talked her out of it. New Avalon was the only other viable option."

"It must have taken a lot of persuasion."

"Not as much as you think," Riahn replied gently. "She knows that she isn't kaesana. She just doesn't feel accepted here the way she does at the canyi. I explained that she'll be able to make a fresh start in New Avalon, and that seemed to catch her interest."

"Have I been that cruel?" Larin asked.

Riahn looked surprised and shook his head. "You? No. You have neglected her, but you haven't been cruel, at least not from Glasnae's point of view." He sighed. "And I don't believe that Linia has been *deliberately* cruel, but that doesn't change the pain she's caused."

"Glasnae must hate her."

"Hate is too strong a word. Glasnae resents and fears Linia, but that's not the same as hate."

It sounded as though Riahn had worked out a reasonable solution that could be acted on relatively quickly. But there was a detail that Riahn had not mentioned that could be an impediment. "Your grandmother's sister, Leah, is the High Priestess," Larin reminded his son.

"I know that, and so does Glasnae. But we've never met her, and as far as I know, she and Linia are not especially close. I told Glas that she has no reason to expect the High Priestess to even notice her, much less cause her any difficulties."

Larin scrubbed his face with his hands. "I don't expect Aunt Leah to cause Glasnae any trouble, but I can guarantee that she'll notice if her great-niece enters the college. And I wouldn't be surprised if she takes at least some interest in her while she's there."

Now Riahn frowned. "Do you think Linia will turn her against Glas?"

"I don't believe that your grandmother would purposely turn anyone against your sister, Riahn." He couldn't entirely keep the reproach out of his voice. Though he recognized his mother's failings, he could not in good conscience allow her to be painted as a villain. "She will likely contact her sister and offer her opinion, but if Leah is anything at all like your grandmother, she'll make up her own mind. And as High Priestess, I would expect her to be open-minded and compassionate. I truly don't believe that Glasnae will have anything to fear from her. I only mentioned it because I didn't want it to come up later as an unpleasant surprise."

When Riahn just nodded mutely, Larin asked, "If I agree to send Glasnae to New Avalon, will you tell me where she is?"

"I have your word?"

Larin crossed the space between them and extended his hand. "You have my word."

Riahn took the offered hand and shook it firmly. Then Larin took the opportunity to pull his son into a rough embrace. "Thank you, lad," he said against his shoulder.

Riahn pulled back gently and met his eyes. Relief, gratitude, and a new sense of trust were written on his face. "She's in her room."

Larin asked in genuine shock. "What kind of hiding place is that?"

"A perfect one." Riahn grinned. "Would you have looked for her there?"

Larin laughed, finally relaxing a bit himself. "Do you think she'd welcome a visit from me?"

Riahn's smile warmed him, and his next words eased the knot in his stomach. "She's waiting for you. I told her you would see her once we'd come to an understanding."

***

A soft "come in" answered Larin's tentative knock, and he opened the door to his daughter's suite slowly, unsure of what he might find.

"Hello, Da," she said shyly. She was standing in the middle of the small sitting room wearing a long, pale-blue nightgown, her hands clasped so tightly her knuckles were white.

Her fearful manner clawed at his heart, even as her use of the word *Da* warmed it. He softly closed the door and approached her slowly, bending down on one knee as he got close. He was low enough, and she was tall enough, that he had to look up at her, and he hoped that would help reassure her. "Are you okay, sweetheart?" he asked gently.

She nodded, copper-red curls bouncing up and down. He gently reached up and stroked the shoulder-length ringlets, missing the waist-long waves that he'd grown accustomed to and hoping it didn't show on his face. He could still remember the day when he'd been told that his child had hacked off her braids with a gardening sickle during an argument with her grandmother. At the time, he'd taken it as a sign of self-destructive willfulness. Looking back on the incident, he realized that his mother was as much to blame for trying to treat the energetic nine-year-old like a living doll when she wanted to be playing in the gardens and forests.

Glasnae didn't move while he followed his own thoughts. Her eyes were aimed at the floor, but she didn't pull away from him. He took that as encouragement.

"I was worried about you."

She glanced up at him briefly, her green eyes red-rimmed but dry. "I was safe."

He wanted to argue but knew that it would be counterproductive. Instead, he said. "I didn't know that. You were upset when you left."

Her next words came out nearly devoid of emotion, but it was clear that she was looking for reassurance. "Riahn said you wouldn't come here until you agreed that I should go to school."

He took both her hands in his own. They felt cold. "You'll go to New Avalon as soon as we can make the arrangements. I'll take you there myself."

She frowned and said earnestly, "You're the governor. You can't leave Maliae just to bring me to school."

She thinks she rates so low in my priorities? he asked himself sadly. *I really have failed my children, but I'm going to do better. Starting right now.*

"I'm your father first, Glasnae. Do you understand that?"

She just stared at him blankly, and he continued. "I know that I haven't been there for you the way I should have been. I don't know if I can ever make it up to you, but I want you to know that I will do everything in my power to protect you and support you. The people of Maliae would never fault me for taking care of my family."

She seemed to consider this for a moment, and her expression brightened slightly. "Can Riahn come, too?"

"I'll contact his commanding officer and make the arrangements."

"He won't get in trouble?" she asked uncertainly.

"He won't get in trouble. The merlins take family matters very seriously. His commander will understand."

She took a deep breath and let it out slowly. Then she smiled. It was a hesitant, shy smile, but it was a start. Very gently, he drew her close and hugged her. She felt so tiny and delicate in his arms. From a distance, she was so fierce and daring that it was hard to believe she could feel so fragile. *She's always been fragile,* Larin thought to himself. *She just hides it well.*

"You must be tired," he said into her hair and then eased back so he could look at her. "Will you let me tuck you into bed?"

Her smile was genuinely happy this time, and she nodded vigorously, curls flailing around her head. He scooped her up, and she giggled as he carried her into the bedroom and tucked her in, settling in at the edge of the bed beside her. "Would you like a story?"

Tears sprang to her eyes, and she asked, "Can you tell me about the day I was born, and how I got my name?"

Larin forced himself to speak past the lump in his throat. "Of course."

He'd told her this story many times before, but not in the past year. When she first came back from Canyi Shaendari, he had used that story as a bridge, a way to connect her to the mother she couldn't remember, and to connect her to him.

"Your mother and Riahn and I went to Canyi Shaendari several days before you were born, since your mother insisted that she give birth among her dragon-kin. One of your mother's cousins had served as a midwife when Riahn was born, but Shae-Lydra trained for months so she could help deliver you.

"You took your time being born." He tweaked her ear playfully and she giggled. "Your mother went into hard labor in the afternoon, and I expected you'd arrive by evening. But no, you weren't quite ready. Your mother walked back and forth across the birthing room to ease the labor pains. Half the time, she wanted me to walk with her, and the other half she ordered me out of the room."

He made a show of frowning and leaned over to her. "You women can be very testy sometimes."

She giggled again and then forced a serious expression. "Childbirth is hard, and we do all the work. We're allowed to be testy."

He sighed theatrically and continued. "Well, that was how it went all night. Pacing back and forth. Calling me to her and then sending me away. Around midnight, your brother went to sleep with the other children, and I could see that your mother was getting tired. But she could only sit or lie down for a little while before she felt the need to move again, and I prayed to Kaestra that you would be born soon so she could rest.

"A few hours before dawn, it started to rain. It was a gentle rain, and your mother wanted to be near the window. She said the sound was soothing and the smell of the rain was refreshing to her. So, I moved the birthing bed right in front of the window and pulled back the curtains. Lydra dropped the shield that usually held back the weather so she could feel the breeze.

"I was worried that it was too cold, but your mother and Lydra insisted that it was fine. I was already used to being overruled by then, so I didn't argue."

"Smart of you," she interjected unexpectedly, her voice pert.

Larin grinned down at her before continuing. "The rain stopped just before dawn, and the rising sun was shining through the trees when you finally arrived. You slipped right from your mother's body into Lydra's hands and shrieked. You looked so tiny, just a wrinkled little wriggling speck of life. Then Lydra graciously allowed me to cut the umbilical cord and help clean you up before placing you in your mother's arms.

"You settled down quickly, and your mother looked so happy. Tired, but happy. She smiled up at me, and then she looked out the window. Everything looked wet and green and glowing in the sunlight, and your eyes seemed to reflect that greenness, so your mother said that green should be part of your name."

He paused and Glasnae picked up the story. "And you said that the word for green in old Irish is *glas*, and Mother liked the sound of it."

"And Lydra said that you should also be named for the rising sun since that's when you were born. She reminded your mother that *nae* is the word for dawn in the kaesana language."

"So, you named me Glasnae," she finished.

"And so, we named you Glasnae," he repeated. "My little green dawn."

He closed his eyes, struggling to hold back tears. A small hand reached up and touched his cheek. "It's okay, Da. I know how much you miss her."

That simple declaration of understanding broke his control, and he pulled her close, letting the tears fall.

He whispered hoarsely, "I'm sorry, Glas. I am so sorry."

"You don't have to be sorry, Da. Atar cries sometimes too."

Atar, he thought. *Mommy. Mariah is her mother, but only a person she hears about in stories. A person who is missed because the people she loves miss her. But Shae-Lydra is and always will be her mommy—her atar—and I'm glad for her sake.*

He was glad. But it wasn't easy. Glasnae had another family, a whole other life. And he wasn't a part of it.

Riahn was, at least to an extent. Riahn considered the Shaendari kin, just as Mariah had. That's what being part of a joined family was all about. But Larin wasn't from a joined family; he'd just married into one.

Not that the Shaendari didn't welcome him. They had been more than willing to accept him as one of their own. But even when Mariah had been alive, he'd always been nervous and unsure of himself among the kaesana. He respected and admired them, but they still felt alien to him. He'd always relied on Mariah to act as a bridge between him and the Shaendari, and after she died, the chasm between him and her dragon-kin seemed too vast to span.

Glasnae hugged him tight, and her willingness to accept his grief eased an ache inside him. He tightened his grip on her briefly and then let her go. "You should get some sleep now." He kissed her lightly on the forehead.

"It's nice having you tuck me in," she said softly before yawning deeply.

He pulled the covers up around her shoulders as she snuggled against the pillow. "Do you want me to stay until you fall asleep?"

"You don't have to," she said in a drowsy voice. Now that she was more relaxed, exhaustion was taking hold.

He reached out and stroked her hair, whispering, "I want to."

She sighed, and he could practically feel her drifting off to sleep. He was about to leave when he heard her mumble, "You sound just like Devya."

He froze, not sure how to respond. After a few heartbeats passed he realized that she was already asleep, so there was no need for a response. He gave her head one last kiss good night and retreated from the room.

He walked to his rooms on unsteady legs. He felt as if he'd been stabbed in the heart by a word: *devya*.

He should have known. He'd never been much of a father, and she'd been raised among the Shaendari as one of their own. He should have expected that she would choose a devya. In a way, it made even more sense for her to have a devya than it did for her to call Lydra her atar. After all, the kaesana were strictly matrilineal, and pair-bonding was not a part of their culture. Children didn't know or care who sired them. A devya was chosen based on his personal relationship to the child, not his role in conception.

It made perfect sense, and it didn't make him any less her father. It just meant that she also had a father of sorts at the canyi. There was no reason for him to feel jealous.

Except that he *did* feel jealous. And not knowing who her devya was made it even worse somehow.

She called me Da, he reminded himself. *She still loves me.*

He repeated those two sentences to himself over and over again that night until he finally fell asleep.

Chapter 6

Naeri was stretched out full-length on the cavern floor, her wings open and lying limply at her sides. Her head rested on her forearms as she studied the jigsaw puzzle in front of her. Now and then, she would lift her head, reach out with one hand, and move a piece or two into place. Then she would resume her contemplation.

Shae-Lydra sat nearby, weaving on a lap-loom while she watched her daughter out of the corner of her eye. The puzzle was one of several gifts that Mirsa had brought with her when she came to visit the previous month. She had stayed with them for more than two weeks, and she and Naeri had spent nearly every moment of that time together. Shae-Lydra knew that the girls met more frequently than either side of the family was openly aware of. She never worried about these "secret" meetings, and wisely never gave any indication that she realized what they were doing. They were young but not careless, and she felt certain that they had far more interest in being together than getting into mischief.

When Mirsa had returned to the Keep, Naeri had been sad to see her leave, but hadn't fussed. But when the day came that she knew her foster-sister was leaving Maliae to go to school in Avrin she had become withdrawn and melancholy.

After a while Naeri stretched, turning her head gracefully to look back over her shoulder at her mother, and sighed. She sat up, folded her wings neatly to her back and wrapped her long tail around her body. When she looked up, Shae-Lydra smiled at her.

"Finished with that puzzle yet?"

"It's more fun when you have someone to work on it with."

Lydra ached to hear the sadness in her voice. "I'll join you for a while," she said lightly. "It's been some time since I worked on a puzzle like that, though. I may not be much help."

Naeri's eyes brightened for a moment, and Lydra moved to sit across from her daughter on the floor. As they started to work on the puzzle together, she could sense the pain building up again in Naeri and decided she had left her child alone with her grief long enough.

Without looking up from the puzzle she said, "Mirsa won't be gone forever, you know. I realize how much you miss her, but she'll be back to visit in a few months, and she's already made it clear to her father that she wants to spend a good part of her vacation with us."

"I know." Naeri also kept her eyes on the puzzle. "But it's more than that. She won't really be Mirsa anymore, will she?"

Shae-Lydra looked up, startled. Tears filled Naeri's eyes and ran down her velvety cheeks. "What do you mean, Naeri?"

"She's going away to school with humans. No one there will call her Mirsa. She'll be Glasnae, and that's all. It was bad enough when she left us to live at the Keep, but at least we were here to remind her. No one will remind her in Avrin."

"Remind her of what?" Lydra asked, already half-guessing the answer.

"Remind her that she's not just human—that she's kaesana too! She's one of us beneath the skin, inside, where it really matters. Now, she'll forget. She'll learn how to think like they do. She won't be my sister anymore."

Lydra reached across the forgotten puzzle and pulled her young daughter into her arms. She rocked her gently, her wings enclosing them both in a soft cocoon as she hummed a soothing song. Naeri cried and cried, and Lydra fought the urge to join her. She was beginning to realize that she had underestimated the bond that held Naeri and Mirsa together. They weren't just *like* sisters. They *were* sisters.

It was a fierce and beautiful love they shared, and a dangerous one for her daughter. She began to wonder if she had been foolish raising them together as she had. Naeri had to realize that Glasnae was human, not kaesana, no matter what fantasies they might indulge in together.

Her child would suffer heartache far worse than this if she didn't come to terms with reality soon.

When the tears came to end, she loosened her hold and looked down at her daughter. "My little Naeri, as much as we would all wish it otherwise, Mirsa is a human being, and the name Glasnae belongs to her as much as Mirsa does." When Naeri did not respond, she continued. "She will always be part of our family. But she cannot change what she is, no matter how much she wants to. She was born human. She will always be human. Even if she stayed with us her whole life, that wouldn't change. And eventually she would become unhappy because she would have longings and desires that she could never fulfill with us."

Naeri looked up, a trace of stubbornness in her face that came as no surprise to her mother; "Our ancestors were like humans once. I've seen The Ruins, Atar. I've listened to the stories. We lived like them once, and we changed. We found a better life. Humans can too. Especially the ones who are already like us, deep down. Mirsa would be happy here."

"Naeri," Lydra said firmly, "as much as I may wish you were right, that just isn't the way of things. Humans are different from us in so many ways, it's a miracle that we can find as much common ground as we do. Yes, we once had a civilization that was *similar* to theirs, but even then, we weren't the same. We are a different species. We evolved on different worlds."

"You and Mirsa's mother were sisters," Naeri said with a child's conviction. "Mariah was happy here. She could have been happy if she'd lived her life here."

The sound of Mariah's name brought on an avalanche of feeling and strengthened Lydra's resolve to make her daughter understand the limits of human-kaesana relationships.

"Yes," she said softly, but firmly, "Mariah and I were as close as you and Mirsa are. We loved each other very much. But we understood that there were differences between us that could never fully be overcome."

"Those differences don't matter."

"They do, sweet child, they do. For one thing, humans and kaesana don't age the same way. Right now, you and Mirsa are both children. But in just a few short years, she will be an adolescent, while you will still be a child. And well before you're ready to join The Dance, Mirsa will be an adult, and may even be ready to have children of her own."

She watched her daughter's face and recognized the moment when that terrible truth, and the even more terrible truth it led to, sunk in. Tears welled up again in Naeri's eyes, and Lydra hugged her close.

"Mirsa will always love you, and you will always love her. I am certain of that much. But if you want to be a true sister to her, you need to accept that there are times when you must let her go."

"Because she is going to grow up and leave me behind."

"Not exactly. But the day will come when she will be the older sister, just as you were once the older sister."

"And someday I'll lose her the way you lost Mariah."

The words came out slowly, as was appropriate for such an unwelcome truth. Lydra wouldn't deny that truth, but she felt compelled to soften it. "Yes, but there are many years ahead of you both before that day."

Lydra held Naeri for a while longer until her tears ebbed, and her sobs faded to sniffles. Eventually, Naeri wriggled free of her embrace and turned to face her.

"I won't let her forget us," she said with determination. "I want to learn human writing, so I can send her letters."

"I can teach you that."

"And I want to learn more about humans and how they live."

"There are many families joined to our clan who would be happy to teach you anything you want to learn."

Naeri looked thoughtful for a moment, and her next words struck Lydra with the force of a physical blow. "And when I have learned enough, I want to live with humans for a while, the way Mirsa lived with us."

She didn't respond for several heartbeats. She *couldn't* respond. She didn't want to refuse Naeri outright, but what her daughter was suggesting was unheard of. Before she could think of something to say, Naeri continued. "Mirsa lived in our world at least part of the time, but I've never lived in hers."

"Just as Mirsa cannot become kaesana, you cannot become human," Lydra warned when she finally found her voice.

"I know that, Atar. But I want to understand humans better, and I want to know how Mirsa felt being among us."

Shae-Lydra wanted to believe that this was just an excuse to try to visit Glasnae in Avrin, but she knew better. Naeri always met others halfway. She always gave as much as she ever asked of anyone else. Why should this situation be any different? Lydra phrased her answer carefully, not wanting to give Naeri too much hope, but also wanting to give her enough that she wouldn't rebelliously do something rash.

"If that is what you genuinely want, then you have a difficult road ahead of you. You have a lot to learn about humans before you can try to live with them, even for a little while."

Naeri's eyes lit up. "You'll help me?" she asked.

Lydra suppressed a sigh as she replied, "I will try."

∗∗∗

"You've squandered your opportunity to earn her trust." Leah imbued each word with the full measure of her anger and frustration.

M'Gan seemed more annoyed than upset to be on the receiving end of her displeasure. "The child overreacted. I was simply trying to get a better understanding of her personality."

"You were supposed to be evaluating the extent of her power and nothing else! I told you that she was already skittish. After this, I doubt that I'll be able to convince her to be in the same room with you, much less allow you to train her."

104

"I merely brushed against her surface thoughts, Leah. It was hardly invasive. A good deal of magical knowledge is passed mind to mind. If she is uncomfortable with that degree of contact, she'll need to overcome it quickly."

"She's only nine years old, and she'd never met you before. Did you really expect her to be comfortable with you listening to her thoughts? Regardless of how minor the contact was, you invaded her privacy. I'm not surprised by her response."

"The poltergeist she created was powerful and dangerous. If things like that are going to happen every time she loses her temp—"

"First of all, the poltergeist was powerful but not large, and it dissipated as soon as she calmed down. Secondly, this was the first incident since she's been here."

"Wonderful. The girl can control herself for nearly two weeks at a time. I'm impressed." His voice dripped with sarcasm, and she wondered how long she'd be able to keep her own temper in check.

"You've put me in an exceedingly difficult position, M'Gan. I was hoping to appoint you as her mentor, but that clearly isn't possible now. You've forced me to consider other options."

"What other options, Leah?" M'Gan asked darkly.

"I need to choose someone who will be sensitive to her needs in a manner which you've proven yourself to be utterly incapable of. And since most of the magical instruction Glasnae has received so far came from her kaesana family, I've decided that her mentor should be well versed in the ways that dragons use magic."

"Who do you have in mind?"

"First Guardian Deirdre Starling," she said levelly.

"Absolutely not! I forbid it," M'Gan all but roared at her.

Leah was not in the least bit perturbed by the man's outburst. As the head of the Magicians Order, M'Gan held a great deal of authority in New Avalon, but she was High Priestess, and even though he didn't technically have to bow to *her* authority, she did outrank him, and he knew it.

"I will do as I see fit."

"The child is too strong. She *must* be trained by a skilled magician."

"Deirdre is powerful enough to guide Glasnae through the process of taming her power, and in addition to being from a joined family herself, Deirdre is probably the foremost expert on kaesana magic in New Avalon."

"As First Guardian, Deirdre has far more pressing duties than mentoring a neophyte."

"You are First Magician, yet you would have found time," she replied dryly. "I am confident that Deirdre will agree to teach Glasnae, especially since I'm making the request a personal favor."

M'Gan glared at her silently for several heartbeats before asking, "Do you think it wise to expose the child to the Guardians at such an impressionable age? What if she becomes enamored of their life? Will you sit back and watch as all that power is locked away, bound into the link of the kae-madri?"

Now he reveals his true fear, Leah thought to herself. Not that she didn't share his concern. Before he touched Glasnae's thoughts, triggering her rather violent response, M'Gan had managed to evaluate her power, and the results he shared with her were incredible. Glasnae was, without question, the most powerful individual he had ever encountered, and by a very wide margin. If her power continued to grow in the typical way as she matured, there was no telling just how much force she would be able to command as an adult. That the gods would bless someone with such an extreme gift had significant implications.

If, as M'Gan clearly feared, Glasnae were to choose to become kae-madri, the largess of that power would be bound into a link with the planet itself for the duration of her life. To become a guardian was to sacrifice the bulk of one's magic to serve the goddess Kaestra as her daughter. Leah had great admiration for the women who so bound themselves, but she believed, as M'Gan clearly did, that for Glasnae, it would be a waste.

"I never said that I intended her to become a novice of the Guardians Order. Priests and priestesses often serve as mentors, regardless of whether their students have any intention of entering their orders or not. If Deirdre chooses to become Glasnae's mentor, I will make certain that she understands that I want to see how the girl's skills develop before any offers are made. Remember that the guardians do not accept petitioners. One joins the Order of Kae-Madri only when invited to do so."

"And do you honestly believe that Deirdre will accept your restrictions once she realizes what she's dealing with? I have no doubt that she will want the child's power at the service of her own order."

She frowned. "Deirdre doesn't think that way."

"And what about *you*, Leah? What plans do you have for this child?"

"The gods must have something special in mind for her. I intend to prepare her as best I can for whatever that destiny may be."

"Are you reconsidering your decision to groom Maylene as your successor?"

"No," she said flatly. "Maylene will serve as High Priestess after me. I know that she will follow my direction without question. I'm not yet sure what the future holds for Glasnae."

"Have you tried to find out?"

Leah did not pretend to misunderstand. "I consulted the Order of Seers yesterday after you left. I received their official response this morning."

"And?"

"And there is currently no record in the Hall of Mirrors involving such power concentrated within a single individual."

He considered this for a moment. "Then we must use our own judgment. You know as well as I do that she belongs in my order. It is as simple as that."

She was inclined to agree, but she disliked his presumptions. "I cannot force her to join the Magicians Order."

"You can guide her."

107

"It isn't as if there are many options for someone of her ability. In time she will come to realize that. Given what I've seen, and what my sister Linia has shared with me, any overt guidance on my part may backfire. I must be subtle."

"It would help if a magician trained her rather than Deirdre. If not me, then someone else."

But Leah had already made up her mind. "I sent a letter to the First Guardian this morning." Before he could protest, she added, "However, I would be willing to talk to Deirdre about enlisting someone from your order to assist her. Someone sensitive, such as Devon Graymoor."

"Devon is little more than a child himself."

"Nonsense. Devon is nearly thirty years old. Young, I grant you, but hardly a child. He's a fully initiated magician and one of your personal students. Moreover, he has a reputation for being patient and understanding. Of all the members of your order, I believe that he possesses the best temperament for this task."

M'Gan looked faintly unhappy. "I don't think that Devon is the best choice."

"He's *my* choice," Leah said with emphasis.

"I have no say in this?"

"You can refuse to extend his services, but I won't accept another in his place."

"Why are you being so stubborn about this?"

"You made a mistake. These are the consequences."

"You would take chances with this child's education simply to punish me?"

"This has nothing to do with punishment. This is damage control. Thanks to your little stunt, she's become wary and withdrawn. It was all I could do to ensure that she wouldn't fear *me* as well. Glasnae needs to learn to control her gifts. In order to do that she needs to trust her teachers. *I* need to trust that her teachers won't give her any incentive to rebel. Your judgment on this subject is questionable at best."

"She's too powerful, Leah. Even if she can control that power, how are *we* going to control *her*?"

Leah fell silent. The man had a point. Considering what Linia had told her about Glasnae's temperament, in addition to her own observations, it was unlikely that the child would easily submit to the will of her elders. On the other hand, the girl gave every indication of being thoughtful, kindhearted, and just. Leah didn't believe that heavy-handed discipline would be required. "She's a good girl. I don't think we need to be concerned with her abusing her gifts."

"Perhaps not," he conceded, "but she's obviously willful. I would feel easier if we had safeguards in place to make sure that she maintains a measure of obedience."

Something in his words bothered her. "If we treat her with respect and consideration, she will have no incentive to disobey."

"There *are* other ways, Leah. Ways that are far more guaranteed to be effective."

She glared at him and said with disgust, "No. That is completely out of the question. I can't believe that you would even suggest doing that to a child."

He shrugged. "It was merely a suggestion. I understand your reluctance, but you might change your mind in another six or seven years, when you're dealing with a stubborn adolescent. By then, it will be far more difficult to influence her, and it may be too late."

Leah paused for a moment. The idea of setting compulsions on an innocent little girl chilled her to the core, but M'Gan's concerns were valid. She shook her head. "No," she said again. "I won't allow it. We'll keep a watchful eye on her, but I see no reason to do anything so drastic."

"So be it," he replied easily enough.

"Does that mean that you will allow Devon to assist with her training?"

"Consider him at your service, Leah."

She smiled gently. "Thank you." Another thought occurred to her, and she added, "Sometimes the influence of a peer can have greater impact than that of a teacher. Perhaps I will arrange for Glasnae to share some of her classes with Maylene."

M'Gan looked thoughtful. "Careful, Leah. Such influence can go both ways."

Leah was completely unconcerned. "Maylene's loyalty to me is unshakable. If I can successfully foster a friendship between the two girls, it should be enough to keep Glasnae in check."

M'Gan bowed ever so slightly. "I hope that you're right."

***

Deirdre sat cross-legged on the ground in front of three youngsters. Two were recent additions to the novitiate of the Order of Kae-Madri. The youngest, Savarrah, was only thirteen and still three years too young to officially enter the novitiate, but she had talked her way into joining the lessons taught to the guardians in training.

The child had been fulfilling her required work hours with various tasks in the guardians' cloisters since she first entered her service years, and it was clear to everyone that Kaestra had placed her mark upon the girl. It was only a matter of time before Savarrah would be of an age to officially join them, and Deirdre saw no harm in letting her get a head start on developing the skills she would need to serve Kaestra.

"A guardian's only true commandment is to maintain the balance," Deirdre began. "This can be interpreted in many ways, but it essentially comes down to this: all things prosper when they exist in a state of balance with one another. Minor shifts are acceptable, and even necessary, but without long term balance, any system will fall apart."

The girls nodded in understanding, and she continued.

"In your science classes, have you all had a chance to use microscopes to examine creatures too small to see with the naked eye?" Again, they nodded, even Savarrah.

"Good. Part of your training here will involve identifying the microbes that live in the soil and understanding how they work together to make the land healthy. But today, I am going to teach you how to perceive them through your magical and intuitive senses."

Three pairs of eyes went wide with curiosity and eagerness.

"Open your senses and watch me closely," Dierdre said, placing her hands palm down on the ground. She carefully sent a tendril of thought along the delicate thread of magic that bound her to the planet. In response, the magic swelled and deepened. To magic-sight, it would appear as if the slender thread of crimson light that joined her to Kaestra had become a ribbon of glowing gold.

Deirdre pushed her awareness into the ground. She felt for the small life forms that manifested as a tingling sensation against her mind, scattered, but more concentrated in some areas than others. Then, she used the power lent to her by Kaestra to flood kaema through the soil around her. Without more focused direction, it wouldn't do much more than enhance the energy signature of the life within this piece of land, making it easier for the girls to detect.

"Oh!" Savarrah exclaimed. "I can feel them. I really can!"

"Me too," Katrine said with a wide smile.

Yasmin was more thoughtful in her response, asking, "Can we only sense them because of what you did?"

Deirdre nodded. "I made it easier for you this first time, but soon, you will be able to sense the life within the land at will."

"Once we become guardians, right?" Savarrah asked.

"Oh no, you won't need to wait for that. Anyone with magical talent and a reasonable level of psychic awareness can develop this skill, but few beyond our order bother."

"Deirdre?" a voice called out.

She turned, saw Freydis approaching, and replied, "Just a moment."

She carefully released the extra kaema back to Kaestra, and her link resumed its normal resting state. Then she turned to her students. "I want you to stay here and take notes on everything you can perceive for

111

the next half hour. Try to feel for differences in the flow of energy and the patterns that form. The kaema I poured into the ground will gradually fade over the next fifteen minutes or so, but I'd like you to try to sense the life-forms even when the power has waned."

"Yes, Lady Deirdre," they said in chorus, each pulling out their notebooks and pencils.

Freydis smiled as she approached and said, "The lessons seem to be going very well."

"I try to be a good teacher," Deirdre responded with a touch of uneasiness.

Freydis narrowed her golden-brown eyes in an expression of amused irritation. Freydis Laylin was in her mid-seventies, a woman in her prime who could probably pass for a youth with little effort. A few faint laugh lines creased her light brown skin around the eyes, but aside from the silvery white hair, she looked nearly thirty years younger.

"You need to learn how to accept a compliment, Deirdre. You are an excellent teacher, and you should be proud of that."

Deirdre sighed and said, "I love that moment when it becomes real to them. Reading something in a book, even seeing it through a lens is so hollow compared to feeling it for yourself firsthand."

"I agree wholeheartedly," Freydis replied. "Now, what is it you wanted to talk to me about?"

Deirdre guided the other woman to a low bench set off by itself under a large tree. The two sat down, and she pulled a carefully folded letter out of her pocket and handed it to Freydis.

"What's this?"

"Read it. I think it speaks for itself."

Freydis lifted the single page and silently read the letter that Deirdre had all but committed to memory.

Dear Kae-Madri Deirdre,

I am asking you for your assistance in a rather delicate matter that I think requires your particular expertise.

Glasnae Maylan, my great niece, arrived in New Avalon a couple of weeks ago to study at the Druidic College. She has significant magical talents, and the first priority in her education is teaching her to manage them. So far, she is having difficulty learning proper control techniques. Most of the magical training she's received prior to now has been from her kaesana kin, and since dragons experience magic quite differently than we do, this could be a large part of the problem.

I know that as First Guardian, you have significant responsibilities, and I do not ask this favor of you lightly. You are the foremost expert in kaesana magic currently in New Avalon. If you could take some time to meet with Glasnae, I would be pleased to hear your assessment of the child's needs and implement any recommendations you might offer regarding her training. If you are able to spend some time mentoring her, I would be particularly grateful. I believe that she would respond favorably to you as a teacher.

As I said, this is a delicate matter. Glasnae is a very gifted child, and I would rather not have those gifts made common knowledge, at least not until she has adequate control. She is quite young and should be able to enjoy her childhood without demands being made upon her prematurely. I trust you understand and will be discreet. I have enclosed a copy of Glasnae's current schedule to facilitate a meeting. I look forward to your response.

I offer my most sincere thanks for your help, Sister.

Warmest Regards,

Leah

"Huh," Freydis said in a huff. "It sounds like she really cares about this child."

"I agree. She didn't even use her title in her signature."

"I noticed that. Of course, Leah is highly skilled in diplomacy and knows how to get what she wants. If she gambled, I'd warn you to never play poker with her."

"This is important, Freydis. What do you think I should do?"

"Seriously, child? Why ask me? If you want to teach the girl, do it."

Deirdre grumbled, caught between the reflex to defer to the woman who'd mentored her since she joined the Order of Guardians fifteen years earlier, and the realization that as First Guardian she was now Freydis's superior. "First of all, you shouldn't call me 'child.'"

"Why not?" the other woman interjected before she could continue.

"Because I'm hardly a child anymore. Last I checked I was thirty-two years old."

Freydis snorted. "Child is a relative term. Since I'm more than twice your age, you look awfully young from my perspective."

"I'm also First Guardian now," she added shyly.

"True, but hardly a good reason for me to give up a comfortable habit. And before you protest, let me remind you that I didn't exactly treat Patricia with any special deference when she was First Guardian."

Deirdre bristled. "You never called Patricia 'child.'"

"Of course not!" Freydis rolled her eyes. "She's decades older than I am. But I did have a few choice names for her—idiot, pain in the ass, bitch…"

"Enough!" Deirdre exclaimed. She took a deep breath to steady herself and said, "Can we please get back to the subject at hand?"

"I don't see what the issue is here. We both know that you're intrigued by this request."

"I may not have time to take on a student."

"Make the time, Deirdre." The older woman held up a hand before she could protest. "And before you say anything stupid, rest assured that none of the kae-madri will have a problem with this. No one will accuse you of shirking your duties or acting inappropriately. No one would begrudge you this opportunity."

"It's not like Leah to ask for something like this."

"No, she usually just demands."

"Exactly. It seems out of character."

Freydis frowned thoughtfully. "Maybe adopting Maylene has softened her. Motherhood can have that effect. Or maybe she's learned that some of us respond better when she doesn't push us around. Only the gods know for sure. But either do this on your own terms or not at all. Don't let Leah dictate how you interact with the child. I believe that her request for help is genuine, but that doesn't mean that she won't try to control the situation."

"I think I can handle her under the circumstances."

"You can't even make a decision without worrying about what the other kae-madri will think, but you believe that you can stand up to Leah Tierney?"

Deirdre straightened and looked her old mentor in the eye. "I may still be getting used to my new position, but I do have a backbone, Freydis."

Freydis smirked at her. "That's exactly what I wanted to hear, child."

"Don't call me child," Deirdre said with some bite in her voice.

Freydis laughed. "Let's not push it."

Chapter 7

Larin knew that the council members were uncomfortable, and he didn't care. After all, the kaesana in attendance were equally uncomfortable, if for vastly different—and in Larin's opinion, far more valid—reasons.

Naeri had spent a great deal of time in Maliae Keep and the village of Mali over the past year, and she seemed relatively at ease, but he could tell that Shae-Lydra was all too aware of the nearness of the ceiling and walls. When Shae-Lydra had asked him to find a way for Naeri to experience living in the human world, accommodations for Naeri's size and wingspan had been his first concern. Though still a child and far from full-grown, she was already six feet tall, and her wings had a span of well over ten feet when fully unfurled. Her mother was nearly twice as large, and even in the large banquet room that he'd chosen for this meeting, she seemed cramped.

He hoped that the meeting would be brief, for all their sakes.

Lydra's gentle mind-voice drifted into his thoughts, a contact he was becoming more and more accustomed to. *I never thought my child would stir up so much concern.*

I'm sure that Glasnae turned the canyi upside down now and then, he replied in kind. *Don't worry. We'll get this settled tonight.*

The councilors were afraid that Naeri's presence at the Keep and in the village was a sign that the kaesana wanted to take a more active role in human affairs. It was nonsense, but Larin had to respond.

The fear that drove the councilors to overreact was deeply rooted. The dragons were native to this world. Humans were not. Human civilization on Kaestra relied upon the hospitality of the kaesana. They were fortunate that the kaesana had been so generous as to grant control of vast amounts of territory to a people who had arrived on their world lost and desperate.

Naeri's decision to live among humans, the way her foster-sister had lived among her people, was without precedent. Larin was frustrated that the child's interest in her foster-sister's people had caused so much unrest, but he firmly believed that the councilors would come to their senses once they met Naeri and her mother. Everyone who had a chance to get to know Naeri invariably came to love and respect her. As young as she was, she was an excellent ambassador for her kind.

Councilor Terena Yandoor, one of the oldest and most experienced of the group, eyed the two kaesana females with open curiosity that bordered on rudeness. But since there was no hostility in her expression, Larin took it as a reassuring sign. Once everyone was settled and refreshments had been brought in, he moved to the center of the room.

"First, I would like to thank all of you for coming. Given the current concerns that have been brought to my attention, I wanted you to have the opportunity to meet Naeri for yourselves, along with her mother, Shae-Lydra, who is a matriarch of the Shaendari Clan." He nodded to acknowledge the two dragons who stood politely near the open balcony doors.

"It is my hope," he continued, "that given the chance to speak with Lydra and Naeri, you will find that we have nothing to fear from our kaesana neighbors. They have agreed to answer any questions you may have so that you will be better able to answer the questions of your constituents."

He then turned to Terena. "Councilor Terena, you have voiced concerns that the kaesana may be looking to expand their territory within our province. Perhaps you can direct your questions to Shae-Lydra?"

Terena looked startled but composed herself quickly. She softly cleared her throat and turned toward the older of the dragons. "Your daughter's presence among us has come as quite a surprise. Is there a special reason for this sudden change in accepted custom?"

"Yes," Lydra replied. "My clan fostered Governor Tierney's daughter, Glasnae. The two grew remarkably close, and my daughter became curious about human culture. She wanted to live among you, to learn about human ways first-hand. The governor, along with others here at the Keep and in the village, have been kind enough to indulge her."

"And that is the only reason?" Terena's tone was polite, but there was no mistaking the skepticism in her voice.

Lydra glanced at her daughter, who stood very still and kept her gaze fixed on the floor in front of her. "Yes, Councilor. That is the only reason. I am a matriarch of my clan, and so I have authority to speak on behalf of all Shaendari. As such, I can tell you that our clan has no desire to change the relationship that we have enjoyed with humans since you arrived on Kaesa Atera—or Kaestra, as you call the world we share. I am grateful that so many of your people have welcomed my daughter and indulged her whim. Please rest assured that this is nothing more than my child's wish to explore your way of life."

"You speak for the Shaendari, but what of the other clans?"

"I am not an elder or a chosen speaker for my species, but I can assure you that no kaesana clan seeks to alter the agreement that was made when your people first came to our world."

Larin watched Terena absorb this. Then Naeri spoke up, her voice slightly lilting. "I didn't mean to upset anyone." She paused, her expression uncertain. Her mother smiled at her in encouragement, and she continued. "Mirsa—I mean Glasnae—and I have always been close, but most of the time we spent together was at the canyi, among my people. I never spent much time with hers. When she left Maliae to go to school three years ago, it became important to me to understand the people she came from better. Living and working among you was the only way I could think of to do that."

Terena appeared taken aback by Naeri's speech, but after a thoughtful pause, she smiled. "I suppose that makes sense. Perhaps we were too quick to read more into this than is really there."

The response among the humans gathered was evenly split between shrugs and nods, but the tension in the room seemed to ease considerably.

Then Naeri asked, with the innocent curiosity of a child, "Is that common among humans?"

Larin held his breath, hoping the councilors would not take offense. Terena quickly put him at ease by laughing out loud. "Yes, my dear, I am afraid it is. If you continue to reside among us, you will soon learn that adult humans often overthink situations, especially those of us in positions of authority."

There were a few chuckles around the room, and Lydra moved to drape a wing over her daughter's shoulder. "Adult kaesana sometimes do the same thing." She shook her head. "I think we could all benefit from listening to our children more often. They have a way of seeing to the heart of things when we are too distracted by our own worries."

There were a few other questions, but they seemed fueled by curiosity rather than fear. As Larin had expected, when confronted with the child in person, the councilors realized just how foolish they had been. It wasn't long before he was seeing them all to the door and wishing them a safe journey home. By the time the last person left, little over half an hour had passed.

Larin smiled up at Lydra. "That was nicely short."

"You're confident that they are satisfied?"

"Satisfied or not, they've had the chance to say their piece. None of us owe them any more than that. If there are any further inquiries regarding this, I can handle them."

There was a mischievous gleam in Lydra's eyes. "Anyone who wishes to speak more on this matter is welcome to come to the canyi. You are free to invite them in my name."

"I may do just that." He chuckled at first, and then grew sober. "I wish more council members were from joined families."

"None who are were here tonight," Lydra commented.

"They saw no need to be. They understand the situation, but nothing they said made a difference to their colleagues." He sighed. "I'm sorry I had to put you and Naeri through this."

"I thought it was interesting," Naeri offered.

Lydra smiled down at her child. "Are you coming home with me, or staying here tonight?"

Naeri glanced at Larin before replying, "I'd like to stay. There's a fair in the village tomorrow that I want to go to."

With the arrangements made, Lydra took her leave, and Larin invited Naeri to take a walk with him around the grounds. It was a lovely night, and Larin took pleasure and comfort in the young dragon's company. Lately he found himself missing his children fiercely and being with Naeri helped ease the ache inside of him.

Larin had promised Glasnae that he would get to know the other side of her family better, and he'd been true to his word. At first, it had been difficult, but now he regretted the time he'd kept himself apart from them. He discovered that with the Shaendari, he could both mourn Mariah without shame and celebrate her life. Her dragon-kin loved her dearly and were glad to share memories and stories with him.

And now, thanks to her curiosity and determination, Naeri had entered his life. Naeri, who delighted him with her innocent sweetness and amazed him with her insight. Naeri, who was beginning to feel more and more like a second daughter to him.

After walking in silence for some time, Naeri said softly, "I have grown very fond of you, Larin."

"And I have grown very fond of you," Larin replied easily.

She looked away, and if avoiding his gaze. "I already have a devya. I chose him many years ago. If I hadn't, I would be tempted to ask you to be my devya."

Larin's throat constricted painfully. Oh, how he understood the significance of that statement, and his eyes grew moist at the honor she paid him. He also felt a twinge of guilt that he had once been jealous of Glasnae's devya.

When he did not respond right away, Naeri turned back to face him. "There is another title that a child can give a male he or she feels a strong bond with. It does not carry the weight of devya, but it is a mark of respect and affection: vanyi."

"What does it mean?"

She frowned in concentration. "I think it's like an honorary uncle. I still don't fully understand human relationships, but that is as close as I can explain it."

"You want to call me…vanyi?" Larin stumbled a bit over the unfamiliar word.

"In my mind, I already do," she said shyly. "Would you accept the name formally?"

"I would be honored," Larin began, "but I'm not sure what responsibilities come with it."

Naeri said softly, "All you need to do is love me."

"I do, sweetheart. I do." He wrapped his arms around her neck, and she returned the embrace. His thoughts drifted back to when he and Mariah had first married. He'd been so nervous around her dragon-kin back then. He would never have imagined that one day he would feel the same tenderness and affection toward a young dragon that he felt toward his own children.

When they separated and began walking back toward the Keep, Larin noticed that Naeri seemed happier and more talkative. Clearly this had been weighing on her mind.

"It's strange, Vanyi"—the title fell from her tongue quite naturally—"that the members of your council seemed so interested in what I had to say. They gave me the same attention they gave my mother, and she is a matriarch!"

Larin chuckled. "In this case, your age wasn't relevant. You were sharing your feelings and experiences, which is what they came to learn about."

"I'm glad that I had something to offer."

"You're young, Naeri, but you are now an ambassador for your clan, even your species. You impressed the people you met tonight. Whenever someone mentions the kaesana, they will think of you. They will remember the lovely young dragon who spoke to them so openly and politely."

Larin could see her growing wiser and more thoughtful with each passing day. He only hoped that she wouldn't grow up too quickly.

Her next words surprised him. "It hurt when Mirsa left us. I was upset, maybe even a little angry, because I didn't want her to go. I thought of her as one of us, and I knew that once she went to school, she would become truly human. I thought I would lose her. Atar said that I needed to learn to let her go so she could become who she was meant to be."

"It is hard to let go of those we love."

"I still miss her, but maybe it was a good thing that she went away. That's why I decided to come here, and I really like working with your people. I have learned so much! Atar has given permission for me to continue for as long as I want, with your approval, Vanyi. And I want to continue for as long as I can."

Larin wished that she wasn't quite so large, because he had the wild desire to sweep her up in his arms and spin her around, the way he used to do with Riahn and Glasnae when they were small. It was that urge that prompted his next question. "How long has it been since you were small enough for me to pick up?"

She looked quizzical. "It's been many years I think, but I'm not sure how much you can lift. Why?"

Larin laughed heartily, and it felt so good to let the joy flow through him. He laughed as the puzzled Naeri watched with concern until he managed to speak again. "I asked because I'd be happy to have you stay with me for as long as you want."

"But I am getting too big?" There was hint of disappointment in her voice.

"No, Naeri, not at all. Kaestra knows there's more than enough room at the Keep for you! I just wish that I had known you this well when you were small so that I could carry you around on my shoulders and pick you up to tuck you into bed."

Naeri's eyes were luminous in the dark. "When I'm a little older and strong enough, maybe I could carry you on *my* shoulders. We could fly together."

"You couldn't," Larin said quickly. "I'm much too heavy."

"I'm not full-grown yet." She said, stretching out her wings. "We'd wait until I was sure it would be safe. It could be great fun!"

Larin told her that they would wait and see. He'd flown with other kaesana and had to admit that it was a marvelous experience. But he felt protective of Naeri and didn't want to encourage her to do something that might hurt her.

They returned to the Keep through the front courtyard. Lightstones set on posts and arranged along the balconies illuminated the area with a soft golden glow. The main doors were open to admit the fresh evening breeze but would be closed shortly. Leaving the main doors open during fair weather was an old tradition that was dear to Larin's heart. It was a sign of welcome and hospitality that reminded him that in Maliae, strangers were greeted with open arms, just as the kaesana had first welcomed his ancestors. Just as the Shaendari welcomed him.

***

"This is a bad idea," Maylene said for what seemed like the hundredth time as they crept down the darkened corridor.

Glasnae waved a hand dismissively. "You worry too much. We won't get caught."

Maylene lacked her friend's confidence. She also lacked Glasnae's motivation for this latest misadventure. "Why are you so determined to torment Lord M'Gan?"

123

"Because M'Gan enjoys tormenting others," she answered sourly. "He deserves this."

"You shouldn't use his name without his title," Maylene corrected automatically. "It's disrespectful."

Glasnae whirled around to face her. "Fine. *Brother* M'Gan deserves whatever torment I can invent for him!"

"That's not the right—"

Glasnae cut her off before she could finish. "Brother is an acceptable title. He may be First Magician, but the 'Lord' is an unnecessary formality. I'm sorry, Maylene, but I cannot bring myself to call that man *Lord*. Besides, given my intentions, it would be hypocritical of me, don't you think?"

They were now at the door of M'Gan's classroom, and Glasnae's eyes took on a gleam that was visible even in the dim hallway. She laid a hand on the doorknob and closed her eyes while Maylene looked nervously around them for any sign that someone might be coming. After a few minutes, there was an audible click and the door opened.

"You're getting better at picking locks," she commented.

Glasnae looked unexpectedly sheepish. "Not really. I think I broke it."

"Next time, he'll use magic to lock the room."

Glasnae snickered. "Maybe, but I can break through his spells easily enough if I have to."

"Not because you understand enough to unravel them."

Glasnae wasn't in the least bit insulted. "True, but there are times when brute force works just fine, and I've got more than enough power."

There were a couple of thumping sounds coming from around the corner, and Maylene's heart thumped even louder in response. "We need to get out of here. Someone's coming."

"Quick—inside!"

"No! We'll get caught!"

"Trust me!"

There was no help for it. Maylene allowed Glasnae to pull her into the room and close the door behind them. They crouched down well below the small window and listened, extending their psychic senses as far as they could to see who might be there. Maylene did sense a presence, but whoever it was—she couldn't tell—was walking away from the room they hid in, and it wasn't long before they passed beyond the reach of her sensing.

"Okay. It's time to get to work." Glasnae sounded far too pleased with herself as she walked up to the large mahogany desk at the front of the room. She carefully removed the first drawer and created a delicate shield over the top. Then she turned it over and put it back in place. She repeated the procedure with the next drawer.

"What do you need me to do?" Maylene asked after she watched her set up the third drawer.

"Just keep watch."

"You said you needed my help!" She didn't want to be here, but now she felt useless on top of it, which added insult to injury. "If we get caught, I'll get punished for something I didn't even get a chance to help with."

"You are helping. You're keeping watch."

"That's not really helping."

"Do you want to set up a drawer?" Glasnae asked sweetly.

"Yes, I do!" Maylene replied without thinking. She really *didn't* want to, but she didn't want to be left out, either. Somehow, Glasnae always managed to talk her into doing things that she didn't really want to do.

She walked over to the desk, and Glasnae showed her how she was building the shield so that it would break when the drawer was pulled back out. It was a tricky spell, which demonstrated that Glasnae could use magic with some finesse when she really wanted to.

They were both so focused on the spell that they didn't notice that someone had entered the room until he was standing right next to them.

125

"What are you up to this time?"

The drawer they'd been holding between them fell to the floor with a crash, and Maylene nearly jumped out of her skin.

"Devon!" Glasnae shrieked in surprise. Then her tone turned accusatory. "What are you doing here?"

Maylene wished the floor would open up and swallow her. *Don't make it worse,* she sent to her friend.

Glasnae didn't reply. She just stood there with her hands on her hips, glaring at Devon who looked more tired than angry.

"I'm not the one who needs to provide an explanation here," Devon replied levelly.

"It's nothing." Glasnae still didn't sound the least bit apologetic. "Just a bit of fun."

Devon shook his head and then looked at Maylene. "I assume she dragged you along as a lookout?"

Maylene nodded, fighting back tears. "Are you going to tell my mother?"

"I haven't decided."

For the first time, Maylene saw Glasnae look faintly nervous. "You don't need to mention that Maylene was here. She didn't even want to come."

He folded his arms across his chest. "She never does." Turning back to Maylene, he added, "I'm disappointed in you, Maylene. I expect you to talk Glasnae out of this sort of foolishness, not allow her to talk you into it."

Maylene cheeks burned with embarrassment as she bowed her head, unable to think of an appropriate response.

"It's not her fault," Glasnae offered after several seconds of silence. "You know what a bully I can be, Devon."

Devon groaned and exclaimed, "Bully, my ass!" Maylene looked up, shocked by his language. "Bullies threaten and torment. You're worse. You wheedle and coerce like…like a…" he trailed off, obviously unable to find the right word.

Unfortunately, Glasnae was in a perversely helpful mood and offered. "Salesman? Maybe a politician?"

"Yes! No! Just be quiet and let me think." Devon sounded as though he was near the end of his rope. "How much trouble do you really want to be in over this, Glasnae?"

Maylene turned and saw that her friend was actually giving the question some thought. Finally, she replied levelly. "I'm willing to accept whatever punishment you think is appropriate."

"Just as long as Maylene isn't punished along with you, right?"

"Bullied or coerced, she's only here because I forced her to come, which makes her a victim. Victims should never be punished."

Maylene frowned, surprised by the vehemence in her friend's voice. When she looked at Devon's face, she saw that the magician was not so surprised, which only confused her more.

"You need to find less destructive ways of expressing yourself, Glasnae," he said after a long pause. "This nonsense has got to stop. M'Gan doesn't care *why* you insist on being a thorn in his side. All he sees is a misbehaving child. The worse your behavior is, the less likely he is to listen to you."

"I don't want him to listen to me. I want him to leave me alone." There was an edge to Glasnae's voice that Maylene usually only heard from adults, which was never a good sign.

"Both of you stay right there," Devon ordered and then proceeded to clean up the mess, right all the drawers and remove all traces of the spells Glasnae had crafted. Then he used magic to repair the damaged lock. When he was finished, he turned his attention back to them.

"I want both of you to go home. I won't mention this little incident to anyone. But it's obvious that you have too much free time on your hands and are incapable of using it wisely, so I think some changes to your schedules are in order. You will both report to me at my workshop first thing after breakfast tomorrow, with copies of your class and duty schedules. If anyone asks, tell them that I've decided to give you some advanced training."

"You want us to lie?" Maylene was grateful for the reprieve but didn't want to compound her mistakes by lying to anyone, especially to her mother.

"You won't be lying," Devon said firmly. "We're going to make the punishment fit the crime. In your case, Maylene, I think that a few lessons in debate and persuasion will help you recognize when you're being led into mischief and make you better able to resist."

He turned to Glasnae. "As for you, it's clear that you're capable of far more advanced magic than your classwork suggests. And it's equally obvious that you still need more practice in control."

"It isn't as if you caught me mid-poltergeist!" Glasnae protested.

"True," Devon replied calmly, "but you do still have them from time to time. Besides, childish pranks like this one are not the actions of a person with proper discipline and self-control, wouldn't you agree?"

Glasnae didn't respond, and there was a stubborn feel to her silence that made Maylene uneasy. After a moment, Devon added matter-of-factly, "You did say that you would accept whatever punishment I considered appropriate. And since Maylene will only benefit from her share of this punishment, you really can't object, can you?"

Anyone else would have accepted the situation with resignation, if not outright gratitude, but Glasnae still sounded defiant when she answered, "Fine. But don't expect me to be happy about it."

Maylene's relief was palpable when Devon ushered them out the door. They were silent for most of the short walk and didn't even look at each other. But when they reached the dormitory where Glasnae lived, she turned to say goodbye and was shocked to see her friend's eyes red with tears.

"I really am sorry, Maylene," Glasnae said softly.

"It's okay," she replied. "Devon's right. I need to stand up to you more, so maybe I do need some lessons in that. Mother won't be angry with me for taking more training, no matter what it is."

"You're a better friend than I deserve."

"You're the best friend I've ever had," Maylene replied sincerely. "You like me for me, not because my mother is High Priestess."

Glasnae managed a grin. "I like you in *spite* of the fact that your mother is High Priestess."

"You don't like authority figures very much, do you?"

"I don't like people who think just because they have a fancy title that they can control other people's lives. Everyone should be able to choose for themselves."

"That means a lot to you, doesn't it? Being able to choose?"

"I think it means everything." Then she went to the door and waved. "See you tomorrow."

On the way home, Maylene thought about what Glasnae had said. They were only twelve years old, so there were some things they couldn't decide for themselves yet. And it wasn't as though anyone was forcing them to do anything terrible. There were rules they had to follow, but even adults had rules. That was just part of living in a civilized society. And since the adults around them had so much more knowledge and experience, she saw no harm in looking to them for guidance.

Glasnae sees harm in it. Despite what Devon had said about control, Glasnae didn't misbehave randomly or without reason. All of her pranks were well thought out and seemed to have a specific purpose, even if she didn't share what that purpose really was.

Maylene realized that she didn't fully understand Glasnae, but it didn't change the fact that they were best friends. At least she was certain that Glasnae cared about her and would always have her back. There was comfort in that thought, and Maylene smiled to herself. *I'd much rather have Glasnae as a friend than an enemy.*

Tarvis carefully observed the gray magestone that hummed with energy, its white-veined surface faintly glowing, and braced himself for any sudden release of kaema. They had taken appropriate precautions, but this experiment was not without risk, and he knew he might need to react quickly.

"It's holding," Orin said cautiously, "but only just barely."

"Considering the amount of kaema we've poured into it, it's holding up quite well." Karimah's tone suggested that she didn't want to push it any further.

"The ability to contain high concentrations of kaema is an intrinsic attribute of all forms of kaeverdine," Tarvis commented absently as he walked around the large rough-cut stone, examining it with a critical eye.

"Not this high," Karimah replied. "And gray magestone is the least stable form. This is dangerous."

"It's well-shielded," Tarvis said, "and we need to know what the limits are. We can't begin experimenting with diverting kaema from the ley lines until we can devise an acceptable storage system."

"I'm merely suggesting that this might not be the best choice of storage material."

"She's right, Tarvis. We're trying to build a battery, not a bomb," Orin added.

Tarvis was about to respond when Malek, the youngest team member present, spoke up. "Gray kaeverdine is readily available in large quantities. That can't be said for any other form of magestone. Besides, it also has the most flexible matrix. If we can determine its raw limits, we'll be better able to calculate how much we need."

"I can already tell you how much we would need," Orin said sharply. "Too much. To store all the kaema in the ley lines in rocks like this, we'd need mountains of the stuff."

Tarvis sighed. Orin was getting on in years, and although he was intelligent and powerful, he lacked creativity. He certainly believed in the rightness of their cause, but he seemed to have a harder time believing that their goals were achievable. "As Malek said, we're still trying to determine the limitations of the *raw* material. Because the matrix is so flexible, we should be able to artificially increase its capacity significantly, but first we need to know exactly what we've got to work with."

He then turned to Malek. "Go ahead and add the next layer."

Malek closed his eyes and poured additional kaema into the stone, which began to vibrate slightly.

"It's too much!" Karimah cried.

"*I'm* holding the shield." Tarvis's response was equal parts reassurance and rebuke. "Continue monitoring and recording."

Before Malek finished adding the last bit of kaema to the stone, it cracked down the center, and raw magical energy was released with explosive force, ricocheting off the inside of Tarvis's shield in all directions.

After taking a moment to recover from the shock, Orin added another layer to the shield. Then Karimah did the same. "Will the shield hold on its own now?" she asked Tarvis with forced calm.

"I think so," he replied thoughtfully. "That was more energetic than I was expecting. You did record the information we needed?"

"Yes." She held up the palm-sized recording disc of black kaeverdine. "It's all here. I just hope that you don't need to repeat this experiment any time soon."

"We shouldn't," Malek answered, reaching for the disc. "Not only did this show us how much energy the magestone can hold, but we've also learned how that energy is released when the limit is exceeded."

Tarvis smiled at the young adept. "You sound eager to get started, and confident of our eventual success."

"Cautiously optimistic," Malek said. "Our ancestors abandoned the use of magical batteries for good reason, but our understanding of how magic works has evolved a great deal since then. Using the records you found as a starting point, I think we can develop the storage system we need."

"This isn't something you're going to be able to figure out overnight," Orin warned.

Observing how the older adept's comment dimmed Malek's enthusiasm, Tarvis reminded them of their common purpose. "We agreed to work together to prevent the gross misuse of magic on Kaestra. That is a lofty ambition and not something that can be accomplished quickly or easily. I expect this task to take years, possibly even decades." He paused to allow the others to absorb his words. "I am prepared to dedicate my life to this effort, but I don't expect the same of anyone else. I will accept whatever aid you are willing to give me, for as long as you're willing to give it."

Karimah and Malek seemed to take comfort from his words, but Orin looked saddened and said quietly, "I'll back you to the end, Tarvis. You know that. But I'm a hundred and twenty-eight years old, and it's a hard thing to accept that the greatest undertaking I've ever had a hand in will probably not be successful within my lifetime."

Tarvis knew that he could very well be correct. But since he was also hopeful that they were well on their way to achieving their goal, and that Orin still had many healthy years ahead of him, he maintained an optimistic outlook. "I believe we'll see success sooner than you'll face death, Orin. But even if we don't, I trust that you'll take comfort in knowing that we are on the right path and that your efforts will be remembered."

Orin looked at him hard, as if sizing him up. "You're too old to be impatient and too young to be complacent. I guess you're well-suited to this task, at least for now. But be careful, Tarvis. The years won't stop for you any more than they will for me. In a few more decades, I'll be dead, and if you manage to avoid killing yourself with these experiments of yours, you'll be an old man like me."

"I should be so lucky," Tarvis said smoothly, hiding the misgivings Orin's words inspired.

Orin said nothing further as they watched the last of the released energy subside enough to be grounded and then dropped the shields. It wasn't until they were heading back to the school grounds that the older man imparted one more piece of advice, this time delivering it silently, mind to mind. *When you're an old man like me, you're going to need someone to keep you motivated, too.*

We have a good team of people here, Orin. I'll have all the support I need.

There's one other thing you'll need, and I suggest you start giving it some serious thought. Orin's tone sounded sharp.

And what would that be? he asked, genuinely curious.

Orin's reply was succinct. *A successor.*

Chapter 8

Aidan pushed through the dozen or so youngsters clustered in the hallway to where Kylec stood in front of the door to the room he shared with Andris. "What's going on here?"

"Nothing," Kylec replied tiredly. "Which is what I've been trying to tell everyone. Andy had a nightmare, and woke up yelling, which startled me. I jumped out of bed before I was fully awake and knocked over a pile of books. The noise woke Jamal and Riley next door, and the next thing I know half the dorm is up and wondering what's going on."

"All right, everyone, back to your rooms."

Dorianne sniffed and said sourly to Kylec, "If Andy's prone to nightmares and you're that clumsy, maybe you should shield the room for sound before you go to bed."

"Mind your own business, Dori," Kylec replied.

The girl whirled around and stomped off before Aidan could comment. It occurred to him that either she had uncommonly good hearing to have been disturbed by the commotion from the opposite side of the building, or she'd been spending the night in a room other than her own. Since that was an issue he was not prepared to deal with until he had a few more hours of sleep, he shooed the rest of the youngsters back to their rooms and stood pointedly in front of Kylec, waiting for an invitation.

"Good night, Master Varano. I'm sorry we woke everyone."

"Nice try," Aidan replied, holding back a smile. "Let's see what condition your room is in."

Kylec seemed to deflate slightly and opened the door just enough for him to enter. Andris was sitting on the end of his bed, looking pathetic. The room was a mess, with books, clothing and other belongings scattered everywhere. At least nothing appeared to be broken. He turned to Andris and asked, "Was it really a nightmare?"

The boy nodded.

"How bad was the poltergeist?"

Kylec jumped in before Andris had a chance to say anything. "It was small, and it stopped cold as soon as Andy woke up."

"I see." Aidan shook his head. "No real damage done, but you've got quite a mess to deal with in the morning."

"It's okay," Kylec replied. "We can take care of it."

Aidan sat down next to Andris on the bed. "Andy? Are you going to be able to get back to sleep tonight?"

Andris finally met his eyes, his expression haunted. "I'll be fine."

He wanted to spell both boys asleep, but he knew it wouldn't be well received, so he stood up to leave. "Andris, I want you to go to Lord Jaron tomorrow right after breakfast. You need to tell him what happened."

"It wasn't his fault!" Kylec exclaimed, subsiding when Aidan lifted a hand in warning.

"I'm well aware of that, Ky. This has nothing to do with blame or punishment. What Andris experienced is perfectly normal, but Lord Jaron is his mentor and needs to know about it so that he can help Andy deal with it."

He turned back to Andris. "You do understand that, Andy, don't you?"

"Yes, sir," came the quiet reply.

Aidan accepted the words and ignored the tone that belied them. "Good. I'll let Jaron know that he should expect you."

"Are you going to tell him what happened?" Andris asked.

Aidan shook his head. "This is between you and your mentor. I'll leave it to you to describe what happened, and I'll let Jaron remind you of why you have no reason to be embarrassed."

He bid the boys goodnight and left, heading back to the apartment that was so conveniently located in the very center of the building. He refused to think of it as *his* apartment; the situation was strictly temporary. He'd only accepted this "tour of duty" as Master-In-

Residence at Jaron's urging because the Archmage had been expecting the very incident that had just occurred.

He climbed into bed with a groan. The last couple of weeks had been brutal. With half the students and nearly a third of the staff sick with a nasty strain of influenza, classes had been suspended and the youngest children sent home. That left the rest of the students with far too much free time.

At least tonight's little incident is Jaron's to deal with, he thought to himself as he turned off the lightstone. He felt more than a little sympathy for Andris, but none at all for the friend who would have to guide him through this next phase of his development. After all, it was Jaron's fault that Aidan would have to deal with the matter of where Dorianne had been spending the night.

***

Jaron was waiting in his sitting room when Andris knocked on his front door. He opened the door, saddened but not surprised by the shame that seemed to radiate from the young man.

"Come on in, Andy."

Andris perched on the edge of a chair, and Jaron took a seat on the couch opposite him.

Realizing that there was no point to dragging things out, he asked, "What's on your mind, Andy?"

"I had a nightmare last night, and…"

Jaron said nothing. He merely sat back, deliberately maintaining a gently encouraging expression. After a while, Andris continued. "…I lost control in my sleep and there was a…a poltergeist," he said. "Only a small one," he added defensively.

"Did anyone see it?" Jaron asked gently.

"Only Ky. But the noise woke half the dorm. Ky told everyone that I had a nightmare and he knocked over some books when I startled him awake. I think the other kids believed him, but Master Varano didn't.

136

He came into the room and saw what happened. He said I needed to tell you."

Jaron paused for a moment before asking, "You're what...fourteen now?"

"Almost fifteen."

Jaron shook his head and smiled gently. "We've discussed this, Andy. Magical power usually grows as a person approaches adulthood, and it's common for it to spike at puberty. You were able to compensate with your internal shielding while the increases were slow and gradual, but it was only a matter of time before your power started growing faster than you could keep up with it. You'll need to refocus your efforts on control for the next year or so. You know that this is perfectly normal."

"Nothing about me is normal!" Andris answered with far more anger than Jaron was accustomed to seeing him express.

"That isn't true." Jaron tried to keep his tone soothing, but it seemed to have the opposite of the intended effect.

"Yes, it is," Andris said hoarsely. "I knew when I first came here that I was different. I accepted that, but I always believed that it was only a matter of time before..."

"Before there would be others with your abilities?" Jaron finished for him, cursing himself for not anticipating this train of thought.

"There aren't, are there? None of the new students even come close, do they?"

There was no point in lying. "No."

The silence stretched between them until Andris asked in a small voice, "What about New Avalon? Do you think that there might be someone there?"

He replied candidly, "I haven't heard of anyone, but I also haven't looked into it."

"Could you?" There was such a plaintive tone to the boy's voice it tore at Jaron's heart.

But he shook his head. "It would be too easy for any inquiries on my part to be misconstrued. But it seems unlikely that anyone with a gift as strong as yours wouldn't be brought to the attention of the Mage Hall. The druidic courses in magical instruction are far more limited than what we can offer."

Andris didn't respond, and after an awkward pause, Jaron said, "Andris, I know that your power sets you apart from your peers, but it isn't as if you don't have any friends here."

"You sound just like Ky."

Jaron's couldn't stop the wry smile as he replied, "Kylec is an intelligent young man, and I think you should listen to him on this subject."

After a moment, Andris spoke quietly. "Kylec's a year older than me, and he hasn't had any poltergeists recently."

It was true, but that didn't make Andris's current difficulties unusual. It was Kylec's lack of them that was strange, and Jaron said as much. "I don't think Kylec has ever had a poltergeist, even as a child. His control is downright unnatural, even Aidan agrees."

"Ky's unique in his own way, isn't he?"

"Thank the gods for that!" Jaron said with a laugh.

Andris smiled weakly. "I just get tired of being different. I know that someday it won't matter, or I might even be glad of it, but right now, it's hard. Ky's a good friend, and he stands by me, but sometimes being around him makes it even harder because nothing seems to fluster him. He's always so confident and in control."

"Did it ever occur to you that he may just be better at hiding his insecurities?"

"No," Andris answered flatly.

Thinking back to Aidan's assertion that Kylec was a lot like him, Jaron replied with a fair amount of certainty, "Trust me, Andy. Ky isn't always as sure of himself as he lets on. He has his weak spots, as we all do. He's just exceptionally good at drawing attention away from them."

Andris didn't look entirely convinced, but he nodded thoughtfully. "I'm sorry I got so upset. But it's been years since I've lost control of my power, and I honestly believed that I was done with worrying about that."

"I'll talk to Master Michaela about adjusting your schedule so we can work together to help you reinforce your shielding. Don't worry. It's going to be fine."

Andris nodded and stood up to leave, only to stumble, grasping the back of the chair to steady himself. Jaron jumped up and was at his side in an instant. "Are you all right?"

"Just a little light-headed."

"Did you have breakfast?" Jaron asked, hoping Andris's sudden weakness was just due to low blood sugar.

He shook his head. "I was so nervous this morning my stomach was too upset for food."

A reasonable assumption under most circumstances, but not with half the school sick. Jaron placed a hand against Andris's forehead and sighed. "Come on, lad. Let's get you to Tam and Jonas's. It looks like you didn't escape this flu outbreak after all."

***

After helping Tamara settle Andris into bed in the room he used to share with Kylec, Jaron joined her in the sitting room. Jonas arrived home a few minutes later.

"I hope I did the right thing in bringing him here," Jaron said to them.

"Absolutely," Jonas replied. "The infirmary is full, and I can take care of him here just fine."

"What about Janari?" he asked as the little girl poked her head around the doorway that led to her playroom.

"She's already had it," Tamara said briskly. "Unfortunately, sometimes Jonas brings his work home with him."

139

Jonas frowned. "You knew I was a physician when you married me, love."

"I know," Tamara said with a soft smile. "I suppose that by the time she's grown, her immune system will be so strong, she'll never fall ill."

Jonas laughed, picked up his bag, and headed for the stairs. "I'll go check on Andy while you call Ky and tell him to get here on the double."

"Why?" Jaron asked, confused.

"They're roommates," Tamara said matter-of-factly. "If one is sick, it's only a matter of time before the other one takes ill."

"You'd better not tell him why you're calling him," Jaron warned when Tamara's eyes lost focus as she prepared her sending to Kylec.

"He's on his way." Tamara smiled with a hint of mischief. "I told him that I wanted him to watch Janari for a few hours."

Janari came into the sitting room and looked up at Jaron, her dark brown eyes far too knowing for a three-year-old. "Andy has the flu?"

"Yes, but I'm sure he'll be better soon," he said.

She sniffed. "Course he will. My daddy will fix him." With that she spun around and went back to whatever she'd been doing before.

"She's mature for her age," he commented to Tamara.

"Three going on thirty," Tamara agreed. "And you were right about the boys doting on her. I'm almost terrified of what they'll teach her as she gets older."

They heard the back door open and close with a bang, and Kylec came running in. "I came as quickly as I could, Tam. How long will you—" He stopped short when he realized that Tamara wasn't alone. Jaron could see him quickly reassessing the situation, no doubt trying to figure out how much trouble he was about to be in.

"Andris just came down with the flu, Ky," Tamara said simply.

"If you wanted me to bring over clothes and stuff for him, why didn't you just say so?" He obviously realized something more going on but was still hoping to get out of whatever was planned for him. Jaron also noticed that his eyes were glassy, and he looked flushed. The boy must have suspected what he was thinking because he quickly added, "I'm a little out of breath. I ran over as soon as I got Tam's sending."

"You're coming down with it, too. There's no sense denying it," Tamara said firmly.

"I feel fine."

Jaron discreetly created a shield around the house, just in case the boy decided to bolt. Kylec was too perceptive not to notice, and his shoulders sagged slightly in defeat, though the light of rebellion still shone in his eyes.

"Come on," Tamara said. "Get yourself into bed."

"I really do feel fine," he protested even as he plodded toward the staircase.

"And if you rest and take care of yourself now, you'll probably only have a light case and will be better in just a few days." Tamara's tone was encouraging.

"What if I don't have it?" he countered. "If you lock me up with Andy now, you'll be *making* me sick. Why risk it?"

"Clever," Tamara replied just as Jaron was beginning to think the boy had a point. "Andy may just be getting symptoms now, but he's been contagious for at least a week if not longer and you've been sharing a room the entire time."

"At least let me stop at our dorm room to pick up some books."

Jaron admired the boy's persistence, but he wasn't about to let him leave the house at this point. "I'll head up to your room and you can tell me what you want."

"Yes, sir," came the grumpy reply as he made his way upstairs.

Jonas came down a little while later. His expression was grim, and Jaron's concern sharpened. "They're going to be okay, aren't they?"

Jonas nodded, but his expression didn't change. "Kylec will most likely have a very light case, but Andy's in for a rough time." He poked his head into Janari's playroom and told her to stay put. Jaron could hear her assure her father that she would do just that and he smiled, thinking that after fostering the boys, Tamara and Jonas had more than earned having such a biddable child. Then they moved to the kitchen where Jonas offered more details.

"Andy's fever is already extremely high, and he feels terrible. I've given him something to bring his temperature down and help with the pain. He claims that he felt fine yesterday, and I don't think he's lying. I've treated dozens of cases in the past three months. When it progresses this quickly, it doesn't bode well."

"He'll be all right?" Tamara asked anxiously.

"Do you need any assistance from Laramy?" Jaron added.

Jonas squeezed Tamara's shoulder reassuringly and shook his head at Jaron before taking a seat at the table. "He's going to be fine, but as I said, he's in for a rough time. Unfortunately, there isn't much that can be done with magical healing that I can't do with conventional medicine for something like this, and Laramy has his hands full right now. Tamara knows enough about magical healing to help alleviate some of the worst symptoms as needed, and if it looks as though he isn't fighting the infection well, I'll ask Laramy to do what he can to boost his immune system. Other than that, we just have to let it run its course."

"You're worried about something," Jaron said when Jonas fell silent.

"Andy told me he had a poltergeist last night."

"He did," Jaron confirmed. "It was during a nightmare. He came to me this morning to tell me about it."

"Is that because he's ill?" Tamara asked. "He hasn't lost control like that in years."

"He's hit puberty, Tam," Jaron replied. "His power is spiking. It's perfectly normal for someone as powerful as he is."

"True," Jonas added. "But right now, it's also unsafe. Several people have experienced high fevers and delirium with this strain of influenza. If that happens to Andy, the results could be extremely dangerous."

Jaron hadn't thought of that. "I can take him back to my house. If anything happens, I can deal with it."

Jonas shook his head, "That's not the answer and you know it, Jaron. All the masters and more powerful adepts who showed signs of having a bad case had their power bound temporarily to be safe."

"No!" Tamara glared at her husband. "As powerful as he is, Andy is still just a little boy. You can't do that to him."

"For his safety and ours, I don't think we have a choice, Tam." Jonas's tone was firm, but his face betrayed his unease. "It's only temporary. He's mature enough to understand why we need to take precautions."

"His confidence has already been shaken," Jaron said softly, his heart sinking. "This will be another blow."

"And what do you think will happen to his confidence if he hurts someone while he's delirious? You have to do this, Jaron. The sooner the better, while he's still able to cooperate."

Jonas was right. Tamara remained silent, a sure sign that she agreed. Binding Andris's power was a reasonable precaution, but it presented problems of its own. Andris was already significantly more powerful than any of the current masters, which meant the process would be difficult.

Jaron considered the best course of action and said, "I'll summon Aidan, Michaela, and Myau-Pei to help me."

"Three more masters?" Tamara's voice had an odd edge to it.

"Andy is more powerful than any master, Tam, me included. You know that. We need to completely encase his core of power and drain away the kaema he's holding. I can't do that without at least one other person to help me, and then we need to complete the binding spell itself. I want to be sure we do this properly on the first try and not subject him to multiple attempts."

"You can't have four people crowding around his bedside, Jaron. You'll frighten him."

"Andris isn't that easily frightened, Tam. I'll explain the situation to him first. I'm sure he'll be fine. Have some faith in the boy."

"I do," she said sharply. "But I'm concerned about him. He may be powerful, but he is *not* an adept or master. He isn't even a mage yet. He's young, and his abilities are still developing. Are you certain that this won't cause any damage?"

"It *could* set him back in terms of keeping his power under control, but I'm confident that he will make up any lost ground quickly once he recovers."

"You really think this is necessary?" Tamara directed her question to both men.

Jonas spoke first. "It is, love. Deep down, you know that."

She took a deep breath. "Would it be better if I told him?"

"I think this would be better coming from Jaron," Jonas replied.

Jaron agreed. "I'm his mentor. This is for me to explain."

***

Jaron knelt down beside the bed where Andris lay. It had been just over an hour since he'd brought the boy to the cottage, but his condition had visibly deteriorated in that short time. There was a fine sheen of sweat on his face, and he looked far too pale. Chasing Kylec out of the room had been surprisingly easy. At first, Jaron thought that he might use the opportunity to talk his way out of the house, but when he locked eyes with him, he understood that Kylec was genuinely afraid for Andris, and wouldn't cause trouble.

"Andy," he said softly, reaching out to brush the hair back from the boy's forehead.

Andris's eyes fluttered open. They were fever-bright and red-rimmed...and confused. Recognition came, but far too slowly. Jaron swallowed hard, silently acknowledging that Jonas was right. This had to be done.

"Master Jaron?" the words were little more than a mumble.

"Yes, it's me." Jaron struggled to keep his tone calm and even managed a weak smile. "Andy, do you remember when Myau-Pei got sick? Do you remember how she was delirious for a few days?"

After several heartbeats, Andris nodded.

"We bound her power for a little while. Just to be safe. Once she was on the mend, we released it again, but it was safer for everyone, including her, for her power to be bound during the worst of her illness."

Jaron waited for a response, but Andris said nothing, looking groggy and slightly disoriented.

Jonas entered the room then and laid a hand on Jaron's shoulder as he said softly, "I gave him painkillers, Jaron. They have a sedating effect, so he's going to be a little out of it."

"Right," Jaron replied, feeling faintly relieved as he recalled Jonas saying that earlier.

Then he turned back to Andris. "Andy, you're going to be fine, but we need to bind your power to be safe. It won't hurt, and it's only for a little while."

Andris nodded, "I…I…understand. I…don't…want to hurt...anyone."

"I know, lad. I know." Jaron took his hand and squeezed it once, reassuringly. "Myau-Pei, Michaela, and Aidan are waiting just outside. You're a powerful sorcerer, and we want to do this as quickly as we can, so they're going to help me."

Andris nodded again and said, "Okay."

"This can be a little unsettling, so I will explain exactly what we are going to do so you know what to expect."

Andris swallowed hard, and when he nodded this time, he remained silent. Jaron squeezed his hand again before continuing. "The first thing we need to do is drain the kaema you are currently holding, and your instinct will be to fight against that. I want you to do your best to stay relaxed and just let it happen. It will feel strange, but it won't be painful. Once that's done, I'll use a spell to surround your core

145

of power and block the channels that would normally draw kaema into you. And that's it."

"Sounds…easy," came Andris's groggy reply.

Jaron half laughed. "For you, it should be. We have the hard part. All I need you to do is relax, okay? And once it's done, you won't need to expend any energy holding your power in check. You'll be able to focus on healing."

"Let's do it." Andris closed his eyes, waiting.

At Jaron's nod, Jonas left the room and a moment later, the other masters entered. Myau-Pei and Michaela sat on the bed that Kylec had recently vacated, while Aidan stood at the foot of Andris's bed. They had already agreed on the division of labor.

After briefly explaining her intentions to Andris, Myau-Pei began reciting a meditation that was commonly used to help sorcerers focus and block out distractions during training. She had a good voice for it, and if they were lucky, the mental exercise would hold Andris's attention so that he wouldn't reflexively resist the draining and binding.

Michaela and Aidan, both of whom had worked with Andris directly in taming his considerable power, took on the role of siphoning away the kaema from his core and grounding it. As they began the process, Andris opened his eyes briefly, looking faintly panicked, but Jaron just squeezed his hand again and said, "Focus on the meditation, Andy. Listen to Myau-Pei. Let everything else fade away. You're safe. Trust me. Trust us."

Andris closed his eyes and took a shuddering breath. Jaron looked up at Aidan who nodded curtly. Jaron monitored the process, which he'd had to perform more than a few times in the past month. The core of Andris's power appeared as an indistinct mass of opalescent light, with dozens of tendrils reaching outward toward the ambient kaema. Michaela and Aidan each used their own power to latch onto a tendril and siphon the kaema through it, away from his core, grounding the power as they did so. Even with the two masters working together, it took quite a bit of time before Jaron noticed any appreciable affect, but eventually, the glow of Andris's core began to dim.

When the young man's inner reserves were nearly empty, the ambient kaema began to travel along the natural pathways, trying to fill the vacuum. It was at this point that Jaron joined the effort. One by one, he blocked off the natural energy channels. He shaped the spell with care, completely encasing the young man's core of power until only the two tendrils that Aidan and Michaela were using to drain him remained open.

"He's empty, Jaron," Aidan said softly after a few more minutes. "Finish the binding."

Jaron nodded and closed off the remaining pathways. As the binding was completed, Andris grimaced and made a soft sound that was almost a whimper.

"Andy?" Jaron asked anxiously. "Are you okay?"

"Tired," Andris replied weakly.

Myau-Pei ceased the repetitive words of the meditation and knelt beside Jaron, gently laying a hand on the boy's head and spoke softly. "That's natural. Just rest, Andy. The more rest you can get, the faster you will get better."

The others filed out of the room and Jonas entered, and Jaron stepped away to give the physician space to check the young man's vital signs and give him another dose of pain medication.

"He'll be fine, Jaron," Jonas said before they exited. "You did the right thing."

"I know," Jaron replied.

When he opened the door, Kylec was waiting in the hallway, uncharacteristically subdued. "I don't want to disturb Andy. I can sleep on the couch in the den," he offered.

"I can't think of anything that will rouse him for the next several hours, lad," Jonas said with a reassuring smile. "And when he does wake up, Andy will feel better having you nearby."

Kylec turned to Jaron, his expression uncertain. He opened his mouth as if to say something but closed it again and looked away. Jaron clapped him on the shoulder trying desperately to convey in the gesture all the feeling that he couldn't find the words for. It must have worked, because the young man met his eyes and nodded. "Andy will be okay. It will all be okay."

Chapter 9

1473 AHS

M'Gan watched the High Priestess carefully as she settled herself into the chair across from him. She had recently celebrated her one hundredth birthday, and though her face and figure remained remarkably youthful, she was beginning to show her age. It was a subtle thing that had far less to do with the white streaks that had recently appeared in her dark red hair or the lines around her mouth and eyes than it did her mannerisms and bearing. It was as if she had suddenly realized that she had more years behind her than ahead of her, and she resented it.

Leah was nearly a decade older than T'Vano had been when he had stepped down from the position of High Priest twenty years earlier, but M'Gan knew that Leah had no intention of relinquishing her position so soon. T'Vano had called for an election to select the next High Priest when he retired, but Leah was following the older tradition of choosing her own successor, and it was common knowledge that her choice had already been made. Maylene was still far too young to assume the role, and he knew that Leah would wait until she was absolutely certain that the girl was ready.

Leah's daughter was not his concern right now. Her great-niece was. It had been nearly six years since Glasnae Maylan first entered the Druidic College, and in that time her magical abilities had increased dramatically. Though she had not had a full-blown poltergeist since her power had spiked a year ago, he knew for a fact that she still struggled to maintain control, and he still feared what would happen if she chose to abuse her god-given gifts.

M'Gan would need to tread softly with Leah, but he also knew how to play on her fears. He began the conversation subtly, trusting that he could bring her around to his way of thinking. "I understand that Maylene is to enter the novitiate of the General Order soon."

She narrowed her eyes, and her tone was suspicious when she replied, "That should hardly come as a surprise to anyone, especially to you."

"I was just thinking that once Maylene begins her formal training as a priestess, she and Glasnae will no longer be spending so much time together."

"Your point?"

"Maylene is moving toward her destiny. Glasnae is not."

Leah frowned and looked down at her lap. He left her to her thoughts for a moment before adding gently, "I did warn you, Leah. The influence the girls have had upon each other was the exact opposite of what you'd hoped for. Glasnae has lost none of her willfulness, and Maylene now questions you in ways she never did before her cousin arrived."

"Maylene is currently transitioning from child to adolescent." The warning in her voice was unmistakable. "She is testing her boundaries and asserting herself. It's perfectly normal for someone her age, and although she may question me from time to time, she ultimately trusts my judgment and remains obedient."

M'Gan knew that he was on thin ice but pressed on. "That may be true, but Maylene is not yet the leader you are preparing her to be. She has also demonstrated that she is all too willing to follow Glasnae, even when she knows she shouldn't. Need I remind you of the numerous transgressions that Glasnae has involved your daughter in over the past few years?"

Leah grimaced. "Youthful misadventures and childish pranks. They never did anything truly harmful, and you know it. Their intent was always mischief, not malice."

"Considering that I have been the target of more than one of their 'childish pranks' as you term them, I'm inclined to think otherwise. Glasnae makes no secret of her dislike for me."

"And that's really what this is all about, isn't it, M'Gan? You've had little success in winning her over to the Magicians Order and now you want me to intervene. I've told you countless times that you would be better served by trying to develop some rapport with the girl than always trying to awe her. She's not easily impressed by authority."

"Because she has no respect for authority," he spat out, annoyed that Leah could be so frustratingly perceptive. "She is willful and self-centered."

Leah regarded him with some surprise. "Willful, yes, but self-centered?" She shook her head. "I don't think you're seeing things clearly. Glasnae is both considerate and generous. She often goes out of her way to be helpful."

"She may be considerate of others, but only on her own terms," he insisted. "She does not respond well to orders and considers her own judgment to be equal to that of her superiors. She is resistant to criticism,"

"She responds well to *constructive* criticism," she said with emphasis, "and though I grant you that she responds more favorably to requests than demands, ultimately, she does what is required of her."

"She has a problem with obedience, and that is going to make it difficult to control her properly. A priestess must submit to the will of the gods and her superiors. I doubt that Glasnae can do that."

"You're terribly concerned about controlling this child, M'Gan. It may simply be that she does not possess the proper temperament to be a priestess. I agree that she is very independent. Perhaps she would be better suited to one of the guilds. She's completed three mini apprenticeships so far, and by all accounts has done well. She has a variety of interests and talents that could be developed into worthy vocations. Maybe it's time to accept the fact that she is not interested in any facet of the priesthood."

M'Gan stared at her in disbelief. He couldn't imagine how she came to such a conclusion. "Leah, we are talking about a girl who will likely become the most powerful sorcerer alive by the time she's fully matured. Without proper guidance and discipline, she could be exceedingly dangerous. Power like hers can exist for only one purpose:

to serve. She must be bound by the proper strictures and her power vowed to the gods. It's the only way that we can be certain that she will not misuse her gifts."

"M'Gan." Leah's voice had an uncharacteristically soothing tone to it. "I *would* prefer that she join your order, but I cannot force her to. As for her misusing her power, I don't think she will. But if she did, the master mages would step in. Foremost among their sworn duties is the obligation to enforce the laws as they apply to all practitioners of magic. If Glasnae should ever require discipline, they would bind her power and eliminate any threat she may pose."

He swallowed hard before replying. "That's the problem, Leah. I'm not sure they *could* bind her power. I told you, she is extraordinarily gifted. I've known many sorcerers over the years. I've even met Lord Jaron, who is reputed to be the most powerful master mage, and I believe that Glasnae's power is already far greater than his. By the time she plateaus in another few years, there's no telling just how strong she will be. Without some sort of leash to hold her…" He trailed off, hoping that Leah would recognize the danger as he did.

She didn't answer right away. Finally, she suggested, "If you feel so strongly about it, *invite* her to join her order. Convince her that she belongs among the magicians."

"If I do that, it will only reinforce her sense of self-importance. She needs to petition for a place among us. If I extend an invitation, it will imply that I want her. It will give her a measure of power over me."

"You *do* want her, so she already has a measure of power over you."

M'Gan closed his eyes, holding his temper in check with effort. "That may be true to a point, but as long as she's unaware of it, it's moot. I need to establish the appropriate relationship. She needs to be prepared to obey me."

Leah scowled. "I cannot give you my consent to set compulsions on her."

Fighting to hide his disappointment he replied, "I didn't ask you for that. I *am* asking for your help. Surely you have some influence over her?"

"Not as much as I would like. Not enough to guide her to you. So far, she has apprenticed with the Healers Guild, the Farmers Guild, and the Foresters Guild. She has shown absolutely no interest in *any* branch of the priesthood. If I suggest such a path, she will certainly question my motives."

"What if Maylene were to suggest it?"

"I can talk to Maylene. But I can't make any promises. As you so bluntly pointed out, Glasnae has not responded to Maylene's influence as I'd hoped. You might get better results working through Devon. He and Glasnae have become close, and it would be more natural for him to try to interest her in the order he belongs to."

M'Gan had already considered that, but he wasn't entirely certain that Devon would cooperate. Given the relationship that had developed between him and Glasnae, he might not recognize the importance of bringing her into their order.

"I will discuss the matter with Devon," he said after a thoughtful pause. "Between his efforts and Maylene's, we'll see what can be done."

Leah's penetrating gaze held him for a long moment before she nodded in agreement. Then he recalled the exact phrase she had used regarding using magic to manipulate Glasnae: *I cannot give you my consent to set compulsions on her.* She would not give her *consent*, but unlike the first time they had discussed the possibility, she had not strictly forbidden it, either. If Devon and Maylene failed to bring Glasnae around to her proper path, he would do whatever was necessary to convince her. If he didn't ask Leah for permission, there would be no need for her to give her consent.

Maylene twirled around the room she shared with her best friend, excitement temporarily overcoming her nerves.

Glasnae smiled at her from where she sat on the end of her bed. "You look beautiful."

"You really think so?" She glanced down at the plain white gown and said, "I'm supposed to look humble and pure."

Glasnae laughed and rose to her feet. "I'll give you humble, but pure might be pushing it."

"I'm pretty pure," Maylene countered, trying to maintain a dignified expression.

Glasnae grasped her by the shoulders and turned her around to face the mirror that hung above her dresser. Maylene was struck, not for the first time, by how different they looked, Glasnae's pale complexion and coppery hair a stark contrast to her own brown skin and black hair. There was nothing surprising about it, though. They might be cousins, but since Maylene was adopted, they had no common lineage. But the physical differences reminded her of how different they were in temperament as well, and she was both amazed and grateful that they had maintained such a close friendship over the years.

Glasnae leaned forward so that her head was resting on Maylene's shoulder, grinning as she asked, "You really think you're pure?"

"More than you are," she pointed out.

"True." Glasnae smiled. "But that isn't saying much, is it?"

Glasnae gave her one last hug and then turned away, and Maylene had to swallow hard past the lump in her throat. In a few short days, she would officially be consecrated as a novice of the General Order. She was excited, but it was bittersweet leaving her best friend behind.

"I'm going to miss you," she said without turning around.

Glasnae spoke in a strangely subdued voice. "You're not going that far. It's not like you'll never see me again."

"It won't be the same." She turned around to face her friend, who was now sitting on the bed with her hands wrapped around her knees.

"No, it won't be," Glasnae agreed. "But nothing ever is."

"You could join with me." Maylene perched on the edge of the bed next to her.

Glasnae shook her head. "I don't know what I want to do with my life yet, but I'm fairly sure that I'm not meant for the priesthood. It doesn't feel right. After all the effort I've put in to control my magical abilities, I want to find a way to actually use them."

After a somewhat awkward pause, Glasnae continued. "There's no rush. I'm only fifteen. I've got plenty of time to figure out my future."

"Are you happy, Glas?" The question came out more abruptly than Maylene intended.

For once, Glasnae didn't try to make a joke of it. "I'm not *unhappy*. I'm not content, either, but I don't think I'm supposed to be. I'm still searching, Maylene, but that's not a bad thing. What about you? Are you happy?"

"Of course." She tried to sound convincing.

"Is this what you really want?"

"It's what I've always wanted."

"No, it's what your mother always wanted for you. Have you ever really thought about what you want for yourself?"

Maylene took a deep breath and answered honestly. "I want to be a priestess, Glas. I've always enjoyed serving in the seasonal rituals, and I want to do something meaningful with my life. Priests and priestesses help people, you know?"

"Your mother expects you to succeed her."

"That's a long time away."

"True, but she's been planning for it since she adopted you. You need to remember that."

"Why does that bother you so much?"

"Because I want you to have a choice, especially for something as significant as becoming High Priestess. I understand that you want to serve, but Leah wants you to *lead*. That's a completely different kind of service. Your life won't be your own. I've seen what that can do to someone."

"I'm not High Priestess yet, and maybe I never will be." She kept her voice light. "I promise that I won't make any commitments I don't want to make. Does that reassure you?"

"For now." Glasnae relented with a smile. "I'm sorry if I'm spoiling this for you. I'm just in a mood."

"I'm excited, but I'm nervous, too. I guess I'm afraid of being lonely."

"You won't be lonely," Glasnae said with conviction. "You already have friends in the novitiate."

"It's not the same…I know that you like me for who I really am."

There was a hint of anger in Glasnae's response. "Do you have reason to believe that your other friends are only pretending to like you?"

Maylene looked down at her hands clasped in her lap. "Not exactly, but I don't trust anyone else to be completely honest with me. When I do something idiotic, you won't abuse me, but you do call me out on it. You know that I'm not perfect, and you don't expect me to be."

"Of course, you aren't perfect. Who is? Besides, perfection isn't something we're supposed to aspire to. The idea of achieving perfection creates a narrow point of view and limits opportunities for real growth."

"You committed that book to memory, didn't you?"

"What book?"

Glasnae's feigned confusion fooled no one. Maylene rolled her eyes dramatically. "*The Value of the Meandering Path.*"

"It's a good book."

"It's a textbook."

"And yet it manages to be both relevant and interesting."

"That's why I'm going to miss you when I enter the novitiate. Only you would challenge me by quoting from a textbook."

"I'm sure that there will be plenty of opportunities for bonding with your new sisters. I just hope your next roommate is a deep sleeper."

"Why?" Maylene was baffled by the sudden turn of the conversation.

"Because you snore."

"I do not!"

"Well then you make noises in the night that sound an awful lot like snoring."

They dissolved into giggles, and Maylene knew she would never lose Glasnae's friendship. No matter what might happen.

***

Deirdre sighed with contentment as she watched Niklas and Glasnae play with the four small puppies under Sorcha's watchful eye. This was her first litter—Sorcha's first, too—and she just couldn't stop smiling.

Freydis stepped up beside her and said softly, "I'll grant you they're cute, but in another year or so, they'll be nothing but trouble."

Niklas's hearing was far too keen. "Glasnae and I are going to help with the puppies, so it won't be so bad," he said.

Freydis glowered theatrically. "Who said I was referring to the puppies?"

Niklas looked confused, and Glasnae nudged him in the ribs before grinning up at Freydis, "You think we're still cute? And that we aren't trouble already?"

"Such sass!" Freydis exclaimed but didn't hide her own smile. Then she turned to Deirdre, "Four is a sizeable litter. Is Subram taking one or two?"

"Only one. This is the third litter Raja has sired in the past five years. Subram only puts him out to stud so frequently because he's in such high demand, not because he's looking for more pups."

"Raja has a lot of good qualities," Niklas pointed out. "He's intelligent, healthy, and has a great disposition."

"He's beautiful, too. Such lovely silver fur," Glasnae commented, then added when Sorcha glanced her way, "Not that you aren't stunning yourself, Sorcha. I would never slight a fellow redhead."

"Looks aren't the important thing, Glas," Niklas cautioned.

"I suppose not," she replied smoothly. "But isn't it odd that this little fellow is nearly black considering what his parents look like?" She held up the puppy in question who promptly licked her nose.

Deirdre shook her head as Niklas, who was fascinated by biology in general and genetics in particular, began to explain how traits such as coloring could be passed down without actually putting in an appearance for generations. He went on to describe how dogs originally only lived to be about fifteen years old, something Glasnae clearly found distressing given the way she clutched the puppy she was holding tighter.

"That was a long time ago," Deirdre soothed. "We can expect these pups to live a healthy fifty years or more."

Niklas eagerly launched into a detailed story about one of the original human settlers on Kaestra who was responsible for increasing the lifespans of several species. He slowly tapered off when he realized that his small audience was looking at him with blank expressions.

Deirdre felt a little guilty for her own lack of understanding when Niklas said, "I guess most people find that sort of thing dull."

"Not dull, Nik," Glasnae reassured him. "Just too complicated for most people to grasp. I've told you before: you're really smart, bordering on the scary side of smart."

"Yes, yes," Freydis said briskly, "Niklas is smart, and Glasnae is trouble, and Deirdre has three puppies to find homes for."

Deirdre glanced sideways at Freydis. She'd planned to spring her news on the youngsters soon, but not quite this soon. Clearly Freydis was impatient to see their reactions.

"Freydis has a point," she said neutrally. "I promised first choice to Marshae as our newest guardian, and she's already shown a preference for the red female."

Niklas laughed. "The one that looks just like her mother."

"Marshae has always been fond of Sorcha. No doubt she's hoping the pup will resemble her mother in temperament as well," Freydis commented.

Deirdre continued. "Since Subram told me that he'll take whichever puppy is left at the end, I'm free to let the next two potential owners pick for themselves, assuming that they're willing to take on the responsibility."

"You have someone in mind?" Niklas asked.

Deirdre beamed at him. "I was thinking of the two people who pledged themselves to helping me raise this litter."

Glasnae practically squeaked. "You mean us?"

"I do."

"Really?" Niklas appeared to be in shock. "You want us to each have a puppy?"

"Really," she answered solemnly. "I just hope that you both don't want the same one."

The two youngsters looked at each other for a long moment, and Deirdre could sense a silent conversation. Then the pair smiled in unison. Having observed their interactions with the litter over the past few months, she wasn't surprised. Glasnae was already holding her choice: the black-furred male. Niklas reached out and carefully picked up the silver and white female. Deirdre was especially glad that he chose that particular puppy since he was the only human that she showed any real affection for.

"I see." She laughed. "I'll let Subram know that he ended up with the red-furred male and that he should give some thought to a name for him. We'll keep them here with Sorcha until they're a full year old, but there's no reason they can't start learning their names."

"Has Marshae decided on a name?" Freydis asked.

"She's still making up her mind. But I think she's narrowed it down to Phoebe or Scarlet."

"Phoebe's better," Freydis replied. "Scarlet is too literal."

"I was thinking of calling my puppy Winter," Niklas said shyly. "Is that too literal?"

Freydis considered for a moment. "No, that's acceptable. Now, if you named her 'Silver' that wouldn't do, but I like Winter for a name."

"You don't have the final say on names, Freydis," Deirdre pointed out.

"Really?" She smirked. "You keep thinking that, dear. Just wait until Marshae tells you her final decision."

Deirdre had no doubt that Freydis would pull Marshae aside at the first opportunity and give her a lesson on naming puppies. She happened to agree with Freydis, but she wasn't about to admit that.

"What about you, Glasnae?" she asked, "Any thoughts on a name for your little boy?"

"Can I have a few more days to think about it?" she asked. "I'm still getting used the idea that he's mine."

"And you're his," Freydis pointed out with a tender smile. "Remember that the belonging goes both ways."

Glasnae snuggled the little dog close and sighed. "I know."

***

Later that evening, Freydis stopped by Deirdre's apartment with a bottle of wine and a satisfied expression. Laughing, Deirdre invited her in.

"T'Vano made this himself." Freydis proclaimed as she filled their glasses and settled herself on the couch beside Deirdre. "One of many activities with which he keeps himself occupied these days. I think he retired too soon."

After taking a sip of the golden liquid, Deirdre replied, "I disagree. As long as this is how he keeps himself occupied, I think he timed his retirement just right."

"He told me how much he's going to miss having Maylene and Glasnae tend his garden now that their service years are coming to an end."

Deirdre knew where the conversation was heading, and she couldn't avoid the subject any longer, at least not with Freydis. "I can't invite Glasnae to join the guardians, Freydis. Not yet."

Freydis grimaced. "She's almost sixteen, Deirdre. And it isn't as if she's immature for her age. Quite the contrary, her penchant for mischief aside."

"I agree, but there might be other options for her that are more appropriate."

"What other options? The Magicians Order?" Freydis snorted. "The child despises M'Gan, and for good reason if you ask me. Besides, the Magicians hardly ever do anything worthwhile anymore. It would be a waste of talent."

"I didn't say I thought she should join M'Gan's order."

"Then what? Leave New Avalon and enter the Mage Hall? That's the only other path I see for someone with Glasnae's talents." Freydis grew quiet for a moment and then added, "That would be a good move for her, if her power was the only consideration, but it's not. I've been watching her, Deirdre. I've seen how she responds to the land. She loves the natural world and all its magic. And she's so close her kaesana family. Kaestra has placed her mark on that child. You have to see that."

"It's not that simple. I made a promise."

"What are you talking about?"

"When I agreed to be Glasnae's mentor, I promised Leah that I wouldn't invite her to join the guardians."

Deirdre expected Freydis to snap back with an angry reply, but the older woman remained silent for a long time, and when she spoke, her voice held a far quieter—and fiercer—kind of anger. "Leah has already mapped out one child's future. Do you plan to sit back and watch her do the same thing to another?"

Deirdre shook her head, "So far, she hasn't mapped out anything where Glasnae is concerned. It isn't as if she's pushing her in a particular direction."

"You're underestimating her. By denying Glasnae certain opportunities, she's effectively herding her in the direction she wants her to go. I've no doubt that she's found ways to make the Mage Hall appear unappealing in addition to keeping Glasnae away from the kae-madri. She's leading the girl right to M'Gan."

Deirdre took another deep swallow of T'Vano's excellent wine, savoring the rich flavor before voicing her fears. "What if we're wrong? What if we only believe that Glasnae should become kae-madri because we covet her power for our order? What if we're no better than M'Gan?"

Freydis reached out and took hold of her hand, squeezing it hard. "You don't really believe that."

"No. But Leah might, and M'Gan certainly will." She took a deep breath. "I'll talk to Leah. She didn't exactly forbid me to invite Glasnae to our order. She just said that she wanted to be consulted in any decisions beforehand."

"And by your tone I take it that you've already broached the subject with her?"

Deirdre nodded. "This past autumn. She said that it was too soon. She thought that Glasnae was still too impressionable and not ready to make such a mature decision."

Freydis arched a brow. "Has Leah met Glasnae?"

Deirdre scowled and continued. "She pointed out that binding Glasnae's power into the link of the kae-madri might be wasteful and once bound, there would be no turning back. She wants to be sure that we don't act in haste."

"Glasnae deserves to decide for herself."

"I agree. But there really is no need to rush. She's only just finishing up her service years. Maybe it would be better to give her a year or two to explore other options."

"What if she chooses to leave New Avalon?"

"I don't think she will."

"But if she does?"

"I'll have to make a decision," Deirdre said flatly.

"You do realize that you're procrastinating because you don't want to lock horns with Leah?"

There was no point in denying it. "Yes, but it's not just myself that I'm concerned about. Right now, Leah and M'Gan are mostly leaving Glasnae alone. If I move too quickly, things could get ugly for her as well as for me. She's still young. She should be allowed to enjoy herself for a while."

"All right. I can see your point. But be careful, Deirdre. If Glasnae is truly meant to become kae-madri, no one can be allowed to interfere with that."

"Glasnae is entitled to make her choice," Deirdre agreed. "And so is Kaestra."

Chapter 10

1474 AHS

The soil was still moist from the previous night's rain, but the land gave impression of being parched. Freydis took note of every detail, from the brown-edged leaves to the bare patches of earth where grasses and wildflowers should have been competing for space. She took a deep breath, noting that the air smelled stale, almost stuffy.

Athens was not a familiar province to her, but when two of the younger guardians requested assistance, Deirdre had sent her in the hopes that her experience would give her some insight. Marshae and Natalya stood watching her now, their expressions both nervous and hopeful.

"Did we miss anything?" Marshae asked after the long stretch of silence.

Freydis continued to survey her surroundings as she responded, "I don't know. The ley line that runs through this area is all but empty. You restored it only three days ago?"

"Yes." Natalya sounded a little defensive. "I began the process, and when I tired, Marshae completed the effort. The ley line appeared to be restored when we left, but now it's as if we did nothing."

"I'm not criticizing," Freydis assured her. "I just wanted to confirm the timing."

"The same thing happened when we first tried two weeks ago, only then it took nearly five days for the kaema to reach this level after being restored. I'd expected it to still be in the process of dissipating today, but it happened much faster this time."

Freydis knelt to touch the ground, reaching out to the ley line with her senses and following the thread that should have burned bright with kaema to see if she could at least determine the direction of the energy drain. The remaining amount of kaema was so minute that it was impossible to be completely certain, but it seemed that the energy was being pulled westward.

164

There were no gateways nearby, nor any significant nodes. In theory, if enough sorcerers were drawing kaema from this ley line to perform powerful spells, it might result in significant depletion, especially since this ley line wasn't particularly strong to begin with. But that didn't explain the repeated draining of energy. Something else was going on.

"That's because it's not dissipating," Freydis said. "It's being siphoned off somehow."

"How?" Marshae asked.

"And by who?" There was a sharp edge to Natalya's voice.

"Both good questions, but we're unlikely to find any answers to either of them here. How large is the impacted area?"

"About ten square miles, maybe a little less," Natalya replied. "It follows the ley line for about four miles each way from where we're standing, but it doesn't extend very far out."

"Have you reported it to Governor Tharan yet?"

"The governor didn't initiate the request," Natalya said. "It came from Mayor Lanston of Cereone. The town is a just a stone's throw to the north. The residents had been complaining to him about kitchen gardens that refuse to grow, scarcity of game in the wooded areas designated for hunting, and similar issues."

"And some of the local sorcerers raised concerns about the decreased amount of available kaema." Marshae added.

Freydis shook her head, mildly annoyed that Deirdre had sent her out on this mission without all the relevant facts. "The mayor should have contacted the governor, who then should have taken up the matter with the First Guardian."

Natalya nodded. "I suspect that the governor tends to turn a deaf ear to these sorts of complaints. I think the mayor came directly to us because he didn't expect any help from the governor."

"He might also have been afraid that the governor would forbid him from contacting us at all if he went through proper channels," Marshae added.

"That makes no sense," Freydis said. She didn't like what she was hearing.

Natalya looked uncomfortable. "I have family in Athens. One of my cousins recently asked me how the Order of Guardians can justify imposing extreme restrictions on hard working people in the name of protecting the environment and then collect outrageous fees for doing it. I told him I didn't know what he was talking about. Apparently, Tharan has convinced a lot of his people that we get paid to make them suffer."

"Tharan is a fool," Freydis said darkly. "And that's what will bring suffering to his people, not us."

"If Lanston hadn't decided to contact Deirdre on his own, we wouldn't even know this was happening," Marshae added.

"We would have found out eventually, one way or another." Freydis was certain of that much. "So, what have you told the mayor?"

"Less than the whole truth," Natalya admitted. "We explained that the ley line was far more drained than we expected and that we'd need more time to remedy it."

Freydis took a moment to evaluate the state of the ley line again, looking for subtleties she may have missed earlier. She noted some unusual resonances in the remaining kaema, which gave her an idea.

"Did you both try to restore the ley line at the same time?"

"No," Marshae replied first. "We took turns."

Freydis nodded, expecting that response. Guardians usually channeled kaema through the ley lines one at a time. It was easier to control the flow of energy that way, under normal circumstances. But current circumstances were far from normal.

"All right, sisters. This is what we're going to do next." Freydis carefully explained how they would all invoke guardianship and flood the ley line with kaema simultaneously.

"Is that safe?" Marshae asked.

"It's no more dangerous than allowing this to continue unchecked," Freydis replied. "I believe that the risk is acceptable."

"Then let's do this," Natalya said briskly, "before I lose my nerve."

The three women knelt on the ground right above the depleted ley line, spacing themselves about ten yards apart along its length. On Freydis's signal, they reached down through their links to Kaestra, invoking the goddess they served and becoming living channels for her power. Then they directed that power into the nearly empty ley line, attempting to fill it.

As the kaema poured into the ley line, Freydis became aware of the energy being drawn westward along the line. The speed with which the kaema was siphoned off was impressive, but not nearly fast enough to match the rate with which it was being filled. Freydis then directed the stream of energy she was controlling to follow the path of the drain, pushing hard. After a few moments, she felt a subtle push back, and the drain ceased.

She told the girls to stop. Natalya and Marshae both sprawled on the ground, exhausted. Freydis held on a heartbeat longer, assuring herself that the ley line was truly restored before she broke her connection to it. She resisted the urge to collapse as the others had done. She was old enough to find such a position both uncomfortable and undignified. But she did lower herself to the ground, sitting with her back against a tree, not quite ready to be on her feet for more than a moment or two.

"Is it fixed?" Natalya asked in a breathless voice.

"I think so." Freydis frowned in concentration. "I think I broke whatever was drawing out the energy. We'll stay for at least a few more days to observe, but I think the problem is solved for now."

"And the land will heal, right?" Marshae asked.

"I see no reason why not. We're in the middle of the growing season. There's still time for the plants to catch up."

Natalya moaned as she rose to her feet and bowed to Freydis. "As you are the senior guardian here, I defer to your judgment regarding how to report back to the mayor about this incident."

"Defer, my ass," Freydis replied tartly. "You're thrilled to be able to toss this in my lap."

Natalya's lips twitched in an effort not to smile. "As you say, Sister."

***

Only the most senior members of the Order of Kae-Madri had been summoned, but Deirdre knew that the rest of the guardians were all too aware of the reason for this gathering. With that in mind, she dispensed with the pleasantries and got right to the point.

"We seem to have a problem in Athens," she began without preamble, opening the discussion.

Everyone conceded that it was unlikely that what Marshae and Natalya had encountered was an isolated incident, but the ensuing debate revealed that there was considerable disagreement as to what they should do about it. Some wanted to take a "wait and see" approach, while others advocated for a more proactive course of action.

Governor Tharan's stubborn refusal to ask for their help was the biggest sticking point, which was further exacerbated by the rumors being spread about their order. Everyone knew that, legally speaking, they had to walk a fine line between doing their duty to the planet and infringing on Tharan's rights as the elected leader of Athens.

Deirdre didn't like the position they were in, but after nearly half an hour of discussion, she arrived at a decision.

"We cannot impose restrictions on the way his people use the land without the governor's consent, and we certainly can't charge for our services. But we can heal the land as needed. We just need to be discreet."

"You mean sneak around Athens restoring drained ley lines?" Gayle sounded dubious.

"If need be, yes," Deirdre said sharply, "And we also investigate this latest incident as well as the general conditions in Athens."

"Discreetly," Freydis repeated with emphasis.

Deirdre nodded and added, "Sisters, I know that this is upsetting, and I appreciate your misgivings. I won't send anyone on an assignment that makes them uncomfortable. From now on, all missions to Athens of any kind will be on a volunteer basis."

Suki, one of the oldest guardians present raised another question. "Do you plan to tell the rest of the kae-madri about this?"

Deirdre replied without hesitation. "Of course. I limited this initial meeting only because I wanted to take advantage of your collective experience before I made any general announcements. However, no one outside the order need be consulted."

Freydis arched a brow. "You might want to consider reaching out to the Archmage," she began in a carefully neutral tone. "Remember, a few sorcerers raised concerns about a lack of kaema to Mayor Lanston, and although we didn't ask, some of them may well have been mages. I can't imagine that this incident wasn't brought to Lord Jaron's attention as well as ours."

"I don't want to involve the Mage Hall or anyone else just yet. Let's see what we can learn on our own. We can always reach out to them later if it seems necessary."

She was relieved when the others indicated approval of her plan. She had only just begun to feel comfortable in her position. Now she had to investigate an incident that defied explanation and posed a serious threat to the environment and the ley lines, all the while avoiding political quicksand. The investigation she could handle. The political quagmire? Well, she would do the best she could. Biting back a curse, she began to understand why Patricia had made herself scarce after she stepped down.

Chapter 11

Four large stones, each as tall as a man and twice as wide, were positioned along the ley line like beads on a wire. It had been relatively easy to find the deposit of gray kaeverdine from which they had been quarried and cutting the material had required little effort. Teleporting the massive objects to this remote area of Athens had been another matter altogether.

Tarvis and his fellow mages had exhausted themselves with the task and had been forced to take a few days to recover before proceeding. He'd been concerned that they might attract too much attention from the locals, especially if anyone had the ability to sense magical talent and thought to look for it. They were all shielding of course, in addition to maintaining simple glamours to hide their identities, but it was impossible to completely hide the power signature of a strong sorcerer.

He had created a simple cover story as a precaution. If asked, he, Orin, and Karimah were from the satellite Mage Hall in Icarus on a tour of the province in search of new recruits. The others, magically disguised to give themselves a more youthful appearance, were potential candidates. He disliked including his Hall as part of their cover story, but it was a simple and plausible explanation.

He needn't have bothered. It was soon apparent that the people of Janus were accustomed to strangers coming and going and were not in the habit of asking questions. The innkeeper had accepted payment and doled out keys without asking for more than names and intended length of stay.

"That wall is oppressive." Karimah shuddered as her eyes strayed yet again to the massive structure that was clearly visible even from five miles away.

"I imagine the Elysians intended it to be," Tarvis said mildly.

"Can the guards see us?" Evyn sounded nervous. "These stones are large enough to be seen, aren't they?"

"We're hidden by the trees." Malek gestured to the branches above their heads. "We can see out from beneath the canopy, but the guards on the wall will see nothing of us from their vantage point."

"Even if they did see us, they wouldn't think anything of it," Orin added.

"Not now, perhaps," Evyn pressed. "But once we start laying in the spells, this place will glow in magic-sight."

Malek waved a hand dismissively. "Elysians are blind to magic."

"All of them?" Karimah sounded unsure.

"So it's said," Malek replied. "That's one of the reasons this place is so well-suited to our purposes. The Elysians can't even sense kaema, and the population on this side of the wall is relatively small and mostly transient. There's little demand for high-level magecraft in the area, so there are no mages living here. Any fluctuations in the flow of kaema should go unnoticed."

"What if we're wrong and the guards notice something? They could report it to the authorities."

Tarvis leveled an icy stare at the young adept. Evyn was annoyingly alarmist. "Your ignorance of the basic organization of our world is appalling." He pointed at the distant wall. "Have you no appreciation for the significance of that monstrosity? The Elysians are isolationist in the extreme. The only reason that border towns like Janus even exist is because the Elysians want our goods. But only certain items, and only under tightly controlled conditions. The Elysian guards that man the trading points aren't even allowed to speak to the people they're trading with! Even if they did see something, there would be no way for them to share the information with anyone in Tarya, because such communication isn't permitted. It's that simple."

"Besides," Karimah pointed out calmly, "we have a contingency plan if things go awry."

"Scapegoats." Orin bit off the word and looked at Tarvis. "Hardly an honorable solution, and one that could backfire."

"The people we've targeted have proven themselves to be of questionable character, and their actions limit the opportunities for legitimate mages in this region," Tarvis replied calmly. "They are exactly the sort of people who are unworthy of channeling kaema, the very inspiration for this endeavor."

Orin grunted. "I agree with your assessment, but the risk remains."

"I'm confident in my ability to manipulate their minds without causing damage or leaving any traces," Malek said solemnly.

Tarvis knew that the younger man's confidence was not misplaced. His psychic abilities were exceptional, and his level of perception was nearly equal to a true sensitive.

Their first attempt at siphoning power from one of the minor ley lines had worked. But it had proved impossible to maintain, especially after the kae-madri interfered. Tarvis had spent years convincing Governor Tharan that keeping the guardians at bay was in the best interest of his people, but obviously at least a few of the local leaders were still willing to engage them.

Unfortunately, he couldn't make any accusations without revealing his own involvement. All he could do was redouble his efforts to discredit the Order of Kae-Madri while attempting to fashion a system that they wouldn't be able to break so easily.

He directed his followers to get into position, two people standing on opposite sides of each stone. The spell was difficult. Not only was it complex, but it also demanded a great deal of power. The efforts of each mage had to be closely coordinated if it was to work. He'd carefully arranged the participants to balance their individual power. He and Malek, as the strongest present, were the farthest apart.

On his signal, they began laying the spell. The first part of the spell was dynamic, requiring a constant flow of pre-shaped kaema to maintain it. This part would create a temporary imbalance in the matrix of the stone that would allow the second, static part of the spell to be set.

It was tiring, but well within the capabilities of those present. Once the first part of the static spell was in place, the weaker member of each pair was able to break off their connection and rest. The stronger members continued with the second, third, and fourth components. By the time the fifth and final layer was ready to be set, the other four mages, refreshed from the brief respite, rejoined the effort and the spell was completed.

The whole process took just over three hours, and when it was over, everyone was thoroughly spent. While the others sat or sprawled on the ground, as exhausted as if they'd run a marathon, Malek joined Tarvis in quietly assessing the result of their labors. The pattern set into the stones was exquisite: a fine latticework that vastly increased the amount of kaema the stones could hold linked to a strong and resilient siphoning spell.

"It's working," the younger mage said after a long pause.

"Indeed, it is," Tarvis responded with cautious optimism. "By this time tomorrow, the kaema along this ley line will be completely absorbed. In another week, all the kaema from the lesser ley lines that connect to it will follow suit."

"That will be the real test." Malek's voice was carefully neutral. "The limiters we've established are the weakest part of this construct. We won't be able to call this a success until we know that the siphoning spell will disengage when the stones reach capacity."

"Then we'll need to use some of the stored kaema to make sure that it begins drawing it in again once the reserves drop below the threshold we've set," Tarvis added.

Karimah, who had been half sitting, half lying on the ground beside them looked up and asked plaintively, "Do we need to stay here for the duration?"

Tarvis chuckled and shook his head. "Not everyone. In fact, it would be better if most of us dispersed over the next few days. You and Orin can head back first, Karimah. You can leave as early as tomorrow if you like."

173

"I won't argue with that," Orin said gruffly.

"Who stays?" Malek's tone made his own wishes quite clear.

Fortunately, those wishes coincided with Tarvis's own. "I'm staying, of course. And I want Malek and Kassen to stay as well."

Everyone seemed content with his decision, and Evyn looked happier than he had since they'd arrived. Tarvis felt some concern that his people had grown too accustomed to comfort, and that they were unprepared to endure the hardships that would likely be necessary. But he said nothing about it as he directed the others to head back to town singly and in pairs to avoid suspicion. It was likely unnecessary, but he wanted to instill a strong sense of caution in the team.

He and Karimah were the last to leave, and he watched her look back at the stones one last time, her face filled with something close to awe. "We really did it."

"This is just one step. But a significant step. If this holds, we can replicate it throughout Tarya and then link the constructs together to create a vast storage web of kaema that mages will be able to access from anywhere."

"How many will we need?"

"It's hard to say. Until we see just how much of a draw this one holds under normal conditions, I can't be certain, but probably a couple hundred or more."

She paled for a moment but recovered quickly. "So, even under the best of circumstances, we have a lot of work ahead of us."

"You're not afraid of a little hard work, are you?"

She laughed nervously. "There's nothing *little* about it. But no, I'm not afraid of doing my part. I am wondering how quickly we'll be able to progress this, though. We'll need to move fast if we're going to finish before someone catches on."

Tarvis closed his eyes and took a slow breath. As usual, she had given voice to his own fears. "I'm working on it," he said softly. "And we shouldn't get too far ahead of ourselves. First, we need to see if this will work as designed."

174

"Agreed." She looked up at him and smiled. "Do you think it's safe to head back?"

"It should be."

They took a meandering path back to town, mostly in companionable silence. Tarvis did his best to distract Karimah from the imposing view of the massive Elysian wall. He understood that it bothered her, as it did many people. But while he agreed that it was an oppressive and rather ugly thing, he also admired the ingenuity and craftsmanship that had gone into its making, as well as the perseverance and zeal of the people responsible for it.

He had obviously never met an Elysian, but he supposed that they were fiercely independent people, determined to protect their privacy and preserve their way of life. He could respect that kind of dedication. After all, he was equally committed to his cause. But he couldn't quite understand why a people would reject all contact with those beyond their own borders and wondered what it was that they felt demanded such extreme measures to safeguard.

At least he didn't need to build any walls. His monuments would be far less impressive to ordinary senses, a mere scattering of stones across Tarya linked together by power and will. But they would preserve their way of life in much the same way that the Elysian wall kept its people safe. His constructs would serve as a wall between kaema and those unfit to wield it.

***

Aidan watched as Jaron paced the length of the long, comfortably furnished room that served as a lounge for the masters who taught at the Mage Hall. He knew the man far too well to be perturbed by his restless movements. He was more concerned that this assembly had been called with little warning, which was uncharacteristic of Jaron. Whatever was bothering him was obviously important, and Aidan trusted that he would explain the situation to the rest of them. Eventually.

Master Seamus was not so patient. "We're here, Jaron. Now tell us why."

Jaron stopped mid-stride and turned to face Seamus, who was seated next to Aidan. The Archmage looked faintly irritated, but quickly apologized. "I'm sorry about the short notice, but I've received some disturbing reports."

Seamus flashed him a look of annoyance but said nothing, and after a few seconds Jaron continued. "There have been problems with the ley lines in Athens."

"What sort of problems?" Michaela asked.

"Specifically, a significant weakening of several secondary ley lines in the far western part of the province."

"What could cause that?"—"What can we do about it?"—"What does it mean?" The questions came from several of the masters at once.

Jaron raised his voice slightly to be heard above the others. "I wish I knew. There is absolutely no precedent for this. All I know right now is that those ley lines have been all but emptied of kaema."

"It's unlikely that this would be a natural phenomenon," Aidan said in a carefully calm tone, even as he struggled to suppress his own rising tension. He had a sinking suspicion that what was happening might actually be deliberate.

"I agree," Jaron replied. "I think that an investigation is in order."

"In the interest of efficiency, we should contact Master Tarvis," Seamus suggested. "He can reach the affected area sooner than the rest of us to gather information. We don't know enough to do much of anything right now."

"There's more to consider," Jaron added. "The environment around the depleted ley lines is showing signs of distress, as if the lack of kaema is affecting the health of the land."

"That's not surprising," Michaela commented. "The connection between the two is well-known."

Jaron looked grim. "What *is* surprising is that none of the kae-madri have yet responded to this incident."

"Have you contacted them?" Aidan asked.

Before Jaron could reply, Seamus interjected, "It's not his place to contact the guardians. It's up to the governor of Athens to request their involvement."

Aidan frowned at Seamus's choice of words. "I take it that he hasn't done so?"

Seamus sniffed. "The Athenian governor doesn't want any of the kae-madri interfering in his province and making unreasonable demands. I can't say that I entirely blame him, but under the current circumstances, it may be short-sighted."

"Short-sighted?" Michaela's voice was sharp. "It's downright pig-headed!"

Seamus shrugged and she added, "And considering the extremity of the situation, why would the guardians wait for an invitation? Isn't it their duty to address this sort of thing?"

Jaron took a deep breath. "I cannot speak for the Order of Kae-Madri, but Governor Tharan has issued what amounts to a ban on guardians performing their duties within his borders, so they may feel unable to act. And while the kae-madri are responsible for correcting imbalances in the ley lines, this is far more than an imbalance. They may not be able to address it at all."

An uneasy silence ensued, and after a moment, Michaela said, "If Jaron wishes to consult with the First Guardian, I will support him."

Jaron looked thoughtful. "Do the rest of you concur with that suggestion?"

Murmurs broke out around the room, but no one else spoke up until he prompted, "I'm asking for your opinions because I value them. Please, if anyone else has any ideas, I want to hear them."

Seamus spoke up first. "I'm not comfortable reaching out to the kae-madri in light of Governor Tharan's position. It could be interpreted as a challenge to his authority. If we're going to do something about this, we can't afford to alienate the Athenian leadership."

"Seamus has a valid point," Aidan reluctantly admitted. There wasn't much value in going to the First Guardian with what little they knew. "Still, we need to investigate as quickly as possible. A group of us could go to the site, but Tarvis is far closer and is just as qualified as any of us."

Jaron swept his gaze around the room, and the other masters nodded their agreement as his eyes met theirs. When his attention turned back to him, Aidan felt Jaron's thoughts brush against his. *I want to speak with you alone after this.*

He inclined his head slightly in acknowledgement, and Jaron addressed the group again. "Consider it done. I will contact Tarvis immediately. In the meantime, if any of you come up with any theories, I want to know."

The gathering broke up quickly. There was no doubt that this problem would be foremost in everyone's thoughts until both cause and solution were found. It wasn't long before Aidan and Jaron were alone.

"I need your help, old friend," Jaron said softly.

"I gathered as much."

"Tarvis is powerful and intelligent, but I'm not sure he's up to this challenge."

"You want me to go to Athens."

Jaron started pacing again, his face a mask of concentration. "Your skills are legendary, Aidan. When we were students together, it took everything I had in me to keep up with you."

"Whoever gave you the idea that you kept up with me?" Aidan folded his arms across his chest and smirked.

Jaron stopped his pacing. "It's been quite a while since you could best me."

"Only because you're considerably more powerful than I am. If the contest were based on skill alone…"

178

"I know all too well what the outcome would be." Jaron's smile didn't quite reach his eyes. "That's why I need you. You're the most qualified to figure out what this is, and who's behind it."

"What have you been holding back?"

Jaron chuckled softly. "You know me too well." He paused and added, "I suspect that what's happening may be deliberate."

Aidan gave him a hard look. "You believe those rumors about independent sorcerers? You think a group of them could be behind this?"

"Maybe." Jaron sounded reluctant. "I know it's far-fetched, but I think I prefer it to the alternative."

"What alternative?"

"That some of our own people are responsible."

An awkward silence fell. Aidan knew that the weakening of the ley lines was almost certainly not natural and had even considered that there might be agency behind it, but he hadn't given much thought to what that agency might be. Obviously, Jaron had, and his conclusions were disturbing.

"Why would anyone want to weaken the ley lines?"

"I'm hoping that you will be able to find out."

Aidan sighed. "Do you have an exact location?"

"The nearest town is Janus, right on the Elysian border."

"A border town?" Aidan sat back, startled. "Do you think this problem could have originated on the other side of the wall?"

"No. Even if the assumption that Elysians have no magical abilities is wrong, the epicenter of this is decidedly within Athens's borders."

Aidan considered his travel options. He'd never been further west than Heraston, and he'd only been there once. But he'd been to Icarus often enough that he could teleport that far. "I can probably be there in as little as three, maybe four days, depending on the train routes and schedules, but I'll have to start in Icarus. It's the only place I know well enough to teleport to. Will that suffice?"

"Do you need to go to the Hall there?" Jaron frowned.

Aidan looked hard at Jaron. "Is there a reason I should avoid the Hall?"

"I want to keep this between us for now." Jaron's face was difficult to read, and there was something just a bit off about the situation that made Aidan feel uneasy. "In fact, I'd like you to travel in disguise. I don't want Tarvis to know you're there."

"Don't you trust him?"

Jaron sighed and fell heavily into a chair. "I think that Tarvis still resents that I beat him in the election, and he can be defensive. I don't want him to believe that I'm questioning his abilities. And I don't want to give any of the other masters more reasons to worry."

"Are you certain that's all there is to it?" Aidan asked, watching his friend's reaction carefully.

It took a moment, but Jaron eventually let his guard down. "I wouldn't put it past Tarvis to try to make me look incompetent here. But if I give him the chance to be the hero, he'll do his level best to get to the bottom of things, and he won't have any reason to question my actions if I defer to him."

Aidan understood. Jaron wasn't just worried about the consequences of outright failure, he was also concerned about how his decisions would be judged by the other masters, even if he did find a solution to the current predicament.

"It will take me longer to investigate if I have to avoid Tarvis while I'm at it."

Jaron nodded. "When can you leave?"

"Tomorrow. I've been helping Kylec prepare for his exams, though he hardly needs my help." Aidan snorted. "He won't complain about me taking time off for a trip, but he'll be curious about where I'm going."

Jaron looked thoughtful. "I wish I could convince him to postpone the exams another year or two. Andris is working himself to the breaking point to keep pace with him."

"He already agreed to wait until Andy turned nineteen so they could take the tests together. I think that if Andy asked him to wait a little longer, he would. But nothing *I* say will convince him."

"Andy won't ask," Jaron said with a sigh. "He wants to prove that he can keep up."

"He's almost a year younger than Ky."

Jaron made a dismissive gesture. "That little difference in age isn't the issue. Keeping up with Kylec is simply impossible."

Aidan smiled. "Commiserating with Andy, are you?"

"Let's just say that I know how he feels."

"Well, since it will fall upon you to oversee Kylec's studies in my absence, perhaps you can persuade him. And you should know that he's been pushing himself to the breaking point, too. In addition to his studies here, he's working toward his journeyman status with the Engineers Guild."

"I thought he'd put that on hold."

Aidan shrugged. "He decided that he could handle it."

"Were we like them at that age?"

"Probably. I suspect the gods sent us that pair as a form of cosmic justice. You know, every mother's curse? 'May the gods bless you with children just like yourself.'"

"And here I thought that remaining childless would protect us."

"The gods are powerful, Jaron." He spoke with mock solemnity. "They aren't about to be thwarted. I hear that my parents howl with laughter when they read my letters, and I suspect that my mother makes special offerings in appreciation for me getting my 'just desserts.'"

Jaron laughed, and Aidan felt the tension in the room ease. "Since you brought up your parents, let's say that you're going to visit them. You can port there without difficulty, so you can even stop there on your way back and give the tale some truth."

"I think I can sell that to Ky."

Jaron nodded. "With any luck, we'll be able to set everyone's fears to rest soon."

***

Aidan could sense the difference in the ley lines as soon as he arrived within the affected area, and he noticed that many of the plants looked wilted or sickly. Though he understood that imbalances in the ley lines could have an environmental impact, he'd never encountered such an obvious correlation. He was glad that he'd taken the precaution of replenishing his internal store of kaema at every opportunity prior to reaching the depleted zone. He was fairly certain he'd have sufficient power to handle whatever came up, but he didn't want to take chances.

He weighed his own curiosity against Jaron's insistence on stealth and decided not to rush directly toward the epicenter of the disturbance. Instead, he meandered out of town, deliberately walking away from the source of the problem until he reached the cover of the forest. Then he began a slow, winding progression toward it, all the while stretching out with his senses to see who, if anyone, might already be there.

He sensed several powerful sorcerers straight ahead of him and paused. If he could sense them, there was a good chance that they could sense him. He tightened his shields as much as he could to mask his presence and waited, listening carefully. After several moments passed, he concluded that he hadn't been noticed, but he thought it unwise to proceed further so he found a suitable hiding place behind a fallen tree and settled down to wait.

It wasn't a long wait. Barely thirty minutes passed before a wave of kaema rushed toward him. He had almost no time to react as the energy slammed into his shields with tremendous force, throwing him onto his back and nearly knocking him unconscious. He lay on the ground stunned for several minutes, his body and mind gradually recovering. He sat up slowly, feeling dazed, and looked around. Nothing appeared different until he shifted his vision to see the magical currents. A faint cloud of raw kaema permeated the immediate area, and the ley lines that had been all but empty moments before were beginning to shimmer with the renewed flow of magical energy.

He stood with some difficulty, feeling slightly drunk, almost giddy. There was a sharp pain at the back of his head, and he gingerly explored the tender area with one hand, wincing as he touched a large lump. He pulled his fingers away and saw that they were smeared with blood. He didn't remember hitting his head, which was hardly reassuring.

He sat back down and forced himself to take slow, deep breaths. He needed to get himself to a healer or physician. But first he had to be stable enough to make the walk back to town without collapsing, preferably without drawing too much attention to himself.

At least he knew enough basic healing craft to stop the bleeding, though even that minor task left him feeling unaccountably weak. Using a handkerchief and some water from his canteen, he cleaned the area as best he could. The process hurt enough to make his eyes water.

While he gave himself a few more moments to recover, he heard a loud noise from the same direction the wave of kaema had come from. A few seconds later he heard voices, and he ducked down out of sight, suppressing a yelp as pain shot through his injured head.

"You can't prove a thing!" a woman shrieked.

"We caught you in the act," a familiar voice said. "You should be grateful that we found you and put a stop to this before anyone was hurt."

Aidan peeked out through a gap between the ground and the fallen tree that hid him and saw several pairs of legs passing unnervingly close to his hiding place. He counted eight pairs in total, three of them moving as if they were being dragged along with considerable force.

"You've got no right to hold us like this." A boy's voice, high-pitched with fear. "Where are you taking us?"

Tarvis spoke again, his voice even and seemingly unperturbed. "We're taking you to the town magistrate. She will then contact the nearest ovates to arrange a trial. Tomorrow, my companions and I will retrieve the evidence of your crimes for examination."

"Stop!" The woman who'd shrieked out earlier threw herself to the ground. Aidan's heart pounded in his chest as he saw a tangle of long blond hair fall inches away from the gap beneath the log. All the woman had to do was turn her head and they'd be eye to eye. He thought about casting an invisibility shield, but it was a miracle that Tarvis and his companions hadn't sensed him already. The sudden flare of magical energy from a spell was certain to draw their attention. He settled for shifting a small leafy branch in front of his face, leaving him the barest space to peek through, and held his breath.

"Up girl!" Not Tarvis. Another familiar voice, but one Aidan couldn't quite place. Probably another mage or adept from Tarvis's Mage Hall in Icarus. Based on what he could see from his limited vantage point, Aidan thought it safe to assume that five of the eight people were from the Hall, and the remaining three were their prisoners.

There was a flurry of movement, and the blond hair disappeared from view, replaced by a pair of worn-looking boots. A heartbeat later, feet were moving wildly in all directions and Aidan lost track of who was who, not that he'd been all that certain to begin with. The frenzied action didn't last long. Aidan sensed magic at work, and soon saw three pairs of legs standing stiffly, as if in military formation.

"Now," Tarvis said, sounding slightly out of breath, "since you are unable to behave, you'll remain under that binding spell until we reach the magistrate."

They started moving away toward town when Aidan heard a new voice, a light tenor that sounded as if it came from an older man. Clearly the binding did not affect speech. "Please," he said quietly, "we meant no harm. Please just let us go."

"Shut up!" screeched the woman again. "Don't say anything. They'll only use it against us."

"Sage advice," Tarvis commented as the procession moved further away. "Perhaps you should heed your leader."

"She's not our leader." The older voice sounded terribly sad, almost stricken.

"As you say," Tarvis replied, his voice getting fainter with distance.

The last words Aidan was able to make out clearly came from the woman, spoken in a tone of pure hatred. "You'll regret this, mage. I swear you'll regret this."

As they moved out of earshot, Aidan glanced at his watch and noted the time. He waited a full hour before rising from his hiding spot, all the while questing as best he could with his pain-dulled senses for any sign that someone might still be nearby.

He stood slowly, testing his balance as he went. The pain in his head was sharp when he moved too quickly, but if he kept his head relatively steady it faded to a manageable throb. He took a breath and considered his options.

He could walk back to town and get the medical attention he knew he needed, or he could examine the evidence Tarvis had mentioned before his team came back to retrieve it. He opted for the evidence, since the source of the disturbance was currently far closer than the town was, and he didn't feel well enough yet to make the longer trip.

The trees began to thin, and he realized he was nearing the edge of the woods. Rather suddenly, four enormous stone blocks came into view. He stood for a full minute just gaping at the huge pieces of gray kaeverdine that couldn't possibly be a natural geological formation. There were no large deposits of kaeverdine for miles. Someone had quarried, shaped, and transported the objects to this location and then carefully placed them in an even row, right on top of a minor ley line.

He shifted his vision and examined the deeper magical structure of the stones. Something was off. He could see that the kaeverdine had been altered, but the spells looked half-finished. Or half-broken.

Of course, he thought. *Tarvis would have broken the spell when he found them. That's what must have caused that violent wave of kaema.*

It explained what he was seeing. Almost. Maybe.

He continued searching the patterns for clues. The remnants of the spell suggested a high level of sophistication coupled with a strange kind of clumsiness. It was as if it had been shaped by someone with limited skill and an enormous amount of luck.

Or by someone with extraordinary skill deliberately camouflaging their work.

The spell seemed designed to draw in and store kaema, and Aidan was reminded of the magical batteries that the earliest sorcerers had experimented with. The intent had been to provide a power source for some of the technology that their ancestors brought from Earth. But development of such batteries had been abandoned when it was determined that kaema could not serve as a substitute for the electrical based energy the machines were designed to use.

To the best of his rather extensive knowledge, there was no modern purpose for such a device. Kaema flowed freely through the ley lines and could be tapped at will. And spelled objects such as lightstones that required stored power were designed to provide their own reservoir, keyed to their specific function and able to be replenished by anyone with the talent and training.

Maybe that was the point: to provide a power source for those without the necessary talent or training.

No, that made no sense. If a person couldn't channel kaema from a ley line, how would they channel it from a stone?

Aidan's pain faded into the background as he contemplated the mystery before him. He'd been too focused on staying hidden to get any sense of what kind of power Tarvis's prisoners might have been able to command, but it seemed unlikely that three sorcerers with no ties to the Mage Hall could manage something of this magnitude. And even if they had, it still didn't explain why.

He pulled a small recording stone from his pocket, intent on documenting the scene along with his impressions, but as he tried to imprint the information, a wave of dizziness overtook him, and he nearly collapsed. He sat down and focused on his breathing as the pain reasserted itself with a vengeance.

Maybe I should find a nice place to sleep it off. No. If I do that now, I might never wake up.

He forced himself to his feet and headed toward town, taking the most direct route. It was a risk, but his life was more important than Tarvis's pride.

He wouldn't be recognized right away. The glamour masking his features was a static spell. Once cast, it drew the small amount of power it needed directly from his body and required no active effort on his part. But the glamour couldn't mask the aura of his power. His shields did that, though even with them working perfectly, he couldn't entirely hide what he was, and he didn't think they were perfect at the moment.

It was well into the afternoon by the time he set out, and the sun was touching the top of the Elysian wall by the time he reached the main road that led into Janus. He carefully placed one foot in front of the other, trying to keep his throbbing head as still as he could.

He was relieved when he reached the road. At least he was now less likely to get lost. He kept moving, even as the world around him turned gray and sounds dimmed. He kept moving. He kept moving. At least, he thought he did.

"Whoa!" A loud voice jarred Aidan back to consciousness. He rolled over, crying out in response to the pain in his head. Faces swam in and out of view.

"He's been beaten, you think?" A woman's voice, sharp with concern.

"Bandits, maybe." A male voice, grim.

"Get him in the wagon. We'll take him to the magistrate."

"No," he said weakly, even as hands lifted him, "no...magistrate...was an accident. I was...exploring...and...fell."

"You're staying in Janus?" A man's face came into view, expression stern but not unkind.

"Yes...room...Archer's Inn," he managed.

The man nodded. "We'll take you there and have the innkeeper call a healer. Now let's get you into the wagon."

They settled him in the back of the wagon amidst what looked like bolts of cloth. He felt consciousness slipping away from him again, and the woman who had climbed in with him must have realized it. She asked in an urgent whisper, "What's your name? We'll need to give them a name when we get you the inn."

"Dan...Marshes." He gave her the pseudonym he'd adopted for this trip after a slight pause that he hoped she didn't notice.

"You rest easy, Dan," she said kindly as darkness claimed him. "We'll take care of you."

***

The other masters left right after he'd presented the results of the investigations. That had been nearly an hour ago, but Jaron remained in the conference room, slumped in his chair at the head of the long table. He stared blankly into its polished wooden surface. The meeting had gone well. He'd managed to put to rest everyone's fears. Except for his own.

Tarvis had succeeded far beyond Jaron's expectations. Not only did he find the source of the problem, but he'd also corrected it and caught the parties responsible. The report he'd sent was very thorough, and Aidan's brief accounting of what he'd seen and heard confirmed Tarvis's findings...more or less.

He frowned, still furious with Aidan for getting hurt, and even more furious with himself for sending him on the fool errand in the first place. As if prompted by his train of thought, there was a knock on the door.

"Come in," he barked.

The door opened and closed quietly as Aidan entered the room. He chose a seat that kept several chairs between them. Considering his current mood, Jaron thought it an appropriate precaution.

"Tarvis discovered a series of constructs resembling the magical batteries our ancestors once tried to use. They'd been placed along a minor ley line and spelled to siphon and store kaema. He found three sorcerers in the act of trying to use that kaema to augment their own power and stopped them." Jaron delivered the summary in a flat voice, deliberately avoiding Aidan's gaze. "Case closed, right?"

"What do you want me to say, Jaron? I screwed up. I was injured and couldn't complete my mission. I can confirm the basic information in Tarvis's report, but I don't have much else to offer."

Jaron paused for a moment, just long enough to set a shield around the room for privacy. Then he hollered at his friend, "Do you really think I give a damn about the mission? You almost got yourself killed!"

"That's an exaggeration, Jaron." Aidan kept his voice level, but he looked shaken.

"Really?" Jaron leaned back in his chair, pinning his friend with a harsh stare. "It was more than a concussion, Aidan. You absorbed too much kaema and it overloaded your system. If it wasn't for the strength of your natural shielding, you could have died on the spot."

Aidan scowled at him. "Laramy shouldn't have shared that with you. Healers are supposed to maintain confidentiality."

"Laramy didn't," Jaron replied. "Your mother did."

Aidan's jaw fell open, "You contacted my *mother*?"

"No. She contacted me. You scared her, Aidan. Badly. Considering that you teleported into her living room and then collapsed in a heap, can you blame her?"

"I should have teleported straight here instead."

"You shouldn't have teleported at all!"

"The healer in Janus said I was fit for travel," Aidan said defensively.

"Travel and teleportation are two different things. The man was treating you without knowing who you really were. As far as he knew, he was just dealing with someone who'd fallen and hit his head. I doubt that he even noticed the affect that the excess kaema had on your nervous system."

"He was a qualified healer," Aidan shot back. "Are you questioning the man's competency? He took good care of me."

"I'm sure he did, within the limits of the information available to him."

"He examined me while I was unconscious. It isn't as if I was able to hide my power at that point."

"I'm sure he realized you were a reasonably powerful sorcerer, but that doesn't mean he knew you were a master mage traveling in disguise. And most healers aren't trained in the kind of nuances that would allow him to recognize the full extent of what had happened to you. Fortunately, your parents' healer is accustomed to treating mages and knew what to do to stabilize you."

"I didn't appreciate how bad it was at first, I'll admit that. I should have booked passage back here as soon as I was well enough."

"No." Jaron fought to keep his voice calm. "You should have sought help as soon as you were injured."

"I explained that. I heard someone coming, and I had no way of knowing who it was. So, I hid."

"And as soon as you recognized Tarvis, you should have announced your presence and requested his aid."

"You didn't want him to know I was there."

"To spare his feelings!" Jaron roared. "Your life is worth a hell of a lot more than a man's ego."

Aidan lowered his eyes and didn't respond.

Jaron took a deep breath. "Seventeen years ago, Celeste Amru paid me a visit. It was her last year as Archdruid, and she came to warn me that there was trouble on the horizon and urged me to prepare for it. That night, she told me that I would need to be very careful about who I chose to trust, and I've heeded her advice."

Aidan looked up with a puzzled expression. "She is a very wise woman."

Jaron nodded. "I have many colleagues and acquaintances, and a fair number of friends. But there are very few people who have my complete confidence. Very few." He paused, looking significantly at Aidan. "You're one of them."

Aidan shook his head in confusion. "And I am honored to be one of your confidants. But I don't understand—"

"I can't afford to lose you!" Jaron didn't shout, but he filled the words with feeling. He needed Aidan to understand just how much he cared, and how badly he'd been shaken.

"You're not going to lose me, Jaron."

"You were reckless."

Aidan arched an eyebrow. "You're calling *me* reckless? Really? Which one of us has the well-earned reputation for leaping headlong into trouble without so much as a second thought? How many adventures did you drag me along on when we were younger? How many near misses did we have because of your absolutely certainty that we'd never get hurt?"

"We were young and stupid. We weren't invincible then, just lucky. And we certainly aren't invincible now." Jaron spoke in a sober tone.

He saw the flicker of fear in his friend's eyes that told him he understood just how narrowly he had escaped permanent injury—or worse.

"I'm sorry, Jaron."

"Prove it," he challenged.

Aidan looked baffled. "How?"

"Take care of yourself. Heal fully before you tax yourself."

"I am ful—"

Jaron cut him off, "Do you want me to ask your mother to confirm that?"

Aidan stared at him, as if trying to gauge his mood. It was a struggle, but Jaron managed to maintain a stern expression. After a long pause, Aidan said softly, "You can't be serious."

He folded his arms across his chest. "Try me."

Aidan shook his head, his expression sheepish. "Okay. I'll rest. I'll even give Laramy consent to keep you informed of my condition until I'm completely recovered, fair enough?"

"More than fair." Jaron stood up and crossed to where Aidan was sitting. He clapped him on the shoulder and said, "I have no desire to invade your privacy. I just want you healthy and whole as soon as possible, so consider yourself on restricted duty until I get the all-clear from Laramy, deal?"

"Deal," Aidan replied amicably enough.

Jaron leaned against the table and stared at the wall. "Since you did risk yourself, I don't suppose you remember anything more?"

"Tarvis's report is accurate enough. I can't recall anything that contradicts it, but..." he trailed off.

"But?" Jaron prompted.

"How did those stones get there, Jaron?"

"The report said that the people responsible for the spell found them in that location. They must have been moved there a long time ago."

"That seems rather convenient, don't you think?" Aidan shook his head. "It's not the only thing that seems odd. I know I probably wasn't very clear-headed by the time I reached the construct, but something about it looked wrong to me."

"Tarvis said it was unstable."

"I suppose it was, but I remember thinking that it looked almost deliberately clumsy." He shook his head again. "I don't know, Jaron. This entire situation seems off."

Jaron sighed. "Most of the other masters are satisfied that the matter is now resolved. They concur with Tarvis's recommendation to the High Court of Ovates that binding the power of the perpetrators is sufficient punishment."

"What do you think?"

"Do you believe that three sorcerers without enough power to rank as mages could do something like this?"

"I don't know. The woman had some training here at the Primary Mage Hall years ago, and she and her father were making a rather good living practicing magic. And the boy has potential—had potential, I guess I should say. That's probably why she took him on as a student."

"So, could they have done this?"

"They were questioned by ovates who confirmed their guilt, but I'm not sure."

"They might have had help."

"Not that they remembered."

That was what worried him the most. It was possible that someone could have tampered with their minds, altered their memories. He could tell by Aidan's expression that he was thinking the same thing.

"There are still a lot of unanswered questions," Aidan said thoughtfully. "Were they acting alone? How did they manage to build that thing? How did they even come up with the idea? Is this going to happen again?"

"No one else is asking, at least not openly," Jaron remarked.

"That may be the most troubling thing of all. Have we really grown that complacent?"

"Tarvis suggested that we should be more careful about those admitted to the Hall, particularly those not enrolled in the standard apprentice system. I don't intend to turn students away without a good reason, but a mandatory ethics class is probably in order."

"Don't let this discourage you, Jaron. This incident isn't your fault."

"No, but it falls upon me to deal with it."

Chapter 12

1476 AHS

"I appreciate your feelings in this matter, Deirdre, but I think it's premature to extend any offers to the child," Leah said calmly.

"Glasnae is not a child. It is customary to extend such offers to candidates between the ages of fifteen and eighteen, and Glasnae is already eighteen."

"She's not just any candidate, Deirdre." There was a note of warning in the High Priestess's voice. "There are special circumstances to be considered."

Deirdre pretended to draw the wrong conclusion. "I realize that she is your great-niece, but I don't understand why that should be an obstacle."

There was a long pause during which a silent war seemed to rage behind Leah's cool demeanor. At last, she said, "Familial relationships are immaterial, though I do admit I feel a certain obligation to her given the close kinship. No, what matters here is the girl's power, which as you know is quite extraordinary. Surely you can appreciate that such gifts are not bestowed lightly. The gods must have something in mind for her, and we must not interfere with that destiny."

"Perhaps we should consult the Order of Seers," Deirdre suggested pragmatically. "If she has such a destiny, I expect that the seers have had some inkling of it by now."

"I have already sought their counsel," Leah snapped, as if offended by the suggestion that she might have overlooked such a thing.

"And what did you learn?" Deirdre asked with genuine curiosity.

"Nothing I can share," Leah said firmly. "But I know that it is far too soon to tie Glasnae into a bond that can never be broken. I expect you to abide by my wishes."

The finality of her tone was a clear dismissal, and she gave Leah a courteous bow before turning to leave, glad that she hadn't bothered to sit. Both the brevity of the interview and Leah's response were what she'd expected.

Her hand was on the doorknob when Leah added, "I trust that your promise still holds."

It wasn't a question, yet it demanded a response. Deirdre thought for a moment, and then decided that it was time to be completely candid. She took a deep breath and turned around.

"I made that promise to you when Glasnae was a still a child and I was her teacher. Circumstances have changed. She is now a young woman exploring options for her future. I believe that she is called to Kaestra, and nothing you say will change my mind on that matter."

She held up a hand to forestall any protests. "However, I have honored my promise. I came to you first. And since you seem so convinced that Glasnae has some grand destiny awaiting her, I'll wait one more year before I approach her. If she has found a path that suits her by then, I'll accept that I was mistaken. If not, I will offer her a place within the Order of Kae-Madri."

"That is not your decision to make!" Leah nearly shouted.

Deirdre forced herself not to flinch at the outburst. "With all due respect, High Priestess, this *is* my decision to make. As first among Kaestra's daughters, it falls to me to seek out those who might serve her and extend exactly such an invitation. As to whether or not that invitation is accepted, well, that will be Glasnae's choice."

"You would dare defy me?" The words were spoken quietly, but there was genuine anger behind them.

"You may see this as defiance, but I do not. I serve Kaestra, not you. From where I stand, I have been more than obliging."

She was out of the room with the door closed behind her before Leah could respond. She realized that it was something of a retreat, but felt she'd been brave enough facing Leah down in her own receiving room.

She still had to wait a year—she always kept her word—but as far as she was concerned, she was no longer bound by the terms of her original promise to Leah. And once the year was out, she would talk to Glasnae. She was certain of what the young woman's answer would be, just as she was certain of Kaestra's will in the matter.

Chapter 13

1477 AHS

"What does ritual magic mean to you?" Glasnae asked. Her head was tilted to one side, and her deep green eyes were narrowed to slits. Devon stared at her, unable to think of a reply right away. They'd been sitting together for over an hour while Glasnae helped him with his mending. Neither of them was particularly good at it, but between them they managed to salvage a few garments from a premature end in the rag heap. They'd barely spoken, enjoying the sunshine and the breeze and the sound of the birds singing in the treetops above them. Her question caught him utterly off-balance.

He finally gathered his wits enough to respond. "Why do you ask?"

"I want to know," she said simply.

For a long time, Devon just looked at her. She gave no outward sign of discomfort or impatience, but her expression revealed nothing of her thoughts either. She was no longer an awkward, exasperating child. She was a lovely young woman who was blooming right before his eyes. And in spite of the fact that he'd been one of the people in charge of her discipline during the more troublesome years of her childhood, they had managed to become friends.

His answer came slowly. Although ritual magic was a central part of the Magicians Order, it wasn't something he thought much about, at least not in a way that he could readily describe.

"Ritual magic is a form of sharing. It's a way for me to be part of something larger than myself, to perform magic that I could never manage alone. It means...fellowship, I suppose. Unity among my brothers and sisters in the order."

She smiled, but her eyes looked faintly sad. "You find joy in losing yourself, in becoming but one of many."

"It's not like that, Glasnae." He felt strangely defensive. "By linking our power, we can accomplish so much more than any of us can alone.

It isn't about losing myself; it's about giving of myself. There is a difference."

"But what difference do you make in the world?" she asked softly, lowering her eyes. "You join your power to that of the other magicians, but what do you do with all that strength?"

It was a hard question. The truth was that though the magicians were dedicated to preserving and protecting the secrets of ritual magic, they rarely used it. When they *did* use it, they usually shaped the kaema into an intention, a kind of magically charged message sent to the gods. Ultimately, the energy was simply grounded back into the ley lines. It was a powerful and profoundly emotional experience, but he doubted that it would impress the young woman beside him.

He decided to offer a more concrete example of ritual magic at work and hoped it would satisfy her. "The great stone circle at the center of the college was built with ritual magic. It was created in a matter of hours. The stones were called and shaped and placed during the course of a single ritual."

"So I've been taught," she said, shaking her head slightly. "But that was centuries ago. What have *you* participated in?"

Devon fell silent. He had not personally participated in any ritual that resulted in anything that she would appreciate.

"I'm sorry," she said softly, misinterpreting his silence. "If your vows forbid you to speak of it, I understand."

Devon closed his eyes and answered, "It isn't that, Glasnae. It's just that since I've been a member of the order, we haven't done anything concrete, nothing I can point to. In the past, magicians performed practical magic as well as the more spiritual, but that was a long time ago. Now, most of what we do is a form of worship. Magical prayers, if you will."

She sighed. "I thought so."

"Things changed gradually over time. They could change again." He wanted her to join his order, but for all the wrong reasons. He had been called to be a priest. If he had not been gifted in magic, he would have joined the General Order. His strength was impressive, but it was nothing compared to what Glasnae possessed. For him to serve the gods and the people of Kaestra with his gifts as a magician seemed appropriate, but he acknowledged that for Glasnae to do the same might be somehow wasteful.

"When you link your power, do you also link your will?" Her voice was deceptively casual, and she kept her eyes focused on the trouser leg she was re-hemming. "It must be difficult to achieve sufficient consensus to be effective."

Devon swallowed hard. "The consensus occurs in advance. Once we join together, we become a single vessel of power, but only one person shapes that power." He didn't add that aside from the wielder, the participants in such rituals were aware of very little beyond the union of power and emotion. He knew all too well how she was likely to respond to that.

"Who does the shaping? Do you take turns?"

The question was not nearly as innocent as it sounded.

"In theory, any one of us can do it," he answered carefully. "But M'Gan is the head of the order, so he usually takes on that role."

"Of course," she responded without looking up.

The ensuing silence felt uncomfortable. Devon sensed that something important was happening, and that he was missing it.

He waited, looking over at her every now and then, trying not to be too obvious about it. In the last couple of years, she'd clearly left childhood behind, and recently his feelings for her had grown beyond friendship. Though there was nothing improper about what he felt toward her, he couldn't forget that she was nearly twenty years his junior and had once been his student. As much as he might want to pursue her, he was unlikely to do so.

Minutes stretched and he stole another sideways glance, only to jump as he unexpectedly met her gaze. Something about the way she looked at him made him feel naked, exposed. It was as if she were peering right through him. He wondered if she had picked up on his thoughts and felt himself flush.

Relief flooded through him when her next words were not about him, but M'Gan. "I don't much like the head of your order," she said in an oddly formal tone of voice, "but I respect his position as well as his knowledge and skill."

He huffed out a laugh. "Your dislike is a matter of public record. But I'm surprised to hear you grant him your respect."

"I grant it grudgingly," she admitted, "but honesty forces me to acknowledge that he is talented."

"It's good to hear you say that," Devon replied sincerely.

"Don't get too excited. I still think he's an ass."

"Glasnae!" He groaned. "Must you?"

"Do you really want me to answer that?"

"No."

She sighed deeply and turned to face him fully. "I need to make a decision, Devon, and it isn't an easy one. You know better than most people just how powerful I am since you helped teach me how to control that power."

She looked away again before continuing. "I need to find a way to use my gifts. I need to decide what to do with my life, and my choices seem far more limited than they did when I first decided to study here. In fact, my choices have narrowed to two: I can join the Magicians Order, or I can leave New Avalon and apprentice at the Mage Hall."

Now it was Devon's turn to look away. She couldn't leave New Avalon. She belonged at the college. He was certain of it.

But her talents would be well suited to magecraft. Even though the Druidic College taught magic to any with the ability, she would have far more opportunities to hone her skills at the Mage Hall.

"Why do I have the feeling that you've already made up your mind?" he asked sadly.

"I haven't." She frowned, and then added, "All right, it's more a matter of when I will leave than if I will leave. I've stayed this long partly because of Galen. I don't want to leave him, and it would be wrong to take him from his mother and littermates too soon. But he's two years old now, and he's already pretty well trained. I think I could arrange to bring him with me if I went to the Mage Hall."

"Galen is only part of the reason you stayed, though," Devon prompted.

His heart caught in his throat when she smiled at him and laid a hand against his cheek. "There are many other reasons I've stayed. I call them friends, and you're one of them. I love New Avalon, and I love the people here.

"I've learned a great deal at the college, and I know that I can continue to learn more if I stay." She laughed and lifted her arms expressively. "I could spend a dozen lifetimes here and still have more to learn. But I've been...blessed...with an unusually strong gift. Every day of my life, I expend effort keeping my power in check. There has to be a reason. There has to be some use for this talent that makes that effort worthwhile. And honestly, Devon, prayers don't seem a good enough reason."

She looked into his eyes for a long moment and then added, "This isn't easy for me. But I need to do what feels right."

"I know," he said in a quiet voice. "But I'm going to miss you."

She shook out the trousers she'd been working on, and stood up, handing the garment to him. He took them as he scrambled to his feet.

"You're leaving now?" he asked, startled.

She gave him an odd look. "I'm scheduled to help serve dinner tonight, so I have to get to the dining hall." She looked at him quizzically for a moment and then huffed at him. "Honestly, Devon! I don't plan on running off just like that. There are things that need to be done and plans that need to be made. Don't worry, you won't be rid of me that easily."

"You won't leave without saying good-bye, will you?" he asked, catching her hand before she could walk away.

"Of course not," she replied, squeezing his hand firmly.

"I'll see you at dinner, then," Devon said, and let her go.

***

When Leah suggested that he enlist Devon's aid to lure Glasnae to his order, M'Gan had hoped that their friendship would be sufficient enticement. He'd avoided being too candid with the other magician, all too aware that he would resist the idea of coercing his young friend. But his subtle attempts at convincing Devon, and Glasnae through him, that she belonged in the Magicians Order had failed. Not only had she shown no interest in joining his order, but Devon also indicated that she was now planning to apprentice at the Mage Hall.

M'Gan shuddered at the thought. The girl was too powerful, and far too independent for his liking. As a mage, there was no telling what she would be capable of. Even Leah would recognize that danger. No. She had to join the Magicians Order. It was the only way that he could be sure that her power would not be misused. The gods had bestowed such a gift upon her for only one reason: to serve. She must be made to understand that.

M'Gan knew that he could no longer rely on Devon to intervene with Glasnae. In fact, he didn't think he could trust Devon to act appropriately at all where she was concerned. His personal feelings for her were clearly overriding his good sense.

It was time to take matters into his own hands. M'Gan knew that Glasnae's personal shields were barely adequate. She'd struggled to learn the techniques necessary to contain her own power, and she had yet to master the art of keeping unwanted influences out. It was common knowledge that she was still an involuntary empath, picking up on the unshielded emotions of others without conscious effort. She should have outgrown that years ago. It was one of the weaknesses he intended to correct when he was in charge of her training, but for now it would serve to his advantage.

In his mind, he began to design a spell that would compel her to stay and present herself for acceptance into the Magicians Order. He had to be subtle. If the spell were too forceful, it would be noticed, if not by Glasnae herself, then by one of her friends.

After some thought, he decided that his aims would be best served by a two-part spell. The first part would address the immediate concern by compelling her to stay at the college for the time being. With that piece, he could be simple and direct. The girl's entire life was now in New Avalon; no one would question a sudden change of heart at the prospect of leaving. The second part would have to take effect more slowly, so as not to be noticed. He would shape a series of layered suggestions to increase her curiosity about the Magicians Order and wear away at her objections. Gradually, she would come to accept that his order was where she belonged. There would be no other options.

She will come to me and offer herself to my order. Her power will be safely controlled and contained. The gift given to her will be placed in service to the gods, as it should be.

***

"Are you sure you want to do this?" T'Vano asked gently. The young woman who sat across the table from him looked unwell, and he wasn't certain that she was entirely in her right mind. Less than three months ago, she'd been planning to seek training at the Mage Hall. She had even come to him for advice on how to proceed.

Then, seemingly overnight, she changed her mind, claiming that she'd grown too attached to the college and her friends. It had seemed reasonable enough at the time. T'Vano knew that she *was* reluctant to leave the people she had grown so close to. Then she signed up for another period of study with the Foresters Guild and seemed content, and he started to believe that she might have found a niche for herself after all.

The contentment didn't last, though. As she began once again to explore new ways to use her talents, something happened. With little warning, she'd fallen seriously ill a few weeks ago. The physician taking care of her concluded that she was run down from being overworked and had likely been fighting the infection for some time. Since she didn't seem to be working herself any harder than usual, T'Vano found that explanation odd, but didn't argue.

She was still recovering, but he had the impression that there was something else affecting her, something he couldn't put his finger on. He was so lost in his own thoughts that he had to ask her to repeat herself when she finally answered his question.

"I said that I'm as sure as I can be." Her voice was incredibly quiet, almost breathless. "I don't know if the Magicians Order is the right place for me, but I feel compelled to try. I won't be making any permanent commitments right away. It will be the same as the temporary apprenticeships I've done. Granted, few enter a novitiate on a provisional basis, but there's no rule forbidding it."

T'Vano sat up straighter as one word caught his attention: *compelled.* Thoughts began to whir inside his skull: *She's so powerful, it never occurred to me that she could be susceptible to that kind of manipulation, but it is possible—and all the signs are there.*

"Glasnae," he began gently, taking her hand in his, "have you had any trouble shielding lately?"

She frowned and lowered her eyes. "No more than usual. I've been ill, though. Are you sensing anything that might be a problem?"

"Have you had difficulty keeping other people's thoughts and feelings out?"

"I'm still pretty open to strong emotions, but my control has improved." She sounded as if he had scolded her.

"I don't mean to criticize." He gave her hand a reassuring squeeze. "It's just that you've been sick, and sometimes people will take advantage of a moment of weakness. Do you think you would know if someone had tried to slip under your shields, maybe even put a spell on you?"

"Why would anyone do that?" There was real shock in her voice. T'Vano was about to reveal his suspicions when a dark shadow passed over her face. She was still weak, and he realized that whatever spell had been worked was still in effect. He could force her to see it, but he might endanger her in the process. And knowing Glasnae as he did, he wasn't sure that she would be able—or willing—to contain her temper once she knew what had been done to her.

He shook his head and came up with a lie she might believe. "Sometimes young men get it into their heads to cast love spells on unsuspecting young women. You are a tempting target, lovely as you are. And you have been ill, which could make you more vulnerable."

She seemed to regain a trace of her old self. "I don't feel particularly enamored of anyone, so I think I'm currently safe. But I'll be on the lookout now that you've warned me." She paused and added with a slight smile. "And I'll be especially careful once I join the Magicians Order, given their skills."

"Definitely be more careful," he said, a little more emphatically than the conversation warranted.

She leaned over and kissed him on the cheek. "It's good to know that you're looking out for me."

**

M'Gan watched Glasnae very carefully. She stood quietly before him and the four other magicians who were present to hear her petition. She had given all the proper responses, and he knew that this was the moment when he should be welcoming her into his order, but he couldn't bring himself to do it. She was here, not out of any real desire to serve, but because she could think of no other way to use her talents.

He also had to consider his own role in her current status as petitioner. His subtle compulsions had produced the desired effect. He had hoped that she would have developed some sense of duty by the time she presented herself, but she had not changed. She promised to obey him in all matters pertaining to the order but gave no indication that she was prepared to set aside her own will and offer her talents in their totality. By the rules of the order, he couldn't *ask* her to do so, but he'd phrased his questions in such a way that her responses would tell him if she was truly willing to offer her gifts in service. It was clear that she would obey him only so far as she had to. She had an independent streak that ran down to the bone.

His spell still held some sway over her thoughts: no matter what happened, she would not leave New Avalon any time soon. He'd reinforced the influence of his magic with more mundane tactics as well, quietly arranging for her to temporarily take over the duties of one of the college librarians who was having a difficult pregnancy, and having others remark in her hearing that dogs tended to be healthier and happier if they spent at least three to four years in the company of their littermates.

He felt certain that between the effects of the spell and her own sense of duty, she would remain in New Avalon for at least another year, even if he denied her petition, which he was now inclined to do.

He knew of only one way to bring her to proper discipline: humility. Perhaps the humiliation of being rejected would be enough for her to reconsider her attitude toward her gifts and her future. Her first reaction might well be anger and resentment, but once the experience had time to sink in, she would realize where she had been wrong.

The candidate's petitions were always heard in public, but usually only a candidate's supporters attended them. Among those who had come to show support for Glasnae, however, were people of importance. Glasnae would, no doubt, feel some shame to fail before them.

After a long, silent deliberation, M'Gan sent his decision mind-to-mind to the other magicians present. They all expressed considerable surprise, but none argued with him, and he was proud that they showed little outward reaction to his verdict. With a nod to the others, he stood and lifted his hands, indicating that all present should rise.

He cleared his throat and spoke with calm authority. "Having heard your petition to join the Order of Magicians, I must regretfully deny you admission at this time."

He paused to allow the surprised murmurs a chance to subside, and then continued. "While you clearly possess great gifts and considerable intelligence and skill, I do not believe that you are currently sufficiently mature to enter the novitiate. You do not yet have the commitment to service that is essential for an aspiring priestess. However, please do not see this as an outright rejection. Instead, look upon this as an opportunity for growth and self-discovery. We shall reconsider your petition after a period of one year. I am confident that by then you will have grown to fully appreciate the value of the Magicians Order and the role you might have within it."

Throughout his brief speech, there had been a low buzz of conversation. It was rude, but he was willing to overlook it under the circumstances. Besides, his attention was far more focused on Glasnae, who, aside from a deep blush coloring her fair cheeks, showed no reaction to his decision.

After he had resumed his seat and the others in the room had followed suit, she responded as was customary, "I accept your decision, my lord. I thank you and the other judges for your time and attention."

He had expected her to say more, but it was clear that she had spoken her piece. He dismissed her. She bowed politely and left the judgment hall. He officially declared the proceedings over, and the rest of those assembled took their leave as well. His fellow magicians looked at him with questions in their eyes, but none of them said a word as they passed him. He remained where he was for a long time, wondering if he had misjudged his control of the situation.

I did what was necessary, he said to himself as he sat in the empty, echoing chamber.

***

T'Vano greeted Deirdre with a hug as she turned from the tray of seedlings to greet him. The young novice with dark curly hair who had brought him to the greenhouse flashed him a bright smile as she left them, and he sighed. He'd come to appreciate such small gestures, especially when offered by attractive young women who were willing to indulge his little flirtations.

He couldn't help but flirt with guardians, even guardians in training. He'd served in the outer court of the kae-madri for several years during his youth, and his love for the women who served Kaestra remained as strong as ever. Something about them stirred his blood in a way that he would have thought impossible at his age. Being in their cloisters was a joy for him, and he only wished that the reasons for his visit were more pleasant.

"I didn't get her name," T'Vano said, embarrassed. "It's shameful to flirt with someone and not ask their name."

Deirdre laughed and shook her head as she struggled to reach a stack of small pots perched on a high shelf. "Her name is Savarrah," she replied. "I suppose I shouldn't be surprised about the flirting. There are some things you never outgrow."

"Let me help you, my dear," he said, easily taking hold of the pots and setting them on the table in front of her.

The woman grumbled. "Being short can be such a nuisance."

"Petite," he corrected, tweaking her braid.

She laughed again and gave him her full attention. "It's always good to see you, T'Vano, but what brings you here today?"

"There's something I need to tell you about Glasnae."

"Go on," she prompted.

"She's being manipulated." He all but growled, his good humor vanishing. "I can practically see it! She's the victim of the foulest use of magic imaginable."

Deirdre said nothing, and he continued. "She was ready to leave New Avalon a few months ago to enter the Mage Hall. I certainly didn't want her to go, but I thought she would do well there and said as much. Then she changed her mind. Granted, women will do that from time to time, but there was something unnatural about it. A few weeks later, she falls seriously ill for no good reason, and while she's recovering, she decides to enter the Magicians Order. That is something she had no intention of even considering before. I may be getting old, but I can recognize the signs of a compulsion spell when I see them. And we both know who has both the ability and motivation to cast something like that."

"He rejected her, T'Vano. He said she wasn't ready. If he had really gone to all that trouble to draw her to his order, you'd expect him to welcome her with open arms."

"But she's planning to petition again. That is utterly unlike the young woman I know. She's more insecure now than she was when she first came here. I think the man is trying to break her spirit, and if this continues, he may succeed. I only waited this long to share my suspicions because I wanted to be sure it wasn't just an old man's paranoia."

"You're not being paranoid," Deirdre said in a low voice. "I suspected something was wrong."

T'Vano cautiously shifted his sight to look at the ribbon of energy that linked her to Kaestra. It appeared untroubled, but he remained alert. When he served in the outer courts, he'd learned to be wary of arousing a guardian's passions, especially the darker ones, such as rage. As long as Deirdre's anger remained her own, the situation was controllable. But if that anger stirred a sympathetic emotion in Kaestra,

Deirdre would become an open channel for power that could tear through friend and foe alike.

"It isn't too late," T'Vano said hopefully. "We can help her shake loose of whatever hold he has on her."

Deirdre shook her head. "How? Confront her with our suspicions? Or confront M'Gan?"

"We can help her reinforce her shielding, for a start," T'Vano suggested.

"I've been doing that anyway." Deirdre turned thoughtful. "In fact, I'd say that her shields have improved so much in the past month that I doubt M'Gan can breach them any longer."

"But the influence he's already had…" T'Vano began.

"Will have to work itself out on its own."

T'Vano felt the burden of his years descend on him all at once. He wanted to help his young friend, but he didn't know how. "There must be something we can do."

"We can be supportive," Deirdre said firmly. "Beyond that, there isn't much else we *can* do."

Maybe we should just tell her what M'Gan did to her," T'Vano said after a pause.

Deirdre's eyes went wide. "You can't be serious. It would kill her."

"You think so?" T'Vano said with a bitter smile. "Frankly, I think M'Gan's life would be the one in danger."

A muffled sob from Deirdre drained the anger from him in an instant and he reached for her. "Are you all right?"

She allowed him to draw her into his arms and whispered, "This is all my fault."

Baffled and desperate to stop her tears, he replied, "M'Gan is a self-righteous, pig-headed tyrant of a man who will stop at nothing to get his way. How could that possibly be your fault?"

"What?" Deirdre sniffled.

"You heard me," he said gently, wiping tears from her face with the edge of his sleeve. "This is M'Gan's doing. None of it is your fault."

Deirdre shook her head. "You don't understand. If I hadn't bowed to Leah, Glasnae wouldn't have been at risk."

"You've lost me, Deirdre. What are you talking about?"

T'Vano listened patiently as she described the promise Leah had extracted from her when she'd first agreed to become Glasnae's mentor. Then he closed his eyes and sighed. Of course, Leah wouldn't want Glasnae to become kae-madri, nor would M'Gan. And yet, now that he thought about it, he knew that there could be no better vocation for her.

"It's not too late. What is a promise made to Leah under duress when compared to Glasnae's happiness? Ask her now."

"Last year I told Leah that I'd fulfilled my obligation. I agreed to wait one more year in case Glasnae found another path that might suit her better. Then she petitioned to join the Magicians Order."

"You never thought she belonged with M'Gan's order."

"No, but I wasn't going to stand in her way."

T'Vano brightened. "But he rejected her."

Deirdre's expression looked positively tortured. "He postponed accepting her. That isn't quite the same thing. She has every intention of petitioning again in a year."

"You can offer her a better choice."

"How will she receive that offer, considering her present state? She may dismiss it out of hand. She may think I'm acting out of pity. And if she does accept, I won't be sure that her heart is really in it. I need to be sure, T'Vano." She shook her head again. "When she petitions M'Gan again, regardless of the outcome, I'll make my offer. She should be free of any remnants of his tampering by then."

"And if she says no?"

"I'll have to accept it."

T'Vano silently reached for one of the small pots and filled it with soil before handing it to Deirdre. She was a guardian. Planting the seedlings would soothe her.

They worked together in companionable silence for a while, and T'Vano could sense her tension ease a bit. After several minutes, a disturbing thought occurred to him, and he risked sharing it with her. "Do you think Leah knows what M'Gan has done?"

"No," Deirdre said with conviction, "but that doesn't mean that she'll believe any accusations made against him."

"You're probably right. But I plan to talk to M'Gan about this." T'Vano raised a hand to forestall her objections, "I am an elder. Even M'Gan gives me due respect. He needs to know that someone has seen through his schemes and will be watching him from now on. Glasnae may no longer be vulnerable, but I'm not willing to take any chances. I won't mention this conversation, of course. Better that only one of us be in the direct line of fire."

Deirdre wiped her hands clean with a towel before handing it to him to do the same. "I'm glad you came. Perhaps you could join us for dinner?"

"I'd be honored," he said solemnly. Then he hugged her again and added, "It will work out. I'm sure of it."

His words, intended to comfort her, held more conviction than he actually felt. But there was one thing he was certain of: M'Gan wouldn't tamper with his young friend's mind again. That much at least, he could guarantee.

Chapter 14

1478 AHS

It was a year later, and the Hall of Judgment was nearly full. Many had come to show support for the young petitioner, but far more were only there to satisfy their curiosity. Glasnae stood before the judges looking respectful and demure in her simple white shift, but M'Gan knew that she was as prideful and stubborn as ever.

His influence was waning. Even if T'Vano hadn't issued his warnings and threats, there would have been little more he could do to control the girl magically. Someone, probably T'Vano, had been tutoring Glasnae on shielding techniques. She was no longer susceptible to his compulsions, and it was unlikely that he would get another chance to bring her under his authority.

He had planned to accept her today, but he'd hoped that she would have learned true service and humility. She hadn't. If he simply accepted her now, he would never have real control over her. There had to be a way to ensure that she learned this first crucial lesson *before* she achieved any status within his order.

He didn't consult with the other judges, not even mind-to-mind. The decision was his to make. He would do what he knew was right and the others would follow his lead. He stood to deliver his judgment:

"I would gladly accept you into our order, Glasnae Maylan. However, I can do so only on a probationary basis. You will be welcomed into the novitiate, but it will be understood that before you are officially granted the full privileges and responsibilities of a novice magician, you must prove yourself worthy of them."

She lifted her head and met his eyes with a gaze so fierce it startled him. "It is your right, Lord M'Gan, to accept or deny my petition. It is also your right to set terms. However, I believe it is *my* right to know what I must do to prove myself.

"I have spent the past year honing my skills, expanding my knowledge, and deepening my understanding of what it means to serve.

I have sought the wisdom of my elders and taken time to mentor those younger than myself. I have demonstrated my abilities and promised to perform my duties to the best of those abilities. I have tried to live a good and virtuous life and to be thoughtful of others. What more must I do to be worthy?"

The words were spoken calmly, without any trace of disrespect or anger, yet she managed to convey the message that she was being wrongfully judged. He could not allow that. He felt his own anger rising and fought for control.

"It is not your skill or ability I question, but your maturity."

"There are many present today who would be willing to testify to the degree of my maturity. Would you be willing to hear them?"

M'Gan trembled with the effort to maintain his calm demeanor. "That won't be necessary. I've already accepted you, though with conditions. The opinions of others are irrelevant here. I must judge you based upon what I know of you, and I know that you are currently lacking in the qualities necessary for a priestess."

Glasnae's face remained impassive. She might have been wearing a mask for all the expression she showed. "I need to know, before I bind myself to your order under such conditions, what I need to do to win your approval. Clearly, I have been unable to meet your standards without specific instruction. In what qualities am I lacking?"

M'Gan exploded. He even shocked himself as he blurted out, "Piety! You lack piety! You do not serve with humility and obedience, but with pride. You do not possess the devotion of a priestess!"

M'Gan watched Glasnae silently survey the crowd before returning her gaze to him. "I understand. I apologize for wasting your time, and that of the other judges. Given your reservations, I do not believe myself capable of meeting the requirements for the Magicians Order. I hereby withdraw my petition and will not trouble you further."

She bowed low to him and the other judges. Then she stood up straight and locked eyes with him one last time before leaving the room. M'Gan felt her thoughts brush against his. *I will not forget this.*

The small garden wasn't easy to find, even for someone who had been there before. Deirdre breathed a sigh of relief when she finally caught sight of the pile of crumbled stone that had once been an archway leading into the space.

This area of the college was largely neglected. The shrubs were overgrown, the grass was almost knee high, and the path had been reduced to a narrow track between the brush. *Well, she certainly has her privacy here,* Deirdre thought.

She moved quietly as she approached the entrance, not wishing to startle the woman she expected to find there. When she rounded the corner, she saw Glasnae facing away from her, head held high. She seemed to be staring into the treetops, though Deirdre suspected her mind was elsewhere. She was still wearing the white robe of a petitioner, but her hair was unbraided and hanging in tangled waves down her back.

Deirdre cleared her throat, in the hopes of drawing Glasnae's attention without startling her. It didn't work. But when the younger woman turned around and saw who was standing there, she smiled.

Deirdre apologized. "I hope I haven't disturbed your meditations."

"You mean wallowing in self-pity, don't you?" Glasnae countered. "It's a more apt description."

"I'm sorry that you had to endure that. M'Gan had no right to say what he did."

Glasnae shrugged and looked away.

Deirdre hesitated, unsure of how to broach the subject she desperately wanted to discuss. Looking around, she asked a question instead. "Do you know the story behind this garden?"

It was the right tactic. Glasnae shook her head, her expression now curious. "I thought it was just a forgotten place, a remnant of something that had once been grand. I think I was drawn here because it reminded me of Kaesa Daerisa."

That made Deirdre smile. "Yes, I can see how someone raised by dragons would find ruins appealing."

"I suppose I should have asked about it, but I was just happy to find a place I could keep to myself."

"This is more than just a garden; it's a kind of memorial." Deirdre's voice fell into the cadence of a storyteller as she closed the distance between them. "A couple of centuries ago, there was a young seeress who was deeply in love with a priest serving in the outer court of the kae-madri. This was their favorite place to meet, and one night, they arranged for a midnight tryst. But when the priest arrived, he found her lying motionless in the grass. She had been overwhelmed by a vision so powerful that it killed her. It is said that he called out to Kaestra, and she filled this place with her presence, trying to comfort him. When she could offer him no solace, she broke the monuments, shattering the stones as a lasting symbol of the grief she could not erase. When the seeress's body was cremated, her remains were buried here."

Glasnae looked around thoughtfully. "Do you know her name? Or the name of the priest?"

Deirdre shook her head. "Their names have been lost to time, but the legend of their love remains, as does this place."

There was a long pause, and then Glasnae asked, "Why did you tell me this?"

"I don't know," she replied honestly. "I wanted to cheer you up, but I didn't know how. So, I decided to offer a distraction instead."

"It's a sad story."

"I suppose it is." Deirdre felt awkward. "But there's something beautiful about it, too."

Glasnae took a deep breath. "I'm upset, but you already knew that. I appreciate the effort to make me feel better."

"I just want you to know that I'm here for you." Deirdre wanted her to know much more than that, but the timing felt wrong.

"I know you are, but I need to make sense of what's happened, and I don't think you can help with that."

It was an opening, and Deirdre jumped at it. "Try me."

Glasnae hesitated for a moment, then said, "When I petitioned to join the Order of Magicians the first time, M'Gan said I lacked maturity and commitment. A year later, he actively attacks my character. If he'd just said that he didn't want me in his order, I would never have wasted my time. Before, I thought he was wary because of the trouble I caused him when I was younger. Now I know that his doubts about me run deeper than that. There's no future for me with the Magicians Order."

"M'Gan *does* want you in his order, Glasnae."

"Really?" Glasnae pinned her with a hard look. "He's got a hell of a way of showing it. Why would he want a priestess in his order who lacks piety?"

"It isn't your piety he doubts, but your obedience. And not obedience to the gods. Obedience to him."

"All novices swear an oath to obey the heads of their orders. I was prepared to make that oath."

"Novices vow obedience in all matters pertaining to their duties within the order. He wants more than that. He wants your utter obedience in all things, in thought as well as action."

Glasnae gaped at her. "What about free will and freedom of conscience? One of the first lessons I learned here was that no one should completely subjugate their will to another."

"M'Gan thinks you're different, Glasnae. From his point of view, your power is too strong to be entrusted to your will." Deirdre paused to let this sink in. She needed Glasnae to understand M'Gan's motives, and his fears, in order to make her point.

When the younger woman did not respond, she continued. "He believed you would eventually accept him as your master in every sense. Then he would have welcomed you with open arms. He trusted that your desire to learn how to use your gifts to their fullest would bring you to him."

Glasnae laughed out loud and said, "So, I'm not fit to wield such power, but he is? Then why did the gods gift me with this ability instead of him?"

Deirdre was groping for a response when the young woman continued. "If he honestly believes that I will come crawling to him, swearing to obey his every whim for the honor of being accepted into his order, he's a fool. I have no commitments here now. I can leave at any time, and I'm pretty sure that I would be accepted into the Mage Hall for training. Does M'Gan really think that he alone holds the key to magical instruction?"

"He assumes that you won't want to leave because your heart is here." Deirdre allowed her emotions to show in her voice.

Glasnae softened. "It is. But I have ties to many places, and I'm not adverse to a new adventure. I want to use the power I was born with, Deirdre. I spend so much effort every moment just holding this 'gift' in check. If I don't use it for anything worthwhile, then what's the point?"

She looked tired and discouraged, but not defeated. Bracing herself for the possibility of rejection, Deirdre finally said what she'd come to say. "I may have an alternative. Would you be interested in joining *my* order?"

Glasnae looked surprised for a second, then her expression went blank. A moment later, her cheeks flushed, and she bowed her head. "I don't need your pity, Deirdre. I have options."

"Do you think I would invite someone into the Order of Kae-Madri out of pity?" She shook her head for emphasis. "Since I first met you as a child, I believed that your place was among my sisters. I've watched you grow into a remarkable young woman who would be a great asset to the guardians!"

"Then why wait so long to ask me?" Glasnae said in a tightly controlled voice. "If you thought my place was with you, why didn't you ever say anything? The guardians don't accept petitioners. One joins only when invited to do so, and you never gave any sign that you'd extend such an invitation."

Deirdre was near tears now, furious that she had given in to Leah's demands. "I wanted to ask you so many times. When I gave you Galen, I thought of what a wonderful companion he would be when you went out on missions. But Leah insisted that I wait. She was afraid that your gifts might be...wasted...if you were to become kae-madri."

Glasnae looked bewildered, and Deirdre couldn't fault her for it. "Leah still doesn't approve of this, but I told her that I believe you are called to serve Kaestra, and I reminded her that this is my decision, not hers."

"Why would you ask for her permission in the first place? You're First Guardian. You swear obedience to none but Kaestra."

"When I deferred to Leah's will on this matter, it wasn't because she's High Priestess, but because she's your great-aunt. I thought she had personal reasons for her request, and that she had your best interests in mind when she made it."

"Whatever her reasons may have been, they had little to do with my interests." Glasnae frowned. "Leah isn't all that different from her sister. Linia always thinks she knows best too."

Deirdre didn't respond to that comment. Instead, she said, "My offer stands, Glasnae."

"And if I say no?"

Deirdre took a deep breath. "Then I would recommend that you go to the Mage Hall and specialize in a field that allows you to work with the land. You have an aptitude for forestry and agriculture. Some mages learn to apply their craft to such fields. It would be a good choice for you."

Glasnae looked thoughtful and Deirdre held her breath. She didn't want Glasnae to find any alternative to the guardians particularly attractive, but she genuinely loved the girl and wanted her to be happy.

"I need time to think about this," she said thoughtfully.

"Take all the time you need."

"And I may have questions."

"I will do my best to answer them."

They regarded each other for a long moment. Then Glasnae took a deep breath and smiled.

"Thank you, Deirdre. Not just for the invitation, but…for everything."

"You're most welcome."

"I won't ever let him know it, but M'Gan hurt me today, and he did it publicly. I don't know if I can forgive him for that. I don't know if I can forgive myself for allowing him to do it."

"M'Gan made a fool of himself today. No one thinks less of you because of what he said, but there are many people who think less of him."

Glasnae looked faintly uncomfortable, and Deirdre sensed that she wanted to be alone for a while. "I need to be going, but I'll see you soon?"

She nodded. "Yes. I promise."

Deirdre turned and left, convinced that the young woman would soon realize what she'd known in her heart for a long time. The World Mother's will was clear: *Glasnae is meant to be kae-madri.*

***

Vreynan soared over the forested hills, looking for a clearing that would make a good campsite. When he spotted one, he reached out with his thoughts to his traveling companion and smiled at her quick response once the connection was made between them.

I see it, Mirsa said mind-to-mind as he shared the image with her, along with the path he'd taken to get there. *We should be there in about five hours.*

I'll go hunting first and meet you there, Vreynan replied in kind.

After more than a week of traveling this way, the rapport between them had grown strong, and he loved the feel of her attention when they shared their thoughts. He was grateful for the extra time with her, even more so than he was for being off that cursed train.

He laughed to himself as remembered how she had taken charge of their travel plans after the third day on the train. He'd stumbled out of the special car designed for kaesana passengers, and after noting that his naturally violet-blue skin had faded to almost gray, Mirsa had stated that that there was no way she would allow him to re-board the high-speed vehicle. She had promptly summoned the conductor and made all the necessary arrangements, pulling out the clothing and supplies she would need for the journey, directing the rest of her possessions to be delivered to Maliae Keep, and sending messages ahead to her family and his new clan to let them know that they would be traveling the rest of the way to Canyi Shaendari by foot and wing, and would therefore arrive far later than originally planned.

They'd spent that first night at an inn on the outskirts of town that had a couple of multi-purpose rooms that could serve as comfortable accommodations for a full grown kaesana. As they'd rested and planned out their route, Vreynan recovered his equilibrium. He noticed that Mirsa's pretty chestnut mare, Darcy, appeared as happy to be off the train as he felt, and her dog, Galen, raced around the property as if to demonstrate that he would have no trouble keeping up when they set out again.

They had talked during the train ride, but the conversations had been casual and superficial. It wasn't until their first night camping in the wild that she had shared her kaesana name with him. He had been taken aback, not just by the fact that she had a kaesana name, but by the weight of meaning associated with it. It had no direct translation in any human language that he knew of. It represented the hope that arises from a terrible loss, like the seeds that begin to grow after a wildfire.

"Mirsa is a powerful word," he'd said softly, "and not an entirely happy one."

"I know," she'd replied. "My foster mother explained it to me when I was old enough. She was mourning my mother when she named me. But I like to focus on the hopeful part of my name's meaning. I brought her joy at an incredibly sad time in her life."

The following day, they conversed frequently mind-to-mind, sharing stories even as they refined their traveling routine. They grew close, and on their third evening on the road, Mirsa shared much more than her name. Joining their thoughts together as they curled up by the fire, she had shown him images of Canyi Shaendari and those who lived there, including her sister, Naeri. He quickly understood that Naeri's name, which meant dawn-fire, was a perfect match for the slender, golden hued female. He suspected that her mother had chosen the name for her exceedingly rare coloration, but from Mirsa's description of her sister, he appreciated that it was also a good fit for her warm, and sometimes fiery, personality.

The mental sharing became their nightly habit, and he was looking forward to showing Mirsa images of his birth clan's home, Canyi Loraeni, tonight. Sighing, Vreynan turned his attention to the business at hand, and began searching out game for their evening meal.

Vreynan had the main fire built and several large fish from a nearby lake cleaned and skewered for cooking by the time Mirsa arrived in the clearing. He'd already eaten a couple of rabbits and another fish since he required far more food than she did, especially when he was covering so much distance. He would have gathered greens and berries to go with the fish, but he was not familiar with the plants in this region and didn't know what would be edible. Mirsa generally foraged during her breaks from riding, and as usual, she had a large bag of gathered food hanging from her saddle when she arrived.

"Hello!" she greeted him with a warm smile as she slid down from Darcy's back.

They quickly fell into the routine of settling into the campsite for the night. After dinner was prepared and consumed and the animals were dozing, he and Mirsa made themselves comfortable. He stretched out and she leaned against him, snuggling under a blanket. He sighed with contentment, and with a feather-light mental touch, invited her to join her thoughts with his. He sensed her pleasure as they slipped into the rapport without effort.

He took her through his memories of his homeland. The hills where his birth family lived were not nearly as grand as the mountains in Maliae, nor were they so densely forested, but they had a beauty of their own that impressed Mirsa. *I wish you could fly with me,* he said into her thoughts. *It is such a rush, to soar over the fields of wildflowers at the base of the foothills.*

An unexpected flush of excitement surged out of Mirsa, quickly replaced with an equally surprising sense of shyness. *Maybe I can*, she told him.

He did not reply in words, but he made no effort to hide his curiosity, and after a pause, she continued. *When we were alone, Naeri and I pretended I was kaesana like her. She helped me craft a mental image of myself as a kaesana so we could fly together in our daydreams. It was difficult for me at first, but eventually, it felt as natural to me as my physical form.*

A thrill went through Vreynan at the thought. Learning that she had such a dream avatar was intriguing, but what really moved him was that she would consider sharing something so personal and intimate with him. He didn't want to push her, but he couldn't hide his eagerness, and she giggled nervously in response.

I need a moment to prepare, she told him as she gently withdrew from his thoughts, asking him to wait for her. When she reappeared in his mind and approached him, he gasped. It was well worth the wait.

She lacked her sister's exceedingly rare golden color or sinuous build, but her slightly oversized wings and deep green skin would certainly have made her stand out in most canyis. He'd half expected her to move like a human and that her wings and tail would appear stiff and unnatural, but nothing could be further from the truth. She hopped lightly on her feet, just as one of his people would, and her tail swished gracefully behind her. Then he remembered that she'd been using this form since childhood, which would account for her apparent comfort in that shape.

You're beautiful. He spoke softly, reaching out with one hand to touch her cheek.

She ducked her head slightly and her wings rustled in a half-shrug. *It's Naeri's doing. This is mostly what she imagined I would look like.*

I think she knows you well.

He realized that he was staring at her and before things could get too awkward, he asked. *Do you want to fly?*

Yes! she replied, sounding slightly breathless.

With that, he grinned and took off at a sprint, racing across the open field of the dreamscape and launching himself into the sky. Mirsa wasn't far behind, and he slowed slightly so she could come up beside him.

Show me everything! she exclaimed happily.

He did just that. He flew with her over the flower fields he'd described, and along the shoreline of Lake Chervi. They wound their way around the tall narrow trees that hugged the base of the hills and soared above the small, silvery green trees that dominated the higher elevations. He showed her the stone-topped peaks and the relatively small doorways that led to the caverns of the canyi hidden beneath them.

They lost track of time in the outside world as he recreated his home canyi for her in the dreamscape, but eventually, her fatigue became apparent. *It's late*, he said with reluctance. *We both need sleep.*

Yes, she replied, her feelings seeming to mirror his own. *We still have days of travel ahead of us.*

They gently disengaged from each other's thoughts and then stood up to stretch stiffened muscles and deal with physical necessities before curling back up together, this time to sleep.

"Good night, Mirsa," Vreynan said aloud.

"Good night." she replied, and then added, "Thank you for the tour."

"You're welcome," he said warmly.

"I hope so," she laughed as she snuggled deeper into her blanket. "Because tomorrow, it's my turn."

True to her word, the next evening found the two of them physically curled up on the ground while their dream selves flew all around Canyi Shaendari and the surrounding forests. And the night after that, Vreynan took her to Kaesa Daerisa, and not just the cliffs overlooking the crumbling city. It took some persuasion, but he eventually convinced her to fly through The Ruins in a private approximation of The Dance.

She was fascinated by the decaying structures and strangely delighted by the way the forest was slowly reclaiming the long-abandoned city. They flew for hours before finally landing on the top of the cliffs where families usually gathered to watch the dancers. They stood side by side on the edge of the cliff, and Mirsa took his hand, seemingly unaware she had done so.

Atar brought me here with Naeri when my brother, Vanek, flew The Dance, she said softly. *I was so afraid I would fall. I'm always so afraid of falling.*

No, you aren't, he responded, confused. *You're more daring when you fly than I am!*

I'm only afraid when I don't have wings.

And then he understood. Mirsa could be fearless in the dreamscape when she wore her kaesana form because she could rely on her own abilities. As a human, she would always be dependent on someone else to keep her safe in a situation like this. He knew that she loved and trusted her kaesana family, but it was equally clear to him that being in control of her own life was important to her.

When he said nothing, she sighed, and leaned her head against his chest. He wasn't thinking when he wrapped an arm around her waist and draped one wing across her shoulder, pulling her close. It just felt right. She didn't pull away or protest. It all felt so natural, so comfortable. He was caught up in that feeling, and nuzzled her neck and head, and then, very gently, he twined his tail around hers.

225

She ripped herself away from him completely, shattering the dreamscape and severing their mental connection with such force that he was lost in a haze of sudden, severe pain for several moments. By the time he had recovered enough to open his eyes, she was half a dozen yards across the clearing, crouched on the ground, head down, hugging her knees while Galen anxiously sniffed at her hair.

"Mirsa?" he asked, hurt and confused. "What's wrong?"

She looked up at him. Between the moon and the firelight, he could clearly see the tears streaming down her face, which was so very pale. He started to move toward her but stopped immediately when he sensed a crude but powerful force field spring up between them. "I'm sorry," he said. "I never meant to hurt you."

"I know." Her voice was ragged, barely above a whisper as she stammered. "It's my fault. You must have thought... I mean, I know I was responding. You did nothing wrong ...but...it couldn't be real. I didn't mean to...but...I'm not kaesana."

Her voice trailed off, and she lowered her head again.

The physical pain of the abruptly severed connection was fading, only to be replaced by a deeper pain, one that he understood would last far longer. Vreynan knew what he had been about to initiate, and so did Mirsa. And she had wanted it, until she remembered that she was human.

They slept apart that night, as well as the remaining two nights of their journey, and though they still spoke mind-to-mind, they limited such contact to words and simple images. They still cared for each other deeply, but there was now a boundary between them that neither would cross. They were kind to one another, which was all they could be.

To be anything more would break both their hearts.

Sunlight filled the meadow where Glasnae and Naeri lay in peaceful contentment. It had been a long time since her last visit, and Naeri had been ecstatic when Glasnae asked if she would like to camp out with her for a few days. They'd spent the better part of the morning trekking through the forest and catching up on one another's lives.

Naeri delighted in sharing her experiences living among humans, and Glasnae especially enjoyed the more amusing tales. She'd laughed until she cried when Naeri told her about the time when she'd been in the massive central kitchen, learning human cooking techniques. The edge of one of her wings had snagged a bag that had been perched on an upper shelf. It had fallen to the ground and burst open, sending up a huge cloud of flour that slowly settled onto everything like a layer of fresh snow. It was only the fact that everyone, including the head chef, had reacted with such good humor that made the story funny rather than horrifying.

Naeri was the first to rise, stretching and yawning. Glasnae lifted her hat from its position shading her face and looked up at her, shielding her eyes with one hand. "Ready to move on?" she asked.

"Ready for something to eat," Naeri announced as her stomach growled.

Glasnae laughed and pulled herself up. She slid her quiver of arrows over her shoulder and picked up her bow. Thus armed, she looked up and grinned.

Naeri recognized the exact moment when Mirsa resurfaced. It was a subtle, but unmistakable change: a slightly feral quality in her expression and a tautness in her bearing. Mirsa was the untamed side of Glasnae's nature, the part that was more kaesana than human. It was what Naeri had feared her sister would lose when she first went away to school. Glasnae *had* changed—so had she—but she was relieved to know that spark of wildness was still there, and the connection they shared had not diminished.

They split up in search of game. Naeri hunted from the sky: taking down birds on the wing or picking out small animals in an open field. She could even fish from the air if there were any fish near the surface of the water. Glasnae preferred to stalk her prey beneath the canopy of the woods, hiding among the trees and undergrowth.

Naeri had good luck in the hunt. No sooner had she leaped skyward than she spotted a flock of waterfowl rising from the nearby stream. It was easy to pick off the last in the line. She made a swift, clean kill that almost went unnoticed by the rest of the flock. Almost. The loud screeching noises they made hurt Naeri's ears and had her flying quickly in the opposite direction.

She circled back and located the camping gear that they'd stored at the edge of the field. Using magic, she quickly plucked, cleaned, and de-boned the bird, then placed it in the large cookpot they'd brought along with water from her canteen. After shielding it to keep out hungry wildlife, she set out to gather wood for a fire and forage for edible plants.

It had been a bountiful summer, and the autumn harvest was only just beginning, so it didn't take long to find what she was looking for. By the time Glasnae emerged from the edge of the woods with two rabbits hanging from her pack and a kerchief full of ripe berries, a delicious stew was simmering. Glasnae handed her the berries and went about the task of cleaning and skinning the rabbits. Like Naeri, she used magic to make the task easier, but preferred to clean the skins with her knife.

She held up the rabbits. "Are you hungry enough to finish these off too?"

Naeri laughed. "Do you need to ask? I'm always hungry."

They set the rabbits to cook on a makeshift spit above the campfire while they savored the stew. Once their hunger was sated, they nibbled casually on the berries and resumed their conversation from the morning, reminiscing and swapping stories.

Naeri understood that in spite of everything she'd learned, she was very inexperienced compared to her foster-sister. In the eleven years since Glasnae started school in New Avalon, the difference in their ages relative to their species had become pronounced. As her mother had predicted, Naeri was now the younger sibling in every way that mattered, and she was beginning to feel left behind.

By human reckoning, Glasnae was an adolescent rapidly approaching adulthood, while Naeri still had decades of childhood ahead of her. Her sister would soon shoulder responsibilities that would make ever-increasing demands on her, and it might be difficult for her to find time for family visits. Naeri pushed those uncomfortable thoughts aside, unwilling to spoil the afternoon.

Eventually, the conversation drifted to Glasnae's journey from New Avalon, and Naeri mentioned the young drake who had accompanied Glasnae to Canyi Shaendari. "Vreynan seems very sweet."

Surprisingly, Glasnae blushed. "He was a good travel companion and spared me the frustration of a formal escort."

"I don't understand."

"Deirdre thought it was too far for me to travel alone, even if I took the train most of the way. She wanted to send a couple of men serving in the outer court to accompany me, but when she found out that Vreynan was coming to Canyi Shaendari, she arranged for us to travel together."

Suddenly, Glasnae's discomfort made sense. "You're not a child, and neither is Vreynan. But traveling together was certainly safer than being alone. You could look out for each other, and it must have been nice to have some company. I'm sure that Vreynan's birth clan was happy with the arrangement, too."

She nodded, but still looked uncomfortable. "The Loraeni were kind. And you're right, Vreynan's mother and older sister were relieved that he wouldn't be alone."

"Kaesana are not accustomed to solitude," Naeri said simply. "Vreynan seems happy here, if a little nervous."

"I suppose that's only natural," Glasnae offered quietly.

"He'll settle in quickly." Naeri grinned. "He's already being courted! Haneyla was following him around and…" She trailed off when Glasnae turned away. "What's wrong?" she asked.

Glasnae didn't answer right away, and when she did, the words came slowly, and were barely above a whisper. "Do you remember when we used to pretend that I was kaesana? We'd join our minds together and imagine that I could fly with you?"

Naeri did remember, but she never thought of it as pretending. To her, they had simply found a way to experience a truth that went deeper than flesh and blood. But she just nodded in response.

Glasnae turned around to face her before she continued, and Naeri noticed that her cheeks were flushed. "The journey took longer because Vreynan and I traveled together. We got off the train after the first few days because it made Vreynan sick. After that, I couldn't ride too fast because then Galen wouldn't have been able to keep up, so Vreynan couldn't fly at top speed, either. We were on the road for weeks. Vreynan would fly ahead, pick out a campsite and hunt for all of us. When I arrived with Darcy and Galen, we'd eat and relax for the rest of the evening. It gave us a lot of time alone together with little to do."

Naeri felt a small pang of jealousy. She wondered if she could travel back to Avrin with Glasnae, but quickly realized that her mother would never allow it. "Did you get bored with each other?" she asked almost hopefully.

"No," Glasnae said, her blush deepening. "Vreynan had a lot of questions about Canyi Shaendari, and I told him all about our childhood together." She paused again for a long moment, biting her lip as if trying to hold back the next part, but eventually she added, "I shared my kaesana form with him, like you and I used to do."

This time, the feeling of jealously cut deep, and Naeri had to fight to keep the hurt out of her voice. "So, you flew with him?"

"Yes." Glasnae's answer came out almost like a sob. "When he saw how you and I imagined I would look as kaesana, he said I was beautiful."

"You are beautiful," Naeri replied automatically. "As human or kaesana."

Glasnae's imagined kaesana form was not as striking as Naeri's own, but no less pretty. Where Naeri had a sinuous build and a golden coloration that was rare among her kind, Glasnae's chosen kaesana form was more typically proportioned and her coloring a clear green that matched her human eyes. Naeri had helped her shape that image many years ago, but Glasnae must have altered it as she'd grown to better match her current level of development. She wanted to ask Glasnae to show her that updated image but sensed that it would upset her right now.

"After that first night, we spent every night lost in our thoughts. Flying together, showing each other our homelands."

Naeri pushed aside her jealousy. "Why would that be a bad thing?"

"Because I'm not kaesana, and I really wish I was. More than ever."

"Because of what you shared with Vreynan?" Naeri asked softly, not quite understanding.

"Because I think I started falling in love with him."

Glasnae's face was bright red now, and Naeri wondered why something so beautiful could cause her sister so much pain and embarrassment. "He seems very fond of you, too. I don't think he would refuse your affection for him."

"Oh, Naeri!" Glasnae laughed even as her eyes filled with tears. "You really are young, aren't you?"

Before she could think of a response to that, Glasnae continued. "I know he cares for me, but what we feel isn't possible between a human and a kaesana."

"Why not?"

"Because that kind of love has a physical expression that requires both people be of the same species. Atar can explain it better than I can."

Understanding came slowly. It would be many years before she was ready to engage in such a relationship, but she was not completely ignorant of the details. She hadn't realized that Glasnae was now old enough to have that kind of bond with someone. That her first experience with such feelings would be impossible to act upon was tragic.

"I'm so sorry," she said at last. "I may be young, but I do know about physical love. I guess I didn't realize how much you've grown up. I didn't mean to hurt you."

"You didn't." Glasnae smiled weakly and said wistfully. "This may be a human thing. In the last few years, a lot of my classmates were having their first romances. They seemed happy and sad and crazy all at the same time. I couldn't appreciate any of it, because I'd never felt that way about anyone. Until now."

Naeri sighed in sympathy. "And because he's not human, it won't work."

"I think it's harder because he feels the same way about me. It's difficult for us both."

"Will it always be?" She didn't want her sister and her new clansman to suffer every time they saw one another.

"No." Glasnae shook her head. "It hurts now, and it feels like it always will, but I know better. Everyone says that the first crush is always the hardest, but it fades."

They fell silent for a long time. Eventually, the easy flow of talk resumed, and neither of them mentioned Vreynan again.

Later that night, when they lay next to each other under a sky filled with stars, Naeri pulled out a small leather pouch from her pack and handed it to Glasnae. "This is for you. A gift from Vanek and me."

Glasnae opened the pouch and pulled out the smooth oval stone that lay inside. It was about half the size of her palm and shaped like a slightly flattened egg. Its deep blue surface was crisscrossed with faint veins of green and had a glasslike finish.

"What is it?" Glasnae asked, clearly delighted.

"A keepsake from Kaesa Daerisa. Vanek told me that it's traditional for new adults to claim a piece of stone or other token from The Ruins when they fly the Dance. When I received your letter that you planned to join the kae-madri, I knew that it meant you were becoming an adult and asked Vanek if he could find a token for you.

"Instead, when we gathered to watch The Dance this spring, Vanek brought me to the edge of the city to look for one together. I'm not allowed to go within the boundaries, but there are small monuments and markers on the outskirts and along the old roads. We found this near a broken road marker where the western road enters the old city."

"It's beautiful, Naeri!" Glasnae exclaimed as she threw her arms around her neck, hugging her close. "I will always treasure this."

As they broke the embrace, Naeri looked her sister in the eye and asked the question she had been holding back ever since Glasnae had arrived for this visit. "Are you ever going to come back to Maliae to live?"

Glasnae's voice was gentle. "I don't think so, Naeri. I'm to become a guardian, and guardians go where they're needed. It's likely that I'll live in New Avalon or somewhere else in Avrin, but I'll probably spend a lot of time traveling. The good news is that once I finish my training, I'll have more freedom and time to visit. I might even be stationed at the gateway in Maliae for a little while. No matter what, I'll come to see you as often as I can. And maybe you can visit me too."

Tears welled up in Naeri's eyes, but she kept her voice even. "I had a feeling that you wouldn't be coming back, and I understand. I'm just glad that you're still my sister, Mirsa. I'm happy that you've found a calling that's right for you. I'm just sad that we won't be together."

"We're always together, sister," Glasnae replied fervently. "Even when families are parted by distance, they're always close at heart."

Naeri sighed and curled up, encouraging Glasnae to snuggle closer. She carefully extended one wing to give her an extra blanket and she drifted off to sleep slowly, savoring the moment. Her mother often told her that growing up happens one piece at a time, each one building on the one before it, giving you time to adjust. Naeri recognized this moment as one of those pieces, and even though this particular piece hurt, she would adjust.

***

Naeri and Glasnae found a surprise waiting for them when they returned to the Keep. Riahn greeted them as they arrived, and Shae-Lydra and Pataerin came down from the canyi soon after. Even Vanek joined them, having just returned for a visit with his birth clan.

Larin had set the arrangements in motion as soon as the girls had left for their campout, summoning the scattered family for a small party by the lake behind the Keep. He took great pleasure in the delighted surprise of the two young females, and silently congratulated himself for his excellent idea.

After the initial flurry of activity subsided, Riahn sat down beside him on a low bench and looked at Galen, who promptly trotted over to be pet. He was quite taken with his sister's new companion and had been dismayed that she and Naeri had left him behind. Larin assured him that Glasnae had the puppy's best interests at heart. Galen certainly hadn't lacked for attention at the Keep, especially since Riahn arrived.

"Your sister is going to have her hands full when she goes back to New Avalon," Larin said with a chuckle. "The way that dog's been spoiled here is shameful."

Riahn laughed. "Even Grandmother seems to like him."

"Oh, she's not as tough as she pretends. She melted when he licked her nose."

"Where is she?" Riahn asked, sounding concerned. "She *does* know that she's welcome, doesn't she?"

Larin hesitated. Linia had made peace with her grandchildren, though their relationship was not as warm and open as Larin would have liked. She had also overcome her dislike of dragons, largely due to Naeri's efforts. The young kaesana's persistent attempts to win Linia over had finally prevailed, and by accepting Naeri, Linia had, to some extent, accepted the people she came from.

Unfortunately, his mother's change of heart was still too recent for her to feel at ease in a gathering like this. Overcoming years of prejudice would take time, and there was no point in pushing her.

"She knows," Larin answered when he'd gathered his thoughts. "But knowing she's welcome and feeling comfortable are two different things. I expect she'll join us later, after everyone has worn themselves out and the party quiets down."

"How do you think we'll all be worn out?" Riahn asked.

"Like this!"

It was Vanek who answered, just before lifting Riahn up by the shoulders and flying him out over the lake. Everyone laughed while Riahn struggled in Vanek's grip and yelled to be let go. Once they were over deep water, Vanek laughed and said, "All right!" releasing his hold.

Riahn didn't hit the water. Glasnae and Naeri worked together to create a force field that caught him just above the surface of the lake. They were guiding him back to shore when Vanek decided he wasn't interested in playing fair. He flew over to Glasnae and lifted her off her feet, breaking her concentration. Naeri, unable to maintain the field alone, shouted an apology and went to rescue Riahn just as Vanek dumped Glasnae in the water. Then Glasnae used magic to pull Vanek in after her and before long, all four youngsters were splashing in the water and making an enormous racket.

Their antics had their elders doubled over with laughter, and one very puzzled young dog whining at the edge of the water. Pataerin patted the animal gently and sent reassuring thoughts to Galen's mind while Larin explained that his mistress and her siblings were just playing. Galen must have understood, because he suddenly play-bowed, barked, and jumped in. He didn't stay in long. Though a decent swimmer, Galen was clearly not a water dog. Shae-Lydra used her magic to dry his fur and then snuggled him close while they waited for the children to make it back to shore.

A few hours later, when the chaos subsided and everyone was content to talk over a leisurely meal, Linia did finally join them. She was subdued but cheerful, and after about an hour she quietly excused herself.

Larin offered to walk her back to her rooms, fully expecting her to dismiss the idea, but she smiled and accepted. "Thank you, Larin. I would appreciate that."

Puzzled and concerned, he gave her his arm and led her into the Keep and up the stairs. She waited until they were out of earshot of the others and said, "I hope that no one was upset by my absence. Or my presence."

Larin answered honestly. "You were missed earlier. But no one was upset, and everyone was glad to see you when you joined us."

"I'd like to spend some time with Glasnae tomorrow, just the two of us. I would've asked her myself, but she's never alone, and I felt…awkward. There are some things I'd like to discuss with her in private. Could you ask her for me?"

Larin took a long look at his mother. She'd been happier these last few months than he could ever remember her being, but at the same time, she seemed unusually weary. It was as if the hard shell that she'd used to keep others out had crumbled away, and it revealed not only the softer side of her nature, but also the weaknesses that she'd kept hidden for so long. He had no doubt that Glasnae would agree to her request. "I'll let her know. She has no commitments tomorrow that I know of. When would you like to meet?"

"She's still an early riser, as am I. Would you ask her to meet me for breakfast, say around seven o'clock? I'll have it brought up to my rooms so we can have some privacy. If she can't make it for whatever reason, just leave a message beneath my door tonight."

They arrived at her suite, and he opened the door for her. "Are you sure everything is all right, Mother?"

"Yes, dear." She kissed him on the cheek. "Everything is fine."

***

Linia smiled at the gentle knock on her door. One thing she could never fault Glasnae for was her punctuality. She greeted her granddaughter and led her inside to the small table set for two. As Glasnae seated herself, she removed the lids from the covered dishes one at a time, setting them on another nearby table.

"I ordered fruit, hardboiled eggs, and bread. There's preserves and butter, too."

Linia took her own seat and picked up a piece of bread, spreading it with preserves, waiting until Glasnae began to serve herself before saying, "To answer the question that you haven't worked up the courage to ask yet, I'm fine. I am in excellent health, and my mind is as sound as it ever was."

"I'm glad to hear that." The younger woman seemed to relax slightly.

"I wanted to speak with you alone because I need your assistance with something."

She paused, wondering how to begin and decided it was best to just get to the point. "I don't think I'm going to stay at Maliae Keep much longer, Glasnae. I hadn't planned to be here nearly as long I have. You were just a baby when Aria asked me to come, and I never really left after that. I'd only thought to stay a few years, but it's been what now, almost two decades? Your father needed me at first, but I don't think that's the case anymore, and I'm ready to move on."

"Move on to what?" Glasnae looked startled. "To where?"

Linia smiled. "I'm not entirely sure. I'd like to travel and see some of the world. I want to visit old friends, and maybe make some new ones. In the end, I'll probably settle down back in Berishire. I miss the

237

old village, and I've kept in touch with many people there. I think it will always be home for me."

"You're certain that's what you want?"

"You're surprised."

"A little. I thought you'd made your home here."

"Sometimes, a person can have more than one home."

Glasnae froze for a moment, as if the words struck a nerve. *Of course*, Linia thought, *she has more than one home herself.*

Since Glasnae didn't look ready to respond, she continued. "I need to get things in order here before I can consider moving on, and as I said, I need your help."

The girl flushed and said quickly, "You know I can't stay. I plan to join the Order of Guardians—"

Linia cut her off with a gesture. "I know that, and I'm not asking you to take over any of the duties I've performed here. Your father's stewards are quite competent. Besides, I'm not planning to leave immediately. I expect to stay for at least another year or so, and I'm sure that I'll be coming back to visit from time to time. I just wanted you to know my plans so that you'd understand the timing of my request."

Linia stared at her plate for a moment, gathering her own courage. "When your mother died, Aria and Micail went through her belongings. They kept a few items, but they left many of her things for Larin to go through at his leisure. They were packed up and have been in storage ever since.

"Your father never touched them. I nagged him about it at first, but it upset him so much that I let it go. I reminded him again shortly after you went to school, and he said that when you were older, you should be given access to see if there was anything you wanted and that I should dispose of the rest."

"What about Riahn?"

"Aria and Micail let Riahn pick out whatever he wanted before they stored the rest. I doubt he'd have much interest in what remained."

"Is there a lot to go through?" Linia could see the eagerness that Glasnae was trying so desperately to hide, and she sympathized. Glasnae had been too young when she lost her mother for the grief to be real to her. But her curiosity about the woman who bore her was powerful.

"Three large trunks. I suspect that they mostly contain clothes. I'd like you to help me sort through them while you're here. It shouldn't take long."

Glasnae stared at her blankly, and Linia turned her attention to her meal, giving the girl some time to think.

"I'm sorry," Glasnae said at last. "I wasn't expecting this, and I'm not sure how to respond."

"Will you help me?" Linia hoped the simple question would make it easier.

"Yes, I'd be happy to help you."

"When would you like to begin?"

Linia smiled when Glasnae suggested that they start immediately. "Father will be busy with court most of the day, and Riahn was going to visit friends. I have no plans, so if you have time now…" Her voice trailed off.

She swallowed a bite of fruit and replied. "It's settled then. We'll get to work right after breakfast."

Glasnae applied herself to the food with enthusiasm, and she turned the conversation to more casual things as they finished eating. Then they went to the storage rooms.

The first two trunks did contain mostly clothes. Since they would never fit her, Glasnae agreed to donate all but two of the items. She decided to keep the blue gown her mother had been married in and a dark red dress that Linia said was her mother's favorite.

Glasnae shyly defended her decision. "I may have a daughter someday who might be able to wear them."

Linia doubted that any child would be interested in wearing something that once belonged to her long-dead grandmother but didn't argue. Glasnae was entitled to a little sentimentality.

The last trunk was slightly smaller and contained mostly books. They lifted them out one at a time, browsing titles and occasionally flipping through a few pages. Some were reference books of one sort or another, likely from Mariah's time at the Druidic College, but most were novels. There were also a handful of children's books. "I'm not sure what Aria was thinking," Linia mused. "These could have been put in the family library."

Glasnae seemed equally puzzled. "Maybe we can put them in the family library now?"

Linia nodded. "I'll see that it gets done later." She lifted out a wooden box from the bottom of the trunk. She grunted with effort as she settled it in front of Glasnae. "This is heavier than it looks."

Glasnae had grown somewhat disappointed sifting through clothing and books, but as she lifted the lid, her eyes lit up. "Journals!"

Linia shifted to sit beside her on the floor and peered into the box. "You should read those later, at your leisure," she said before the girl could open the first leather-bound book. "Let's see what else is inside first."

Glasnae's impatience was palpable, but she set the books aside and lifted out the remaining items, one at a time: a simple but beautiful jewelry box that held Mariah's small collection of adornments, a small decorative perfume bottle, a framed picture of Mariah and Larin on their wedding day, and a neatly folded piece of fabric.

Glasnae carefully unfolded the fabric and looked down at it, her expression confused, almost alarmed. It was a richly embroidered stole, the kind worn by novices of the druidic orders on formal occasions.

Very gently, Linia asked, "Do you know what that means?"

The stole revealed a secret that Linia had been sworn never to speak of, until such a time that Larin or one of Mariah's children discovered it on their own. In leading Glasnae to the item, she was bending the terms of that promise, but she believed that Glasnae deserved to know the truth.

Nearly everyone assumed that Mariah had been a novice of the General Order, but the stole that Glasnae now held wasn't embroidered in the rainbow-colored patterns indicative of that order. It was not the black and silver of the Magicians Order, the green of the Order of Kae-Madri, or the brown and blue of the Shamans Order. It was violet, with intricate swirls picked out in silvery lavender.

Glasnae's voice was barely a whisper. "How long have you known?"

"I learned about it shortly after your mother's death. Aria summoned me here hoping that I could pull Larin out of his depression. She didn't want to tell me, but she knew who my sister was and realized that I might find out by accident. She begged me to keep the secret because that was what Mariah had wanted.

"When she and Micail left here, I promised her that I wouldn't tell anyone what she'd divulged to me. But I made it clear that if your father, or Riahn, or you ever learned about it some other way, I would no longer be bound by that promise. I knew that someone would have to open these boxes eventually, and that the contents might reveal the truth. When I realized that your father would never do it, I knew it would fall to you."

"Am I sworn to secrecy?" Glasnae asked uncertainly.

"You've made no promises. You are free to do as you see fit."

"Father really doesn't know?" Glasnae looked at her in disbelief. "How could he not have known that his wife was a novice of the Seers Order?"

"Your father met Mariah here, in Maliae. He was a merlin cadet stationed in the village of Mali, and like all the young cadets, he frequently came to the Keep. Your mother was home for an extended visit, and…" She shrugged. "One thing led to another. I've never seen two people so devoted to each other. Their relationship developed quickly, and their feelings ran deep and strong. Your mother chose to leave the novitiate and marry Larin. Seeing that her only child was now eligible to succeed her, Aria added her name to the list of candidates, and she was elected her heir. She and Larin stayed here. The rest you know."

"But how could she keep this secret?"

"Seers are very reclusive, and I think that your mother kept it something of a secret even in New Avalon. As I understand it, her gifts were…erratic. She had the Sight but was not particularly strong in it. Some novices of the General Order serve as liaisons to the Seers Order. I believe that Mariah pretended to serve in that way while she learned to control her gift, as much as anyone can control the Sight."

"But she left."

"She chose a different life."

"It was the Sight that killed her, wasn't it?"

There was no point in pretending. "Yes. Ultimately, the Sight proved stronger than Mariah."

"She could have lived longer." Glasnae sounded almost angry. "If she'd isolated herself in their cloisters, she might not have died so young."

"Your mother was forty-eight when she died. Most seers are lucky to see their thirtieth birthday, so she was more fortunate than most. If she had chosen a life of seclusion, it's possible that she would have lived a decade or so longer, but then you and Riahn wouldn't be here."

"You wanted to tell me." There was a note of wonder in the young woman's voice. "Every time I asked about my mother, you became evasive. But it wasn't that you didn't want to talk about her. You were afraid you'd break your promise if you said too much, so you said nothing."

Despite her best efforts, a few tears escaped Linia's eyes. "I loved Mariah like a daughter. She was sweet and caring, and she made my son happy. I was angry with her for a while, right after she died, because she left Larin, and you and Riahn. It took time to forgive her, and once I had…well, let's just say that I'd fallen into certain habits that were hard to break."

"Everything is different now, isn't it?" Oh, the hope that reverberated in that voice.

"I am no longer bound by promises of secrecy," Linia replied carefully. "And I will tell you what I can. But you shouldn't expect too much from me."

Glasnae looked again at the journals. "Perhaps these will tell me more about who my mother was. I wonder if she knew what would happen. Do you think she foresaw her own death? Do you think she foresaw what the future would hold for her family, for us?"

Linia hesitated, and then said, "You may gain some insight from Mariah's journals, but I wouldn't expect a record of visions. If your mother did have glimpses of her own future, I doubt she would write about them. My sister once told me that it is forbidden to ask a seer if they've ever glimpsed their own future. One hopes that the gods never condemn anyone to such personal knowledge, but if they do, it would be wrong for anyone else to remind them of it. Some things are better left unknown."

There was a long silence, after which Glasnae said, "Is it wrong for me to be curious?"

"No, child. It would be surprising if you weren't. I just don't want you to get your hopes up too high."

"I don't know how to tell Father and Riahn about this."

"Then don't tell them," Linia said gently. "At least not right away. Give yourself time to come to terms with what you've learned. When the time is right to share this with them, you'll know. Trust your instincts."

Linia rose awkwardly, stretching stiff muscles. "I'm getting too old to be sitting on the floor," she commented with a groan. "You can stay here as long as you want, though. I can ensure that no one disturbs you."

Glasnae stood as well and turned to face her, then slowly lifted her arms, her expression faintly wary. Linia stepped into the offered embrace and hugged her close. "It will be all right, child. Even if you don't find all the answers you're looking for, there's no harm in asking questions."

She sighed as Glasnae leaned against her and said softly, "Thank you, Grandmother."

Chapter 15

1478 AHS

The storm was fierce, the pouring rain punctuated by flashes of lightning and sharp cracks of thunder. It matched Deirdre's mood all too well as she stood by the window, her expression as dark as the sky. The guardians' cloister felt echoingly empty, with less than half the usual population in residence. So many governors and local leaders had requested their services lately that it was hard to keep up. Deirdre couldn't remember a time when there had been so many kaema imbalances. Most had been easily corrected, but it was the underlying nature of the problems that worried her.

Four years earlier, the Mage Hall had publicly issued a detailed statement that a small group of sorcerers had created an experimental construct that caused localized environmental disturbances in Athens. Deirdre had read the report with interest, especially in light of the drained ley line that the kae-madri had restored just months earlier. But she had refrained from contacting Lord Jaron to pose the questions that the document had raised. She was beginning to regret that decision.

None of the current imbalances were as severe as the earlier ones in Athens, but they were similar, and widespread. If they were the result of some deliberate action, she needed to know.

There was a polite knock on the door, which opened before Deirdre could answer. Freydis walked in sat down on the edge of the desk. "We need to do something," she said after a long stretch of silence.

"Really?" Deirdre's voice oozed sarcasm. "I thought we could just ignore it."

Freydis glared at her. "Aren't we being snippy?"

"What more can I do? We've studied the affected areas and found nothing." She couldn't quite keep the desperation out of her voice. "I'm in over my head, Freydis. Nothing could have prepared me for this."

The older woman's demeanor softened. "You've done very well under the circumstances, but we need to get to the bottom of this."

"I'm open to suggestions."

"I think it's time we asked for help."

"You think I should contact the Archmage?"

Freydis shook her head. "Let's start with someone a little closer to home. I think it's time that you consulted the Order of Seers."

Deirdre shuddered. It was a reflexive reaction that had no rational basis. The seers were often consulted during times of crisis, whether of a public or private nature. The current situation certainly qualified as a crisis, and she wondered why she hadn't considered going to them herself.

"It hadn't occurred to me, but you're right," she said in a quavering voice.

"It occurred to you on some level, Deirdre." Freydis's voice was warm, but her eyes held a penetrating sharpness. "You just wouldn't let the thought rise to the surface. Your reaction just now was quite revealing. You're obviously afraid of what they might tell you."

She realized that Freydis was right: she *was* afraid. But she wouldn't let fear keep her from doing what was necessary.

She nodded mutely, and Freydis continued. "Their insight can only help us, and we need all the help we can get." She paused significantly and added, "And there's one more thing you can do to help the order."

"What?" Deirdre asked.

"Glasnae should be initiated sooner rather than later. With her strength, we'll be better equipped to deal with the present situation."

Deirdre shook her head. "Novices train for three to four years, and Glasnae has barely been with us for one. It wouldn't be right."

"Glasnae would have been with us well over four years by now if you'd been free to act when you wanted to. With all the time she's spent working with the Foresters Guild, she's learned enough about the practical side of guardianship, and she's been a quick study since she joined us. I think she'll be thrilled to take the final step, and there isn't a sister here who won't welcome her."

Freydis's reasoning seemed sound, but she still wasn't sure it was fair to push Glasnae so quickly. She'd hoped that one of the other novices could be initiated before her so that she would have the opportunity to see what the process entailed, but no one else would be ready for at least two more years. Freydis was obviously confident in her position, and Deirdre felt her objections giving way before the other guardian's determined expression.

"I'll talk to her when she returns from Maliae, and we'll see what arrangements can be made. But it won't be until summer at the very earliest. I can't possibly prepare her before then."

"I'd like to stand as her sponsor," Freydis said as she rose to leave. "Unless you wanted that honor for yourself. You've been her mentor since she was a child."

Deirdre's smile came easily this time. "I would love to sponsor her, but it wouldn't be appropriate. As First Guardian, I should lead the rite of initiation, and I don't want to be accused of playing favorites. Since you've also mentored her in recent years, I'd be happy for you to stand for her."

"Then it's settled."

"Yes," Deirdre agreed. "I'll contact the First Oracle first thing tomorrow, and when Glasnae returns, I'll speak to her about initiation."

Freydis walked to the door. When her hand touched the handle, she turned and added, "She's ready, Deirdre. This will be the best thing for her, and for Kaestra."

"She's had some difficult experiences growing up, and her power has always set her apart, but I think she's been happy here. I hope that she feels that she belongs with us."

"She does belong with us, Deirdre. In her heart, she knows that."

The images that filled the viewing chamber beneath the Hall of Mirrors were unsettling at best. First Oracle Chu-Lin Sadray ruthlessly suppressed her emotional response and forced herself to view the scenes with a critical eye. She was still mourning the recent loss of the previous First Oracle and knew that if she gave into her feelings, she would be useless to anyone. Perrin had been more than an able leader: he'd been a good man, and a much-loved friend. With his passing, it fell to her to guide the Order of Seers, and she felt unequal to the task.

Her eyes passed over the image of the tainted ley lines, and she fought the instinct to cringe. She'd thought it would be easier to view the recording this time, but if anything, it was even more frightening.

"These images are far more solid than when we last viewed them." Reed's voice trembled slightly, and Chu-Lin knew that it had nothing to do with the vision. Perrin and Reed had become lovers in recent years, and he'd been at Perrin's side when the man drew his last breath. She would have preferred to give him more time to grieve, but the current situation demanded their attention.

As Second Oracle, it was essential that Reed be kept informed and involved. Unlike the other druidic orders, the Order of Seers were exceedingly cautious when it came to succession. The matters that they were entrusted with were too important, and their life expectancy too short, for them to take any chances that the order would be left leaderless. Third Oracle Vanarra Holan had been chosen only hours after Perrin's death, and now, less than three weeks later, she was being called upon to offer her opinion on a matter that could mean the end of their world.

Chu-Lin shook her head to clear her thoughts, then responded to Reed's comment. "Each subsequent time we've viewed this, there have been more details. I've never seen that happen with any other recorded vision. It could mean that these events are on the brink of unfolding."

"Did the vision call to you?" Vanarra asked hesitantly.

Chu-Lin regarded her thoughtfully for a moment. At more than seventy, Vanarra was old for a seer—incredibly old. Unlike most gifted with the Sight, her abilities had not appeared in late childhood or early adolescence. Vanarra received her first vision on the morning of her sixty-third birthday. In many ways, she had more in common with the youngest novices than she did with the senior oracles, but her life experience gave her insight no other seer possessed. That was the primary reason she'd been chosen for the position of Third Oracle.

The uncertainty with which she asked her question revealed her lack of confidence, and Chu-Lin answered with care. "No. I asked you to view this vision with me again because of a request I received from the First Guardian. There have been numerous environmental problems throughout Tarya, and her order has been struggling to correct them. Both the nature and magnitude of the imbalances are without precedent, and they haven't been able to determine the cause. Lady Deirdre has officially asked us for aid."

Reed replied. "If the guardians have requested our aid, then the time to share this with them has come."

"I agree that Deirdre should be informed," Chu-Lin said with conviction. "The question is how."

"I don't understand." Vanarra sounded confused.

Reed answered her. "We could describe the vision to Deirdre, and give her the benefit of our interpretations, or we could simply arrange for her to view the message for herself."

Chu-Lin nodded. "When someone views a recorded prophecy, if they are familiar with certain aspects of it, those pieces will reveal themselves to that person so that they will be recognized. If Deirdre is acquainted with any of the people or other elements of the message, she will be able to discern things that we cannot."

"But for the untrained, viewing a recorded prophecy can be overwhelming," Reed noted.

"I thought only seers were permitted to use these viewing chambers." Vanarra said softly, almost to herself.

Reed nodded and explained, "This level of immersion is far too intense for those who haven't experienced such visions first-hand. Instead, Deirdre will be given access the recording upstairs, in the Hall of Mirrors itself. While she will be able to mentally connect to the vision, the mundane surroundings will keep her grounded, lessening the impact."

"Perhaps we should explain the options and allow the First Guardian to decide for herself."

Chu-Lin smiled at Vanarra's proposal; the wisdom of her selection reinforced. She glanced at Reed who nodded his assent and said, "I will contact her right away. I expect she will want to see it for herself, so we should prepare accordingly. And we should expect her to have questions."

"But will we have any answers?" Vanarra asked.

"Perhaps not, but we can listen, and offer what we can."

Vanarra turned in place, taking in the overwhelmingly grim panorama. She paused before the image of the three glowing lights merging into one and said, "At the very least, we can remind her that in the face of devastation, hope does remain."

***

Deirdre chose to visit the Hall of Mirrors at night. First Oracle Chu-Lin had told her to come whenever she felt most comfortable and had arranged for an escort to guide her. The young priest who met her was not a seer himself, but a member of the General Order. Deirdre was unsurprised. Most seers were extremely sensitive and preferred to live in the semi-isolation of their own cloisters, so members of the General Order served as aids and messengers.

Brother Wistan had a calm demeanor, and Deirdre was grateful for his presence. She had only visited the Hall of Mirrors once before, and then she had only been accompanying a friend and hadn't actually gone inside. The atmosphere of the place set her nerves on edge. Wistan offered her his arm in an old-fashioned display of chivalry, and she accepted it with a smile as they climbed the stairs and went inside. The priest standing watch at the entrance opened the door and then closed it quietly behind them without a word. Wistan assured her that no one would be permitted inside until she was finished.

She began to say that such precautions were hardly necessary given the late hour but stopped herself. Both Wistan and the priest at the door acted as though such late-night visits were commonplace, which made her feel less self-conscious about the timing of her appointment.

They crossed the large foyer and passed through another set of doors that led to the main gallery. Deirdre felt jittery, and when the lightstones brightened in response to their entry, she paused in surprise. Her escort glanced at her with mild concern and then smiled. *He's seen people react this way before,* she thought.

The room was quite long, but only about twelve feet wide. The niches that covered the walls were not set in a regular pattern but appeared scattered across the walls at random. The lowest were set about four feet off the ground, and the highest were maybe seven or eight feet from the floor. Step stools that could also serve as chairs were strategically placed along each wall, and Deirdre was comforted by the practicality of it. Wistan guided her about a third of the way down the long room and stopped. With a graceful wave of his hand, he indicated a niche just above Deirdre's eye level, covered in a white cloth.

She swallowed hard and nodded. He pulled the cloth to one side and tucked it behind a simple wooden peg. "I will wait in the foyer for you," he said gently. "If you need anything, please call for me."

"Thank you."

She waited until he'd left the gallery before turning her attention to the black mirror, about a hand's span in diameter, that lay nestled within its niche. As she had been instructed earlier, she went through the process to engage the spell that would reveal the message it held. With one hand, she reached out, her fingers not quite touching the mirror as she gracefully traced a simple clockwise spiral, beginning at the outermost edge of circular surface, winding inward and imbuing the gesture with the faintest touch of kaema. When her fingertips reached the center, she opened her mind to the vision.

As the power of the message enveloped her consciousness, she wept at the image of Kaestra turned barren and cold and lifeless, the ley lines filled with poison, twisted and sickly. The hopelessness of it began to overwhelm her when she saw three ghost-like figures moving across the ground.

The misty shapes looked faintly human and glowed with a dazzling brilliance. One of them seemed familiar to her, its light tinged a faint green. After a moment of reflection, she knew who it was.

Glasnae.

She watched with wonder as the three figures moved across the barren landscape and drew close, forming a brilliant triangle of power. A column of light appeared in its center, and energy radiated outward from it, cleansing the kaema that was Kaestra's life blood and restoring her. As the planet was healed, the vision faded from her thoughts.

Then, because she couldn't help but look, she opened her mind once again. This time, she focused her attention on the part of the vision where the ghost-like beings first appeared. She carefully studied the one formed of green mist and found the sign that she was searching for: A delicate thread of power connected the misty shape to the world it walked upon. Then she examined the other two forms, wondering if she would see the same thing. But there was nothing, just the warm radiance that could work miracles.

Not three guardians, she thought, not sure if she was relieved or frightened. The message of the vision was clear: their world was dying as the result of some unknown menace. But it could still be saved. Three powerful individuals, one of whom she knew was her young novice, would be able to restore the balance.

She called out softly, surprised that her voice was as steady as it was, and Wistan hurried to her side. He dropped the curtain back into place and offered his arm again. "The First Oracle awaits you in her cottage,

First Guardian. But I was told that the meeting could be rescheduled if you would prefer some time to yourself."

Deirdre smiled up at him weakly. "There's no sense in waiting. I'd be pleased if you'd escort me to First Oracle Chu-Lin now."

"As you wish."

He said nothing more as he led her deep into to the seers' cloisters where the First Oracle waited.

She considered Freydis's insistence that Glasnae be initiated as soon as possible and thought, *You were right, Sister. The sooner Glasnae becomes a guardian, the better. I can only hope that the other two spirits I saw will be found soon and that they will be as willing to help as I know Glasnae will be.*

Chapter 16

1479 AHS

"I'm not trying to make you uncomfortable, but I need to be certain that you understand," Deirdre began, feeling awkward herself. "The date for your initiation has been set, and you only have a couple of months left to take care of this."

Glasnae's cheeks flushed a deep crimson. "I understand." She looked down at her feet as she spoke. "I plan to participate in the bonfire dance at Summer's Dawn."

Deirdre forced herself to maintain a neutral expression. "That's a very sweet idea, and I appreciate the symbolism, but I don't think you want to take any chances with your first time. A man caught up in the heat of the moment may not be prepared to treat a virgin with the gentleness and patience she deserves. I recommend that you seek out someone known for their skill and restraint. There are several men in the outer court who would consider it an honor to ease you past this obstacle. I could introduce you, if you like."

Glasnae stood silently for a long moment, and Deirdre wondered if the young woman had truly never been touched by passion. It was possible, but something about Glasnae's demeanor suggested that there might be another explanation. Deirdre had a nagging suspicion that the girl *had* known romantic love but hadn't acted on it for some reason.

When Glasnae finally responded, she spoke quietly but with conviction. "I wasn't going to leave it to chance. I've asked…a friend…to meet me at the fires. He's…older than I am…and has a patient nature. I know I'll be in good hands."

Deirdre wanted to ask Glasnae whom she had chosen, but she suppressed her curiosity. Given the way Glasnae had phrased her response, it was obvious that she didn't want to divulge the identity of this friend, and she wouldn't intrude on her privacy. Instead, she focused on trying to reassure her as best she could.

"The last thing I want is to pressure you into this, Glasnae," Deirdre said softly. "But it isn't just a matter of tradition. The link simply won't form in a woman who is still a virgin. Just as it won't form with someone born male."

"I wonder why that is," Glasnae mused aloud.

Deirdre shrugged. "There are theories, of course, but no one knows for certain. Regardless of why, this is a reality that has been born out through countless attempts over the centuries. It is a limitation we need to accept."

"I do accept it, Deirdre," Glasnae said firmly.

"I don't want you to think of this as something to be endured. If your partner cares for you and has a reasonable amount of skill, you have nothing to fear. The experience should be pleasurable. Glasnae, please know I didn't expect this to be an issue when I set the date for your initiation."

"I suppose it seems strange for someone my age to still be a virgin."

"It may be unusual, but that doesn't make it strange, or wrong. You shouldn't feel bad in any way for waiting. It is a very personal decision, and I think it's admirable that you haven't been casual about physical intimacy. Too many people rush into sexual relationships before they're ready and then regret it."

Glasnae flashed her a wry smile. "I don't know if it's admirable or not, since it was less about choosing abstinence that lacking any appealing opportunities. I'm not opposed to sex. I just haven't met another human being who stirred those feelings in me. If I had, we probably wouldn't be having this conversation."

Deirdre chuckled softly and shook her head. "That may be, but I can't help but feel that I'm pressuring you."

"You aren't. Glasnae said quickly. "This is my choice."

"If circumstances were different, I would suggest that we wait another year, but the order needs you, Glas. Not just your strength, but your skill and sensitivity as well."

"I'll admit that I'm a little nervous, but I'm also excited." Glasnae's tone was reassuring. "I just want my first time to be special, which is why it's so important to me to do this at Summer's Dawn. I may not be in love with my partner, but I care about him very much, and I think that the ritual will add a different kind of romance to the occasion."

Deirdre recalled her own experiences at the fires of Summer's Dawn, and she had to admit that the ritual did imbue the act with a certain extra…intensity. When she finally shook her head clear of memories and met Glasnae's gaze, the younger woman looked bemused and asked, "Reminiscing?"

Deirdre laughed and replied, "Let's just say that I think you may have made a good choice."

***

Freydis was in the kitchen herb garden with a couple other guardians, tending the beds. Deirdre caught her eye, and the older woman excused herself and they met beneath the large oak tree at the far end of the garden.

The air was still chilly this early in the season, and the branches that arched above their heads had not yet leafed out, but the scent of spring was in the air. Freydis gave her a knowing look, chuckling slightly. "I told you that it wouldn't be easy."

"It wasn't that bad. I think I was more embarrassed than she was."

"But she'll be ready for initiation?"

"Yes." Deirdre laughed softly. "She'll be ready."

Freydis looked at her quizzically for a moment. "Anything happen that you want to share?"

"No," Deirdre replied airily, "I just took a short stroll down memory lane."

"Hmm." Freydis seemed to weigh the merits of pressing her further, but she turned the conversation back to the immediate issue at hand. "You managed to make the arrangements quite swiftly given your initial reservations. I assume that your visit to the Hall of Mirrors had something to do with it?"

Deirdre sobered instantly. She hadn't shared what she'd learned from the seers, and Freydis hadn't asked until now. She should have known that the older woman was merely waiting for the right time to bring it up.

"Whatever you learned upset you," Freydis added when she didn't respond. "You don't have to tell me anything you don't want to. I trust you, as a friend as well as First Guardian. You will do whatever is needed, and you certainly don't need to consult with me."

"I appreciate your confidence, but I don't think I can do this alone. The seers have been protective of this knowledge, and with good reason, but I shouldn't be the only guardian to know the full extent of the danger we're facing."

"I'm here for you, Sister. Whatever you want to tell me, I'll listen."

"They showed me the imprinted record of an incredibly old prophecy. I recognized Glasnae in the vision, and in it, she was kae-madri. You were right about how much we need her strength. As for the details…I don't know if I can describe it. Perhaps Chu-Lin would allow you to view it for yourself, if you're willing."

Freydis's eyes filled with understanding. "Some things cannot be put into words. If the First Oracle agrees, I will go and see for myself. Perhaps then I can help you."

Deirdre nodded. "The seers will understand the importance of having at least one other member of our order familiar with this prophecy."

"Prophecies and portents aside, Glasnae will make a good guardian, Deirdre," Freydis said briskly, her demeanor changing from sober to cheerfully enthusiastic in a heartbeat. "I am looking forward to her initiation."

Deirdre knew that Freydis was trying to cheer her up, and she was more than willing to let her. She smiled warmly and responded in kind. "It's always a joy to welcome a new sister."

***

Paper lanterns in calming shades of blue and green illuminated the interior of the large tent where Freydis and Glasnae waited to be summoned to the gate. The sun had just begun to set when Freydis had led the young novice to the tent that had been set up a few hundred yards beyond the boundaries of the gateway where the ritual of initiation would take place. Since then, night had fallen, and Freydis watched Glasnae move restlessly around the enclosure like a wild animal in a cage. When her attempts at calming the girl failed, she tried distraction instead, keeping up a running conversation that focused on the pragmatic aspects of what was going to happen.

"You are going to be *physically* linked to Kaestra during the ceremony, so you will experience a number of physical sensations, including a moment or two of pain."

Glasnae nodded, her attention clearly divided. "Deirdre told me that. My menses will be triggered during the ceremony. She said that the suddenness of it could be painful."

"It will make life easier afterwards," Freydis added with a slight laugh. "You'll be as regular as the calendar."

Glasnae stopped her pacing and stared at her. "You make it sound so…mundane. So ordinary. Deirdre did, too. But it isn't ordinary. After tonight, nothing will be the same for me."

Freydis crossed the distance between them and caught Glasnae's hands in her own. "Are you having second thoughts?" she asked seriously.

There was a slight pause before Glasnae shook her head. "No. This is what I want. But I'm not sure if I'm worthy. I'm not sure that Kaestra will accept me."

Freydis pulled her gently into an embrace. "Kaestra has called you, my dear. There isn't a guardian here who doesn't know that in her heart. Don't doubt yourself."

Glasnae returned the hug and whispered, "I hate to admit this, but I'm afraid."

Freydis held her at arm's length, searching her face. "It's natural to be nervous, but you have nothing to fear. Every woman present tonight has gone through this same ritual and are gathering to support and welcome you. And I will be at your side the whole time."

The girl's eyes lit up for a moment, hope warring with doubt. With a wavering smile, she asked, "What is it like? I know the format, the responses, the gestures, but Deirdre didn't tell me anything about what happens behind the words and symbols."

"She didn't tell you because she couldn't. Not because of secrecy but because some things just can't be explained. Initiation is a momentous thing, too difficult to describe. It's emotional and magical, and terribly personal. Until you've experienced it, no explanation can ever be enough, and once you have, I suspect that you will be equally at a loss for the words to encompass it."

Glasnae took a deep breath and smoothed imaginary wrinkles out of the sleeveless, calf-length white shift she wore. "Will the ritual be starting soon?"

"I expect so. Once it begins, it will feel natural. I promise."

"Thank you."

"You'll do well, child."

As she predicted, it wasn't long before one of the other guardians entered the tent and announced that the gathered kae-madri were ready for them. With a soft sigh, Glasnae reached for Freydis's hand. After one last reassuring squeeze, Freydis gestured for her to precede her along the path that led to the gateway.

The moment they left the tent, she noticed the soft thrum of power that surrounded them. It was both potent and soothing, and by the time they arrived at the circle, Freydis noted that Glasnae's nervous energy had abated to the point where she seemed almost calm.

More than two thirds of the kae-madri were in attendance, nearly two hundred women dressed in long hooded robes who stood shoulder to shoulder within the circle defined by rough-hewn waist high stones. Th guardians were singing softly, and the wordless melody rose and fell in rhythmic waves. The night was clear, and the moonless sky was lit by a multitude of stars. Even more light seemed to gently radiate from within the circle itself, as if the combined power of those gathered could not be fully contained.

As Glasnae and Freydis approached, the guardians nearest to them parted just enough to allow them room to pass. Glasnae glanced over her shoulder to watch the circle close again behind them, and Freydis caught the girl's eye to offer her a reassuring smile.

The power rising from the circle was incredibly strong, not only seen in the soft glow, but also felt as a tingle in the air and a low throbbing in the ground beneath their feet. It thrummed with expectation.

In the center, Deirdre stood alone, her small figure silhouetted against the fire that burned behind her. In front of her was a ring of polished black stone about six feet across, set into the ground, filled with a fine white sand that shone as if made of starlight.

They stopped a pace away from the circle of sand. Deirdre then lifted her arms above her head and the music ceased.

She called to the assembled guardians, "Daughters of Kaestra, we are gathered here, in this sacred place, to celebrate Kaestra's presence among us, and to offer our support to the candidate who presents herself before our mother."

She lowered her arms and focused her attention on Glasnae. "Glasnae Maylan, daughter of Mariah Maylan, daughter of Larin Tierney, daughter of Shae-Lydra, why do you present yourself before us this night?"

Glasnae hesitated, no doubt surprised that Deirdre had deviated from the usual form of the ritual by naming Shae-Lydra as one of her parents. Freydis knew that the gesture was more than a kindness, it was an acknowledgement that Glasnae's connection to the kaesana went far beyond merely being part of a joined family.

After the briefest of pauses, Glasnae responded as she'd been taught. "I come to offer myself in service to Kaestra. I offer up my body and soul. I offer myself to her totally, to be her eyes and her ears, her voice and her hands."

Deirdre continued. "Do you make this offer freely, knowing that once accepted by Kaestra, only death will sever you from her service?"

"I do."

"And do you pledge yourself to the care of this world, her physical form, and all those who depend upon her for life?"

"I so pledge myself."

Deirdre lifted her arms and her voice, directing her words to the assembled guardians. "My sisters in Kaestra, do you accept Glasnae Maylan among you, to be a sister of our order from this night forward?"

Freydis heard Glasnae draw in a ragged breath, waiting for the answer, but she never doubted the response that reverberated through the circle. "We accept and welcome Glasnae among us."

Glasnae released the held breath in a barely audible sigh, and Freydis smiled as Deirdre responded, "By the will of all those present, I declare Glasnae Maylan a candidate for guardianship. If it be the will of Kaestra, she shall leave this circle as kae-madri, linked to Kaestra, and through her, to us all."

She lowered her arms and directed her next words to Glasnae. "Come forward now and submit to Kaestra's judgment."

Freydis helped Glasnae step into the white circle and kneel upon the sand, then arranged the skirt of her candidate's robes neatly about her before rising and moving to stand directly behind her. Deirdre's eyes were shadowed in the dim light, but she thought she saw a hint of a smile when the woman spoke again. "Glasnae, you have chosen to offer your life to Kaestra. Should she accept, the union between you shall be sealed in blood, and you shall be joined to the goddess in flesh as well as in spirit. This is more than a vow—this is an unbreakable spell. If you have any reservations, now is the time to make them known."

Glasnae swallowed hard, and Freydis understood all too well. This was her last chance to reconsider her decision. She couldn't recall a record of any candidate making it all the way to this point only to walk away, but there was a reason for this part of the ritual. At her own initiation, she had allowed herself nearly a full minute to be sure that she was making the right choice.

Freydis knew that for Glasnae, there really *was* no other choice. It took several heartbeats for the girl to come to the same conclusion, but there was conviction in her response when it came. "I reaffirm my offer of service. My life is Kaestra's, if it be her will to accept me as her daughter."

"So be it," Deirdre said solemnly and laid a hand upon Glasnae's head. The moment had come, and as Freydis watched, memories of her own initiation decades earlier came unbidden to her thoughts.

The power that had been building inside the gateway since they had entered rose to a fever pitch, and Glasnae was caught up in the flow of that power like a small twig being carried upon the current of a strong river. Freydis watched Deirdre remove her hand and step away. The other guardians began singing again. The rhythm of the music matched the flow of energy that would soon come to a focus deep within the novice.

A fierce roaring sound filled the circle, and Freydis winced in sympathy when Glasnae gasped, remembering the pain that inevitably accompanied the forging of a guardian's link. She forced herself to remain calm as she watched the girl stiffen, her body frozen where she knelt as Kaestra's power swirled around and through her. The energy gradually coalesced into the thin ribbon of power that was the link of the kae-madri. Then Glasnae cried out and fell forward, her hands sinking into the fine sand as she caught herself before falling flat on her face. Freydis quickly crouched beside her, offering support.

Now that the purpose of the ritual was concluded, the gathered kae-madri wasted no time. The power that had been raised was quickly and thoroughly grounded, with minimal formality. Deirdre and a handful of others joined Freydis and helped her to gently lift Glasnae from the circle of sand that was now stained with the blood from her womb. Come morning, a seer would come to read the omens in the patterns of that stain, which served as physical proof of the bond that had been forged.

The newly made guardian tried to stand, but was too weak to do so, and they eased her onto the litter that had been readied for her. Freydis took a moment to assure herself that Glasnae's link to Kaestra was strong and sound before urging her to rest. She stayed by her side as Glasnae's hold on consciousness slipped away and whispered softly into her ear, "Welcome, Sister. And well done."

***

Deirdre walked into the room just in time to see Glasnae snap at Jenry, who was trying to help her out of bed. "I can get up by myself!"

"I know." Jenry sounded patient. "But I'm here to help you, so why strain yourself?"

Glasnae's response came out in a growl. "Getting out of bed shouldn't be a strain."

Deirdre quickly made her way to Glasnae's side. "It won't be a strain for long," she said as she slipped an arm around the new guardian's waist. "The adjustment period should be over soon, and then you'll feel stronger than ever."

Glasnae's expression darkened. "I don't think so, Deirdre. I don't think I'm going to survive this adjustment period." No sooner had she finished the sentence than she doubled over, gasping in what appeared to be agony.

Why is she suffering so much? Deirdre thought to herself as she crouched down beside her. *It doesn't make sense.*

"Is it always this hard for new sisters?"

Deirdre looked up at Jenry, scolding herself for forgetting that the novice was still there. She answered truthfully. "No, Jenry. This is unusual."

"Are you afraid she'll change her mind if you tell her the truth?" Glasnae gasped out, shifting to sit on the floor and hugging her knees. "I know I would have."

Deirdre caught and held Jenry's gaze as she answered Glasnae's question. "I'm not lying. Some discomfort for the first few days is normal, but nothing this severe." She turned back to Glasnae. "If you give me a few minutes, I may be able to figure out what's wrong."

"Do you need anything?" Jenry asked quietly. "Is there anything else I can do?"

Deirdre shook her head. "Go. I'll send to you if I need you."

Jenry bowed and practically fled the room. Deirdre watched her leave and then turned her attention back to Glasnae. She shifted her sight to see the currents and patterns of kaema and examined the link that now bound Glasnae to Kaestra. What she saw explained a great deal.

The slender ribbon that ran between the new guardian and the planet throbbed angrily, kaema flowing back and forth along its length in disjointed, fractured pulses. The shielding that contained Glasnae's core of power thinned and thickened in a matching rhythm, pushing against the link instead of flowing into it. The resulting dissonance was having a terrible impact on the girl. The pain that Glasnae was experiencing was only a symptom. If the situation was not corrected soon, there was a risk of permanent damage.

"Glasnae," she said firmly, "I can see what's wrong. It shouldn't hurt this much, and it doesn't have to. You can make it stop."

"What are you talking about?" Glasnae cried, tears welling up in her eyes. "My insides are being torn apart!"

"No, Sister, they are not. You're resisting the link between you and Kaestra. You're holding on to your power too strongly. Most of that power is now bound to Kaestra through your link. The tension is causing the pain."

"I'm not resisting!" she protested, sobbing now.

"Maybe not intentionally, but you are. Which means you have the power to stop it."

"What if I can't? And if Kaestra rejects me, what happens then?"

Deirdre held her close. "Kaestra has already accepted you, Glasnae. The bond is made and there's no turning back for either of you. The link will hold for as long as you live. The pain will last only as long as you continue to fight it."

"I'm not fighting!" Her voice was tinged with the beginnings of hysteria. "I'm...I'm not doing this...on purpose."

"I know." Deirdre tried to keep her voice soothing. "But you're holding onto your power too tightly. You need to relax your hold on it."

"I don't know how." The words came out as a whimper. "All my life, I've struggled to control my power, to hold it in, to keep it chained. When I failed, terrible things happened. I don't know how to let go."

Deirdre took a deep breath, beginning to understand more fully. "You can do this, Glas. Kaestra holds the largest of your power now. You don't need to worry about it anymore, or waste your energy and attention trying to control it. Just relax your hold. You *can* do this."

Glasnae began to argue, but it only came out as muffled whimpers, and Deirdre shushed her. "Trust me, child, trust me. Let me in. Let me help you."

In her distress, Glasnae had tightened her shields, and it took effort for her to lower them enough to give Deirdre access to her mind. Deirdre moved slowly, calming and soothing as she eased her way into her consciousness. *Easy, child. Easy. Trust me, now. Just relax. Release your hold on your power. Trust me, it's safe. Easy now, just release it. Release. Release. Release.*

Deirdre repeated the word in her mind over and over until it became a mantra, all the while directing Glasnae's awareness to the ribbon of magic that now bound her to Kaestra. She could feel the force of that connection and the energy that ebbed and flowed along its length. Glasnae tried to recoil from it, but Deirdre wouldn't allow her to turn away. Instead, she urged her to embrace it. *This is part of you now. You cannot turn away from yourself. You are kae-madri, a daughter of Kaestra. Accept this and calm the link. Restore the balance within yourself.*

I don't know how.

Yes, you do—it's instinctive. Release your hold on your own power and the link will settle. Trust me.

Deirdre held her as she struggled against years of training and discipline. Glasnae clung to Deirdre as she relaxed the stranglehold she kept on her power, desperate to stop the pain that consumed her. Gradually, she managed to loosen her grip, and Deirdre felt her relief as the physical pain eased.

She continued to urge her to soothe the link. With each effort, the pain lessened, and the ribbon of magic that bound Glasnae to Kaestra calmed. It took time, but eventually the balance of energies within her was restored and her link became a warm and golden glow joining her own power to that of the planet itself. Then it faded and thinned, assuming the appearance of a delicate crimson thread as was typical of a guardian's link when at rest.

Deirdre gently withdrew from her thoughts but continued to hold her. "You see? I knew you could do it."

Glasnae eased back in her arms and took a shaking breath before she began to sob again, a lifetime of frustration and pain pouring out of her. Deirdre held her wordlessly as she cried, rocking her gently as a mother would. She understood all too well. After Glasnae's long struggle to master a gift that she'd never asked for, she was finally free. By the time the flood of emotion ran its course, the young woman was utterly exhausted, and didn't argue when Deirdre tucked her back into bed.

"Rest now," Deirdre said softly, holding her own fatigue at bay. "I'll come to see you when you wake. I promise."

When she left, Deirdre wanted nothing more than to take a nap herself, but duty came first. Now that Glasnae was settled, she needed to seek out Jenry and make sure that the novice understood what had just transpired, and that the circumstances that had caused Glasnae so much distress did not apply to her.

***

Freydis picked her way through the overgrown grass, trailing behind Glasnae, who practically skipped along the narrow track that could only loosely be called a path.

"Are we nearly there?" she asked in a deliberately aggrieved tone of voice.

"Nearly," Glasnae tossed back over her shoulder with a truly glowing smile.

She shook her head and chuckled. It warmed her heart to see the girl so happy. They were still dressed in their ceremonial regalia, having come from directly from a small reception formally welcoming Glasnae as the newest member of the Order of Kae-Madri. The long robes were ill suited to the current venture, but Glasnae had been so keyed up following the gathering that she had suggested they take a walk. The girl had responded by dragging her out here to see her special garden in the full bloom of summer.

Glasnae looked lovely in the gown, made of the special cloth that was woven and worn only by guardians. It held over two dozen different shades of green thread, woven into a subtle pattern of overlapping leaves. It reminded Freydis of a forest in springtime, seen from a distance. It suited their newest member quite well.

"This way!" Glasnae called back, dancing around a cluster of shrubs before disappearing from view. Freydis hurried to catch up with her only to pause as she made her way past the bushes, and the garden appeared before her.

It was lovely in a way that only a space being reclaimed by nature can be. The edges of the shattered stone sculptures were rounded and smooth, softened by wind and rain and time. The flowering shrubs were overgrown, but beautifully so, and a rainbow of wildflowers filled the space with little regard for the boundaries of defined flower beds. Glasnae stood in the center, practically bouncing in delight. "It's beautiful, isn't it?"

"It is," Freydis said simply. "Deirdre told me that you'd discovered this little remnant. I trust she told you the story?"

Glasnae's smile faltered for a moment. "It's a sad story," she said softly, "but this has always been a peaceful and happy place for me."

Freydis wanted to kick herself for dimming the girl's pleasure. "I think that it depends on how you look at it," she said, walking toward her. "A young woman died here, true. But she also knew great joy here. I think it is the joy that endures."

The smile returned. Freydis could see how such a place would appeal to a woman raised by dragons. Glasnae had found her own miniature version of Kaesa Daerisa. "So," she began gently, "why did you really want to bring me here?"

A look of mild annoyance passed over Glasnae's features before she sighed. "I've been in seclusion for over a month. Now that time is over."

"And you wanted to come here first?"

"There's more to it than that." Glasnae fingered the narrow band of dark red embroidery that edged the sleeve of her robes, drawing Freydis's attention to it. That tiny crimson ribbon that graced the hem, sleeves and hood of a guardian's robes symbolized their link to Kaestra, an unbreakable chain forged in blood.

When Glasnae didn't continue, Freydis prompted her, "What's bothering you, Glasnae? You seemed happy a moment ago."

"I am happy." Glasnae looked up. "Happier than I've ever been. But...I'm reluctant to leave the cloisters. With my new sisters, I feel accepted. I feel safe."

"And you don't feel safe beyond those walls?" The idea alarmed Freydis.

"Not unsafe, exactly. But I don't know if I'm ready to face…certain people."

Freydis understood. "You are kae-madri now, Glasnae. No one can change that or deny your new status. Not M'Gan. Not even Leah. I understand that you may feel uncomfortable in their presence, but they have no right to influence your life in any way. Accept that, and the rest will fall into place."

The girl still hesitated. "Do you think that either of them will confront me?"

"I doubt it," Freydis said honestly. "They lost, Glas. They tried to herd you in a direction of their choosing, and you took a different path. You took charge of your own life and found fulfillment. Don't let them dim your joy in that new life."

Glasnae took a deep breath and let it out in a sigh. Then she looked around and her brilliant smile returned. "Thank you, Freydis."

"You can thank me by letting me return to the cloisters so I can change into something less cumbersome," she replied tartly.

Glasnae readily agreed, clearly reassured. As they made their way back along the path, Freydis felt a small pang of unease and hoped that she hadn't offered false comfort. Neither M'Gan nor Leah were inclined to accept defeat graciously. But she hadn't lied. Glasnae was beyond their control now.

And thanks be to Kaestra for that! she thought.

***

The novice magician trembled before the heavy wooden door that led to M'Gan's private workroom. She was here at his request, but his moods had been unpredictable over the past few weeks, and no one wanted to be on the receiving end of his temper. She took a deep breath, gathered up her courage and knocked. There was no reply, but the door slowly swung open, and she entered.

She wasn't surprised when the door closed soundlessly behind her, or that M'Gan kept her waiting with his back to her, his attention on the various books spread out on the table in front of him. She *was* surprised, however, when he finally turned around.

Sahana's first impression of M'Gan had been that he was a man who had never been young and would never be old. There was a timeless quality to his face and form that made it impossible to guess his age, and his mannerisms and voice were elegant and refined.

It was hard to see the First Magician she knew in the man who stood before her now. His skin held a deathly pallor, almost gray, and his eyes were sunken into a face that looked drawn and gaunt, as if he were wasting away. He was dressed in his usual gray work clothes, but there were dark stains down the front of his tunic and on the sleeves, and they looked wrinkled and in disarray. She swallowed hard when his eyes met hers, momentarily forgetting why she'd been summoned.

His voice was uncharacteristically gentle, as he asked, "Has Glasnae left the guardians' cloisters?"

"Yes, Lord M'Gan," she replied warily.

"Did you see her yourself, or was this news passed along?"

"I saw her myself. She was speaking with Winala in front of the main library."

"Good. I knew she wouldn't hide forever, but I thought she might try to avoid being seen for a while longer. It's good to know she has more backbone than that. You've done well, Sahana. You no longer need you to waste your time monitoring the activities of the guardians. You may tell Devon that you are free to resume your studies with him."

Sahana bowed her head and left, grateful for the dismissal. After she had put a fair amount of distance between herself and the head of her order, she allowed herself to think about the unsettling state Lord M'Gan was in, and his unexpected reaction to the news she'd brought.

Everyone in the Order of Magicians knew that M'Gan and Glasnae had quarreled more than once, and that he'd denied her entry into their ranks. It was also no secret that he'd been furious when Lady Deirdre offered her a place within the Order of Kae-Madri. Sahana, like most others, could only speculate about these things. She would have liked to ask Devon since he and Glasnae were friends, but that seemed unwise.

She knew that Devon was occasionally uncomfortable around her, as if he suspected that she was there to spy on him as much as learn from him. When Lord M'Gan first took special notice of her, she'd been honored, believing that he'd singled her out because of some special talent or potential he saw in her. Now she wasn't sure, and it was becoming painfully obvious that being M'Gan's favorite was isolating her from her fellow novices, and even some of the fully initiated magicians. M'Gan was respected, but not liked.

Once she felt herself beyond M'Gan's range of sensing, she slowed her pace. By rights, she should've hurried to inform Devon of the First Magician's wishes, but something held her back. She took a meandering route to the pavilion where Devon would likely be at this time of day.

When she reached the pavilion, she heard Devon talking to someone and she slowed her steps before coming around the wall, wanting to give them time to finish their conversation before interrupting. When she recognized who Devon was with, she stopped to listen.

"I don't really care," Glasnae said with a hint of temper in her voice. "He excluded me from the Magicians Order. I'm excluding him from my life. Nothing he says or does has any bearing on my choices. It's as simple as that."

"I'm not suggesting that you try to appease him. I just think it would be a good idea for the two of you to talk and put the past behind you. There's no reason for continued animosity," Devon replied reasonably.

"Believe me, Devon, I'm not nursing ill feelings. I wish him the best of luck. I just don't want to be in his company. Why is that so hard to understand? Besides, he hasn't requested to see me, at least not in the last few days. I can easily assume that he's lost interest since he's no longer bothering the honor guards at the inner court of the cloisters."

"Glasnae, please. Trust that I have my reasons. It will be so much easier if you offer the olive branch. He isn't well. The reason he hasn't been pestering Deirdre isn't due to lack of interest. He's in no condition to pester anyone. I know you have no love for the man but show some compassion."

"If he's ill, he needs a healer, not a guardian. Unless he's accidentally transformed himself into a tree or a piece of farmland. Has he?" She sounded amused.

"This isn't funny, Glas. I'm serious. He tried crafting some sort of spell that backfired on him. No one knows exactly what, but I have reason to suspect that it might have something to do with you."

"I don't see how."

"Seven days after the dark moon, he stationed several of us around the perimeter of the gateway. For more than a month, only kae-madri had been allowed near the place since they were preparing for your initiation, and that was the first time since then that he could gain access. I don't know what he did, but he looked like a walking corpse afterwards. Fallon and I helped him back to his rooms and took care of him as best we could. He wouldn't allow anyone else to see him, not even Sahana, his new favorite."

There was a long stretch of silence, and Sahana began to sweat. Hearing her own name had startled her and made her wonder if they sensed her eavesdropping. After a few moments, Glasnae answered, and she exhaled in relief.

"If he was trying to open the gate without a guardian, it might account for what happened to him, but I can't be certain. I may be kae-madri now, but I still have a lot to learn. I could ask another guardian to check the gate. They might sense something that could help."

"No, don't do that." Devon sounded tired. "I'm not trying to dig up trouble."

"Neither am I."

"He's the head of my order, Glas." Devon's tone became almost pleading. "Whatever personal difference we've had, he was my mentor for many years, and I still believe he's a good man. I know how it must look to you, but I don't think that he's motivated strictly by personal ambition. He must have had reasons for his actions.

"You think he had some kind of altruistic motives for his attempts to run my life?"

"No, I think he feared you—and still does."

Sahana listened in shock to the flat and utterly convinced way Devon spoke that last sentence. It had the ring of truth. The audible gasp that Glasnae gave indicated that she recognized it too. When she answered, her voice was gentler.

"I'm sorry, Devon. You may be right. But if you are, he should be relieved that I became a guardian. Most of my power is bound now."

"Your power isn't gone, Glas, just…changed. You're now the most powerful guardian that ever lived. There may be limits to the ways your power can be used, but it's still a part of you. Besides, I think that he's more frightened by the fact that *anyone* could have so much power than he is of you personally. He thought that if you would bend your own will to others—his own, especially—then you'd be unlikely to use your gifts to control anyone else."

"He feared my ambition?"

"You've always been independent and never showed much deference to authority figures. He worried that you might want to rule over others."

"The only person I want to rule is myself."

"I know that. He doesn't. If you go to him now, you might be able to reassure him. And you might be able to help him, or at least prevent him from doing himself any further harm."

She sighed loudly. "You're a good friend, Devon. To both of us. M'Gan doesn't deserve your loyalty, but since you feel so strongly, I'll think about it. Besides, I owe you a favor, don't I?"

"I've told you before, you owe me nothing. And you have a standing invitation to visit my bed whenever your heart desires it." Sahana had never heard that tone in Devon's voice before, and she was shocked by what he implied.

"You removed the last stumbling block barring my initiation, and it is a memory I will always cherish." There was a slight pause before she continued. "I wish I felt that way about you, I really do. But I can't pretend. I love you, but as a friend."

"Men hate hearing that from women," he responded, a touch of humor blunting the pain in his voice.

"Women hate saying it for that very reason. Let it go for now, Devon, please? I want you to be happy. I'd promise you Summer's Dawn next year if I thought it wouldn't be leading you on."

"If you promise to meet me at the fires, I'll promise not to be led on, fair enough?" Now the humor overpowered the pain in his voice.

Glasnae laughed. "Agreed. If we're both in New Avalon at Summer's Dawn next year, we'll celebrate together. Unless, of course, you acquire any attachments that prevent it."

"And if you have any such attachments?"

"They'll have to accept that I have a previous commitment."

"Done!" Devon said happily.

"And…I will visit your old mentor," Glasnae added soberly. "I won't make any promise beyond that. I can't be certain what to expect from him, or myself."

"I know this is hard for you."

"I won't say I'm looking forward to it, but I'm beginning to think that you're right. I need to put the past behind me. Facing him is probably the best way to do that." There was a long pause, and when she continued her voice was far more lighthearted. "I'll try to see you again before I go, but I'm leaving for Maliae the day after tomorrow. "

"You always know where to find me."

Sahana waited until she was certain that Glasnae had left before retracing her steps and choosing another path. Approaching the pavilion from the other direction, she waved and called a greeting to Devon as if nothing had happened.

***

"I'm surprised that you came to see me," M'Gan said with more candor than he was accustomed to showing.

"That makes two of us."

Glasnae looked as uncomfortable as he felt. Unsure of where to begin, he fell back on simple courtesies and gestured to the chairs opposite his desk. "Please, have a seat. Would you like any refreshments?"

She accepted the chair but declined further hospitality on the grounds that she couldn't stay long. He nodded and resumed his own seat. The heavy wooden desk that stood between them felt like a wall, but a welcome one. He had always feared the power that Glasnae wielded, but he had never really feared *her*, until now.

She sat up straight in the chair, hands folded in her lap, and began what sounded like a pre-rehearsed speech. "Deirdre said that you've been asking to see me for the better part of the past month. It seemed only polite to respond, belated though it may be."

He smiled weakly, hoping that the depth of his fatigue wasn't too readily apparent. "Belated is a good choice of words. We both know why I wanted to see you, Glasnae. I was hoping to talk you out of your decision, but it's too late for that now."

Her voice held a trace of suspicion when she replied, "If that were true, you would've stopped immediately after my initiation, but you continued to ask for me up until just a few days ago."

Uncertain if she would be able to sense a lie, he was as truthful as he dared. "I thought there might still be a chance to reverse the process, but I now know that's not possible. Even if it were, it's clear that you wouldn't reconsider."

Glasnae stared at him for long moment before her eyes lit up with comprehension. "That's what happened to you! You tried to sever my connection to Kaestra, and the power you used doubled back on you when you failed."

M'Gan didn't confirm her statement, but he didn't deny it either. Instead, he asked, "Did it ever occur to you that there must be a reason you were given so much power? That you had a responsibility to use that power in service to others?"

She looked baffled. "And what is it that you think I've done? I've given my life in service to Kaestra, to the life of the very planet we live on! The power I was born with is now bound to that service. Why would you want to change that?"

"Because it's a waste!" He couldn't hold the words back. "You could have done great things. As a magician, you could have given your service to all the gods, not just one. In time, you could have learned to do things we can only imagine now. I thought that eventually, you might even become my successor." He hadn't meant to say that last part out loud. He had barely allowed himself to think it and would never have admitted it under normal circumstances. He was worn out, body and spirit, and he could not remember a time when he felt so weak and exposed.

Glasnae looked thoughtful. "And what kind of leader would I have become if I'd bent to your will? You would have stripped me of my independence and taught me to follow you so blindly that by the time you were willing to step down I would've been utterly unable to shape my own path, much less lead anyone else. You wanted to use my gifts as your own and mold my life to suit *your* ambitions. I *am* willing to serve. I've proven that. But I am *not* willing to be less than what I am."

"And what is it that you think you are?" he challenged.

"An individual."

M'Gan took a mental step back. Her response had been delivered in a direct, matter-of-fact tone. He heard no trace of the pride or self-importance he expected, but still, he was convinced that it was there, just beneath the surface.

"You're stubborn," he said at last. "You refuse to heed those with greater wisdom and experience. That makes you unpredictable, and potentially dangerous."

"Maybe," she conceded, much to his surprise, "but the same can be said of almost anyone. I believe that we are given free will for a reason. I can't see much point to a life spent in mindless submission. I will gladly offer service to others, but I will *never* be another person's slave."

"I wasn't asking you to be," he countered quietly.

"Are you sure? I think you should look more closely at your own motives. I'm not the one whose ambition led me to try to manipulate another person. I haven't dared forbidden magic in an attempt to counteract the will of a deity."

Her words hit their mark. M'Gan lowered his eyes, unable to think of a suitable reply. He felt the beginnings of shame, and it angered him that she was able to stir such feelings in him.

After a few moments of silence, Glasnae added, "I haven't come here to quarrel with you. I thought we had unfinished business, and that it would be better to clear the air so that we could both move on with our lives. If you have nothing else to say, I'll leave."

She was halfway to the door when he found his voice. "Please stay. Please, just a few more minutes."

She paused and turned back to face him. He knew that he should have let her go, but he needed something from her first.

"You're right, Glasnae," he said reluctantly, "I have attempted the forbidden, and no doubt I'm being punished for my sin. I have no right to ask this of you, but would you give me your word that you won't tell anyone else what I've done?"

They both knew that her knowledge of what he had attempted gave her a measure of power over him. But if she gave him her word now, she would be honor-bound to keep it and he would never have reason to fear betrayal at her hands. The choice was hers.

Fortunately for him, she seemed to be in a generous mood. "You have my word that I will never tell anyone what you tried to do. I would rather forget it altogether."

He allowed his relief to show. It seemed only proper. In response, Glasnae's expression changed, and he saw genuine concern in her eyes. "Healers are sworn to protect their patients' privacy. If you need help, your secret would still be kept."

Her sympathy was unexpected, but strangely gratifying. "I thank you for your promise and I'm touched by your concern, but I assure you that I will recover. It will just take time."

She nodded, looking uncomfortable again. "I should go."

"Thank you for coming." He came out from behind the desk to open the door for her. With his hand on the doorknob he added, "I intended to seek you out eventually, though I'm not sure what I would have said. This was…easier, I think."

"I'm leaving tomorrow to visit my family. When I return, I'd like to put this behind me. I don't expect that we will ever be friends, but I don't want to be enemies either."

He nodded. "I am not your enemy, Glasnae. You are now kae-madri, a daughter of Kaestra. Whether or not I approved of your choice, you are now to be accorded all the deference due to a sister of that order. Besides, whether you believe it or not, I've always respected you."

She looked dubious at first, but then her face softened into a slight smile. She bowed slightly in a common gesture of respect. "Thank you for the compliment. I really must be going now."

"Of course. I won't keep you any longer."

As he opened the door for her, she studied his trembling hand. "I think you would recover more quickly and thoroughly if you ask a healer for help. There's no reason to suffer any more than necessary."

Her continued concern was mildly surprising. "You have a generous nature, Glasnae. Some people in your position would delight in my suffering."

"I don't like to see anyone suffer."

He sighed. "You're still young. I can only hope that time and experience does not blunt your compassion."

Glasnae looked puzzled. "Is compassion only for the young?"

M'Gan decided this would be his only chance to warn her of what might lie ahead. "No, but it is not uncommon for people to grow more cynical and callous as they age. And you are bound to Kaestra now. Your feelings are linked to hers, and she is not always the gentle and benign mother of all. She can also be fierce, even cruel."

Glasnae bristled, as he expected any guardian would. "Kaestra does what is necessary for life to continue."

"Of course. But what is necessary is not always kind. Sometimes harsh, even brutal, measures are needed. Sometimes the individual must be sacrificed for the greater good."

"Are you speaking from personal experience?" There was a slight edge to her voice.

"I'm speaking as someone who has lived far longer than you have. Knowing the power you can wield, I wonder what will happen if you are ever called upon to be the hand of necessity."

"The daughters of Kaestra are not warriors sent out like merlins to fight battles in her name and bring down her enemies, M'Gan. Our purpose is to heal the land and maintain the balance."

She clearly didn't understand. He recognized that this was a lesson she could only learn on her own, and the thought frightened him. "You're right, of course," he replied. "But balance is a delicate thing, and sometimes a diseased limb must be removed to save the tree." He shook his head and took a deep breath. "Enough. Your sisters will instruct you, I'm sure."

He wasn't sure of that at all, but there was nothing else he could do. "I wish you well, Glasnae. Enjoy your visit with your family. When you

279

return, I will greet you gladly as a fellow servant of the gods. Perhaps one day, we will be on better terms."

Glasnae held his gaze for a long moment, as if weighing his words. Then she nodded and left.

M'Gan closed the door behind her and replayed the encounter in his mind, trying to determine if he could have done anything differently. He eventually abandoned the endeavor as futile. He couldn't turn back time. What was done was done.

It is up to Deirdre to teach Glasnae what it means to be kae-madri. And what it means to become kae-raeva.

Chapter 17

Malek held out a slim folder and said flatly, "I'm sorry, Master Tarvis. I can't see any way to avoid the environmental effects of our experiments. If we continue, we will impact the land."

Tarvis took the folder and flipped through the pages inside. Then he searched the younger man's face for traces of uncertainty and found none. The evidence was compelling. What was more, Malek was convinced, and Malek was rarely wrong.

It wasn't entirely unexpected. The connection between the flow of kaema in the ley lines and the health of the land was well known. It was the basis for the considerable influence that the guardians wielded.

Jaron's interference had derailed their more ambitious endeavors. They'd been forced to resume their more limited experiments in the hope of finding an alternative means of achieving their goal. Unfortunately, the environmental disturbances were far more pronounced when they confined their efforts to a smaller area. In addition to attracting unwelcome attention from the Order of Kae-Madri, it suggested that this methodology could seriously damage the land itself.

Tarvis took a deep breath. "There's little point in taking control of the ley lines if we destroy the entire ecosystem in the process. We'll have to find another way."

"I said that we were having a negative effect, Master, not that we were destroying the ecosystem." Malek's tone was impassioned. "I believe that the disturbances are only temporary, and my research proves that the severity of the problem is exacerbated by moving too slowly. By trying to do this piecemeal, we're creating severe localized imbalances. I think we need to resume working on a larger scale."

Tarvis considered his suggestion as he reviewed the information in front of him. After a few minutes, he countered, "We've only managed one truly large-scale attempt, and there was still a noticeable effect to the environment."

"We weren't able to let it run its course. I believe that given a couple of weeks to adjust, the land would recover."

Tarvis considered it. "We can't be sure."

"We need to conduct further tests. If we try again and there's no sign of recovery after a few weeks, we can reverse the spell."

"I wanted to do this gradually, preferably in such a way that no one would notice until it was too late to stop us," Tarvis said as much to himself as to Malek.

"We've already been noticed. And based on my research, I no longer think it's possible to complete this the way you'd hoped we could."

"If we make too bold a move, we risk being caught. We're not ready."

"I agree, but if we work carefully, we *could* be ready in just a few more years. I'm close, Master Tarvis. I just need a little more time to work this out."

Tarvis smiled indulgently. "I didn't realize this was so important to you."

"I may not have been aware of the danger until you pointed it out to me, but I can't help but see it now. Our way of life is at risk, and we need to act."

Tarvis considered how far Malek had come in the past decade. He had every confidence that the adept would eventually succeed, but by devoting so much time and attention to this project, Malek had postponed other matters that were also important. "All right. We'll see what we can come up with. But first, you have some unfinished business that I want you to attend to."

"Unfinished business?"

"When you agreed to join me here, you had every intention of completing your studies and sitting your exams for mastery. You've put that effort on hold long enough. I want you to take the next year to prepare yourself and petition for testing. I'll even accompany you to the Primary Mage Hall for the exams."

Malek's reaction was interesting. His expression revealed a mixture of pride and embarrassment. "Preparing for the exams will take valuable time away from this project."

"Then we will redouble our efforts *after* you achieve the rank of master. You're nearly ready, Malek. I want your status formally recognized before we take over, so that there is no doubt in anyone's mind that you've earned it."

He watched the adept compose himself before replying, "Are you sure?"

"I'm sure, Malek. We'll sit down tomorrow and lay out a training schedule. Once I'm confident that you can pass, we'll contact Lord Jaron and set a date for the exam."

"And when I achieve the rank of master, we'll pick up where we've left off." He gestured meaningfully to the folder Tarvis held.

Tarvis glanced down and scanned the pages again. Putting their project on hold to focus on Malek's bid for mastery would serve another purpose. By the time they resumed their efforts, the effects of their experiments would fade from the land, and hopefully from the minds of those who had been paying attention, particularly the other master mages and the kae-madri. He was confident in his ability to manage the former. The latter might prove more difficult.

"We'll have to be careful. The guardians could be a problem," he mused aloud.

Malek frowned. "It won't be easy to keep them at bay. They are watching Athens closely, and have already approached the governor to offer aid."

"Yet Governor Tharan has refused their help," Tarvis said with a satisfied smile. "It doesn't much matter what they suspect. They cannot defy Tharan, at least not openly. But we should do everything we can to prevent them from looking in our direction. Lady Deirdre is persistent.

We can't be completely sure that she will continue to abide by the governor's wishes if conditions become too severe."

"Is that why you are content to wait?" Malek asked.

"I want you named master," Tarvis said firmly. "But yes, there is an advantage to pausing in our efforts. By next year, there will be no reason for the kae-madri to turn their attention toward Athens."

"But you will continue to cultivate your influence with Tharan?"

"Of course," Tarvis replied smoothly. "I have every confidence that Tharan will be governor of Athens for many years to come, and as long as I have his ear, I will have a measure of control over the workings of the Athenian government. We'll need that control to ease our way when we move forward."

"There are many facets to your plan, Master, and I won't pretend to understand them all. I'm only glad that I can contribute."

"And yours is a most valuable contribution. Never doubt that."

Chapter 18

It was raining outside. It wasn't much of a storm, just a gentle rain that should have been soothing to the nerves, but Aidan was certain that the young man standing before him was anything but soothed.

"I've reached my peak, haven't I?" Kylec wouldn't quite meet his eyes.

"I can't be certain, Ky. You're only twenty-six. Some people continue to develop their powers well into their thirties." It wasn't a lie. It had been known to happen. However, most people born with magical talents gradually increased in strength during childhood, spiked at puberty and reached a plateau shortly thereafter. Kylec had followed the usual pattern thus far, but while it was unlikely that his power would grow significantly at this point, Aidan didn't want him to give up hope.

"So," Kylec responded, "I *might* become a little stronger over the next few years. Let's assume for now that I won't. Am I strong enough?"

Aidan closed his eyes. Kylec and Andris had each petitioned to test for the rank of adept and there was no question in anyone's mind that both would succeed. They were still young, but Jaron had only been a year older than Kylec when he had made the grade of adept, and seven years later he'd achieved the rank of master.

It was the master rank that was actually in question for Kylec. It was customary to gauge a candidate's potential to achieve mastery when they successfully made the rank of adept. Most did not, and it was deemed both cruel and wasteful to allow such individuals to spend years in a fruitless pursuit. It was also wise for those who *did* have the ability to know as soon as possible, so that they would have ample opportunity to make the most of their gifts.

The testing process had two phases: a private evaluation by a master or senior adept, and a formal exam before a panel of masters and adepts.

The second phase was little more than a formality, since no one was sent before the panel who couldn't pass, but it ensured impartiality.

Jaron had already completed Andris's evaluation, which was the easier task. Andris had more than enough power to be master, let alone adept, and his skills had developed impressively. Aidan had the greater challenge in assessing Kylec's abilities. Kylec's power was far from small, and he would easily be among the most powerful of adepts. But Aidan wasn't sure if he was strong enough to become a master.

He sensed Kylec's impatience. The young man didn't like waiting, especially when it came to important matters. Still, he remained quiet and respectful while Aidan pursued his own thoughts. After a few minutes, Aidan opened his eyes and asked, "Will you let me in, Ky? I want to get another look at your power."

Kylec nodded and closed his own eyes. Aidan waited until he was certain that the younger man had lowered his shields, which were the strongest he'd ever encountered and would be a formidable barrier if he ever tried to force his way in. As Aidan entered Kylec's mind, he focused on his purpose. Though the young mage allowed him entry, he wouldn't be pleased if he took the opportunity to pry. There was no fear of wandering into a stray thought. Kylec's mind was carefully ordered, at least when another was permitted inside. Aidan's impression was of a long corridor lined with closed doors. Eventually, he came to one that was open wide. This was the representative location of Kylec's power within the mindscape. He entered and took a long and careful look.

The core of Kylec's power appeared as a shimmering sphere of energy, with delicate tendrils reaching out to absorb ambient kaema. It was not quite as large as that of any master Aidan knew, but there was a richness and intensity to it that he'd only seen in other masters. And there was a strange perfection to Kylec's core of power. Unlike other sorcerers, whose power softly radiated at the edges, giving a fuzzy or soft texture to the image, Kylec held the kaema within him so completely that it seemed to radiate back in upon itself, giving the impression of a perfectly smooth sphere.

He knew that this was the result of Kylec's impressive shielding ability, but he didn't know how the young man did it. Kylec didn't really know either, since he'd formed the initial shield instinctively when he was very young, and while its strength had grown as he had, this particular barrier was now outside of his conscious control.

This too-perfect containment was why he couldn't be sure if Kylec was powerful enough to be a master. As Aidan withdrew, he held his thoughts tightly to himself. When he opened his eyes again, he saw Kylec watching him closely.

The younger man spoke first. "You aren't sure."

"You still can't consciously drop the shields that hold your power?" he asked, not for the first time.

Kylec shook his head. "I've tried, but they're just *there*. They have been for as long as I can remember."

Aidan ran his fingers through his hair. "I'm sorry, I just can't be certain."

"Should I try anyway?"

"When I meet with the panel, I will inform them that you *may* have the potential to be a master. I'll explain that it's a very close thing, which I believe it is. It is entirely up to you what road you choose to pursue, but I don't think that further study will be a waste of your time, even if you don't achieve the master rank.

"You have unique skills, Ky, which could benefit the entire Hall. You'll be welcome to join the faculty, and there are plenty of employment opportunities here if you aren't interested in teaching. Besides, adepts traditionally stay at the Hall where they train for a couple of years to hone their skills."

"I take it that I passed the written exam, then?" Kylec seemed more at ease than he had a moment ago, though Aidan knew that appearances could be deceiving.

"A perfect score, as usual."

The young man smirked. "So, what do you have in mind for the practical part of the test?"

Aidan directed Kylec to perform a series of increasingly difficult spells, which he executed flawlessly. Aidan watched with pride as he manipulated matter and created elegant illusions. Passing solid objects through each other, changing solids to fluids and back again, moving objects from one point to another instantaneously, all were child's play to him.

Kylec could also do what few but masters could: he could safely teleport living things. He had been initially reluctant to experiment, but as his confidence grew, he'd agreed to try. Plants came first, then insects, fish, and finally small mammals. All came through unharmed. Aidan believed that with a few more years of practice, Kylec would be able to transport himself via teleportation. It was one more reason to believe that he had the potential to be a master, because only masters could do that, and most did it rarely.

Aidan brought out a large empty aquarium and asked Kylec to create a small swamp, complete with appropriate wildlife, for use in the science class he taught to the youngest students. He smiled wickedly, remembering the pond that the boys had turned their bedroom into years ago, much to Tamara's consternation.

Of course, *that* had only been an illusion, though he'd had some difficulty convincing Tamara. The spell had been very convincing, fully engaging all the senses, and he doubted that any woman would want a pond in her home, even an illusory one.

Kylec recognized the reference and looked at Aidan with a falsely innocent expression. "Do you want an illusion or the real thing?"

"I've seen you do plenty of illusions. Stretch yourself a bit and give me the real thing. Just make sure whatever plants and animals you bring in are ones I can care for in the classroom."

A few hours later, Aidan sat back and admired the little marshland in a box. There were a dozen distinct species of plants, including three beautiful flowers, a pair of miniature turtles, several different snails, and

288

a scaleless mahori snake—a lovely native creature that resembled Terran snakes only in its sinewy structure and lack of limbs. The frill that ran along either side of its body undulated as the creature moved, and the rich coral color made it look like a living jewel when it curled up to sleep.

There was no doubt in Aidan's mind that the young man could not only pass the test for adept, but that given a few more years of study and practice, he could pass the standard master's test as well. The question was whether or not the other masters would disregard Kylec's lack of power and accept him based on the results he achieved. His understanding of kaema and the ways it could be manipulated allowed him to craft spells that needed far less power than was usually required.

Sadly, Aidan knew that at least a few of the masters would resist his admission to their ranks even if he could do everything they could. For some, power mattered more than skill. At least it would be a few more years before Kylec was likely to petition for mastery. There was no need to borrow tomorrow's trouble today.

**

Storm clouds loomed in the distance, but for the moment it was sunny and warm, and Tarvis could tell by the way the young man looked out the window that Kylec would rather be outside enjoying the nice weather while it lasted.

He'd requested assistance in evaluating some textbooks as a pretense to spend the afternoon with this particular adept. He had expected the young man to be flattered, but instead, he had the distinct impression that Kylec was merely being polite and had little interest in currying favor.

Tarvis had arranged to spend some time with Andris a few days earlier, and his disappointment had been sharp. Andris was utterly loyal to Jaron, and would never question the Archmage, much less turn against him. Tarvis had been careful not to tip his hand, but the visit had left him uneasy that Andris might have sensed his true intentions. The young man was extraordinarily gifted, even more so than the rumors had led him to believe.

Kylec, on the other hand, was more of a mystery. He was very self-contained, and Tarvis found him difficult to read. He showed great respect for Jaron but did not seem awed by him or any of the masters. He behaved appropriately deferential toward Tarvis but was more familiar with many of the other masters, including Jaron, suggesting that he had developed friendships that transcended rank.

"Most of the texts here are acceptable," Kylec said, drawing Tarvis out of his musings, "but I wouldn't recommend these." He held up three of the books, all produced by the same publisher.

"Are they deficient?" Tarvis feigned more interest than he felt.

"They're poorly written," Kylec responded. "The information is accurate, but the language is confusing and convoluted. They're supposedly geared toward beginners, but the explanations are anything but clear. Books like these hinder the learning process rather than help it along."

Tarvis raised an eyebrow, impressed by the insightful comment. "Lord Jaron told me that you're teaching several of the introductory classes here, and I'd hoped that you would have some good advice. I see that I was right. That publisher has a good reputation. I would not have expected their products to be so poor."

"It depends on your perspective, I suppose," Kylec replied. "Some teachers believe that clear explanations make students lazy. I don't agree. There's no reason to make lessons more difficult than they need to be. I've found that the more a student learns, the more he or she wants to learn."

"You must have learned a great deal then," Tarvis said with a charming smile. "Since you've decided to continue your own studies here while teaching, you must have considerable interest in furthering your knowledge."

"I plan to test for mastery in a few more years. I need to prepare if I want to succeed."

Tarvis frowned slightly. "Yes, it's a difficult test, and not one that everyone can pass. It takes great power and great skill, and a fair amount of pure nerve. Malek has been on edge since we arrived. I have every confidence in him, but it will be a great relief tomorrow afternoon when it's behind him."

"He must be glad to have his mentor here to cheer him on."

"It's been too long since my last visit. I must confess that I came as much for my own pleasure as I did to reassure Malek, though I'm happy to offer what support I can. I remember my own test as if it were yesterday. I was just as nervous as Malek is now. Fortunately, I was able to meet the standards set by my judges, and I trust that he will be able to do the same."

Kylec looked embarrassed and began stacking the books. "That may not be the case for me. Aidan believes that I already possess the skill, but I may not meet the minimum requirements for power. It'll be a close thing."

"And you believe that if you sufficiently impress the other masters that they may be more lenient with regards to pure strength?" Tarvis asked neutrally.

"Something like that," Kylec admitted. "But I'm also hoping that my power will increase. Aidan told me that some people continue to gain strength into their thirties."

Tarvis did not respond right away. Here was the opening he needed into Kylec's psyche. The young man had great potential, but that potential might be overlooked. Though Tarvis was certain that Jaron, Aidan, and the other masters Kylec had befriended would welcome the young man into their ranks, they hardly comprised a majority. Under different circumstances, he would also be loath to grant anyone the rank of master who did not meet the requirements in every respect.

However, these circumstances were unique, as was the young adept currently sorting books on the table in front of him. By all accounts, his intellect was astounding. Such a mind could solve problems no other could. It was even possible that Kylec would be able to find a solution to the problem that continued to challenge Malek. Still, he would have to tread carefully. Kylec was nothing if not observant, and Tarvis suspected that beneath that quiet nature the younger man was as devious and insightful as he was.

"It must be frustrating for you," Tarvis said with a hint of sympathy. Nothing too strong, nothing obvious. "It takes a great deal of time and energy to prepare for mastery. Most who follow that path do so with the conviction that they stand a good chance of achieving their goal. That you have such doubts so early on yet continue to persevere is admirable."

"Some would say it's foolish." There was a trace of bitterness in the boy's voice. "I'm also a journeyman with the local branch of the Engineers Guild. As soon as the paperwork has been completed, I'll be formally recognized in that rank by the Druidic College in New Avalon. I could pursue engineering as a career, but I'm not ready to give up on mastery in magecraft yet."

"Pursuing a goal that matters to you is never foolish," Tarvis said. He was beginning to like this young adept. "But it is good to have options."

He started loading the textbooks that Kylec had approved into a trunk as he continued. "I wish I could say that most of the master mages would recognize your talent and accept you as one of us, but I can't. *I* would give you a fair chance and would consider all of your abilities when making my decision, but many of the masters are set in their ways. I don't think that you can expect all of them to be open-minded."

"I know." Kylec sounded sober, but not defeated. "Lord Jaron has had a difficult time convincing the other masters that his new policies will benefit the Hall. Every change seems to be followed by complaints."

"What do you think of his changes?" Tarvis asked conversationally.

"I think we're going in the right direction, but time will tell. Of course, I'm here partly because of Lord Jaron's willingness to take chances, so my opinion may be biased."

"An honest answer!" Tarvis declared. "I admit that I have my own reservations, but as you said, time will tell."

"Is that why you haven't instituted the new policies in your own Hall yet?"

Tarvis had not expected such a direct question, or that Kylec would know anything about his own school. Fortunately, he excelled at thinking on his feet, and knew enough to wrap his lies around a core of truth.

"It's one of the reasons," he said after a pause that he hoped seemed thoughtful rather than suspicious. "But the size of my school has been the deciding factor. We don't have the faculty and resources that you have here. Everything is geared toward the standard apprenticeship and journeyman program. Paying students would expect a greater degree of flexibility and diversity in their studies, which we can't provide without disrupting the routine for the apprentices. I send some of our more exceptional students here since I am unable to offer them the full range of opportunities that the Primary Hall can. It's the same with those students requiring extra instruction in certain areas. We simply can't accommodate special needs."

He shook his head as if regretting a sad truth. "I must also admit that at my age, it is one thing to be open to an idea in concept, but quite another to put those ideas into practice."

Kylec's expression turned speculative, and Tarvis mentally verified that there were no weaknesses in his psychic shielding that might be exploited. Satisfied that the young man would not be able to read his thoughts, he relaxed somewhat, but the quality of the adept's attention was unnerving. After a long pause, Kylec said quietly, "I don't think you're giving yourself enough credit. I think you could meet just about any challenge if you set your mind to it."

"That's kind of you to say," Tarvis replied uncertainly.

"I tend to speak my mind," Kylec countered.

They finished packing the rest of the books with little conversation. Tarvis was caught up in his thoughts, and the young adept didn't intrude. When Kylec offered to return the unwanted books to the store for him, he gladly accepted and dismissed him.

He wanted to enlist him on the spot, but he resisted the temptation. Kylec might not be pleased with the possibility of failure in his bid for mastery, but that wasn't enough to turn him against the institution that had trained him. That might change when the moment of truth came, but even then, his friendships at the Hall might make him hesitate.

Tarvis also had some misgivings about the boy's perceptiveness. It was almost as if Kylec *knew* him in ways he shouldn't have been able to. He didn't miss much, that was certain, and Tarvis needed to know more about the depth of the young man's loyalties before he approached him. He already suspected that the lad knew too much.

There was time. He would keep in touch with Kylec and work toward winning his trust. It wouldn't be easy, but it could be done. It would help if he could drive a wedge between Kylec and Andris, but trying to interfere in that relationship would likely backfire. The two young men were like brothers in every sense. Of course, quarrels happened, even between the best of friends, and some disagreements could turn ugly. History was full of examples. But whatever triggered such a rift could not come from him, at least not directly.

He had to remain patient. Tomorrow, Malek would face the mastery exam, and Tarvis had no doubt he would triumph. Then it would be time to bring this visit to an end. They would take their time returning to their own school; the journey would double as the fortnight new masters traditionally spent with their mentors to celebrate and adjust to their new status. Tarvis wanted to use that time to reinforce his relationship with Malek, so that the younger man would continue to respect and trust him.

He wondered if he might establish a similar relationship with Kylec someday. He was impressed by the boy's skill and insight, and he found him intriguing.

Though his interest was piqued, Tarvis knew that he couldn't afford to get ahead of himself. Now was not the time for foolish risks. It was too soon to predict how his plans would unfold, but, as Kylec had said, time would tell.

Chapter 19

1481 AHS

Responding to her mother's mental summons, Brianna hurried to the barn through the covered hallway just in time to see a bedraggled trio hurry inside amid a fierce rush of snow. A couple of men quickly shut the large wooden door against the weather, but not before Brianna caught the edge of the chill and shivered.

Her mother, Nessa, waved her over as soon as she saw her and gestured at the new arrivals. "Look at this pathetic lot!"

The grooms immediately took charge of Darcy, cooing to the pretty chestnut mare as they led her to a warm stall. Her younger brother Tomas was on his knees petting and fussing over the dog, whose thick, dark fur sported so many balls of snow and ice that it was a wonder he could walk. Brianna knew both animals well, but the woman who was with them looked so unlike herself that she barely recognized her.

"We've had a rough time of it, Nessa," the woman, not much older than Brianna, said ruefully.

"I should say so," Nessa replied. "What did you do? Fall in a lake?"

"Something like that," came the embarrassed reply. "I'm not used to traveling in the winter. There was a partially frozen stream hidden under the snow, and I fell in. Darcy and Galen helped me get out before I froze to death."

Nessa's manner softened as she joined them. "Come on, Glasnae. Let's get you all taken care of."

"Could you have a tub of warm water brought to the barn?" Glasnae asked, a little breathless, "I want to clean the snow and ice from Galen's fur. He can stay out here until he's dry."

Brianna snorted out a laugh as Nessa snapped back, "I will do no such thing! You're family. Tomas will take Galen to one of the small bathing rooms and give him a proper bath, and he can dry off beside the hearth. Meanwhile, Brianna will see to it that you have a bath as well."

Glasnae opened her mouth to protest but stopped herself before she said anything. Brianna sympathized. Her parents ran the Traveler's Haven with hospitality, kindness, and an iron will. Nessa treated every guest as a favorite child, coddling and chastising as she saw fit.

She gestured to Glasnae, guiding her to the hallway that led from the barn to the bathing houses.

"Do you think Tomas will mind giving Galen a bath?" Glasnae asked as she followed her.

"You are tired!" Brianna laughed. "Didn't you see his face? Tomas is ecstatic! He loves dogs, and Galen is an absolute favorite."

Brianna brought her to one of the larger bathing rooms. "Mother will have a room made up for you and make sure you get some supper."

Glasnae groaned as she helped her remove her cold, wet clothing, and pile it in a basket near the door. The large sunken tub in the center of room was already filled with steaming water, and Brianna told her to sit and soak for a while.

"How were you able to prepare a bath so quickly?" Glasnae asked.

"Good timing," Brianna replied with a grin. "The gentleman who ordered the bath will only need to wait a few more minutes."

Glasnae looked guilty. "That doesn't seem fair."

"He's been warm and dry all evening, enjoying the common room. I'm sure he won't mind the minor inconvenience."

Brianna waited until Glasnae had settled herself into the bath before she ducked out with the basket of clothes. "I'll be back in a few minutes."

Having noticed quite a few scrapes and bruises as Glasnae disrobed, she paused for a quick word with her mother on her way to the laundry rooms. "I think we should see if there's a healer available for Glasnae."

"Anything serious?" Nessa's concern was sharp.

She shook her head. "Just bumps and bruises, and likely a few strained muscles."

Nessa nodded. "I'll make arrangements for tomorrow morning. A hot meal and a good night's rest will hold her till then. Besides, timing like this happens so rarely. I trust you've not spoiled the surprise?"

"Of course not! I want to see the reunion as much as you do."

Then her mother looked at the basket. "The rest of her clothing is already at the laundry. Do you have something you can lend her for the night?"

"I'm sure I can find something. We're not that far off in size."

"That's my kindhearted girl."

Brianna smiled at the warmth and pride in her mother's voice.

"Consider Glasnae your only charge for the rest of the night," Nessa said. "Once you've got her settled, get some rest yourself."

By the time Brianna slipped back to the bathing room where she'd left Glasnae, the young guardian was close to nodding off in the tub. She set down the basket of clean clothes and toiletries and then approached her with a sponge and bar of soap balanced in one hand, and a hairbrush in the other.

"Thank you, Brianna," Glasnae said with a faint smile. "I guess I'll be needing those."

"Mom said that everything you'd brought with you was soaked through, so I thought I'd lend you a few basic essentials."

"Here," she continued, handing Glasnae the sponge and soap. "You hold on to those while I see if I can get some of these tangles out of your hair."

Glasnae's voice was rough with fatigue. "I think I can manage on my own."

"You look like you've been through a battle, and I'm guessing your arms are sore enough without having to do another battle with a hairbrush. Don't worry," she added soothingly, "I'm very gentle."

She carefully worked the brush through the wet and matted hair and then helped her finish bathing. While Glasnae dried herself and donned the long-sleeved pajamas, soft house slippers and dark blue robe she'd brought her, Brianna drained the tub and tidied up the room.

Glasnae sighed gustily. "I think I could sleep for three days, I'm so tired."

"I don't think Mom will let you go to bed without a meal in you," Brianna said seriously. "I'm sure she's whipping something up for you and Galen in the kitchen as we speak."

"Your night-hearth stew has always been more than enough for me and Galen," Glasnae answered earnestly. "It's the best I've ever had, and I've been to quite a few inns and rest houses."

"But the Traveler's Haven is your favorite," Brianna added with a mischievous smile.

"No question about that. You mother was right, you know. I do feel like family here."

"Well then, let your little sister lead you to supper. Tomas should have Galen washed up by now. They'll probably be in the common room waiting for you."

Glasnae frowned at her attire. "I don't think this would be appropriate for the common room."

"Why not? In the summer, many of the guests come to the table half-naked. You're perfectly decent, so come on."

Glasnae laughed lightly as Brianna led the way to the common room along the enclosed walkways. In the warmer seasons, the passages were open to the air on both sides to allow breezes to blow through, but now they were long windowless hallways, illuminated by lightstones spaced along the walls.

"The floors are warmer than I remember," Glasnae commented.

"Dad will be happy you noticed. He installed a new heating system beneath the floors this summer."

"It's wonderful."

They arrived at the main entrance foyer of the Haven, and Brianna smiled with amusement at the young man stationed at the front desk. He was new to the establishment, and his bored, almost sleepy expression made it clear that he didn't find the late-night shift particularly exciting. Since they'd entered through one of the smaller side doors, he didn't notice them until they were only a pace away from the desk, at which point he jumped back with a startled yelp.

"Sorry about that, Derek." Her tone was more amused than contrite.

He grinned. "I suppose I deserved that," he admitted, "and I'd rather have you sneak up on me than your mother. No offense, of course."

"Of course," she said as solemnly as she could manage. Behind her Glasnae laughed.

"This is Kae-Madri Glasnae Maylan," Brianna introduced the guardian. "Kae-Madri Glasnae, this is Derek Holmes, one of our newer employees."

They exchanged greetings, and Derek gestured to the common room door. "Nessa is setting out dinner for Kae-Madri Glasnae near the west hearth."

Brianna nodded her acknowledgement and led Glasnae inside.

The common room was a large space, with massive fireplaces at each end, and a bar set on one side running the full length of the room. An assortment of wooden benches, chairs, and low cushions were clustered around the hearths, and several wooden tables designed to accommodate parties of varying sizes were arranged at the center of the room.

Brianna guided the other woman toward the hearth on the left where a small table had been moved close to the sitting area, set for two. Glasnae looked at her in confusion over the extra place setting, but before she could say anything, she was swept up into a fierce hug, and Brianna laughed out loud.

"Riahn!" Glasnae exclaimed when the young man set her down. "What are you doing here?"

Riahn grinned broadly and winked at Brianna, clear blue eyes twinkling merrily. "Nessa opened her arms to this weary traveler barely an hour before you dragged yourself across her threshold. I was heading back to Maliae Keep from my latest post when the weather turned vile. I thought it made more sense to wait it out."

"Did you know about this?" Glasnae whirled on her.

"A nice surprise, don't you think?"

"A wonderful surprise!" She suddenly looked wide awake.

"I'll leave you in your brother's capable hands, then."

Before she could leave, Glasnae pulled her into a quick embrace. "Thank you," she said softly but fervently.

"You're welcome."

***

Riahn pulled out a chair for his sister, and she gratefully sat down.

"You're heading to the Keep?" Glasnae asked brightly as a server brought over a basket of bread and a crock of butter.

Riahn reached for a roll and gave her a quizzical look. "I thought you must be on your way there, too."

She looked baffled. "Why would you think that?"

"Didn't you get Father's message?"

She shook her head. "I've been roaming much of southwestern Tarya since just after the Turn of the Year. As a rule, only letters marked urgent are forwarded to guardians in the field."

"Why all the travel at this time of year?" Riahn asked around a mouthful of bread, just as the server returned with bowls of stew and mugs of hot tea. Glasnae laughed lightly when the girl rolled her eyes in his direction, and he flushed in response.

When they were alone again, she answered his question, "I've been addressing environmental disturbances and restoring imbalanced ley lines."

"What kind of imbalances occur in the winter?" The situation sounded serious.

"Imbalances can occur any time of year," she countered, but then added, "although I'll admit that we're rarely summoned in the depth of winter, except perhaps in the southernmost provinces. People tend to notice these things more readily during the growing season.

"But in this case, some of the ley lines have been weakened, almost as if the kaema were being drained. It causes localized imbalances that manifest in strange ways: unusual storms, isolated areas where spring arrives months too soon, evergreen trees dying for no apparent reason…" She trailed off and took a sip of tea. "Kaema is the life's blood of Kaestra. When there is a disturbance in its flow, the natural cycles get thrown off-kilter and we are summoned to deal with it."

"What could cause something like that?" Riahn wondered aloud, not really expecting an answer.

"I don't know," Glasnae replied slowly. "The First Guardian has been studying the problem since it began several years ago, but the cause remains elusive. We have more questions than answers."

Riahn sensed that she was holding something back, but he understood that Glasnae belonged to a religious order and was not necessarily at liberty to share everything with him. He trusted that she would tell him anything he really needed to know.

There were still aspects of his sister's new position that were a mystery to him, so he decided to ask a few questions. "If the ley lines themselves are imbalanced, how can you correct it?"

"I use my link to Kaestra to draw power from the heart of the planet and direct it to restore the flow within local ley lines."

"Really?" She made it sound like a simple, commonplace thing, but he knew it was far from it.

"You sound surprised."

"It sounds…difficult."

She shrugged. "The stronger her link, the more kaema a guardian can channel to replenish the ley lines. That's why only the most powerful of us have been sent out on these missions."

"You've found a good use for all that power after all, then."

Her smile lit up her face. "Yes."

There was so much happiness in that single word, it was infectious, and Riahn smiled in response. Then they fell into a companionable silence, enjoying the delicious stew.

When a yawning, but happy-looking Tomas brought Galen in, Riahn immediately called them over, delighted to see the dog. "What a beauty you are, Galen boy." He laughed as the large dog enthusiastically licked his face, tail wagging fiercely.

Tomas gave him a hard look, and then turned to Glasnae. A shadow of concern crossed the boy's face and he announced loudly, "Mom said Galen could sleep with me tonight…as long as it's okay with you, Kae-Madri Glasnae." His expression stated clearly that there would be tears if she didn't say it was okay.

Riahn watched his sister struggle to keep a straight face. "I think that's a grand idea," she replied solemnly. "And you did an excellent job bathing him. Thank you very much."

Little Tomas beamed. "It was no trouble! I'll give Galen a bath anytime you want." Another yawn. "I think we should go to bed. It's getting late. Don't worry, I already fed Galen while he was drying off."

"Then you two have a good night, and I'll see you in the morning." Glasnae gave both dog and child a light pat on the head.

Riahn ruffled Galen's fur one last time and added, "Okay, Galen-boy, you go with Tomas now. Be a good guard dog. Good night."

Galen woofed softly once and obediently followed Tomas out of the room.

Riahn watched them leave, dimly aware that his sister had focused her attention on him. "I think you need a dog," she said.

"I wouldn't refuse one," he said more quickly than he intended.

They chatted lightly as they finished their meal, catching up on one another's lives and swapping amusing stories. But by the time the server came to clear away the dishes, Riahn's thoughts circled back to the circumstances that had brought them to the Haven.

"You never received Father's message…" he began uncertainly.

"No. I assume it was nothing urgent, or you would have told me so right away."

He weighed his words with care. "Father wants to call for an election to select his heir."

"Is he well?" There was sharp concern in her voice.

"He's healthy and strong, only tired of ruling all alone. He wants to step down, but not immediately. An elected heir will provide him with assistance as well as continuity for when he does retire."

"When does he want to hold elections?"

"According to the letter I received, sometime next year. But he's having preliminary meetings over the next few months to meet potential candidates."

"I see."

He didn't think she did. "Can you come with me to Maliae Keep?"

Glasnae bit her lip, a childhood habit that made her look younger to Riahn's eyes. "I hadn't planned on it."

"But Father *did* plan on you coming. He sent—"

She cut him off. "Letters that I never received."

"Glas, please come. You're a priestess. Wouldn't you agree that Fate arranged for us to meet like this?"

"Coincidence."

"You believe in coincidence? Even before you went to Avrin, you always said that things happened for a reason. The kaesana taught you that."

"Sometimes we outgrow the beliefs of our childhood."

"And sometimes we deliberately deceive ourselves when faced with a difficult situation."

Glasnae stared at the table. "I don't want to travel anywhere until after the Midwinter festival," she said at last. "I'd hoped to be back in Avrin by then, but I'm in no condition to travel right now, and I want to celebrate the high day with friends, not spend it on the road."

"That's fair enough. I'd like to take a few days to rest myself." It would give him more time to wear down her objections.

She glared at him. "If I do go with you to Maliae Keep, you should know that I will be informing Father that I will not be a candidate for succession."

I guess she understands after all, Riahn thought.

"It's your decision to make," he said, unable to keep the disappointment out of his voice.

They watched each other in silence for what seemed like an eternity. Glasnae finally said, "I have responsibilities that would conflict with the position. You know that."

"I do," Riahn answered with reluctant acceptance. "But there's no law forbidding priestesses from serving as elected officials."

"It's different for kae-madri, Riahn. I have to put Kaestra first."

"I think that the people of Maliae would be content to be ruled by a guardian, even knowing that their needs would come second in your priorities." He countered. "There are many people who see you as Mother's true successor. The people of Maliae have always preferred to be ruled by women, and they expected Mother to become governor, not Father."

Glasnae frowned. "The people voted Father into office, and they've been happy with his rule. He's a good governor, and…"

She trailed off, but the unspoken *you would be too* hung in the air between them.

Riahn said nothing. He'd always hated politics, but he was prepared to accept the position of governor if it seemed to be best for his people.

"Riahn." Glasnae reached across the table and took his hand in hers. "I'm sorry, but I can't become a candidate. Priests and priestesses may sometimes serve as elected officials, but guardians do not."

"I understand, Glas," he said gruffly.

She looked stricken. He didn't want to admit it, but in a strange way her discomfort made him feel better. "There must be other acceptable candidates," she suggested, "The governorship has been in our family for eight generations. Maybe that's enough. If there are other people presenting themselves for consideration who are worthy of the task, perhaps you don't have to list your name either."

Riahn forced himself to meet her eyes. He tried to smile but couldn't quite manage it. "As far as I know, there are at least two other people under consideration who would be suited for the job, but that doesn't mean I can walk away. At least one of us has to be among the candidates."

"Why? To satisfy some outdated tradition?"

"For the sake of our people, who value that tradition."

"You don't want to lead." It sounded like an accusation. "Is tradition a good enough reason for you to give up your freedom?"

"Maybe it is," he said slowly. "It's a question of duty. If the people of Maliae want me as their next governor, I will bow to their will."

She looked at him incredulously. "You've always felt the call of duty more strongly than I have, but I didn't realize how much you were prepared to sacrifice."

"You're as bound by your commitments as I am, you just chose different ones."

"I gave up nothing that I value."

"You gave up the bulk of your power to become kae-madri."

"And I don't miss it!" she exclaimed, then glanced sheepishly at the other people in the room who until that point had been politely ignoring their little drama.

"You've made your choice, Glas. I have to make mine."

Glasnae's reply was gentle. "I can't stay in Maliae indefinitely. I have other responsibilities."

"As do I," Riahn responded swiftly. "And I'm not suggesting that either of us settle in for the duration, but I think it would be wise to stay a week or two. I've been granted six weeks of leave, but I don't plan to spend all my time at the Keep. I was thinking I'd tour the province and if you're willing to join me, I'd enjoy your company. I realize that you have your own schedule to keep, but I'd be happy for any time you can spare."

Glasnae sighed. "I'll go with you, but I'm not making any promises about how long I can stay. I'll contact Deirdre in the morning and inform her of my intentions. As long as she has no need of my immediate service, I'll leave with you after the holiday celebrations are over."

"Thank you, little sister. I appreciate this."

"I'm a bit old for you to be calling me 'little sister,' don't you think?" Her voice was lighthearted, but she looked like she was holding back tears.

"You'll always be my little sister." He was barely holding his emotions in check. "Always."

Glasnae stood up and excused herself. He rose as well and hugged her close, wishing her a goodnight.

"Will you meet me for breakfast tomorrow?" he asked.

"Of course." She squeezed his hand one last time and retreated.

Hours later, Riahn sat before the hearth, snuggled into an overstuffed chair with his feet resting comfortably on a hassock and a glass of brandy in his hand. He tried to relax, but he couldn't. He was too upset, and angrier than he wanted to admit. The anger only added to his distress, because he didn't know *why* he was angry. He wasn't short-tempered by nature. He was generally a level-headed and rational person, but right now, he didn't feel at all rational.

He took another sip of brandy, rolling it on his tongue. He'd been nursing the drink for nearly an hour as he watched the other patrons trickle out of the common room, heading for their beds. Now the room was nearly deserted. A few older men, traders by the way they were dressed, huddled around a nearby table, talking about the upcoming festival. There was also a woman sitting alone near the fire, knitting, who had the resigned look of a chronic insomniac. Riahn envied her perseverance.

He'd imagined that Glasnae would succeed their father and that he might serve as one of her stewards. He now understood that wasn't possible. She had a valid point: as a guardian, it wasn't appropriate for her to govern a province. He supposed he'd always known that on some level. He'd just been unwilling to accept it.

Without Glasnae among the candidates, it was likely that he would be elected.

"How I hate politics," Riahn muttered under his breath.

The politics were especially ugly at the moment. The provincial governors were in unfamiliar territory as they tried to address problems, both real and imagined, that no one had dealt with in centuries. Crime rates were up, economies were weak, and according to his sister, there were new natural disasters looming. Something was very wrong in Tarya, and it was not a good time to be a leader.

The bar was closed, the tables cleared, and only a single server remained to see to the guests, a young man sitting comfortably in a chair, distinguished from the patrons only by the blue and gray uniform he wore. Riahn drained his glass and went to set it on the bar, but the server rose and took it from him before he had the chance, asking if he wanted anything else.

"No," Riahn answered wearily, "I'll think I'll go up to bed."

"Pleasant dreams, sir," the lad answered brightly. Riahn decided that he must be a night-owl by nature. Few people could be so cheerful after midnight. As he left the common room, with all its warmth and cheer, he wondered if he wasn't blowing things out of proportion. Things might not be as bad as he believed. He hoped that was the case.

***

Linia hugged herself for warmth as she stepped out onto the open-air terrace and into the bite of the wind. The elegant space on the topmost floor of the Keep was frequently used for formal gatherings during the warmer months, but tonight, there was only one other person there besides herself.

Glasnae stood at the railing, gazing up toward the sky. At first, Linia didn't think that the girl was aware of her presence, but Glasnae glanced back over her shoulder briefly before resuming her study of the heavens.

"Our ancestors came from out there somewhere," she said without turning her head again. "One of those points of light might be Earth."

Linia wavered between concern and annoyance. "I doubt it," she said as neutrally as she could. "As I recall, the first settlers were thrown so far off course that they couldn't determine where Earth was. If we could see it from here, surely they would have been able to find their way back there."

"Maybe." Glasnae's voice was distant, as if her thoughts were as far away as the stars.

Linia sighed, growing tired of this game. "I knew you would say no."

Glasnae spun around and glared at her. "It was the right thing to do."

"I never said otherwise."

When Glasnae didn't respond, Linia stated the obvious. "You must be freezing. Come inside where it's warm."

Glasnae hesitated for a moment, but then nodded and followed her inside. Linia led her to a small alcove used to store coats and cloaks during receptions. There were a few folding chairs leaning against one wall, and she handed one to her granddaughter before unfolding another for herself and sitting down.

"You chose a good place to hide," Linia began. "My choice may not be as picturesque, but it's private, and has the advantage of being warm."

"It wasn't that good a hiding place if you found me," Glasnae pointed out.

"I know you," Linia said as gently as she could. "This wasn't the first place I looked but it wasn't too far down the list."

"Why *did* you look for me?"

"Your father isn't pleased with your refusal to become a candidate for governor."

"I didn't expect him to be."

The words were delivered with more bitterness than she was accustomed to hearing from her granddaughter, and she chose her next words with care. "You are not your mother, Glasnae. Your father needs to accept that."

Glasnae just stared at her, silent. After a long pause, Linia added, "Mariah loved you, and I'm sure that she would have been happy to see the young woman you've become. Your father is proud of you as well, but he's making the mistake of seeing you as Mariah's daughter rather than as your own person. He's struggled with this ever since your mother died."

"I don't want to hurt him, but I can't be governor of Maliae. I'm a guardian now, and that changes everything. Hopefully, Father will come to understand that."

"In time, he will." Linia said very quietly. "He's been a good governor, but it was never a position he planned to hold. And lately, there have been difficulties that anyone would be hard-pressed to cope with. Electing a successor isn't just about preparing for the future. It's about selecting a suitable person to help right now. While your father is training the governor elect, Maliae will have two elected leaders to care for the province."

Glasnae nearly shouted, "I understand that! What I don't understand is why Father thinks that person has to be me."

Linia narrowed her eyes at the girl's outburst. The gesture wasn't lost on Glasnae.

"I'm sorry," she said, her tone appropriately apologetic. "But I'm frustrated."

"You should talk to him. The other candidates will have left by now and he should still be in his study." She stood up, ready to leave.

Glasnae did not rise with her. Instead, she looked at the floor and said, "I don't know what more I can say."

Linia took hold of her chin and forced her to look up. The girl met her eyes reluctantly. "Tell him the truth, Glasnae. Tell him the *whole* truth."

When the meaning of her words sank in, Glasnae's eyes went wide, and she swallowed hard. "You can't possibly think that sharing Mother's secret will make any difference."

"It makes all the difference in the world!" Linia insisted. "Mariah knew she was unlikely to live long enough to become governor. She must have realized that your father would be considered as her replacement, which means she thought that he was the best choice for Maliae. He believes that he's merely been holding a place that is rightfully yours as Mariah's daughter. He needs to know that isn't the case. Maybe then he can think more clearly about the future."

The girl nodded after a moment, clearly holding back tears.

"Good night, Glasnae," Linia said before she walked away.

"Good night, Grandmother." The response floated up behind her and she didn't turn around. She didn't want Glasnae to see the tears in her own eyes.

***

"Has she gone?" Larin asked as he stared out the window, squinting against the early afternoon sunshine. His head ached. His heart ached.

"She left about an hour ago," Riahn answered.

"Was she...all right?"

"As well as can be expected. She didn't want to leave this way, but Deirdre's summons was urgent." Riahn paused and then added, "It does prove her point."

"I know."

The silence stretched. When Glasnae refused to be included as a candidate, he'd been angry. He wished he was still angry. The anger had been easy to deal with. The pain that had taken its place was not.

"She must have had a good reason for not telling us about Mother until now," Riahn offered.

They'd both been shaken by the secret Glasnae had divulged. But while Riahn believed that she'd always intended to tell them eventually, Larin wasn't so sure. He suspected that the only reason she'd shared the information now was to bolster her position. Her words still echoed inside his head:

I'm not my mother. She chose to leave New Avalon before she vowed herself to the Seers Order. She chose you, Father, not just to be her husband, but to be the leader of Maliae. I also made a choice: I became a guardian, and there's no undoing that decision. I can't leave the order. It simply isn't possible. And I cannot be both kae-madri and governor of Maliae—that, too, isn't possible.

Larin took a deep breath and turned toward Riahn. "You realize what this means, son?"

"Yes," Riahn said with an air of resignation. "I will most likely be elected the next governor of Maliae."

Larin said nothing. He clapped his hand on his son's shoulder and squeezed for a moment. He loved both his children, and though he'd always expected Glasnae to succeed him, he knew that Riahn would make a superb governor.

He hoped that Glasnae wasn't too upset. She'd been called away very suddenly, and though they'd parted on good terms, there was still hurt on both sides. He knew that time would ease the hurt. He only hoped that it wouldn't take too long.

Chapter 20

The meeting hadn't gone as well as Tarvis had hoped. He appreciated that the others had their reservations, but if they didn't make a decisive move soon, they would be better off abandoning the project altogether. Fortunately, as reluctant as everyone was to take chances, he knew they were just as reluctant to give up. What they were doing was not only right, but imperative. Malek's new plan had its drawbacks, but the potential for success made the risks worthwhile. He trusted that in time the others would see this.

Karimah didn't leave with the rest. Instead, she poured herself a glass of wine and curled up on one end of the sofa. Her expression and posture were just short of provocative, and he had no doubt that she had posed herself with deliberate care. With well over seventy years behind her, she was entering middle age, but time had been kind to her. She remained beautiful and possessed an allure that transcended the physical. Being with her made him feel young.

They'd long since given up any pretense that their relationship was a secret, and though she still maintained an apartment of her own on campus, Karimah rarely spent the night there. There was now a second dresser in his bedroom, and a portion of his closet had been set aside for her use. He'd even turned one of the smaller guest rooms into an office for her convenience.

The arrangement was unexpectedly agreeable. She was much more than a lover and companion; she was a partner in the truest sense, listening to his ideas and acting as devil's advocate when needed. It was a role she played remarkably well.

He regarded her for a moment, and she smiled at him over her glass, her eyes saying all too plainly that she knew the direction of his thoughts.

He rose to the bait. "So, what do you think of Malek's newest proposal?"

"It's far more daring than anything we've attempted so far."

"Too daring?"

She shrugged. "As you so aptly pointed out, our overly cautious maneuvers are getting us nowhere. We're at a crossroads."

"You know that I will do everything I can to minimize the risk to us."

"Minimizing the risk isn't the same as eliminating it."

He frowned at her. "Since when did you become a coward?"

"I'm not. I just want to make certain that you're seeing the situation clearly. Since he resumed his experiments, Malek has been careful to avoid any disruption to the ley lines that would draw Jaron's notice."

"But we *have* attracted the attention of the guardians."

"Jaron poses a far greater threat than the kae-madri."

"I'm not so sure. The guardians wield a fair amount of power, both magically and politically. Right now, we have them chasing shadows, but Deirdre has become increasingly aggressive in her investigations."

"Yet Tharan continues to hold her at bay," Karimah reminded him.

"Which further draws her attention to Athens, and potentially to us."

"He's acting at your direction, Tarvis. Would you rather he invited the kae-madri here?"

"No. I don't need those women exploring my domain. I was merely pointing out that we cannot expect to elude them forever."

"If we follow through with Malek's new proposal, we'll have Jaron *and* the kae-madri to contend with."

"If we succeed, that will hardly matter. We will have control of a sufficiently large piece of territory to protect ourselves and our interests while we expand our sphere of influence."

"And if we fail?" she prompted.

He took a deep breath and walked to the window. He kept his back to her, gazing into the neatly landscaped yard. "I won't pretend that failure isn't a possibility. Even Malek has his doubts. But I've reviewed his calculations, and I concur with his conclusions. If we create a large enough construct along a primary ley line where a minor line crosses it, we should be able to siphon off sufficient power to drain all the ley lines in the region in a matter of days. We will be able to access kaema through the stone, but no other sorcerer in the area will be able to draw in any power at all. We'll effectively be in control."

"Let's say that you're right and Malek can pull this off, what happens next? By siphoning off so much power, you'll be creating a huge imbalance of energies. The kaema flowing through the other ley lines will begin to fill the vacuum and the entire system will become unstable.

"Malek acknowledged that a certain critical mass of magical energy will need to be brought under our control before the system becomes self-sustaining. That could take months, even years. Until then, we'd be vulnerable. If Jaron chose to retaliate, he'd surely have the backing of the Senate and the Council of Governors, and they'd place the merlins at his disposal. It wouldn't matter if we crippled his ability to use magic against us, he would still be able to destroy us."

Tarvis closed his eyes and leaned his head against the glass of the window. Karimah was right, but he wasn't ready to give up. He had devoted too much time and energy to this endeavor to walk away. This was to be the crowning achievement of his life. His legacy.

Then he smiled to himself, thinking of what he hadn't shared with her yet. Taking advantage of the fact that she couldn't see his face, he took a deep breath and put as much gravity into his voice as he could. "You're assuming that I'll publicly claim responsibility as soon as Malek completes the first phase."

He heard Karimah rise and approach him, then felt her hand slide up his back and grip him on the shoulder. She leaned against him and said softly, with a smile audible in her voice, "We've underestimated you again, haven't we?"

He turned to face her and noted that despite her words, it was exasperation and not contrition that colored her expression. He reached up and stroked her silky hair with one hand. "I see no reason for us to reveal ourselves prematurely. We've successfully used other sorcerers as a shield in the past. I see no reason why we can't do so again."

"You could have explained this during the meeting."

"I don't want the others to become too complacent. As you so carefully pointed out, minimizing the risks isn't the same thing as eliminating them. I'll call another meeting in a few days and inform them of my intentions. That should take the edge off their fear without entirely blunting their sense of caution."

"What about Malek? Since he needs to execute this plan, he'll be taking the lion's share of the risk. Have you informed *him* of your intentions?"

Tarvis briefly considered lying to her, concerned about how she might react to how deeply he had taken the younger master into his confidence, but in the end, he offered the truth. "Malek knows. As you pointed out, he will be taking the biggest risk. If he's caught, I'll have no choice but to disavow him."

Her tone sharpened, bordering on anger. "Have you shared *that* with him as well."

"Yes," he replied flatly.

"I see." She bowed her head, hiding her face from him. "He's more devoted to you than I thought."

"What do you think of him?" he asked on an impulse.

She looked up and met his gaze without flinching. "I think you've found your successor."

Her response didn't come as a complete surprise. He'd realized for some time that he needed to plan for the day when he would no longer be able to lead his people, and he'd confided in her about his concerns. He fully expected to see the first phases of his plan brought to fruition, but he also acknowledged that the full extent of his grand design wouldn't be realized within his lifetime.

Even if they succeeded in seizing control of the ley lines within the next few years, it would take decades of effort to reorder the governance of sorcerers throughout Tarya. And once that was accomplished, there would still be much to be done. The use of magic was woven into the very tapestry of life in Tarya, and the impact of what they were doing would reverberate for generations.

The position of Archmage was currently an elected one, and Tarvis believed that eventually it would be again, but not in the immediate future. Until his reforms were accepted by the majority of the people, it was essential that the Mage Hall have someone at the helm who would not be swayed by popular opinion, someone handpicked to follow his carefully constructed plan, ensuring the continuation of their way of life.

Malek was the obvious choice. He was the only other master fully engaged in their project, and his personal contributions were central to their success. What was more, Tarvis was utterly convinced of his loyalty. Malek did *not* blindly obey his every command; he wasn't some mindless yes-man. He frequently challenged Tarvis's strategies, giving him the full benefit of his intellect, but he never questioned his intentions or motives. He was committed to Tarvis's vision of the future.

But Tarvis still hesitated. His reservations had nothing to do with Malek, and everything to do with the long reach of his ambitions. Musing aloud he said, "I was hoping for someone younger."

"Kylec Dracami is Jaron's man, Tarvis. Through and through."

He blinked at her, startled by her insight. "I wasn't speaking of anyone in particular," he said defensively.

"Come now, you've been obsessed with that boy since you met him. But your attempts at attracting his interest haven't been very successful. He has no intention of leaving the Primary Hall. He's loyal to Jaron, and you risk arousing his suspicions if you continue to pursue him."

She knew him too well. "I admit that I want to recruit Kylec to our cause, but I honestly wasn't referring to him when I said that I was hoping for someone younger. I'm just thinking of the future."

"And no doubt that's what so many of our colleagues were thinking of when they elected Jaron in the first place. Malek isn't exactly old. He's what, forty-five?"

"Forty-seven," Tarvis replied thoughtfully.

"Young enough, Tarvis. You don't need a child. Malek is a man in his prime. Let him find some adolescent to groom as *his* successor. He's proven that he's willing to risk his freedom, even his life for you. Isn't that enough?"

Tarvis took a deep breath and let it out slowly. Once again, Karimah proved her worth to him. "You're right, my dear. Perhaps I've just been looking for excuses to put this off."

She smiled knowingly. "Choosing the person to follow you is not the same thing as stepping down. You'll still be in command for as long as you want to be, if not longer. And it isn't an indictment of your age, either. Malek may be at the beginning of his prime, but you haven't seen the end of yours just yet."

"I know that," he said, though he secretly acknowledged that until *she* said it—and with such fervor—he hadn't really believed it.

"Announce it before he leaves, Tarvis. Before he places himself in harm's way for the sake of your dream, let him know the role you envision for him. He deserves that much."

He turned the idea over in his head, his objections wearing thinner and thinner. At last, he said, "I will. In a few days I'll call everyone together for one more meeting. I'll explain the more subtle nuances of my plan that I previously withheld, and I'll formally announce that when I *am* ready to step down from command, Malek will assume the position of Archmage."

"We're almost there," Karimah said with quiet conviction.

Buoyed by her confidence, he replied with equal assurance, "Yes, we're almost there."

Grim faces filled the room, and it took every bit of discipline Jaron possessed not to turn around and run the other way. Instead, he gently closed the door behind him and took his place at the head of the long conference table. Since his fellow masters were well aware of the reason they'd been summoned, he skipped the preamble and got straight to the point.

"We need to address the situation in Athens. Immediately."

He unrolled the large map he'd brought and spread it out in the center of the table, using a light touch of magic to hold it flat. The affected area had been highlighted and looked like an elongated blob with nearly a dozen outstretched tentacles. Varying colors showed how its relative size and shape had grown and changed since the problem was discovered a few days earlier. The pattern suggested that the progression of the phenomenon was slowing, but continuing to spread, and his calculations indicated that it would cover nearly a quarter of the province of Athens before it stopped. *If* it stopped.

"It looks like a bruise," Renee said softly, her expression as curious as it was troubled.

"That's not a bad analogy. This shows the extent of the ley line depletion."

"Depletion?" Seamus countered. "That isn't what I heard. Haven't the ley lines been completely drained?"

Jaron conceded the point. "For all practical purposes, you're correct. We need to find out how it happened and how to reverse it."

Michaela glanced at Renee and then turned to Jaron. "That much is obvious, but do you have any idea how to accomplish it?"

"Actually, I do." Jaron tried to imbue his voice with an optimism he didn't feel. "But first, I want to know if any of you have suggestions."

A tense silence followed, but Jaron could tell by the expressions of the assembled masters that there was a good deal of conversation going on. Normally, they would just whisper to each other, but the gravity of the situation dictated a greater degree of decorum. He waited patiently, trusting that eventually, someone would speak up.

His patience was wearing thin by the time someone did. "Have you reached out to Master Tarvis?"

Jaron wasn't surprised that Seamus asked that and was glad he had a ready answer. "Of course. Fortunately, his school is well beyond the impacted area, but he's had his hands full keeping the students and staff calm. He was able to confirm what the other mages in the area reported. The ley lines have been drained for no readily apparent reason. Practitioners can still use the kaema stored within their own bodies, but once they've exhausted their internal reserves, they have no way to replenish them."

"What about those strong enough to access more distant ley lines?" Master Renee asked.

"As the condition spreads, the number of people able to reach beyond it is diminishing quickly. I've suggested that any mages currently living within the affected area move beyond it for the time being."

Seamus sounded outraged. "You've ordered an evacuation?"

"No, I made a suggestion," Jaron corrected calmly. "Once they've burned through their stored kaema, they're effectively powerless. If they head to the outskirts, they will be able to tap into those ley lines not yet affected, but they'll still be nearby if they're needed."

"Needed for what exactly?"

Aidan's sudden entry into the discussion was unexpected, but Jaron maintained his composure as he replied, "I'm not entirely sure just yet. The weakening of the ley lines has also caused some kind of blight in the affected area. We should be prepared to offer whatever help we can."

"I agree that we should offer aid, but I don't see that there's much we can do," Jarvais said. He was the youngest master present, a vibrant and energetic man known for his generosity and passion, if not his patience. His frustration showed in his voice.

320

"Right now, our ability to help within the affected area is limited, but if we urge our people to move to the outskirts, they can continue to offer the rest of the population the benefit of their services."

Michaela looked worried. "Healers are also affected, aren't they?"

"All sorcerers are." Jaron understood her concern but had little to offer by way of reassurance. "But remember, there are plenty of non-magical remedies and treatments for common ailments and injuries. Not all villages have healers in residence. Many people rely solely on the services of physicians. I'm sure that the leaders of the impacted localities will evacuate anyone truly in need of a healer."

"You might want to initiate that suggestion yourself," she noted. "The magistrates and town councils will already have their hands full. They might not think of it on their own."

"I'll see that a message is sent right away."

"This resembles what happened eight years ago, though certainly more severe. Could the same group of people be responsible?" Seamus sounded doubtful, even as he asked the question.

"They've been ruled out," Jaron replied. "Tarvis bound the power of the individuals involved as the High Court of Ovates decreed. He also kept discreet watch over their activities, just in case. The same question must have occurred to him, because he told me that there was no way they could be behind this before I even had a chance to ask."

"But it could be someone else with similar intentions, and similar knowledge," Jarvais countered. "If this is another group of sorcerers intent on increasing their power, we could stop them only to face the same problem in few more years when someone else decides to make the attempt. I don't like to say this, but I think we should confer with the Senate and the Council of Governors. Perhaps new laws are needed to ensure that such abuses don't continue."

Jaron closed his eyes, considering. He had to admit that the concerns were valid, though he was loathed to initiate any measures that needlessly restricted sorcerers' rights. In the end, it was the desire to prevent an overreaction that made up his mind. "Agreed. I will request an audience with the Senate and bring this matter before them."

"I suggest that we bring our attention back to the real matter at hand," Seamus said gruffly, "It's all well and good to ponder what we can do to alleviate the suffering caused by this damnable blight, but shouldn't we be focusing on eliminating it at its source?"

"We should ask Master Tarvis what he can do to help," Renee suggested.

"I already have. He's offered to send a select group to investigate, but he's unwilling to put the members of his staff in harm's way, and I don't blame him. They will only enter the area for short periods of time and will exercise the utmost caution."

"Do you expect them to find anything useful?" Michaela sounded hopeful.

"I'm not sure," he replied soberly. "Unfortunately, the epicenter is nowhere near the train lines, and I don't think that anyone here is familiar enough with the area to teleport there directly. Tarvis's people can be there within just a couple of days and can scout for clues. It will take us more than twice as long to make the trip, and we can't tell what conditions will be like by then."

"If you have so little faith in their abilities, why send them at all?" Seamus made no attempt to hide his irritation.

"I don't mean to malign anyone, but several mages and even a few adepts have already tried—and failed—to figure this out. I'm happy to have Tarvis's aid because every piece of information we can gather could help, and it *is* possible that they will see something the others missed. But we can by no means count on them to do so."

Aiden met his eyes for a moment before pointedly looking away.

"What about the guardians?" Michaela asked, her tone brightening. "Shouldn't they be doing something? They *are* charged with maintaining the environment and the balance of kaema."

Jaron shared what he knew. "I believe that the kae-madri are doing what they can, but Governor Tharan has forbidden them to take any action within Athens itself."

"That makes no sense," Michaela argued.

Jaron shrugged. "I can't pretend to understand his motivation."

"It's likely that Tharan doesn't want to abide by any restrictions they might impose," Jarvais said. "Once the guardians become involved and provide their recommendations, the governors and local leaders are bound by law to carry them out. The kae-madri put the wellbeing of the land ahead of the comfort of the people and enforcing the rules they establish can be difficult." Jarvais surprised Jaron with his knowledge, and he nodded his concurrence.

"Earlier, you said you had an idea," Aidan said neutrally. "Perhaps now is the time to share it with the rest of us."

Jaron met his eyes and suppressed a sigh. He'd intended to take Aidan aside *before* the meeting began, but he'd been delayed. Now, his friend was forcing him to issue a public command rather than a private request.

"It's fitting that you should ask," he began. "Since I was hoping that you would play a critical role."

Aidan gestured for him to continue.

"I want you to travel to the epicenter of this phenomenon, determine the cause, and if possible, neutralize it."

"Is that all, Jaron?" Michaela asked. "You make it sound like you're asking him to fix a leaking pipe."

"It's all right, Michaela," Aidan said. "I'm perfectly willing to accept this assignment."

Seamus grumbled. "How do you expect one man to accomplish all that? You've already said that no one else has been able to uncover anything useful."

Jaron nodded. "That's true, but I think all of us will concede that Aidan's ability to decipher magical patterns is without equal." He paused to let the assenting murmurs subside. "He will go in to assess the situation, and I will decide on further action based on what he discovers. If it seems appropriate, others will follow, but for now I want to minimize the number of people exposed."

The room came alive as everyone began talking at once. This was not the buzz of quiet conversation, but an audible expression of concern and doubt. Jaron waited for the noise to subside before adding, "I understand that you may not agree with my decision, but unless anyone has a better idea, I'm going to stand by it."

"I understand why you chose Aidan, but why send him alone?" Jarvais asked. "There are others here who could help."

"Are *you* volunteering?" Seamus asked.

"As a matter of fact, I am," Jarvais responded without hesitation.

"I appreciate the offer, but it isn't necessary, at least not yet." Jaron smiled at the young master, admiring his conviction as well as his courage. "But I will keep you in mind if reinforcements are needed."

"So, that's it?" Seamus asked. "That is your plan? It's not a plan. It's barely the beginning of a plan."

"Considering how little information we have to go on, I think that Lord Jaron's actions are appropriate," Michaela replied.

"You *would*," he snapped back.

"Enough!" Jaron put just enough force into the word to recapture everyone's attention. Then he started issuing orders.

"Jarvais, I want you to prepare a letter for mass distribution to the local officials in the impacted towns and villages. Encourage them to evacuate anyone who might need magical medical care and let them know that we will have mages and adepts stationed at the outskirts to help however they can. Then instruct adept Simon to teleport copies to every message center within the affected area."

He then turned to Myau-Pei, who had remained silent throughout the meeting. "If I remember correctly, you have a sister in the Senate."

She inclined her head. "Yes, Lord Jaron. Marla is one of the Senators representing Tikal."

"Would you be willing to talk to her about this matter? I'd like to hear her opinion before I formally contact the Senate."

"I will send to her immediately," Myau-Pei said solemnly.

"Unless anyone else has something to add, this meeting is adjourned," Jaron said with a note of finality.

He sat down and watched the others file out. Aidan remained behind without being asked. Jaron pulled the map closer and traced the outline of the shaded area with one finger. "Do you approve of my actions?" he asked once everyone else had gone and the door had closed.

"Does it matter?"

"As far as the others are concerned, no. But between the two of us, yes, it matters."

"If I had any other ideas, I would have spoken up. Your plan is as good as any I could come up with."

"But something's bothering you."

"You've placed an enormous responsibility on my shoulders, Jaron. I just hope that I'm as good as you think I am, especially considering what happened last time."

Jaron looked at him hard. "I expect you to exercise more caution this time around, naturally. I also don't intend to send you alone."

"That isn't what you told the others."

"You'll be the only *master* I send for now, but I want you to take a small team with you."

"And this team will include who, exactly?"

"Once you reach the drained ley lines, you'll only have the energy contained within your own body to draw from. I'm relying on you to figure this out, but by the time you do, your resources may already be exhausted. Andris can hold more kaema than anyone else alive. He's also skilled and can take direction."

"Andris doesn't know how to teleport," Aidan pointed out.

"I don't want you porting this time," Jaron replied. "It won't be an easy journey, but you need to conserve as much power as possible. I also want you to approach this area slowly and keep alert. I suspect that the answers we're looking for are at the center of the affected area, but there may also be clues further away that could shed light on the situation."

"I may be exceptionally good at decoding spells and magical patterns, but my psychic senses are within the average range. If you're hoping that I can detect trace psychic emanations or similar subtleties, I'm going to disappoint you. I'm not a sensitive."

"I know. That's why your team will include someone who is."

"You have someone in mind?"

"Tamara Kallyn. Not only is she a sensitive, but she's also a powerful and skilled adept."

"If Andris and Tamara are to be part of this team, why not include Kylec as well and make it a family outing?"

"He's your student more than mine these days. Do you want him on a mission like this?" Jaron was not entirely opposed to the idea, but obedience wasn't Kylec's strong suit.

"Better to have him with me and under my command than trailing us on his own. He won't be content to stay behind once he finds out what's going on, and I honestly don't think we stand a chance at keeping this a secret from him."

"I'll leave that decision to you. But if you include him, please do what you can to keep him in line."

"Will we be traveling in disguise again?"

"No. I don't want you broadcasting your rank or mission to every person you meet, but there's no need to hide. And this time I want you to route through Icarus and check in with Tarvis. With any luck, he'll have more information for you by then."

"Of course," Aidan replied soberly. "Should I inform my team of our mission, or did you want to handle that yourself?"

"Have a seat." Jaron waved him into a chair. "I'll summon them now, and we can break the news together."

Freydis and Glasnae had been gone less than a day, and Deirdre was already second-guessing her decision.

She'd learned about the dire situation in Athens the same day it began, not because Governor Tharan or any other elected official had turned to her for aid, but because she'd left standing orders at every grove house within the province that she was to be contacted at the first sign of trouble.

Governor Tharan may have forbidden the members of her order from conducting any active investigations within his province, but he had *not* prohibited members of the General Order in Athens from sending information back to New Avalon. Even if he'd wanted to, he'd have no viable way to prevent such communication. There were plenty of priests and priestesses with sufficient power and training to perform a long distance sending on their own. They didn't even need to rely on mages for aid.

The mages. Deirdre's thoughts kept drifting back to them. She didn't believe that the overall organization was responsible for what was happening, but that didn't mean that every mage was innocent in all this. She knew that many of her sisters considered it a possibility that at least a few of them were involved. Since the incident in Athens eight years earlier, the Archmage had not intervened in the restoration of the destabilized ley lines. In fact, as far as she could tell, he was unaware of what they recognized as an ongoing problem. No doubt he'd noticed the rise in ecological difficulties, but he hadn't made it his business to get involved, and she wasn't inclined to criticize him for that. After all, the mages were not charged with Kaestra's well-being. The kae-madri were.

The current situation was different from the previous incidents, and far more severe. She hadn't received confirmation yet, but she expected that Lord Jaron was fully aware of what was happening and was already taking actions of his own. She could only hope that whatever he chose to do wouldn't make things worse.

That was one of two reasons why she was now second-guessing herself. The other kae-madri were against involving the mages, even the majority who believed they were blameless. Their reasons were varied, but in Deirdre's opinion they all arose from a subtle yet persistent prejudice and vague distrust. Though she disagreed with this consensus, her own views on the matter were not strong enough for her to defy the collective will of her sisters.

And then there was Glasnae. The current crisis bore all the signs of the vision in which Glasnae played such a vital role. If the moment of prophecy was indeed upon them, she had sent her to meet her fate. The problem was that she couldn't be certain what that fate might be.

The vision had faded before revealing what would happen to the three individuals chosen to restore Kaestra. She didn't know if they were meant to survive the ordeal. And she still didn't know who the other two people were.

No prediction was perfect. She had no guarantee that they would come together as they had in the vision. She had no guarantee that they would triumph even if they did. She had no guarantees at all.

She closed her eyes, fighting back tears, but the effort was futile. She sobbed quietly as she prayed, her heart aching for her young friend. *Kaestra, I beg you! Please protect her. Please keep her safe, even while she's giving everything in her to save you.*

Chapter 21

1482 AHS

"We're definitely headed the right way," Tamara said briskly, turning back in her saddle to meet Aidan's eyes. "The team Master Tarvis sent out may not have been able to gather much information, but at least they got the direction right."

Aidan snorted. "I should hope so. It isn't exactly difficult to sense the depletion."

Tamara sighed and added, "I meant that the source of the problem is consistent with what we were told. I can feel the draw point from here."

Aidan took a deep breath and bit back the sharp reply that Tamara in no way deserved. He had no doubt that she was just as frustrated and ready for this journey to be over as he was.

It had taken nearly a week to get as far as the satellite Mage Hall that Tarvis ran. They'd taken trains where they could, but the kaema-powered vehicles didn't go to every city, much less the smaller towns like Icarus. And as they approached the impacted area, scheduled runs were canceled altogether since they would not be able to recharge the engines that ran the trains. They had left the satellite Mage Hall three days ago and had at least as many days left ahead of them.

"Maybe we should take a break to stretch our legs and water the horses," Andris suggested.

Aidan smiled, all too willing to agree. Though Kylec was generally considered the more perceptive of the two young men, he had noticed that it was Andris who was more in tune to people's emotions and that he had a knack for defusing tense situations.

They soon found a promising spot just off the road. There wasn't much by way of grazing, but after a little scouting, Kylec found a small stream where they could fill their canteens and let the horses have a drink. After an undeniably graceless dismount, Aidan kindly assisted Tamara out of her saddle and offered her his arm as she steadied herself.

"I think I hurt worse now that I'm off the horse," she muttered, kneading a fist into her hip.

"I know some general pain-relieving spells," Kylec offered. "I haven't actually learned how to treat sore muscles yet, but I can still offer some relief."

"I appreciate the offer, but no thank you. We need to conserve all the kaema we can, and this is just a touch of soreness."

"Ah, I can help with that—no magic required!" Andris pulled a small jar of salve from his saddle bag and tossed it to her. "Arnica, eucalyptus and lavender. Perfect for sore muscles." He pointed to a cluster of shrubs a short distance away. "That should give you a bit of privacy."

Tamara thanked him on her way to the suggested location, and Aidan smiled broadly.

"Andy, putting you in charge of supplies was definitely one of my better decisions."

Andris smiled back, but then grew serious, looking at something over Aidan's shoulder. He turned to see Kylec staring intently into the trees on the other side of the road.

"What do you see?" Andris asked before he could.

"I'm not sure. Tamara said that the epicenter is west of here, right?"

"Mostly west, and a little south," Aidan clarified.

Kylec pointed almost directly south and said, "There's a fairly significant ley line not far from here, running almost exactly east-west. I can't feel the pull the way Tam can, but the energies feel, I don't know, turbulent?"

Aidan couldn't see anything, even with magic-sight, but using Kylec's words as a cue, he opened his deeper senses, reaching outward along the indicated direction. It *did* feel strange, but he couldn't express it any better than Ky had. When Tamara returned, they shared the discovery with her, and she grimaced.

"The kaema is being pulled through the ley line toward…something. I can't quite see the flow from here, but I can feel it."

"I don't feel a flow," Kylec argued.

"Neither do I," Andris added. "It feels more like a whirlpool."

"It's the vacuum." Aidan spoke his epiphany aloud. "As the ley line empties, the ambient kaema is rushing into it to fill the void."

Andris bent down to touch the withered grass. "And that's what killing everything. The plants need a certain amount of kaema to survive."

That statement sobered everyone. With a renewed sense of urgency, they soon returned to the road, and Aidan hoped that they would be able to deal with whatever they found at the end of this journey.

It wasn't just fatigue that was wearing on Aidan. As Jaron had requested, they'd stopped in Icarus to confer with Tarvis. The older master welcomed them, but it had been an uneasy visit. Students and teachers alike were nervous, no doubt worried that the school would close in response to the crisis. But no one voiced this concern aloud, so he hadn't broached the subject, not even to offer reassurances. After all, with so much still unknown, perhaps their fear was justified.

Master Malek Shandry and two adepts had explored the perimeter of the affected area in some detail but had discovered little. He would've liked to speak with them directly, but Tarvis explained that they'd traveled quite a distance around the drained ley lines in search of clues and had not yet returned.

When they'd left Icarus, Master Tarvis had wished them good luck, but Aidan could tell by the worry that had etched itself into the older man's face that he didn't have much faith that they would discover anything useful. Tarvis's reaction was disheartening, but not unexpected. He was one of the most conservative Masters, and he didn't hold a particularly high opinion of the "younger generation." No doubt he expected him to fail and was preparing for the worst.

***

By the time they reached their destination, Aidan wanted nothing more than a hot meal and a soft bed.

A tight-faced groom silently led their horses into the stable and started removing their tack while they took their saddlebags and went to the main entrance of the inn. A few minutes later, a weary looking woman led them to the establishment's best suite, which consisted of three bedrooms that shared a common sitting room and bathroom.

The price quoted by the clerk at the front desk was far below the usual rate, giving notice of just how bad business was. "You're mages?" the man asked with a trace of disbelief.

"Yes. We're just passing through." Aidan kept his tone casual, though he couldn't hide his fatigue.

"Seems to me you're headed in the wrong direction. Most sorcerers are leaving."

"I don't think we'll be staying very long either."

A shadow passed over the man's face. "If this doesn't stop, no one will be. It's as though Kaestra herself has taken ill. No offense, Mage, but I wish we had some guardians passing through instead of you folks. They might actually be able to help."

Aidan accepted the key with a slight nod, unable to think of an appropriate response. The man was right. The lack of kaema in the ley lines was causing an obvious blight. If Tharan would just get out of the way, the kae-madri might be able to help.

Once they reached their suite, Tamara let out a soft moan and Aidan turned to see her stretching her back, face tight with pain. He walked up behind her and gently kneaded her shoulders. "Why don't you pick out which room you want and get settled. Then you can take a hot bath before we have dinner and then turn in early."

"Don't we need to get started?" she replied.

"Not until we're rested. I want everyone at peak performance. Tomorrow morning is soon enough."

Kylec dropped his bags and donned his sword belt. "In that case, I'm going downstairs to run through some drills in the yard. No sense in bathing or showering when I'm just going to work up a sweat."

Aidan suppressed a groan. The younger man's obnoxious display of energy just made him feel more tired. "I think we have very different definitions of resting."

"I'm all tied in knots from riding. If I don't work out the kinks, I'll be stiff as a board by morning."

Andris snorted. "Hardly. You're just frustrated and want to beat on something."

"You want to spar with me?" Kylec asked, looking hopeful.

"Do I look stupid? Sparring with you is the equivalent of signing up for a beating. Sorry, but you'll have to amuse yourself."

Tamara chuckled. "Some things never change."

She poked her head into each of the available rooms and settled on the one with a view of the lake behind the inn. "I'm taking your advice, Aidan," she said after dropping her bags on the bed. "You boys had best make use of the facilities while you can. Once I get in there, I don't want to be disturbed for at least an hour."

Andris headed for the bathroom immediately. "She means it, Aidan."

It didn't take long for everyone to settle in according to their preference. A few hours later, Aidan ordered room service. They ate with plates balanced on their laps and discussed what they'd learned so far and what their next move should be.

Tamara quickly summarized what they had encountered enroute, including the subtleties that only she had sensed. "Something is aggressively drawing kaema from the ley line and concentrating it. I'm not kae-madri, but I can feel how the entire system of ley lines has been unbalanced. I think that it's trying to naturally correct itself, but something is preventing it."

"What could do something like that?" Andris asked.

"A battery?"

"What did you say?" Aidan turned toward Kylec, who'd spoken so quietly, it sounded like he was talking to himself.

"If someone was using the kaema in the ley lines to charge a magical battery, it might explain what's happening."

"What do you know about those?" Aidan kept his tone deliberately neutral.

Kylec answered slowly. "I came across some references to them in my studies with the Engineers Guild. The subject piqued my curiosity, so I did some research. They were kaeverdine constructs encoded with a spell to store kaema. Our ancestors tried to use them to power some older technology when they first came to Kaestra, but it didn't work."

"Why not?" Tamara asked, sounding intrigued.

"The technology from Earth used a different kind of energy…a form of electricity. From what I understand, kaema wasn't a viable alternative."

Aidan paused for just a moment before asking him, "Could you build one?"

The young adept caught the hesitation and gave him a knowing look. His answer fell between them like a stone. "With enough time to work out all the details, yes."

Aidan turned to Andris. "And you?"

"Is that a challenge?"

"It's a question. Just answer it."

Andris grimaced at his sharp tone, but then turned thoughtful. "I don't have the familiarity with these magical batteries that Kylec seems to, but I've configured lightstones, wards, and other items that store and use kaema, so theoretically I suppose I could. But right now, I wouldn't know where to begin."

"What haven't you told us, Aidan?"

Tamara's eyes bored into his as Aidan weighed the consequences of trying to evade her question. He opted for the truth. The others listened in silence as he recounted a somewhat abridged version of his involvement with the previous occurrence. Although they were well acquainted with the formal report from Tarvis, that version had not included Aidan's observations. He filled them in on the relevant details, including what he remembered about the construct that Tarvis has disabled.

When he was finished, Kylec shook his head. "You really believed that three sorcerers with no formal training could pull something like that off?"

"One of them did have training at the Mage Hall," Aidan pointed out.

"If she was able to figure out how to make something like that with just a few years of formal education in magecraft and limited power, she's a genius. Did you interview her?"

"No. Master Tarvis did, and he didn't say anything about her being a genius. He implied that they'd just gotten lucky."

Kylec scowled, his doubts about that theory evident, but he said nothing. Aidan continued, "This is far more severe and widespread, but the similarities are unmistakable. If you're right, Ky, we need to find this construct and figure out how to disable it."

"I was just thinking out loud, Aidan. From Tamara's description and my own observations, it seemed like a logical explanation, but I'll be the first to admit that it's flawed. For a magical battery to effectively hold this much kaema, it would have to be massive. Something like that would be difficult to hide."

"How massive?" Andris asked.

Kylec closed his eyes, and Aidan could tell he was running calculations in his head. When he opened them again, he said, "At least the size of this building, probably larger. And it would have to be right on top of one of the major ley lines for the effects to be this widespread."

Just moving an object that large would take an enormous amount of power. Or would it? "What if someone used an existing object, something that had always been there and therefore wouldn't be noticed?"

Tamara's eyes widened as she saw where his train of thought was headed. "Like a boulder or stone outcropping."

"Or a piece of bedrock." Kylec looked like he'd just had an epiphany. "The soil in this region is shallow. Just a few feet below the surface there's solid rock. It's mostly granite, but there are also large deposits of gray kaeverdine."

"An entire field of raw magestone," Tamara breathed.

"With a large enough piece in the right location underground, the task becomes much simpler," Andris offered.

"They'd still have to alter the matrix enough to hold the charge and then shape a spell to siphon the power into it," Kylec replied. "I know I said I could build a battery given some time to figure it out, but creating something on this scale would take months, and an awful lot of raw power."

Aidan silently thanked the gods for the impulse that had made him bring Kylec along. The boy's skill was already on par with his own, and his knowledge of geology and engineering had been invaluable.

"Whoever is behind this must also have set up blockages to prevent kaema from replenishing the depleted ley lines," Tamara added.

"If this is about acquiring and hoarding kaema, why prevent the ley lines from refilling? Why go to so much trouble to maintain an imbalance that's obviously damaging the environment?" Andris asked.

"Assuming our theory is correct," Kylec said, "the storage capacity for such a device, no matter how large, would be limited. If the power continued to flow into the ley lines being tapped, the construct wouldn't be able to hold it, and it would fail."

"I take it that would be bad," Andris commented.

"Catastrophic would be a more apt term," Kylec responded.

Andris swallowed hard. "Coming from you, that's especially frightening."

"If we find it, can we destroy it safely?" Tamara asked.

"I think so," Aidan said thoughtfully. "First, we'd need to break the siphoning spell. Then we'd have to create holes in the storage matrix to allow the kaema to be grounded back into the ley lines."

"It won't be easy," Kylec said. "Skill alone isn't enough. What you're describing will take an enormous amount of power."

"Good thing I'm here, then," Andris said with a forced smile.

Aidan scrubbed his face with his hands. "We can all sense the location, so finding it shouldn't be a problem at this point. I'm surprised no one else noticed."

Tamara looked thoughtful. "I can feel it acutely, but I'm a sensitive. I don't think any of you would have picked up on it if you weren't looking for it."

"True," Aidan said. "But Malek and his team *were* looking for it."

"They never got this close," Andris said flatly. "Tarvis reported everything they discovered, but he said they explored the outskirts of the affected area. I bet they never got close enough to sense this."

"What about finding those responsible?" Aidan asked Tamara. "Do you think you'll be able to sense anything about who did this?"

"I might be able to detect a psychic signature, but without someone to compare it to, that doesn't necessarily help. And given the scale of this, it seems likely that multiple people have had a hand in this. That will make it harder."

"All right. Tomorrow we'll track this back to the source. If it is what we suspect, our first priority will be to disable it. Then we'll attempt to track down the ones responsible."

They retired to their respective rooms, and Aidan lay awake for a long time, staring at the ceiling. He believed that they were on the right track, but that wasn't necessarily comforting. If their theory was correct, chances were slim that this was the work of some random sorcerers trying to increase their power. Even worse, Kylec's assessment of the previous incident reawakened his own doubts about the official report and its conclusions.

He'd always thought it improbable that a small group of sorcerers with limited training and even more limited power could create something strong enough to noticeably weaken a ley line. And the circumstances surrounding the incident—the four kaeverdine monoliths so conveniently located—stretched the credibility of coincidence to its limits. But they had confessed, and from what he remembered, they'd been enraged that Tarvis had thwarted them.

But did he really? Aidan asked himself again, his suspicions renewed by Kylec's well-reasoned doubts. *What if Tarvis was so anxious to prove himself to the rest of us that he seized the first sorcerers he came across and set them up to take the blame? No one outside of his own people had the chance to talk to them directly, and Tarvis is a gifted mage. He could have used a manipulation spell to convince them that they were guilty, even if they weren't.*

Aidan couldn't accuse a fellow master without proof. The only evidence he had was circumstantial at best. He felt a twinge of guilt that he wasn't prepared to challenge a verdict that had stripped three potentially innocent people of their power, but he consoled himself with the knowledge that they'd suffered no other punishment, and by all accounts had moved on with their lives.

What made his blood run cold was the fear that the real perpetrators had completely avoided detection, allowing them to refine their technique and further their ambitions.

What do they hope to achieve? he asked himself. *And how can we stop them?*

***

Malek stood beside the waist high protrusion of stone that was the only visible piece of his carefully crafted reservoir. He stroked the rough gray surface, admiring his handiwork. He could feel the well of kaema deep beneath him, intoxicating in its richness. Reaching out to touch the top of the exposed stone, he drew in a small portion of that energy, replacing what he'd depleted, temporarily pushing aside the frustration he felt at having to abandon his creation.

The process of draining the local ley lines was nearly complete, and everything had gone according to plan. He should be moving on to the next site to set up another reservoir in an adjacent area and expand their sphere of control, but instead he was preparing to retreat.

Tarvis's urgent sending had been wrenching. He trusted his mentor's judgment but couldn't help but think that he was overestimating Jaron's people. Still, if he were caught, the consequences would be severe.

He'd argued that they'd anticipated the possibility that Jaron would react and had prepared accordingly. But Tarvis indicated that it was the special combination of skills this team possessed that made them such a threat.

Leave quickly, Tarvis had told him. *Aidan and his companions will be there in a few days. One of them is a sensitive, so you need to be at least fifteen to twenty miles away before you teleport back here. If you attempt it when you're within her range, she may be able to trace it. Don't take chances.*

They didn't discuss what would happen when he left the construct undefended. If Aidan located the access point, he could potentially reverse the spell, and lay waste to all their hard work.

Malek bit back a curse, ruthlessly buried his frustration, and focused on practical matters. He addressed the four men standing a few yards away. "I want this monument guarded at all times. Do you understand?"

"It's not much of a monument," one of them scoffed.

"Not to you perhaps, but it holds tremendous sentimental value for my family." Malek stroked the hair of an illusory beard as if in deep thought. The glamour was a reasonable precaution. He didn't want anyone in the area to know his true face.

When the man grunted, he added, "If mages arrive here intent on restoring the ley line, they won't care about what they destroy in the process. This object is worth a great deal to me, which is why I'm willing to pay you so well to protect it."

"You expect us to defend this chunk of rock against mages?" The man was aghast. "We wouldn't stand a chance."

"Mages are only human, and without the ability to access the ley lines, their power will be limited. I'm told that you're the best hired swords to be had. Surely you aren't afraid of a little magic?" He smiled as he appealed to their egos.

The leader nodded, but still looked uncertain, and Malek realized that without an extra push, they'd run if confronted. This was little more than a last-ditch effort to secure the result of his work, but he would make it count.

The men *were* skilled with weapons, but their psychic abilities were barely average, and their shields were nothing to a man of his talents. It took little effort to slip beneath their defenses and plant a simple but powerful suggestion. By the time he left the clearing, the four of them stood at attention around the stone, prepared to do whatever it took to keep it safe.

If Jaron's people haven't completely exhausted their reserves getting here, those mercenaries won't stand a chance, Malek thought uneasily as he mounted his horse, but he pushed the feelings aside. Instead, he focused on covering enough distance to safely teleport home before morning. If Tarvis's estimates were correct, Aidan and his group might already be nearby.

But if they'd already burned through their power by the time the guards confront them, they'd be the ones at a disadvantage.

He slowed his horse to a walk when he realized that the compulsion he'd planted in the men's minds might be strong enough to push them to extreme measures, possibly even murder. He almost turned around to alter the spell with the addition of some safeguards, but common sense reasserted itself and he spurred his mount back into a gallop. *The spell wasn't that invasive. They won't harm anyone if it isn't already in their natures to do so, and if they are killers, then no prompting from me—one way or another—will change that.*

Chapter 22

Fields of withered crops, trees shedding their leaves months too soon, and a faint but ever-present scent of decay further dampened the spirits of the small band of travelers heading into the very heart of the blighted lands.

Freydis swallowed hard against the bile that rose in her throat. At first, her body's response to Kaestra's distress had been easily ignored, but as they drew closer to their destination, she felt increasingly ill. She turned in her saddle to see how Glasnae fared. The younger guardian was deathly pale, and Freydis marveled that she was able to stay in the saddle. She signaled to one of their two escorts, a young merlin who'd suspended his commission to serve in the outer court of the guardians for a year. Yuri approached and bent his head toward her. "How can I help you, Kae-Madri Freydis?"

"Stay close to Glasnae. She's weak and might slip from the saddle. I want you to be at the ready."

Yuri's young face looked troubled. "If she's ill, perhaps we should rest."

"Soon," Freydis assured him. "But not yet. We're nearly there. I can feel it. I want to be just a little bit closer before we make camp."

The young man bowed and eased his mount back until he rode beside Glasnae. She watched as he deftly covered his protective stance with conversation. Glasnae made some effort to respond at first, but when he failed to fully engage her attention, they lapsed into a companionable silence. Freydis returned her attention to the path ahead, leading them toward the source of the devastation.

The urge to invoke guardianship and restore the lands they passed through was strong, but she resisted it and made certain that Glasnae did the same. Healing the land a few acres at a time would quickly exhaust them, and ultimately wouldn't help. Until the balance within the ley lines was restored, the environment would continue to deteriorate.

They needed to get to the heart of the problem, and they were drawing close.

She stopped abruptly when Glasnae called out, a wordless cry that had Yuri on the ground and easing the young woman from the saddle by the time she'd turned around to see what was happening. Freydis surveyed their surroundings, noting the scant vegetation and sluggish trickle of water that under better conditions would have been a free-flowing stream. It was as good a place to stop as any.

"I can't go any further," Glasnae announced weakly. "Whatever we're going to do, it has to be here."

Freydis dismounted and hurried to her side as Yuri guided her to a seat on a fallen log. Conrad joined them a moment later with a small wooden bowl that he handed to Glasnae. "Drink this," he told her. "It should help."

Conrad was a fully qualified healer, and a powerful one at that. Freydis knew that he wanted to exercise his full range of talents to ease their suffering, but she'd hobbled him early on.

"You need to conserve your power," she'd told him, her tone a clear warning that she would not be disobeyed. "If any of us are seriously injured, *that's* when we'll need magical healing, not before. In the meantime, we'll drink your potions and follow your advice, at least within reason."

He glanced at her now, the unspoken question in his eyes. She shook her head, and he turned his attention back to Glasnae. "Feeling any better?"

She nodded. "I'll be all right. But I can't go any farther. I'm sorry. I just can't."

Freydis paused and stretched out with her senses. "Maybe you won't have to."

She walked away from the others and bent down to touch the earth with one hand, sending a questing tendril down into the ground, reaching, tasting, searching.

Aha! she thought with satisfaction. *We're closer than I thought. The ley line runs parallel to this stream. We should be able to work from here.*

She returned to the others and said, "Make camp."

"It's still early, are you sure?" Yuri asked.

"Glasnae and I can do what needs to be done from here, but we should rest first."

"I'll get a fire going and prepare some food," Conrad offered. "Something guaranteed to tempt your weak appetites. Something restorative."

"Thank you," she replied.

An hour later, with stomachs filled by Conrad's excellent stew, Freydis and Glasnae lay side by side on a makeshift mattress made of bundles of dried grasses and a heavy blanket. Freydis's thick cloak covered them both, and Glasnae curled against her, sound asleep. She felt drowsy herself and suspected that more than restorative herbs had been added to the meal Conrad had prepared, but she was grateful for it rather than annoyed.

Late morning sun filtered through a thin veil of clouds, and everything was quiet. The men sat nearby, tending the fire and keeping watch. They were as safe as they could be and needed the rest, so she gave herself over to sleep, confident that they would soon correct the terrible imbalance that plagued this land. Then they would truly find peace.

***

Freydis woke first and took some time to examine the ley lines before she gently roused Glasnae. "How do you feel?"

"Still faintly ill," Glasnae replied as she eased into a sitting position. "But better than before."

It was well into the afternoon, though sunset was still a few hours off. Glasnae stood up and stretched, still looking groggy. "When we stopped you said we could do what was needed without going any further. Were you just trying to humor me?"

"No. As soon as you're ready, we'll get started."

"You know what we need to do?"

Freydis nodded grimly. "I know what *you* need to do. I've worked it out, and I think that you'll have to break the blockages alone. If we try to do this together, we could upset the balance even more."

She imbued her words with more conviction than she felt. There was no need to burden Glasnae with her doubts.

Clearly Glasnae had doubts of her own. "What if I fail?"

Freydis glanced back over her shoulder to make certain that Conrad and Yuri were out of earshot before responding. "You're the only one who *can* do this, Glasnae. Have faith in yourself."

"Why me?" Weariness and no small amount of fear colored Glasnae's voice. "Because of a power that I never asked for?"

Freydis held her own fraying temper in check, keeping her voice even, but firm. "In part, yes. But it's more than that. You not only have the power to do this, but you also have the skill and the determination."

"What if I fail?" she asked again.

"You won't fail. I have faith that you are here, in this place, at this time, for a purpose. I believe that you were meant to do this." Freydis had promised not to mention the prophecy, and she would keep her word. But she thought that the younger guardian might find some reassurance in believing that Fate had had a hand in bringing her to this point.

She'd thought wrong.

"Don't I have the right to choose for myself?" Glasnae cried.

Caught off-guard, it took Freydis a moment to respond. But her reply forestalled any further argument. "You are kae-madri. Is there any choice left to make?"

Freydis watched as her words sank in. Glasnae could no more turn away from this duty than she could stop breathing, and they both knew it.

"What do I need to do?"

Freydis explained that the blockages were not the real concern. They were contributing to the imbalance of energies, but they were not the primary cause. The source of the problem was an unknown force that was drawing in and holding kaema. It was similar to the earlier disturbances that they had both encountered, but far more extensive. The epicenter was nearby, situated along the same ley line that ran through their camp.

She carefully walked Glasnae through the steps she would need to take.

"First, you'll need to establish a rapport with Kaestra. Then you must reach through the link and draw in as much power as you can, directing it into the drained ley line as quickly as you can."

"That's a terribly simplistic solution for a problem of this magnitude. What makes you so sure that this will work?"

"Instinct, mostly."

Glasnae's eyes went wide in response to her candor, and Freydis continued. "But I'm not relying on my gut alone. I studied the area carefully while you slept. If you ignore the severity, this is just like any other magical imbalance, so it follows that we correct it the same way. The only difference is that since we have reason to believe that *this* imbalance was deliberately created, we need to do more than restore the ley line. We need to push enough kaema through it to overwhelm whatever is causing the drain and break the peripheral blockages."

"How much power, and for how long?"

Freydis struggled to keep her voice and expression calm. She didn't want to frighten Glasnae too badly, but she wouldn't lie to her either. "As much as you can channel. As for how long, that's impossible to say. It usually takes only a few minutes at most to restore a weakened ley line, but this is unprecedented. You'll have to keep going as long as you can."

Glasnae regarded her in silence for several heartbeats before she asked in a quavering voice, "This will push me to my limits, won't it? And even then, you're not sure that I'll succeed."

"Nothing is certain. All we can do is try and pray that it's enough. I'll be right here with you. I promise you that much. I only wish I could do more."

Glasnae studied the ley line herself for several minutes and then commented, "You're right. We can't work together on this. It would be next to impossible to synchronize our efforts to replenish the ley line, and even the slightest deviation could aggravate the problem."

"Do you want to rest a little longer?" Freydis asked quietly.

"No. I'm as ready as I'll ever be."

Her decision made, Glasnae took a deep breath and turned slowly in place, arms outstretched, as she used all her senses to pinpoint the exact location of the ley line. When she found just the right spot, she sank down on one knee and reached out to touch the ground. The long grass was dry and brittle and the soil beneath was parched and cracked.

Glasnae closed her eyes and Freydis watched with a mixture of fear and hope as she reached down the length of her link to touch the well of power at the heart of Kaestra that was the source of all magic. The link that was ordinarily visible as a slender crimson thread expanded and deepened, becoming a hundred times greater and a thousand times stronger. Pure, potent kaema surged through it, flowing through the young guardian only to return to its source in an endless loop. Then Glasnae altered the flow of energy from Kaestra's core and directed it into the ley line that ran beneath her outstretched hand.

There was a brief moment of dissonance, as if the ley line was attempting to refuse the energy being poured into it, but it passed quickly. Soon it was drawing the power into itself, greedily devouring the offering and demanding more. Glasnae gasped and Freydis watched helplessly as the girl lost all control of the process, becoming little more than an open channel through which the hungry ley line could feed. It left her completely helpless as it drew kaema through her much as a child might draw water through a paper straw, and with as little regard for her wellbeing.

It seemed to go on forever, and Freydis wondered if the gaping chasm would ever be filled, *could* ever be filled. When Glasnae began to sway on her knees, she caught her in her arms and gently eased her to the ground. She whispered her name over and over, but it was apparent that Glasnae's consciousness was so far removed from her body that the girl couldn't hear her. She tried to send soothing, reassuring thoughts into her mind, but she felt as if the young woman was slipping beyond her reach.

The ley line continued to siphon energy from the core of the planet through Glasnae's link, and Freydis feared that it would leave her raw and bleeding inside. *Kaestra!* Freydis called through her own link. *Please, Mother, please help her!*

It was a desperate plea, a prayer offered up only when all hope that it would be answered seemed lost. But Kaestra *did* respond. Freydis cried as she sensed a flood of warmth and tenderness caress Glasnae's battered spirit. It fell short of true healing, but it seemed to renew the girl's strength.

Freydis forced herself to set aside her fears and doubts. What remained was a cruel kind of clarity. She knew that Glasnae was dying in her arms, ravaged by the power tearing through her. The ley line was finally becoming whole again, but at a terrible price.

She began to prepare herself for the moment when Glasnae's strength failed entirely and she would have to take over, when something caught her attention.

Another surge of power, nearly as potent as what Glasnae was channeling, raced toward them along the ley line. She watched, unable to react, while the energy collided with the kaema coursing through Glasnae and severed the connection with an explosion of force.

Reeling from the impact of the colliding kaema, Freydis shook off her initial shock and turned her attention to Glasnae. She was incredibly weak, but stubbornly clinging to consciousness and trying to sit up. Her link had been returned to its normal resting state, abruptly and violently.

"Sweetheart, lie still." Freydis couldn't keep the fear out of her voice.

"Did it work?" Glasnae croaked.

"Hush now," Freydis admonished before turning her head to shout, "Conrad! Come quickly. We need you now!"

"Did it work?" Glasnae asked again, a desperate question from a woman who believed she was dying.

"Yes, dear." Freydis stroked her head and neck. "It worked. The ley line is restored. The land will heal."

"As will you," a deeper voice said.

Freydis looked up at Conrad, clinging to the hope that his determined tone inspired. He was an exceptional healer. He wouldn't let Glasnae die without a fight.

His strong hands moved over the girl's body with calm professionalism, and Freydis breathed a sigh of relief as his touch appeared to ease her sister's pain. At his direction, she helped him get her into a sitting position. He held a bowl to her lips and said, "Try to drink this down."

Glasnae eagerly swallowed the contents of the bowl, and soon afterwards she drifted into sleep. Freydis hovered at Conrad's side as he began the lengthy process of repairing the damage, ready to assist him however she could. He had little need for her help, but she stood and watched, unable to move away while Glasnae's life seemed to hang by a thread.

He's a good healer, she told herself firmly. *He won't let her die without a fight.*

By the time they found what they were looking for, it was well past noon. Aidan struggled to hide his irritation, which would only make the task ahead more difficult. They'd gotten a much later start than he'd planned, since both Andris and Tamara had been slow to wake up in the morning. He reminded himself that it had been a difficult journey and that everyone would work better if they were well rested, but he was anxious to get on with the task at hand.

They followed the subtle pull away from the village and through a stretch of woodland. When Tamara indicated that they were close, they dismounted and tethered the horses and continued on foot.

"There's someone up ahead," Tamara whispered, then added silently, *They don't feel particularly friendly.*

Could they be the ones causing this? Andris asked in kind as they continued moving forward, exercising both caution and stealth.

I don't think so, she replied. *I'm not sensing any magical talent. But they are definitely at the focal point.*

Guards, Kylec sent decisively. *Probably protecting the construct.*

If it's what we think it is, Aidan cautioned.

Kylec turned to him and frowned. *We're close enough to see it, Aidan. Look for yourself.*

He shifted his sight and surveyed the area. The ground beneath their feet was giving off a faint glow. Looking more closely, he concurred with Kylec. Their theory was correct.

A massive deposit of kaeverdine was located just a few feet below the surface. The deposit was natural, but the way in which it was currently storing kaema was anything but. On a hunch, Aidan tried to connect with that energy and draw in a small amount, but he couldn't tap it. It was as if the power was locked away, and he didn't have the key.

Come on, he sent to the others. *Let's get as close as we can without being seen.*

We could cast invisibility shields, Tamara suggested.

No. I want to avoid using any magic until absolutely necessary. I'm not entirely sure what it's going to take to break through this.

They crept closer, using the vegetation for cover. As wilted and wasted as many of the trees and shrubs were, there was still sufficient foliage to hide them from sight as they approached the edge of the woods, and the center of the kaema-hoarding stone.

The meadow beyond the tree line was little more than a parched hayfield, the grass and wildflowers all but scorched. About a hundred yards into the clearing, a dark gray stone thrust out of the ground. It was roughly rectangular in shape, its top nearly level with the waists of the four men who stood surrounding it, expressions grim and swords at the ready.

Now might be a good time to use some magic, Andris commented, gesturing to the men. *Unless you can think of another way to get past them.*

I can, Kylec's mind-voice sounded far too eager. He loosened his sword in its sheath, and Aidan grabbed his arm.

What do you think you're doing? Aidan's mental tone was fierce.

Why use magic when we can take a more direct approach?

Just because you sneak in a few hours of fencing with the merlins now and then does not qualify you to take on four trained swordsmen. What were you thinking?

He wasn't. There was an edge to Tamara's words and expression that made Kylec wince, and he released the hilt of his sword, eyes downcast.

It was just a suggestion.

Aidan scrubbed his face with his hands. Realistically, it wouldn't take much power to remove the threat posed by the men, and for the most part, they'd managed to avoid using magic since they crossed into the affected area. All four of them were nearly at their full strength, but since Aidan still wasn't sure exactly how much power it would take to break through the spells on the construct, it was imperative that they use their resources wisely. They would only get one chance at this.

He considered their options carefully and came to a decision.

Tamara, can you cast stunning spells on all four of them simultaneously?
She nodded.
Good. Do it.

He watched as Tamara shaped her power and released it toward the men. Her skill was considerable, and they barely had a chance to look surprised before crumpling to ground in near unison.

"Move now!" he shouted, running toward the fallen men. "Do any of you have some rope or cord?" he asked belatedly.

"Here!" Tamara handed him a neatly coiled length of rope that she pulled from her knapsack.

"Bless you, Tam." He cut the rope into lengths and used it to secure the men, binding their hands and feet together. Andris and Kylec helped him to move them a little bit away from the stone, laying them side by side and tying their bindings together with the remainder of the rope.

"Can you keep them under control if they wake up, Tam?"

She nodded. "I've barely touched my well of power. I've more than enough to handle them."

"Good. With any luck, there won't be any reinforcements."

"I don't sense anyone else in the immediate area," Tamara replied.

"Are you sure?" Andris asked.

Tamara closed her eyes. When she opened them again, she said, "There's a small group of people about ten miles north of here."

"Can you sense anything else about them?" Aidan asked.

"Not from this distance. I think they have some magical ability, but I can't determine how much. I'm sorry I can't tell you more."

"It's enough. They're still at a fair distance. If we move quickly, we should be able to finish undoing this mess before they can get here, *if* they're involved at all."

"What do we do?" Andris asked.

Aidan looked at the young Adepts and said slowly, "I need some time to work this out. In the meantime, I want you both to try to do the same."

They spent the next couple of hours studying the stone in near silence. During that time, the guards started to come around once, but Tamara had no trouble sending them into a deeper sleep, ensuring that they wouldn't cause any trouble. Aidan focused on the magical patterns that had been woven into the matrix of the stone itself. It was skillfully done. Far too skillfully for him to believe that some independently trained sorcerer had crafted it. To his refined perceptions, it looked like the work of a mage. More specifically, it looked like the work of a master.

He filed the thought away in the back of his mind. Discovering who had made it was not his primary mission, destroying it was. He traced the patterns back into the kaeverdine deposit, probing deeply. It was an intricate spell that reminded him of the one that had made the battery Tarvis had disabled, but this was far more complex. It was as if the battery spell had been repeated over and over again to create a tightly coiled chain that burrowed deep into the kaeverdine, fundamentally changing the stone into something else entirely: a power sink.

Once he broke the code, he was confident that he could also break the spell, but first he conferred with Andris and Kylec, wondering if they had seen the same thing. Andris was close to arriving at the same conclusion, and Aidan was proud to see how far his skills had progressed. Then Kylec offered his opinion and he reeled for a moment, slightly stunned.

"The underlying spell is fairly complex, and is repeated over and over, doubling with each repetition. The doubling appears to increase the power of the chain exponentially."

"Are you sure?" Aidan turned his attention back to the construct.

"I'm certain," Kylec said firmly. His tone was neither patronizing nor boastful, merely confident, and Aidan realized that the day he'd been expecting for some time had come. His student had surpassed him.

Show me, he sent, opening his mind and asking the younger man to guide him through the pattern. Kylec did so, and as the subtle detail became apparent, he knew that his original solution needed revising.

He pulled out a pad of paper and a pencil from his pack and sketched out his first solution. "I know this won't work, but it's a starting point."

"I think I'm a little out of my depth here," Andris commented while Kylec moved closer to examine the drawing.

"Don't sell yourself short, Andy," Aidan replied, unable to shed the instincts of a teacher, even in these circumstances. "You're far cleverer than you give yourself credit for, and since you'll be the one executing this, you need to understand how it works."

By the time they'd worked out the exact pattern needed to break through and unravel the spell, another hour had passed. Aidan sent out another silent prayer of thanks to whichever god inspired him to include Kylec on this mission. The young man's skill would likely be the difference between success and failure.

"That's it then." Aidan gathered up their scribbles and slipped them into his bag. They were only notes. The full design of the spell was too complex to draw on paper, but the image was firmly fixed within his mind, as he was sure it was in Kylec's. Andris still looked uncertain, but Kylec declared that he could pass the details of the matrix to him mind-to-mind without difficulty.

"We have a special technique," he said simply.

"That explains a lot," Aidan replied dryly, noting that neither young man volunteered any further details.

Andris took up position a couple of yards away from the stone and glanced back at them over his shoulder. "This would have to be a dynamic spell," he grumbled.

Kylec snorted. "If it weren't, I'd take care of it myself."

Aidan watched as they both closed their eyes. Kylec sent the details of the pattern to Andris, who raised his hands and began shaping kaema into the specific form required. When the first tendrils of power reached the stone, there was a crackle of energy, visible as sparks to magic-sight. A few minutes later, the full force of their counter-spell had wormed its way into the stone, burrowing deeper and deeper as it slowly released the trapped power back into the ley line.

It was a maddeningly slow process, and Aidan felt a breath of concern for the young adept who continued to feed into the spell the massive amount of power required to make it work. Andris's stamina was impressive, but he eventually started showing signs of fatigue.

"Aidan!" Tamara called out in an urgent tone. "There's a swell of power coming toward us."

"What?" Aidan pulled his attention away from Andris and the stone to look where Tamara was pointing. His senses lacked her acuity, but it didn't take a sensitive to discern the massive surge of kaema that was rushing through the ley line, heading straight for the construct. Struck with horror, he realized that if it reached the stored energy inside the stone while the spell was still in force, the entire thing could explode.

Andris had already unraveled more than half the spell, but the holes he made wouldn't be enough to release the pressure of the wave when it hit. Before he could think of what to do next, Kylec yelled, "Keep going, Andy. I've got this."

Andris redoubled his efforts, pushing the spell deeper into the stone, while Kylec created the magical equivalent of a dam across the ley line that would reflect a portion of the power back towards its source. Taking the cue from his protégé, Aidan followed suit with a second barrier positioned behind the first, adjusting the design so that it scattered a portion of the energy rather than reflecting it. Then he and Kylec joined efforts to create a third wall that would slow the power moving through it, buying Andris a little more time.

When the surge of kaema hit the first dam, its power was roughly halved, with the portion that passed through moving at a reduced speed, and the second barrier effectively reduced the force traveling through it by half again. The third barrier did nothing to reduce the overall amount of kaema that passed through it, but by slowing its speed to a mere fraction of what it had been, it gave Andris several more minutes to work.

Even so, the force of the collision was enough to rebound along the thread of energy that Andris was feeding into the counter-spell, severing the connection and knocking him to the ground. Kylec rushed to his side. "Andy, are you all right?"

Andris sat up and shook his head, looking slightly stunned. "I think so. What the hell was that?"

"I'm not sure." Aidan searched the magical patterns for some clue. Even has he watched, several waves of energy pulsed from the stone, rings expanding outward until they dissipated completely. The sensation threw him off balance and he reeled on his feet for a few seconds before steadying himself. For a moment, he nearly panicked, remembering the last time he'd been hit by a wave of violently released kaema. But when he assessed himself for internal injuries or disruption, he found nothing amiss.

"Are the rest of you okay?" He asked urgently, "Check yourselves for any internal energy imbalances."

"I'm fine." Kylec replied after a pause just long enough to assure Aidan that he had truly taken the time for a self-assessment.

"Me, too." Tamara added a moment later.

Andris took a minute longer before responding, "I'm a little shaky, like I took a bit of a shock, but nothing serious. I'm also low on kaema – not fully drained or even close to it, but I definitely feel depleted."

"Let your core refill naturally." Aidan ordered. "Don't deliberately draw in from the ley lines."

"The kaema in the ley lines feels normal again to me." Tamara said. "Why shouldn't we replenish what we've used?"

"You and Ky can." Aidan replied. "But Andy should wait since he took the brunt of the feedback, just to be safe."

Andris nodded. "I understand. Hopefully we've done all we need to here."

Aidan examined the area looked again, but he couldn't find any trace of the spell that had transformed the kaeverdine deposit into a magical reservoir. In fact, barely any trace of excess kaema lingered at all, and the nearby ley lines had almost returned to normal.

Questions took shape in his mind, and he turned north, where the surge of power had originated from. It was the same direction in which Tamara had sensed a small group of people. If they were the ones who'd created the construct, then it was likely that the flood of power was intended to destroy any evidence that would lead back to them. There was only one way to find out.

Aidan wasted no time. First, he took the time to replenish his internal reserves of kaema, relieved when the action caused no unexpected side effects. Then he rallied the others and issued his orders. He directed Kylec and Andris to fetch their horses. Then he had Tamara release the sleep spell on the prisoners and crafted a basic binding spell to ensure that they would pose no threat during the journey back to town. When he reached out to touch the mind of the first man, he recoiled. Someone else had been there ahead of him.

The manipulation spell compelling the man to protect the construct was simple, but elegant. Aidan carefully removed it before replacing it with the less invasive binding. He repeated the process with the other three men and relayed his discovery to Tamara.

"So, these men are victims," Tamara said sadly.

"Maybe." Aidan wasn't entirely convinced. "But they can't be released until we have a chance to question them properly."

Once they were safely under the thrall of his spell, he removed their physical restraints and got them to their feet. Kylec and Andris returned with the mounts, and Aidan helped Tamara into the saddle. Arranging the prisoners in a line behind her, he commanded the men to meet his eyes. He pointed at Tamara and said, "You will obey this woman without question. You will follow her and take whatever direction she gives you. You will do no harm to anyone. Do you understand?"

The men nodded as one. He climbed into his own saddle and gestured for the boys to do the same. "The three of you are to go back to town and ask the magistrate to hold these men until I return. Make sure that they are treated well. Until we know what part they played in this, we have to assume they are innocent. Then I want you to go back to the inn and wait for me."

Tamara nodded, unasked questions in her eyes.

Andris looked confused. "You aren't coming with us?"

"I need to find out what caused that surge of power. I'll meet up with you later."

"Andris and Tamara can handle the prisoners." There was an edge to Kylec's voice that made him nervous. "I'll go with you."

"No," Aidan replied firmly. "Go with Tamara and Andris."

"They don't need me. You do."

"I can take care of myself."

"You don't know who or what might be out there. You need someone to watch your back."

"Enough, Ky," Aidan growled out. "This isn't a discussion."

"But I can help you," he protested.

"Adept Dracami!"

Kylec froze in response to the sharp tone and formal address. Knowing he had his full attention, Aidan continued. "I'm giving you a direct order, and I expect it to be obeyed."

A bright spark of rebellion glinted in the young man's eyes, and Aidan wondered how much time he would have to waste fighting with him. Then Kylec looked away and growled back, "As you wish, Master Varano," and he pulled at his horse's reins, turning the animal to fall into line behind Andris.

Aidan was about to leave when Kylec twisted in the saddle and called out in a vastly different tone of voice. "Aidan?"

"Yes, Ky?" he replied, his patience wearing thin.

The lad looked downright tortured. "Be careful, okay?"

Aidan managed a smile. "I will be. Don't worry about me. Just get yourselves back to town and I'll contact you soon."

He turned his horse northward and set off at a gallop. The countryside sped by in a blur, and Aidan focused on his goal, following the path of the ley line and hoping that it would lead him to the answers he sought.

***

With sunset only an hour or so away, Freydis had to make a decision. While Conrad took care of Glasnae and Yuri broke camp, she carefully weighed her options. The ley line was restored. If its failure had been the result of some natural occurrence, she would have considered the mission complete and let the matter rest. But that wasn't the case. The kaema had been deliberately drained, and this might be their only chance to find the people responsible.

"How far are we from the nearest village?" she asked, a plan forming in her mind.

"We passed a small settlement about half an hour's ride back along the road," Yuri answered.

"Good," she said briskly. Turning to Conrad where he still crouched beside Glasnae, she added, "Can you ride while holding her in the saddle in front of you?"

He nodded. "We'll have to go slow, but we'll manage. I'd feel better if she had a comfortable bed to sleep in tonight."

"I agree." Freydis walked to where the horses were tethered and began adjusting her gelding's tack. "I want you and Yuri to finish breaking camp and head to the village. If they have an inn or a boarding house, rent us a couple of rooms. If not, secure hospitality for us wherever you can. If you need additional help for Glasnae, you have my permission to do whatever you need to, but don't reveal that she is kae-madri if it can be avoided. Tharan's edict against us may not be

359

particularly popular with the locals, but I'd rather avoid any complications."

She swung up into the saddle just as Conrad replied, "And where do you think you're going?"

"South," she said. "Glasnae healed the ley line, but we still don't know what drained it in the first place, or what caused that backlash of power. I need to trace it all the way to its source before whoever is responsible has a chance to cover their tracks."

"Give me twenty minutes to finish breaking camp and get Conrad and Glasnae on their way, and I'll go with you," Yuri said, jumping to attention.

"No. Every minute I wait is a minute wasted. I need to move now, and I need *you* to keep Glasnae safe. She needs your protection far more than I do."

"You shouldn't go alone," Yuri protested, but Freydis's mind was made up.

"I am kae-madri. I can take care of myself. Right now, I need you to guard Glasnae."

"Freydis is right," Conrad said, unexpectedly taking her side. "A guardian of her age and experience knows how to stay safe." The statement was said with conviction, but he silently added, to her alone, *Don't make me a liar.*

Freydis nodded and turned back to Yuri. "One more thing. You need to move soon, but don't be overly hasty. When you leave this place, I want there to be no trace that we were ever here, understand?"

Yuri looked startled and she added, "Your training as a merlin did include such procedures, did it not?"

"Yes," he replied, "but I never expected to use those particular skills in service to the Order of Kae-Madri."

"These are strange times." She glanced at the sun, sliding ever westward behind the thinning clouds. "I need to go. Take care of Glasnae and contact me if you encounter any problems. I will send to you as soon as I have something to share."

"Or if you need help," Conrad added placidly.

"Or if I need help," she conceded. "Travel safe."

She pulled lightly at the reins and headed south. She touched her heels to her horse's flanks, and he took off at a gallop, following the narrow track that ran along the edge of the sluggish stream.

She stayed alert and watchful, extending her senses outward even as she kept her eyes on the path ahead. Her caution was not misplaced. When Freydis detected another rider on the same trail, heading toward her and moving fast, she slowed her mount and moved off the trail, holding the gelding steady while she waited for the other rider to appear.

He must have sensed her as well, because he had slowed to a trot by the time he came into view and halted a few yards away. She took in his appearance in a single, sweeping look: a man at the beginning of his prime, in his late forties or early fifties. He sat tall in the saddle, had a slender build, and the hands holding the reins suggested little experience with manual labor. His skin was a light brown, with dark auburn hair and striking, jade green eyes. His expression was equal parts determination and wariness as he scanned the surrounding area before focusing his attention on her.

"Are you alone?" he asked abruptly.

She blinked in surprise before narrowing her eyes in irritation. "Under the circumstances, that question can be interpreted as either an insult or a threat. Which did you intend?"

Now it was his turn to be surprised, and she was oddly gratified as his cheeks darkened with a blush. "Neither, lady. I spoke without thinking."

"It's a common malady," she replied, trying to take his measure. "Does it afflict you often?"

He remained mute, staring at her in something close to shock. Despite his rudeness, he didn't look the part of a villain, but their meeting was more than coincidence. Shifting her sight to see the magical currents, she studied his aura, the faint glow of shielded power confirming her suspicions.

He's a mage, she thought to herself, her heart sinking, *and a powerful one. At least an adept, possibly even a master.*

When he found his voice, he didn't reply to her question but asked one of his own. "Have you seen anyone else near here? Perhaps a group of mages or sorcerers?"

His question made her reassess the situation. If the man was involved in the draining of the ley lines, why would he be hunting a group of magic-users? Another possibility sprang to mind, *Perhaps we're looking for the same thing.*

Hopeful that she was dealing with an ally rather than an enemy but remaining appropriately cautious she shook her head. "None except for you, Mage."

He sucked in a breath, eyes burning with frustration. After a moment, his expression softened. "Forgive me, Kae-Madri."

Freydis wasn't surprised that he recognized what she was. Nothing could hide the link of the kae-madri from magic-sight, not even the most cleverly crafted glamour. She and Glasnae had avoided doing anything that might draw attention to the fact that they were guardians, but they'd known that they couldn't hide it from anyone who thought to look.

She suddenly felt at a disadvantage. The mage, whether friend or foe, now knew without question where her loyalties lay, but she had no idea if she could trust him. "Why are you here?" she asked.

He hesitated, and she didn't know if he was trying to decide how much he could tell her, or if he was thinking up a lie. "I was sent here by Lord Jaron to restore the ley lines. My companions and I were in the process of doing just that when we felt a surge of energy approach from this direction. I came to investigate."

He seemed sincere, but appearances could be deceiving. "How can I know you're telling the truth?"

"You can't," he said sadly. "You'd have to trust me."

"I don't," she said flatly.

The man bit back a curse, waves of frustration radiating from him. She watched him closely, and although her instincts told her he was being honest with her, there was simply too much at stake for her to take any chances.

After a moment, his eyes lit up. "What if I opened my mind to you. Would you believe me then?"

Depending on his skill, he might be able to let her inside his thoughts and still lie to her. It was unlikely, but possible. But there was someone else that would know instantly if he was telling the truth, someone who would be able to see through any lie.

"Will you allow me to invoke guardianship first?" she asked. "Will you open your thoughts to Kaestra as well as to me?"

He swallowed hard, eyes bright with fear. But after a moment, he replied, "If that's what I have to do to earn your trust, then yes."

Freydis sent a gentle query along her link and felt Kaestra's strength fill her in response. Once the rapport was established, she nodded, indicating that he should lower his shields. He did so after only the briefest of hesitations, and she entered as gently as she could.

Show us, she said into his thoughts.

There was another hesitation, followed by a pervasive feeling of resignation. *I will share everything I know.*

The man was true to his word. She watched his memories unfold before her. As his knowledge became hers, she felt the warmth of Kaestra's approval, and knew that everything she'd seen was true.

When he was finished, she withdrew with the utmost gentleness and said aloud, "Thank you, Master Varano. I believe you, and I trust you."

"Can you help me?" he asked.

Freydis dismounted and gestured for him to do the same. They led the horses to a pile of tumbled boulders near the stream and she said, "Let's sit for a moment like civilized beings."

"I suppose the need for haste has passed," he said. "I assume that you were responsible for the power that flooded through the ley line…" he trailed off, then added, "I still don't know your name."

"Freydis Laylin," she replied, feeling guilty for not sharing it sooner. She'd learned his name, along with his rank, the moment she'd entered his mind. "But please call me Freydis."

"Freydis," he said softly, as if getting a feel for the name. "You may call me Aidan."

"I'm pleased to meet you, Aidan. Though I wish it were under better circumstances." She fought the urge to smooth the worry lines from his forehead, as she would have done with her own son. They were roughly the same age, and even though it had been many years since she'd seen her son, some habits were ingrained.

"Was it you?" he asked, returning to the matter that concerned him.

"Not me personally," she began. What followed was a strictly factual account of what had occurred, devoid of any emotional overtones, or any mention of Glasnae by name. She explained what her sister had been trying to accomplish and her impression of how it had gone awry.

When she finished, Aidan took her hand in his own, "Will your sister recover?"

"I hope so," she replied flatly, without even thinking. She looked up and met his gaze and added, "I believe so. She's in good hands. The gods willing, she will mend."

"I pray that she will."

"I need to get back to my people, and you need to return to yours." She rose to her feet, and he stood with her.

He wordlessly helped her into her saddle before climbing wearily into his own. The sun was quite low in the sky, and he offered to escort her back to her companions. She gently refused, assuring him that she didn't have far to go, and reminding him of his own responsibilities. "Your boys will be driving that dear woman quite mad," she said with a smile, thinking about the two young men reflected in his memories.

"I'll tell you the same thing I keep reminding my own escorts of: I'm accustomed to traveling alone, and I am well-equipped to take care of myself. Don't worry about me."

"All right." He chuckled weakly, a faint sound that revealed his fatigue. In a more sober tone, he asked, "Do you think this is over?"

Freydis thought of the prophecy that the seers had revealed to Deirdre. It seemed to have played itself out, and yet she felt as if something was missing. Something important. By the look on his face, it was clear that Aidan did *not* believe it was over, and as much as she wanted to reassure him, she couldn't.

"For now, yes. But without knowing who was behind it or what they hoped to achieve, it's all too possible that this could happen again."

"I agree," he said. "If this does occur again, I hope that we can work together."

"I think we already have." She smiled at him.

He acknowledged that truth with a nod and waved good-bye, heading back in the direction he'd come from to rejoin his companions. Turning in the opposite direction, she did the same. The light was fading fast, forcing her to concentrate on the path ahead as she navigated between the trees in the gathering dark. She didn't mind. In fact, she was grateful to focus on something so mundane for a while. There would be plenty of time later to consider what had happened, to ponder the possibilities, and to worry.

Chapter 23

"Aidan must have destroyed the reservoir," Malek said. "My connection was severed a few hours ago."

"I expected as much." Tarvis failed to keep the disappointment out of his voice but added more optimistically, "At least you escaped detection, so no one will have any reason to suspect us. We remain free to try again."

"You still want to try again?" Malek asked, hope warring with doubt in his voice.

"Of course."

"I failed you."

"No, you didn't. Your spell was working. The failure was mine. I underestimated Jaron, but I won't make that mistake again."

"How can we defend against him while we build our bank of power?"

Tarvis sighed. "We need to rethink our strategy, but I am confident that together, we'll make this work. We're close, Malek. Don't let your disappointment blind you to what we've accomplished."

"What *have* we accomplished?" the younger man asked, sounding plaintive.

Tarvis smiled, glad that he had at least some good news to share. "We may not have control of the ley lines *yet*." He stressed the last word, pausing before he continued. "But thanks to your work, we've made significant progress on another front."

Malek's expression changed from disappointed to curious in an instant. "Tell me everything."

Tarvis waved him to a seat and replied, "With pleasure."

***

Jaron dropped the two reports that Aidan had provided on the coffee table and said, "Very conscientious. It's usually a struggle to get someone to complete one report, much less two."

"I thought there were certain things you would prefer to leave out of the official account, such as the guardians' involvement. Considering that they were acting against the orders of Governor Tharan, it seemed to be in their best interest as well," Aidan replied, sitting back against the soft cushions of the sofa.

"Very considerate. And your editing proves that you know me far too well."

"Have you already circulated the public version?"

"I had little choice. The demand for updated information has been constant. I can only hope that this explanation will hold."

"It did last time."

"You weren't able to learn anything from the men you found?"

Aidan shook his head. "They were mercenaries hired to guard the construct and had no direct involvement. As I explained in my report, they were victims of a manipulation spell. I was able to pull an image from their minds, but it was likely a glamour."

Jaron's already sober expression became downright grim. "You still believe that some of our own people might be involved."

Aidan had given the matter a lot of thought during the journey back, and he hadn't shared the results of his musings with anyone until now. "Tarvis went out of his way to be helpful last time, and I have good reason to believe that he fabricated that story about the sorcerers' involvement, planting the information in their minds to fit the evidence. At first, I thought he did it to boost his standing with the other masters, but now…I think that there might be more to it."

"You think he may be directly involved." It wasn't a question.

"I don't know."

Jaron sighed deeply. "So, what do we do now?"

"There's nothing we can do. We have absolutely no proof that he's done anything wrong."

"But you believe that he bound the power of three innocent people after manipulating their thoughts so that even *they* believed they were guilty."

Anger and frustration drove Aidan to his feet. He paced the length of the room before answering, "I can't prove it, Jaron. And I could be wrong."

Jaron's expression was positively tortured.

"What is it?" Aidan asked, not sure that he wanted to hear the answer.

Jaron replied in a leaden voice, "While you were gone, a new proposal was placed before the Senate, despite my best efforts to block it. It would require all individuals above the age of sixteen who possess any magical talent to register with the government and submit to a panel of inquiry once every five years to ensure that they aren't abusing their powers. The penalties for neglecting or refusing to do so are rather severe, including the binding of their power and imprisonment."

Aidan gaped at him. "Something like that will never pass."

"It already did." Jaron bent down and cradled his head in his hands. "Only by a slim margin, but enough. The Council of Governors ratified it this morning, and the new law is set to take effect at the end of the year. The High Court of Ovates is already in the process of establishing the necessary procedures."

"I don't believe it." Aidan felt numb with shock. The idea chilled him to the core. This new law would treat every sorcerer like a criminal on probation, facing trial every five years for the duration of their adult lives. "This can't be happening. Not in Tarya."

"I'm afraid it is, and as master mages, the enforcement of this new law will fall largely to us."

"Can you refuse?"

"I'm a citizen, just like everyone else. I don't get to choose which laws I follow."

"This one is wrong."

"I agree. Perhaps, in time, enough people will see that, and the law will be repealed. Until then, we have to live with it."

It occurred to Aidan that if the perpetrators of the recent catastrophes were brought to justice, they might be able to restore faith in the magical population as a whole. Or it might just give the rest of the people greater reason to fear them.

"This isn't over yet, is it?" Jaron asked when Aidan fell silent.

Feeling lost and soul-sick, Aidan replied quietly, "No, it isn't over."

***

"It's over." When Deirdre rehearsed the simple phrase in her head, it had sounded authoritative and confident, but spoken aloud before the senior oracles, the words came out as a plea.

Chu-Lin's expression was grave, and Deirdre looked at Reed and Vanarra in turn, searching for some reassurance, knowing she'd find none.

"I'm sorry, First Guardian," Chu-Lin said gently. "But the prophecy remains. As trying as these events have been, the vision is yet unfulfilled."

"How can you say that? All the pieces were there: the environmental disaster, the weakening of the ley lines...and Glasnae." The last part came out as a sob. "I recognized her in the vision, and she pushed herself to the limit to heal the land. She succeeded, so it must be over."

"You only recognized *one* of the chosen. In the vision, there were three." Chu-Lin was firm. "I assure you: this is *not* over."

"If this crisis wasn't the one predicted, then what was it?"

"A preview." Reed's voice sounded weak, his expression shadowed, to the point that Deirdre wondered if he was in the thrall of the Sight as he continued. "The catastrophe that was prophesied has been foreshadowed by these trials. This has been but a taste of what is yet to come."

369

"Foreshadowed?" Deirdre's searched the faces of the other two seers who gazed at Reed with sadness. Whatever was happening, it was beyond her understanding.

Chu-Lin laid a hand upon her shoulder. "I'm afraid so, Deirdre. We have been granted a little breathing room, but we must be vigilant. You must prepare."

"How?" Deirdre cried, frustration mingling with fear. "How can I prepare when I know so little?"

"I wish I had the answers you seek, but we've already shared everything that has been revealed to us."

"And what good is any of it?" Deirdre lashed out at the First Oracle. "What good are portents and prophecies when they don't tell us how to avoid the disasters they predict? What's the point of knowing that the blade will strike when you don't know what direction it will come from? I can't defeat an enemy I can't find. I can't prevent an evil that remains hidden from me!"

"It is not for us to question the will of the gods," Reed intoned.

"The will of the gods? *Which* gods? Do you think that it is Kaestra's will that we allow her to die?"

"We do not know the sum and total of the future, Deirdre." Chu-Lin sounded almost angry. "The Sight doesn't work that way. We can't choose what we see."

Deirdre looked back at Reed, who stood still and pale, his eyes unfocused. She thought about how young he was, how young Chu-Lin was, and the likelihood that neither of them would live as long as she already had. It was with greater compassion that she said, "I'm sorry. I meant no disrespect. I know that you've done everything in your power to help, and I will do my best to make the most of the knowledge you've shared with me."

She bowed to them, about to take her leave. Before she did, she locked eyes with Vanarra, who'd remained silent throughout her visit, and the older woman stepped toward her and spoke. "I could use some fresh air. Would you mind if I walked with you for a while?"

"I'd be pleased to have your company," she replied, curious.

They took a roundabout route to the guardians' cloisters, walking side by side in uneasy silence until Vanarra asked gently, "How is Glasnae doing?"

"She's recovering." Deirdre was gratified by the concern in her voice. "The healers assure me that the damage done isn't as bad as it seems. They say that it's mostly exhaustion and that she'll soon be on her feet again. Her condition is already much improved since she returned, but it's upsetting to see her so weak."

"Wouldn't it have been better for her to remain in Athens until she regained her strength? The journey must have been a strain."

"Freydis tried to convince her to wait, but she was desperate to come home. No one wanted to cause her further distress, so they returned as soon as she was able to travel." She remembered all too clearly what the young guardian looked like when she'd arrived in New Avalon less than a week earlier. Pale as a ghost and unable to stand without assistance. Deirdre had hardly recognized her. She *was* recovering, though. In fact, she had improved to the point where she was beginning to chafe against the restrictions imposed by the healers, but Deirdre wasn't about to let her overtax herself too soon.

"Perhaps she knew best, then," Vanarra suggested. "No doubt being among her sisters has helped her heal. She can draw on your strength while hers returns."

It was an interesting thought, and almost made Deirdre smile. Almost. Since Vanarra had shown such concern for Glasnae, she ventured a question of her own. "Is Reed all right? He seems...unwell."

Her reply came slowly and was colored by pain. "He falls into trance easily these days, and as his gift grows stronger, he grows weaker. It's unlikely that he'll live to be First Oracle or see the events of this particular prophecy unfold."

"I'm sorry, Vanarra." She could think of nothing else to say.

Vanarra shrugged as if resigned, but there were tears in her voice. "As seers, we are taught that the price of our gift is a greatly foreshortened life. The other members of my order accept this as a matter of course, but I can't. Reed is younger than my own children, and he's fading away before my eyes. I know that there's nothing I can do for him and that he has already made his peace with this, but that doesn't change how I feel."

"How *do* you feel, Vanarra?" Deirdre asked without looking at the other woman.

"I feel helpless."

"That makes two of us."

Vanarra stopped walking and turned to face her. "You aren't helpless, Deirdre, and you mustn't lose hope."

"When I asked you to read the omens after Glasnae's initiation, what did you see?"

Vanarra took a physical step back. The unexpected question obviously startled her, which was exactly what Deirdre had intended. She'd hoped to learn as much from her reaction as from her answer. "You already know what I saw. I recorded everything in the formal declaration of omen."

"In the declaration, you claimed that while she would face great trials, she would persevere. Does that mean that she will defeat the force that threatens us? That she will triumph?"

"You know that it doesn't work that way. Omens and portents— even full-blown visions—offer glimpses only. There are no absolutes. Nothing is certain until—"

"—it is past," Deirdre finished for her. After a pause she continued, "You also said that Glasnae would find fulfillment and happiness. Do you stand by that prediction?"

"What do you want from me, Deirdre? Guarantees? I already told you, I have none to offer. You have my official recording of the omen I saw in Glasnae's spilled blood. There is nothing else I can tell you."

Her tone and choice of words suggested that she was being honest, but less than candid, prompting Deirdre to ask, "Did you leave anything out of that account?"

372

Vanarra didn't even flinch. "No. The declaration I sent you was a complete and accurate depiction of what I saw in the blood that stained the sands."

She's telling the truth, Deirdre thought, holding her gaze, *but she's holding something back.*

"If you knew anything else that might shed some light on what we're up against, you would share it with me, wouldn't you?"

"Of course!" The response was swift and heartfelt. "You have my word, Deirdre. If I learn anything that might help you, I will tell you right away. I'm on your side, please believe that."

"We both serve the gods," Deirdre said, nodding.

"It's more than that. I'm your friend, and I care."

Deirdre didn't doubt her sincerity. Whatever Vanarra was withholding, she didn't believe that it had any bearing on the current situation. Her assertion was reassuring, as was the reaffirmation of friendship, but Deirdre couldn't get past the look on Chu-Lin's face when she announced that the prophecy still loomed ahead.

There had been compassion there, yes, but from a distance. Even in the face of such a pervasive threat, the woman had been detached, almost cold. She knew that the seers cultivated such detachment as a means of self-preservation, but she also thought that it made their judgment questionable at best. If they couldn't *feel* for the rest of humanity, how could they possibly be trusted to make decisions that would affect the entire world?

Vanarra was unlike most seers. Her age and experience gave her a connection to those around her the others lacked, as well as a heightened perception of other's feelings, as evidenced by her next words. "You shouldn't judge us all by Chu-Lin's responses, and you shouldn't judge her too harshly. The last few years have been hard for her, and she's changed because of it. She's also preparing herself for Reed's death."

"You say it so calmly." Deirdre couldn't hide her shock. "I thought you said you weren't resigned to it."

"I'm not. But a person can only cry for so long. For the moment, I can hold the grief at bay."

Deirdre imagined how Vanarra must feel, and she shuddered in sympathy. "I wish I had your strength. I'm so afraid that I can't do this."

"You're one of the strongest people I know." Vanarra sounded confident. "If anyone can get us through this, it's you."

"But *I* wasn't chosen, was I?" Deirdre knew by the look on Vanarra's face that she'd made her point. "I'm expected to sit back and watch while someone I love like a daughter risks her life."

"You don't know that."

"The vision doesn't reveal the fate of the three individuals chosen to fight this threat. Even if they succeed, we don't know that they'll survive."

Understanding blossomed across Vanarra's features. "That's it, isn't it? You're just as afraid of success as you are of failure. You're afraid of the cost."

"Glasnae is even younger than Reed, and unlike him, she has *not* reconciled herself to a foreshortened life. How am I supposed to send her to her death?" She'd lost all control, but at that moment, she didn't care. "Foreshadowed—that was the word Reed used. This is only a preview, he said, merely a hint of what awaits. And this *preview* nearly pushed that child to the very limit of her endurance. How much more can she take before it kills her?"

"Deirdre!" Vanarra's sharp exclamation cut through her hysterics, silencing her outburst. "Don't discount the other two people in the vision. She was on her own this time. When the threat rears its head again and the prophecy plays out in full, she *won't* be alone. Whoever the other two individuals are, they'll be with her, and I believe that together they *will* prevail."

Shaking from the force of the emotions coursing through her, Deirdre felt a subtle stirring in the link that bound her to Kaestra. For a moment, she feared her goddess's reaction, but the feelings that seeped through the ribbon of power were warm and soothing. Having regained some semblance of balance, she responded, "I'm not a seer, but I do know a few things about prophecy, and about destiny. Glasnae is uniquely gifted. Such gifts rarely come without a price. You of all people should know that."

Vanarra took both of Deirdre's hands in her own. "Don't mourn her yet. I know you're afraid but have faith. I don't think such an extreme sacrifice will be demanded."

"How do you know that?"

"I don't. It's just a feeling."

Deirdre considered that. Coming from anyone else, that statement would seem like nothing more than a weak attempt to comfort her, but coming from Vanarra, it carried far more weight.

"All right." She took a deep breath. "Chu-Lin said that we have some breathing room. I'll use that time to prepare Glasnae as best I can for whatever may lie ahead for her."

"Do you intend to tell her about the prophecy?"

The question hung in the air between them while Deirdre pondered all the possible consequences of telling Glasnae, and then all the possible consequences of *not* telling her.

"I didn't ask for this burden," she said at last, "But it's mine to bear. Sharing this with her won't help me, and it won't help her, at least not now."

"I understand," Vanarra said softly. "And for what it's worth, I agree with you."

"Thank you."

"Just remember one other thing, Deirdre."

"And what is that?"

"Just like Glasnae, you are not in this alone."

Glossary of Terms

Adept – a mage who has completed advanced Mage Hall training and passed the necessary exams. Equivalent to master rank in a druidic guild.

Archdruid – the title used by the elected governor of the province of Avrin.

Archmage – the title given the master mage elected to lead the Mage Hall. Anyone who holds the rank of mage or higher is eligible to vote in this election.

Atar – kaesana word for mommy.

Canyi – the kaesana term for community. Most canyis are built into mountains and often incorporate natural caverns. Each kaesana clan has their own canyi.

Council of Governors – a governmental body made up of the nine provincial governors. The functional executive branch of government.

Devya – kaesana word for a chosen father. Kaesana are matrilineal and do not have any equivalency to marriage. The male who sires a child is rarely known. A devya is chosen by the child based on a personal connection. A child can only have one devya.

Druid – this term applies to any person who has achieved some rank within any of the druidic orders or druidic guilds.

Druidic College – the center of learning in Tarya. Physically, it is a vast, sprawling campus that serves as the home to teaching facilities, libraries, guild facilities, religious facilities, government buildings, museums and associated support structures. It is located in the city of New Avalon and comprises most of the city.

Druidic Guild – a professional organization that provides training and sets standards of proficiency in a particular trade or field of study.

Druidic Order – a religious organization that serves the gods and the people of Tarya. Members of the druidic orders are called priests and priestesses, though some bear other titles specific to their orders. They serve in both spiritual and practical ways.

Gates or Gateways – points where at least three primary ley lines cross. At these points, there are also connections to the core/heart of the planet that usually remain passive. However, a gate can be opened by guardians to channel kaema directly from the heart of the planet.

Governor – the elected leader of a province. The Governor of Avrin carries the title of Archdruid and presides over the Council of Governors. However, the Archdruid has no more political power than any other provincial governor.

Healers Guild – guild for sorcerers who use magic for healing.

The High Court of Ovates – The highest judicial body of Tarya, sometimes referred to simply as "The Ovates".

Kaema – the magical energy that permeates everything on Kaestra and is concentrated in the ley lines. Also called the blood of Kaestra.

Kae-Madri – a priestess of the Order of Kae-Madri (also known as Guardians). The contraction kae-madri means "daughter of Kaestra", and the kae-madri are sworn to protect the planet/environment and maintain the balance of kaema in the ley lines. Only sorcerers who are born female can become kae-madri. Their initiation links them to the planet through magic. The "link of the kae-madri" is visible to those who can see magic as a thread of crimson light.

Kae-Raeva – this is term used to describe a guardian who has become partially possessed by Kaestra. The contraction kae-raeva means "window of Kaestra" or "doorway of Kaestra", though many people incorrectly believe that this term means "reflection of Kaestra". This condition usually occurs when a guardian's emotions, especially the darker ones such as rage, stir a sympathetic reaction in Kaestra. A guardian in this state becomes an open channel for power that is only loosely under her control.

Kaesa Atera – the kaesana name for the planet as well as their world mother goddess.

Kaesana – the native sentient species of the planet Kaestra. They superficially resemble some of the dragons from human mythology, and so they are sometimes referred to as dragons.

Kaestra – the "shortened" form of Kaesa Atera adopted by humans and sometimes used by kaesana.

Kaeverdine – a form of stone capable of holding a magical charge. It occurs in a variety of colors and configurations which can be utilized for different purposes. It is also referred to as magestone.

Ley lines – natural veins that crisscross the planet in which kaema is concentrated. There vary in size and strength. The most powerful are referred to as primary ley lines.

Mage – a sorcerer who has completed a Mage Hall apprenticeship and passed the necessary exams. Equivalent to journeyman rank in a druidic guild.

The Mage Hall – this refers both to the organization that governs all mages as well as the school that trains them.

Magician – a priest/priestess of the Magicians Order. Members of this order primarily serve as teachers of magic at the druidic college and preserve the secrets of Ritual Magic.

Master Mage – a mage of exceptional power and skill who has passed the necessary exams, which are rigorous. This rank exceeds that of any rank within a druidic guild and was established approximately 700 years ago in response to the increased power and skill that developed in a small percentage of the magical population.

Merlin – a person who serves in the combined police force/army/national guard of the country of Tarya.

Nodes – points where at least three ley lines cross.

Ovate – a judge.

Physicians Guild – guild for medical professionals who lack magical ability and rely solely on mundane medical techniques.

Poltergeist – the term used when kaema suddenly and forcefully erupts from a sorcerer in an uncontrolled way, most often manifesting as something resembling a miniature tornado with the sorcerer in its center. The term "magical seizure" is sometimes used as well but is considered to be a slur against sorcerers.

Seer – a priest/priestess of the Seers Order. Seers are gifted with the power of prophecy. They experience visions that they record in scrying mirrors for others to view and react to. For reasons unknown, the power that grants them such visions also greatly reduces their lifespans. Living in semi-seclusion among their own kind can extend their lives somewhat, as it decreases the number of visions they experience.

Senate – the legislative body of Tarya. Each of the nine provinces is represented by nine senators.

Sensitive – a person with a high level of psychic sensitivity and perception.

Shaman – a priest/priestess of the Shamans Order. Members of this order primarily serve as counselors and spiritual healers.

Sorcerer – the term used for anyone with magical ability.

Vanyi – a lesser title of affection a kaesana child can bestow on an adult male they feel close to. A child can have multiple vanyi.

Pronunciation Guide

Below are some general guidelines for the pronunciation of kaesana words and proper names.

<u>Vowel conventions:</u>

ae = this letter combination is always pronounced with a long a sound, such as in way or date.

i = this is always pronounced as a long e sound as in fee or weed

ey = this is always pronounced as a short e sound, as in pet or red

y = when used as a standalone vowel, this is always a long i sound, like my or pie

a = this always has a soft "ah" sound as in pa or la

<u>Emphasis conventions:</u>

In two syllable words, the emphasis is always on the first syllable, as it is in words like winter and mother.

In words of more than two syllables, the emphasis is always on the second syllable, as it in words like returning and attention.

Hyphenated words are pronounced as if they are two separate words in terms of where the emphasis will fall.

Geography of Kaestra

There are three human nations on the planet Kaestra: Elsysia, Neweden, and Tarya. There is also a small territory in the north that the native kaesana have reserved for themselves.

The nation of Tarya is divided into nine provinces:

Athens
Avrin (considered the capital province)
Baikal
Jenolan
Kalahari
Kyushu
Maliae
Ratatosk
Tikal

Made in United States
North Haven, CT
04 August 2022

22293989R00209